Praise for *The Happy Valley*

A knotty, philosophical mystery dense with lingering regrets.

—*Kirkus*

Benjamin Harnett's trippy, ambitious debut novel . . . is steeped in fond remembrance of childhood games, and reading [it] is not unlike the experience of opening a D&D game box. Dense with historical and cultural references and perceptive insights into human nature on both an individual and societal scale . . . *The Happy Valley* is a poetic, delightfully inventive work of modern mythmaking.

—Edward Sung for *IndieReader*

One of the most intriguing, beguiling, and thought-provoking books I read this year.

—Diana Spencer, author of *Varro's Guide to Being Roman*

The story doesn't just open. It grabs . . . From cards containing great power to the ironies of disparate forces that find themselves unexpectedly on the same side, Harnett's juxtaposition of social discord and angst are nicely done . . . The profound realizations experienced by the characters in this story will attract and captivate mature teens and audiences interested in the concurrence of past, present, and future . . . Powerful, gripping, and tempered by mystery and intrigue, *The Happy Valley* resides in a category of its own—that of a unique and compelling work of art that blends social and historical inspection with the trajectories of everyday young lives.

—D. Donovan, Senior Reviewer, *Midwest Book Review*

Fabulous and engaging . . . richly creative!

—Glenda Burgess, award-winning author of *So Long As We're Together*

The Happy Valley offers fascinating insights about the relationship between the past and the future, anchoring its philosophical musings in a personal story of rediscovery. To blend the abstract with the concrete, to mash-up genres with intention—neither is any small feat, and this novel pulls off the sleight of hand necessary to bring its distinct vision to life.

—Nathaniel Drenner for *Independent Book Review*

www.thehappyvalleynovel.com

The Happy Valley

Also by Benjamin Harnett:

Animal, Vegetable, Mineral

Gigantic: Stories From the End of the World

The Happy Valley

X

Benjamin Harnett

Serpent Key Press

THE HAPPY VALLEY

www.benjaminharnett.com

Published by Serpent Key Press, Cherry Valley

www.serpentkey.com

ISBN: 979-8-9867445-6-8 (Hardcover) / 979-8-9867445-4-4 (Paperback) / 979-8-9867445-8-2 (eBook)
LCCN: 2022914725

Cover and jacket design by Benjamin Harnett

10 9 8 7 6 5 4 3 2 1

For Toni, who gave me the key

Remembrance of the past may give rise to dangerous insights, and the established society seems to be apprehensive of the subversive contents of memory.

—Herbert Marcuse, *One-Dimensional Man*

I found that region of country . . . a "burnt district." There had been . . . wild excitement passing through . . . I can give no account of it except what I heard from Christian people and others. It . . . resulted in a reaction so extensive and profound, as to leave the impression on many minds that religion was a mere delusion.

—Charles G. Finney, *Autobiography*

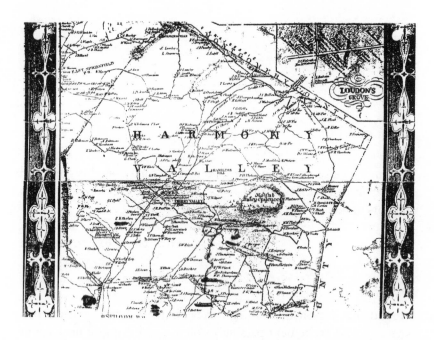

Map of Harmony Valley with Loudon's Grove inset, 1835

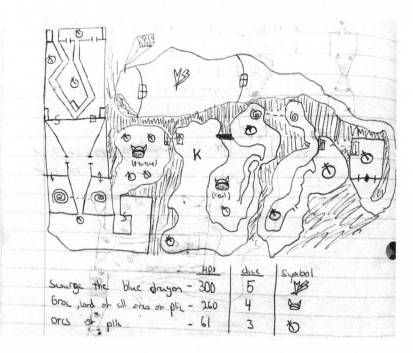

	HP!	dice	Symbol
Scourge the blue dragon	300	5	
Groc, lord of all orcs of plic	260	4	
orcs of plic	61	3	

A map from "The Game," from Brian's notebook, 1992

Contents

THIS IS A TRUE STORY. It's just that some of it hasn't happened yet. It's a coming-of-age tale—about first love, and about inevitable disappointments. About the sorrows and pleasures of growing up. Not only the growing up of a single person, but the coming of age of an entire society.

It's about everything that isolates and pushes us apart, and the thread that binds us all together. Why isn't it more clear, how the future works? Are we any clearer on how things work now? I know we have the tales we tell ourselves. They are myths—democracy, freedom—and we have been honing them a long time.

Or we have been honing ourselves against them so that all their fragmented truths and misfit parts feel smooth.

Ask a child, their understanding is more fresh, more accurate. Aren't these children too articulate, too intelligent? Yet I was just as they are. I believe you were too. I think we've both lost a step since then. It's not our fault. Everyone has lost a step. How could we not? We have been sleepwalking through the ages.

Why is our hero so hapless, so removed? Is he the hero? Aren't we all the hero of our own story? Not one of us has our "own" story, though, do we? Every story is the story of who we are bound to, the web of past and future relationships that constitute a life.

It may be unbelievable for us now, this story of how everything that has been going wrong in the world goes right—a fantasy. But it's a mystery, too, I mean how we relate to it, how it can come to be: how our little peregrinations around the local space-time of this cockeyed, rocky orb can resonate together to leave great change in their wake.

Read this like a gothic tale, but know that real life is more gothic: more grotesque, mysterious, and desolate, but it doesn't have to be.

Like Dorothy's story, this one begins on a farm. Then we find a key.

"It was a game," she said. "Children played it. But the stakes were real, and the consequences were our entire world."

I.

The Farm

Chapter
1

I T WAS WHEN the Sioux were dynamiting Mt. Rushmore that I heard from her again after so long a time. They hosted livestreams every Friday afternoon, detonating one president at a time. Even those who affected moral outrage at the destruction—I was not one—would replay over and over on their personal screens slo-mo videos of half of Washington's face sliding away from the other, or watch Teddy's pince-nez shoot out in a cloud of dust over his bully mustache and shit-eating grin.

"Can you help me?" her message said.

This was the penultimate contact I had with June before she disappeared. (In the sense of the one before the last, a waning sense of the word—June herself used to use it in its current sense of "the most awesome," and when I challenged her on it, she accused me of pedantry, and asserted it was a folly to try to hold back the tide of society. This was a strange stance for someone so interested in, even obsessed with, the past.) Her plea was a mirror of the first encounter we had ever had, at school, when she poked her head out with that same request from behind a pillar in the library.

Her message, which this time popped up on LinkedIn, came after several years of complete radio-silence. But that was normal for our relationship. Ever since that disastrous 11-month sublet and double bed we had shared in Brooklyn—"I have never made a worse mistake," she told me one time, but that was hyperbole—we had maintained an intense but intermittent friendship.

I was more surprised by the venue than the message itself. June was prescient, though. LinkedIn—after an abrupt and complete 180° on privacy (from scofflaw to earnest preserver), combined with the bland, almost invisible nature of its corporate-tuned advertising (it was like the slightly-shiny beige walls and upholstery in business hotels, designed to reject any stain)—was in the process of being taken over by teens, who, out of an initially ironic impulse, began to saturate the service with their youth, and litter it with imaginary CVs. In a year they would own the place, making it useless for employment purposes, and anyone who was anyone wanted to hang out there. I wasn't anybody, and I kept my own presence there out of the same inertia that had long dominated my life.

Leave it to June to know which way the wind blew.

Maybe she meant it as a clue. Her mind worked like that. It took me a while to respond; I was wary of being dragged into something (it had happened before). When I did, at last, she replied cryptically, with a time, and a date, but no place. It was a test of the telepathic connection neither of us believed in, but that somehow always seemed to work. We finally met up. What she needed was a favor. I had no choice but to grant it. We lost touch again.

If you recall the tumult and turbulence of that time, its tribulations, I don't think you can blame me. Nevertheless, I felt that it had been my fault; that I had lost her.

When I made an effort to contact her again, I discovered that she really was lost—June had gone missing. The more I thought about it, the more I realized our last meeting had been for her a cry for help. A provocation.

I decided to take it up, at last.

June's message to me had been a key, and only after I set out did I discover its use—that it unlocked a deep mystery, an adventure. I should have known—she was like that, everything about her that seemed normal later grew in significance. Our entire life had been a great unfolding, like one of those old USGS topographical maps we had pored over in Boy Scouts. It all started in mid-October 1993, with a disembodied voice calling out for help.

I had turned twelve that year. The early months had been good for snow so we had more than our usual time off from school. I had saved my allowance and, together with the

Easter money, upgraded by mail order the RAM in my home computer. I finished reading the last Sherlock Holmes story in the omnibus collection, and discovered the wry voice of Mark Twain. That summer my friends and I engaged in an intense campaign through a series of inhospitable but ingeniously crafted dungeons in the clubhouse at the farm, in the hours between our arrival and the communal lunch. In August, I had my birthday.

After that, seventh grade began: our rural school accommodated all grades, K-12, and so the transition to middle-school was one only of degree.

But what happened next was the catalyst for a wholesale transformation.

In the library, when you took the stairs up to the second floor, you entered the Media Lab. It was just four Apple IIe computers set on four desks arranged around a central pillar. There was a big dot-matrix printer, a wall of reference books and the librarian's desk. She had a basket where you'd put in requests for interlibrary loan, and an outbox where they showed up, as if by magic. One day in October, engrossed in a game called "Wizard and the Princess" I was startled almost completely out of my orange, plastic seat.

"Hey!" a disembodied voice called. I was shocked, because no one was ever up there in the lab, and if they were, it was usually someone like me: a shy nerd loathe to make any noise, let alone call out to a stranger. Her face shot out, freckled, bright-eyed, under a slash of dark hair. Even more awkward to me, she was a girl. "Can you help me?"

June had been sitting at the computer directly opposite me, obscured by the pillar.

I stammered out that I would, not knowing what was needed, and moved to her side in a somewhat spastic manner. A dark prompt obscured her screen. I knew at once what was needed, and helped her to find the appropriate disk in the box to swap into the drive to resolve it. Then I took over her keyboard, unable to help myself, and got the game moving.

June had already known how to do it, of course. She'd known almost everything, all along. This had been an excuse to strike up a conversation; it was—due to my poor social development—something of a failure. After rendering that overbearing assistance I stopped abruptly and shuffled back to my own game without anything more passing between us than a nod. But weeks passed, and over time we developed a pattern of incidental chatting.

She found out many things that I had observed, about teachers, student cliques, parents, and the town. She elicited things from me I had never expressed to a single soul. She had come to school midway through the year, a rare stranger in this place, and entered a grade back of where she should have been by age, and two grades ahead of me (she was in ninth—already a high-schooler).

We met because we both avoided the lunch room ("It smells like wet gym socks!" she said), and preferred spending the noon hour in the library, playing computer games in the "Media Lab," a pretentious name for what was just those four, already archaic computers—curved CRT monitors sitting on two floppy drives like cinder blocks, themselves perched on the body of the typewriter-like CPU, and upon which you could play *Wheel of Fortune* and *Oregon Trail.*

As the ice broke, I discovered that June was a crack squirrel-shot, and could carry her family across the prairie on a diet of wild rodent alone. She always risked fording the river, and never seemed to plan, whereas I catalogued my many barrels of salted meat and always laid in an extra yoke. Though she had moved here recently, June seemed to know a lot about our small Upstate New York village. We were very much off the beaten path, although within comfortable driving distance of the city.

Then it was noted for the beauty of its maples, which used to burst out with their deep reds in early fall—now global warming has made them all stumps.

There was a single burger joint on Main St. that did a slow business, where old farmers sat drinking bitter coffee in diner cups, and the occasional visitor was delighted to mix in fresh cream from a local dairy. It was one of only three restaurants in town.

"Did you know," said June, "the bus used to stop there?"

"The school bus?" I said, puzzled.

"No—the Greyhound." she said. I had had a vague sense there were other kinds of buses than the ones we rode every day. Buses not just for students but for all kinds of people. When she realized I didn't know, she explained, "Haven't you ever seen them—they have a slender dog on the side. Anyone can buy a ticket, and take them to many different places. This one went from Albany to Syracuse until they finished the new highway."

The driver would get out to stretch, have a cigarette and chat with the locals. In the space behind the restaurant was a bowling alley that had closed in the early 80s. It didn't have pin-setting machines, but relied on local kids to do it. I've heard from the kids, a dozen years older than me, how some bowlers would throw so hard you had to jump out of the way, and that others, like Mrs. Emilia Webb, would roll the ball with so little force that the ball might come to a complete stop almost a foot away from the lead pin. They said a coat hanger, twisted into a hook, couldn't be seen from the other end of the lane, and in the shadows a spare pin or two might be helped down with its aid.

I have stood in the empty space back there, where the honeyed-wood was ripped up long ago. Nevertheless, something of an essential, communal feeling remained. Was it only some nostalgia brought on by the faint scents of old tobacco smoke and beer soaked into the rafters—maybe. By my late childhood, neglect had left all the buildings as faded as an old Polaroid; some even had the air of a tintype in their decrepit reality.

I have seen a daguerreotype of the bank from 1848 (by Samuel Morse), and absent the garish backlit sign, the building has not changed. The street was dirt then, and seemed wider. There were tall curb-stones in front of the fancier houses, to step up into carriages. There were four or five thousand inhabitants. There could be four-hundred now.

Main St. has lost buildings at a rate of one or two every few years. Usually to fire. (There had always been fires, but their impact became more evident once any effort at rebuilding ceased.) Sometimes, for variety, we got an epic collapse instead: a long, slow rot of all internal components followed by total catastrophe. Some English fop had called the place Loudon's Grove when it was hard on the periphery of the colonies, and its lone citizens could be fairly regarded as "pioneers."

Improbably enriched by a trade of maple sugar and potash, then colonized by Scottish lawyers who had gotten plugged into Albany graft, the village finally incorporated in 1812 as Harmony Valley, sometimes called "The Happy Valley," on account either of the felicity of its richest residents or the lithium reputed to infuse its wells. Imagine: streets thronged with black-suited men and well-dressed women, to meet the grand entrance of Governor Clinton. Several Presidents too. The ones you'll hear television anchors swear never existed: "President Millard Fillmore? No, that's some kind of joke. Impossible."

And me? Imagine someone so caught up in stories from books that far from being a prime mover in some great action, they are barely an active participant in their own life; someone with so little understanding of their own character that they could not imagine it coming across as bad; someone who lives only for uncovering secrets; finally, someone who through it all has done one thing well: remain.

Picture the past, that time before, when the springs could be bitter cold, before so many trees died, and all the lawns; before the drones lit up the sky in the evening, lights like flashing stars; before the fires; before the big truck route change. Before the high-tension lines.

We are almost on the other side of it all.

We can almost imagine a past as vibrant and present as now. Even then, when we regarded pictures of the still, frozen lives of a generation before—faded, wreathed in darkness, flattened by a flash, in strange clothes and hair piled up—we thought them ancient, felt no connection to the incidentals of their lives, just as they, on their shag carpet in the den, with the fake wood-grain TV set, looked at black and white photos with deckled edges, and wondered that a time had ever been when those photos were new. It was all very hard to believe. June believed in it all, though, and she asked me to, as well.

"WHAT ARE THEY LIKE?" she said one day, asking about my parents. After I had just shrugged in response, she said, "They must be nice." They were. I loved them, but my home life was so simple, so easy, it was as if they had faded into the background. I realize now how hard it was for my parents to make that so.

"My parents," she said, "have gotten religious." She explained one day how they told her—when she had brought a rock crusted with fossils to show them—how God had put them in the shale, these brachiopods, crinoid stems, the occasional trilobite, even bones, had laid down the earth in strata, warped it, thrust up mountains from the sea, and eroded them to nothing, and otherwise had tempted man—with a special eye to geologists, I assume—to imagine an earth older than the 4,004 years since our eviction from paradise (a figure derived from the ages of all the patriarchs of the Bible, cross-referenced against recorded history).

"Total shit!" she said.

June cursed a lot. It excited me, promising the possibility of running amok, of breaking through; I was stuffy, too good, and I wanted to imagine letting go. I pretended to myself that I didn't act on impulse at all, but in fact I had just entered the age of impulses. I would like to say that I perceived in her uncharted depths of cunning, despite her devil-may-care attitude, and some deep potential that I had to connect with. It's more likely that she perceived something in me, some use, something I was good for. Not in a selfish way, nothing was ever selfish with her, even if I have thought so at times.

My curiosity about June grew until it felt boundless, but my wits were incapable of extracting much from her, and everything I discovered she handed to me. Were these discoveries like the dead mice and birds a cat brings to its human, or were they more like breadcrumbs left to guide a lost child home; or were they desperate flags waving from the deck, or smoke signals—dots and dashes spelling out S.O.S.?

What I picked up from her—inferred from hints and errant revelations—was that she had been home-schooled most of her life, that her family had moved here recently from Ohio, that she had a sister and a brother, that there had been, before she was born, another sibling who died in a house fire. Her father had been forced earlier that year, into changing jobs, so that her mother had had to take on work, nights, at the hospital. This is what had ended the home schooling, and raised tension at home to a high pitch. And last, that her "father" wasn't her actual father, but only a man her mother had met named Tim. It was with Tim that the fervor for the gospels had arrived.

I knew these to be facts, could even feel some of them, but only at a surface level. I didn't truly understand what it all meant—to be tense at home, to have a lost brother that was only ever a spirit, a name, a shadow from a place they shared that you knew only from rumor, where your own family had once dwelled without you.

How can we know anything without living it ourselves?

JUNE'S HOUSE, TO WHICH they had moved only in September, was a ramshackle, 18th century farmhouse. It had been the home of her maternal ancestors, most recently held by June's grandmother. June's mother had stayed away on account of a bitter feud between them, the cause of which I have not been able to discover. But on the grandmother's death, with no last testament and no other heirs, the estate went to the daughter.

It had once been the seat of an extremely profitable farming enterprise, with goats, sheep, and cows. The house was originally built in the Federal style, then had great Greek-revival columns and a long portico appended. Various additions followed that doubled and tripled the size. The woodwork was impeccable, if eclectic, and the carriage path that brought visitors to the door made a leisurely arc to the house flanked by plane trees that cast their ragged bark on a trim lawn with a large stone fountain as its focus.

A prodigious barn stood behind the house, and it had been painted, ostentatiously, yellow with white trim, instead of the standard, cheaper red. In the barn, dusty, stuffed full of acorns and chestnuts by enterprising squirrels, and partly covered by hay, remained the smart gig the young gentleman used to race from there into the village.

A village in incorporation, it had shown every indication, at its height, of first taking over the county seat, then growing to assume a mantle of importance, perhaps even becoming the capital. All on the strength of its situation on a main turnpike. You can guess the series of shocks that followed: first, the canal, which seemed to increase the importance of this star of the map with the traffic of its building, but upon opening, shifted the locus of transit away just enough to block the wildest aspirations of its populace. Then the railroad. And the turnpike diverted. Then a disastrous crop blight.

The fortunes of June's ancestral home followed those of the village: The fountain cracked, and stopped being repaired. The pastureland was sold, a parcel at a time. The animals, dying, were not restocked. The paint chipped of the wood. The siding underneath greyed. The great porch took on rot, and buckled. The pillars split. One wing was closed off as un-heatable. The barn slumped. It took three generations to go from a respectable relic to an absolute ruin. So, now this was June's house and June's life.

She took walks in the woods that had grown over the old farmland. She took refuge in the hidden places of the barn. She found treasures she kept and wondered over. Her stepfather, Tim, rejected the overwhelming family legacy that inhabited the house like a malevolent force. But June learned things, discovered secrets, and these secrets made a place for her, let her recover the past, and stand facing the future with something of her own to grow.

The single, sparkling, most amazing thing I discovered about June was a fact about this home—about her farm: When she talked about the hayloft, and the old wooden farm tools hanging, or the chicken coop, or the copious raspberry patch; when she talked about the big, leaning porch and the layers on layers of cracked paint, I felt a pang of recognition. It could be any farm. But did I know this place? I believed I did.

I began to ask her more specific questions, wary of tipping my hand and revealing myself as ridiculous. I had, in the past, made the mistake of too openly declaring my private thoughts through unfiltered statements and questions, realizing only after a shocked or derisive reply that I had shown something I shouldn't have shown of what was in my brain, what was in my heart.

It was in the afternoon, en route to Study Hall, after we passed Mr. Grimmon, one of the gym coaches who often oversaw middle-school recess, that it all came out. He was a small man with a big head, a tiny face, and long, thin nostrils stretched over a sunken nose. Mr. Grimmon had a face that looked like a skull. His beady, black eyes were shadowed in their sockets. His lips were always pursed into a small, black "o." A shag of dark gray beard and salt-and-pepper hair encircled his bone-pale skin.

"A cow skull," June whispered to me, "a cow skull grown into the fork of a tree."

That June should make this observation, and that I should have known the exact cow skull she meant, might not seem of that much moment. But what it meant for me, personally, I will shortly explain. What it meant to June I came to understand later. And what it meant to the world seems so fantastic that I myself hardly believe it.

It was Tiffany, on one of her visits to my modest little cabin far out past the weather stabilizers, on a particularly snowy day, all those years later, after the revolution, who pointed it out. She had, in a mysterious way, become someone of importance in this new world, yet she continued to see me, as if I were a kind of ward of hers—a favorite. One time she asked, pointedly, "What was it like, for you, then?" Meaning: before everything, back when we were all still so young.

FOR CHILDREN THERE is a thorough flattening of life. The adult sorts events into categories of significance, but for eleven-year-old me, whatever was in front of me was of the utmost significance and to all else I was indifferent. One moment, strangers in the news from halfway around the world could be as vital and present as some happening in my immediate, actual life, then I would find myself fully invested a thrilling hover-car chase I was reading in an old Tom Swift book.

That year was a year of great incident, like all years, I think. Comprising incidents I've mostly had to look up. If I read them to you, you might say, "Ah, yes, I guess that was important," or, "How did we forget that so quickly?" Clinton inaugurated. Waco. The latter I remember for the way the fatal fire pixelated on the TV screen as I stood too close, a bright, rolling, artificial orange and red. The split of Czechoslovakia. The first Trade Center bombing. This I saw in the newspaper, only a black and white picture, smoke billowing out of a concrete car park.

To what extent were the events of that year part of the foundation of what was to come after? To a young boy they were little more than background, pictures tacked to the wall. What I have learned in preparing to tell this story is that maybe the child is right. Maybe things mean more and less than we make of them, and maybe it is precisely the things that touch us that touch the world.

I have been reading a lot in preparing to tell this story; for context, and also to more accurately sketch out the vast gap between what life was then and what life is now. Now, on the other side, and then, just at the lip of history, blend in my mind, with only a vast, dark crater in the center, that long period of misery, that coming of age.

To paraphrase one historian: by 2034, the big and small movements which had maneuvered American society into its present place of stability and shared prosperity had quiesced. We were, at last, living in equilibrium with the environment and with the balance of humankind.

It had meant a smaller, more insular focus. It had only come through a period of spirited revolt and much sacrifice. It had happened more quickly, by far, than anyone expected, as revolutions tend to.

Now we live as though we have always lived this way. We should not forget the past, but it is unavoidable. When you have been sick, stuck in bed, feverish, a headache so bad you can scarcely see, the day grinding forward gruelingly, minute by minute, and then the fever breaks, you suddenly open your eyes without pain. You have lost, in an instant, all connection to that terrible, sickly feeling, could not remember it if you had to. So much the better.

Or not. I find myself peering back over this past as if it were a void across which a ladder is stretched. There is purchase on the far side. I can see myself crossing over it to myself, rung by perilous rung.

AFTER JUNE'S COMMENT about the skull, I couldn't hold off any longer. I knew because June's house was also the farm where, in the summer, my friends and I were dropped off by our parents while they worked, to be cared for by an older woman and her daughter who had rented the empty place for a day-care. That is, before June and her family came back to live. I wondered, at once, with some dismay, if the summer arrangement, a defining fact up until that point in my life, could continue now that June and her family were there. The fact exposed in an instant an entire terrain we shared beyond the few computers on the second floor of the library.

"I know the one you are talking about!" I said. "In the tree, in the barnyard, just before the cornfield. You're living on our farm!"

"What do you mean 'your farm'?" she said, sharply.

I might as well have blurted out, "I love you," I was so mortified. I had inadvertently revealed something deep, a secret. Now I would have to explain.

Mr. Grimmon had a face like a skull.

It had started out of necessity, and a thunderstorm.

Chapter
2

"**M**AYBE," SAID JUNE, half-serious and half-teasing, after I had told her something about my time at the farm, her family farm, "the farm belongs more to you than me."

"No," I told her, "It is yours. I mean, I guess it will come to be yours the same way we came to own it—by your being there, and by exploring."

"Hey," June said—we were peering over the balcony, from the "Media Lab" down toward a table in the back of the library where four kids were sitting, heads bowed intently over a scatter of notebooks and paper—"what are they doing?"

A clatter of colorful dice rolled into the middle, and Eric, the slightest of the four, groaned loudly, which was followed by the shush of the librarian from behind her desk.

"They're playing 'The Game,'" I said.

"You mean *Dungeons & Dragons*? We have that in Ohio. I mean, some people I knew were into it. They were strange, you know? These kids seem kinda, I don't know, ordinary. Is that Brian?"

"Yeah, that's Brian," I said, pointing to the eldest—she knew him because they were in the same grade—"and Aaron, and Eric, and Max. It's sort of like *D&D*, but it's something we made up." I paused a second, then added, "At the farm. At your farm."

"Why aren't you playing?" she asked.

I told her that I did, sometimes. It didn't feel the same, to play at school, as it had over the summer. And I didn't say that since I met her, my enthusiasm had further waned. She pressed me more.

"Why not just play *Dungeons & Dragons*?" she asked,

and, "What made it better on the farm?" and, "Can I play?"

It had started out of necessity, and a thunderstorm.

The farm, June's farm, was a fertile green rectangle of fields that flanked a meandering stream through bottomland, a thick loam with pockets of clay, a gently sloping plain which ultimately met the Mohawk and the Erie canal. On most weekdays in the summer, while our parents worked, we were kept there, at a sort of day-camp.

There was an hour or two of outside play, Tonka trucks and Transformers, bounding through the thickets, feeling vaguely threatened by the wandering roosters, picking raspberries.

Then, a bit before noon, some of the more-responsible charges were tasked with making sandwiches, peanut butter and jelly on Wonder Bread, a great stack of them, cut into small triangles, fit for all ages. The select would also mix up the lemonade and iced tea from powders, in translucent pitchers.

After lunch it was time to get ready for the walk to the swimming hole. We each got towels, selected from a motley pile, and changed into bathing suits, and then got in a line. An adult at each end, and along the road, I remember periodically touching the guardrails to see how blistering hot they had gotten in the summer sun.

Single-file then down a short leap from the concrete that held the high culvert pipes—to us, vast tunnels—onto a dusty path. There was the ginger clambering, down to the tree with the rope you could swing out on and drop straight into the water. We lived in constant fear of a snapping turtle rumored to sit at the bottom. You never let your feet drift down through the "cold zone," imagining its probing nose and vicious mouth waiting. There were hornets and wasps that lived in the bank. I was stung several times. For this you could apply a layer of cool clay, of which there was a long seam by the rocky beach. It went on smooth and baked hard in the sun. It was good for all manner of disguises.

Afterward, we rinsed ourselves of clay and mud, gathered up the towels, made our way up the shoulder of earth to the railing, still hot in the sun. We felt equal parts relief, for it was exhausting, and sadness, for every leaving was like another exile from Eden, as we trudged back to the farm. Gradually as swimsuit and hair dried, as the whole earth warmed and was suffused by light, you got to feeling settled and content again. Then we'd have ice pops (my favorite was the coconut), or play another game with trucks, or eat so many raspberries we felt sick, while the shadows lengthened until our parents came.

"BUT WHAT ABOUT 'The Game'?" asked June.

I had been waxing on, lyrically, and was in danger of losing the thread. I had just wanted so much to explain to her what the place was to me, to us.

"Rainy days, we'd be all cooped up in the house, looking for something to do."

I told her about the living room, with the enormous, Jurassic-looking jade tree that one year had flowered dramatically; the constant drift of dust through it all.

When it rained we could sit at the dining room table with colored markers and draw, or play with Tinkertoys or Lincoln Logs in the den, a cozy room stuffed with mismatched, comfortable furniture, and lined with bookshelves. Maybe there was a baseball game on the woodgrain-framed television there, all white noise and washed-out green.

Or we could sit on the wide porch, and watch the storm roll in over soybean fields. It would be sunny where we sat, but we'd begin to feel a cooler breeze against our skin. The sky in the distance was dark, cloud piling up from the horizon. Colors would become more vivid. All the trees around the drive, each a hundred years old if a day, would start to rustle. At last we'd feel the spray of the rain on our cheeks and rush inside, the screen door slamming behind us.

One time they had us make butter, and we spent the whole time shaking fresh cream in jam jars. It took hours, and left our arms feeling like rubber.

I saw June had her arms crossed, impatiently.

"'The Game,' yes!" I said, "Getting to it. I promise.

"It was on a rainy day like that, this summer. Brian came to me with a notebook."

I explained how some time before that there had been a *Dungeons & Dragons* rule book randomly shelved at the toy store in the mall—the sad, shabby mall in Oneonta—and I had bought it, and showed it to Brian. It had a set of dice clipped to it with a poly-bag. At that time, there was no internet where things could be privately and exhaustively explored. We didn't want to ask our parents about this; there were stories on the local news and an attitude among the adults that this was something bad—something evil, demonic. In retrospect I don't think our parents, who had more of an open-minded attitude about everything, shared that feeling, but how could we know?

There had been a few other *D&D* items there, but my allowance wouldn't support getting them. Brian came back from a trip with his parents with two campaign books and a set of advanced rules. By ourselves we worked our way through it all, trying to wrap our heads around the complicated and seemingly contradictory instructions. But it was more work than video games or taking a walk in the woods, and sometime during the school year I had given up trying to puzzle it out.

But when I saw the notebook Brian handed me I realized he had not given up.

He had created his own set of simple rules, formulated for ordinary dice. Now, on rainy days at the farm that summer we began a long period of elaboration, not yet playing, but devising new rules—creating magical and ordinary objects with all their associated characteristics in excruciating detail. We invented dozens of characters, and baroque backstories for each. We created pages of spells and items, each with precise numerical impacts.

While the rain gurgled into catchment barrels and thunder rumbled, we huddled in a corner of the den, where two bookshelves full of mystery and thriller paperbacks met, behind a natural barrier formed by the back of a leather recliner and a side table. It was a unique fortress we defended against all comers. At last Eric came, to find out what we were doing.

He was a year younger than I was, thin and lanky. He refused to leave. Finally we let him in.

Eric flipped through the pages of our notebooks where we had laid out the grand theories, our complications, and our simplifications. We had borrowed names, objects, concepts from a universe of fantasy novels, video games, cartoons, and movies. You could idly sketch out the family tree of a famed weapon and its magic powers, or build up an encyclopedia of spells, their effects, their limitations, and inventors. We would have kept it up forever, except for Eric.

"Okay," he said, "let's play!"

Eric had already called Brian's sister and two of the younger kids over. Soon everyone had created a character. Most of the time, Brian was the mastermind, and I alternated the lead of the party with Eric.

We had taken the blueprint of a role-playing game and adapted it to our terrain and circumstances. One of us would be the "Dungeon Master," scratching out a map of a treasure-laden dungeon filled with small and large villains, and talking us through our adventure. Each enemy had their own hit points, magic skills, and strengths. Every action was ruled by the roll of the dice. And we each had a sheet with our own characters on it, and as our rolls let us strike down monsters of increasing difficulty, or outwit traps our levels and skills increased, in rough imitation of our own development.

First we only played in bad weather. But we quickly commandeered the treehouse that some neighbor kids had built before heading off to college (and furnished it like a bar, with a big *Miller Lite* sign and red vinyl barstools, the yellow padding of which was starting to flower through). The treehouse smelled like old, sun-baked carpet. A small, empty mini-fridge buzzed, while some bluebottles beat lazily against the window.

The dice clattered on the "bar-top." The Tonka trucks sat, abandoned, in the muddy thicket, and were grown over.

I WAS ABOUT TO TELL June about an incident with Eric but I realized she had left my side and was starting to walk down the stairs toward my friends. She caught my eye and waved me to come with her. I followed, reluctantly.

I was hesitant to share her with them. Already jealous.

"Hey," said June, and everyone at the table looked up from the game. "This looks fun." They all turned their heads down again, sheepishly. Not one of us had any social grace, certainly not in the presence of a girl, and certainly not one like June. She was undaunted. "Brian, right?" she said. He nodded.

"Hi," he said, then looked down again.

"June wants to play," I said, arriving beside her. "Maybe next Tuesday?" The period was almost over. Games were Tuesdays and Thursdays; other days people needed time to catch up on school work. On Wednesdays Eric had extra soccer practice. Of all of us, he was actually athletic.

"I don't know," said Max. "We are right in the middle of this dungeon. It would be weird."

"Come on, let her play," I said. At first I had been reluctant, but now I took umbrage at their refusal to open up.

"It's alright," said June, "when will you be finished?"

Brian leaned over to Eric and they whispered back and forth. Finally, Brian said "How about Tuesday the week after?"

"Sure," said June.

"Won't you play, too?" Max asked me.

"Sure," I said. Anything for June.

*The Tonka trucks sat, abandoned, in the muddy thicket,
and were grown over.*

A tall but gnarled figure, bent over a leather-bound tome set on a stand made entirely of human bones.

Chapter
3

"**T**HAT WAS FUN**," said June, after we had spent all of lunch and recess playing "The Game" with my friends. June didn't have a character of her own, but she took over a recurring character Brian and I had created. The character had entered our game sessions over the summer at the farm, a female wizard, appearing and disappearing at opportune moments to prod us along with an inscrutable hint or blazing magical aid, toward a goal she alone knew and focused on, whether for good or ill had remained to be seen.

The way June took up the wizard character as if it had been her all along was disconcerting. I realized that, like June, the wizard had appeared first from behind a pillar. The wizard concealed her power; pretended to be weak, injured. She followed us for a while in the dungeon before we began to understand that her "following" was, in reality, leading from the back. She tossed out questions that became hints, which were, finally, commands. She vanished when we confronted her, only to reappear to me alone when I had become lost, separated from my companions.

I secretly loved her, this character, though I had barely known what love meant. She left me, and returned, and left again as I wandered. In game time it was decades. Finally, battered by relentless campaigning, hair going white, I stumbled upon a group of strangers, who I only gradually understood to be my friends, changed to me as much as I must have seemed changed to them. Now we had a real quest. Each told the same story of becoming lost, separated, of the wizard woman with the dark hair who came in and out of their path, sometimes guiding, sometimes holding them back.

I saw desire sparkle in their eyes, though it was entirely unspoken, and at once I felt sick with jealousy and utterly despondent. Still, there had been a shared vision, a shining cup. I suppose this was Brian pulling from the grail legend. The rest of the adventure is cloudy in my mind. So yes, the wizard had been June's, what? Her harbinger? Or had it been June herself?

In a state of, perhaps, confused fever, I wondered, had Brian known her before? But it seemed preposterous, as preposterous as my idea that he was himself traveled back from the future like Sam out of "Quantum Leap," inhabiting his own younger body, but with sure knowledge of the future.

Much later, I was struck with the momentary conviction that June wasn't real at all. One spring at college I found myself lunching every day with the philosophy kids. It had been a banner year for concept films and the students would erupt into heated discussions of them around the lunch table. The first was the movie about the 80s Wall St. trader and serial killer, "American Psycho," then it had been "Face/Off," followed by "The Matrix," but it was "Fight Club" that engaged them the longest. And I found myself wondering if, as in that movie, June was only a fragment of my own psyche, waiting to be reabsorbed.

The fever passed. She was real. But even now if you told me, in some dream voice, that after a gaming session in the clubhouse at the farm I had wandered down to the vegetable garden, sat on some crates, and, mesmerized by the stark blueness of the sky, had fallen into a stupor and dreamed my entire life up till now, I would have believed you. I would wake, a little sunburnt, blurry eyed, watching a purple thistle come into focus. It would all, everything—the forty-odd years, June, the revolution—vanish into smoke, and I would go on and live out a different life, in a world that knew nothing of this one, of its tragedy and its wonder.

When June had said that "The Game" had been fun, I asked, "Do you want to keep playing?"

She was quiet for a while, contemplating. "Nah," she said, "I'm good. But I think it's so cool. You took something that was"—she paused, looking for the right words—"strange, and incomplete, that was just words and hints, and made something out of it, something alive. I don't know."

June was older, and periodically her comments deeper and more penetrating than I think I could understand then. As adults, in general, we forget how intelligent and insightful children of all ages are—we underestimate them, and overestimate our own reckoning.

YES, I REALLY HAD met June in "The Game" first, met them all, before I met them: There was the old, hairy ogre, keeper of the key and of a harp of unsurpassed musical beauty only he could release. The hermit collector who would whisper only likenesses of ideas twisted outside of all understanding, not the ideas themselves. There were the sirens, alluring women whose calls heeded were death. There was the vampire, undying, and his young familiar. There was a host of goblins, skeletons, warlocks, witches, noble steeds, spiders as big as dogs, dogs as big as houses, forgotten castles, trackless wastes, forests of night, springs of youth, all of them I encountered. I met farmers; I met innkeepers.

I had met them all in advance, but these meetings of the imagination were no preparation for what came next. It was just like what happened with Eric, over the summer, the incident that I had wanted to tell June about.

Nothing had been going right. Dead ends, bad rolls, inconsequential victories with limited gains. Somewhere, past a hundred twists and turns in the underground fortress, past creaking gates, pitfalls and spikes, grumbling goblins scraping and sniggering along, locked doors with niches waiting for glowing gems, was a cavernous room filled with parchment scrolls and spiderwebs.

Behind two towering, green-glowing candles, in a robe of dark crimson embroidered with silver and gold stars, planets, suns, and comets, stood a tall but gnarled figure, bent over a leather-bound tome set on a stand made entirely of human bones. His grey beard, curling over the page, crawled with spiders and moths, and a long centipede surged through it, breaching here and there like an ocean mammal.

He was contemplating a great spell to wrap the entire world under crushing dominion. We were only a few ragged companions, leveled-up only so far, escaping his notice by our sheer powerlessness, the absence in our presence of any threat.

"Nothings!" Eric burst out. "We are total nothings! That wizard could crush us with a thought."

Brian raised his eyebrows. "That's the point."

"You mean if we were just a little bit more powerful he would stop us? But every time we play, it's the same. We are a bunch of weak nothings. Then . . . somehow, we win anyway."

We were all looking at Eric now.

He continued. "We always win. We always find a way. We are just all a bunch of nobodies and in the middle of some big doing. Some amazing adventure."

"But," I said, "that's the game."

"We should be just making it," he said. "We should be lucky to steal from some rich travelers. We should be eating dirt out in the woods! Why is every step we take a step closer to shining 'destiny'?"

"That's the point!" we all yelled at him, at last, unsure of what else to say. That's the point. The point of every book, of every movie, every game. That what you are, and what you experience, is of global significance. And to each of us, then, it couldn't have possibly felt different. Here we were living out our own importance, our summer of freedom; we could pull adventure out of the air, harden it into words and build a castle.

Eric rolled the dice glumly after that. We ground on in silence. There were some missteps. Then a dramatic fight. A secret object was revealed under the skeleton of a long-dead beast. Through its broken, prison-like ribs, we pulled out a dusty scepter with a crystal head. Eric rubbed it clear with his cloak, and it began to glow. He was drawn back in.

As kids, we never talked about anything real, except unconsciously. I sensed, from what he was saying, that there were things roiling about in Eric's home, and that this was at root of what he was saying. Whatever it was, it was soon righted, and Eric never posed such existential questions again.

Ever since then, though, I have had an uneasy feeling. Your heady illusion of unshakable centrality, your inherent significance, either solidifies into insane egotism over time or fades as you come to grips with your inescapable obscurity.

I PRESSED JUNE: "BRIAN, and the others—they'll be disappointed if you don't keep playing."

"No," said June, "I had fun in 'The Game,' but I got what I needed. It's not really my thing, you know? Anyway, I think I found something." We were sitting side by side in front of a keyboard, taking turns hunting, on a joint traversal of the Oregon Trail.

She grew conspiratorially quiet, and then she grabbed my arm. Two things: it was startling how hard her grasp was, and startling in the way I felt it over my entire body. A kind of thrill, but like an animal, frozen, feeling the bite on the nape of its neck.

"Do you know about Clyde Duane?" she asked in a prophetic tone. "Do you know about his secret?"

*Shaggy green grass brushed her tires where it grew
in patches through the ruin.*

Chapter
4

THE TWO TEENS at the end of the block called to Tiffany as she skipped down her stoop. "Looking fine, Tiff!" shouted the first.

"Will you escort me to my court date, good lady?" added the shorter of the two.

His friend elbowed him.

"Sorry," said Tiffany, as she unchained her scooter from the iron fence, "I'm not bailing your young ass out of the joint."

Rebuffed, and mildly chagrined, they resumed their grim posturing. There were some candles behind them, and a few cellophane-wrapped flowers stacked like logs. A white plush unicorn, trailing a rainbow, had a bedraggled look, as if it had been outside too long.

The whitewashed wall curving into the corner store—a bit of architectural folly meant to suggest a Moorish palace, supporting a sad terrace with a few withered tomato plants—was notched with bullet holes. A few weeks back, a stranger from Detroit, just out of prison and looking to make a name for himself, had come here to Utica and shot five times—loud pops Tiffany had heard while sprinkling water over her nasturtiums—into the gathering usually collected there.

The bullets had only found the wall, but Sammy (aka "Biggs!") had clutched his chest and toppled over on the spot. When the ambulance finally came, almost an hour later, he was stone dead.

It was a plum locale, on the border between two police precincts that neither was inclined to patrol. Two youngsters, one from each of the rival factions contesting the area, stood together there out of solidarity against the actions of the foreign interloper. Tiffany's father had bought the building as an investment property when she was about ten. Now he was living in the basement apartment with his girlfriend. Though he grumbled about the black and Puerto Rican gangs, the gangs had more-or-less let them be, and when Tiffany, to be closer to work and keep an eye on her aging father, had moved into the second floor apartment, she had been received by the locals with an open, if fumbling, acceptance. The teens on the street postured, but were as apprehensive as anyone about the real violence that sometimes erupted.

As Tiffany scootered by the pair of faux-toughs, children really, she grew angry again over her father's racist dismissals of the local "punks." Intellectually she grasped the idea that marginalized groups, immigrants like her family, directed their repressed anger from their own mistreatment against other powerless groups, but it felt stupid and pointless, and hypocritical, to spit on people that were just as scorned as they were. Nobody here coughed and said nasty slurs to her as she passed (she shivered, thinking how it had been in Boston), but her father always said, "They're thinking it, Tiffany. Never forget, it's always in their minds."

The punks had something else in their minds, which also would not have made her father happy, as she passed, upright and imposing on her silver scooter, in dark wool skirt, kitten heels, and white blouse open around her neck. She wore a helmet, mirrored aviators, and black leather gloves. This was the view that had caused her boyfriend James, when he had still been a random stranger walking down the street, to slam his shin straight into a fire hydrant, and left him with an enormous purple bruise, and a quest to find out who she was, where she came from, and where she was going.

She took a few turns on a zigzag of quiet back streets, cobblestone still peeking out from under asphalt that flowed like cooled lava, here and there a rail from the long-gone streetcar, now buffed to a bronze shine by the tracks of age, all looking old as Pompeii. Shaggy green grass brushed her tires where it grew in patches through the ruin. In about five minutes more, she reached her destination.

The firm of Jeremiah & Jeremiah inhabited a white clapboard house with a short deck; straight pillars with simple wooden capitals that held up a short roof decorated with long, irregular dentation; matte black wood shutters; and a hand-painted sign with the firm's name and an established date of "1788." Four-score years, or so, before Utica's high-water mark, when its vast water-powered woolen mills had manufactured all the uniforms for the Union Army. The decline thereafter had been, except for a few bright spots, as steady a march downward as Sherman's to the sea.

Jeremiah & Jeremiah was like a fly in amber, except better: it was alive, kept freshly painted, never changing, every piece well-oiled, replaced when needed. And there had always been a Jeremiah at the helm. And always of some indeterminate age, between fifty and sixty-five, with mutton chop whiskers the color of campfire ash and narrow eyes with big black pupils and thin, violet-flecked irises whose hue changed with the weather.

When she first started work, Tiffany would arrive early, which was on time, fifteen minutes before 8 AM. Then Jeremiah would sit with Tiffany, and in his baritone voice declaim on special points of the law, and ask her questions, in preparation for her bar exam. They did this until 9, when the paralegals came in. They'd work two hours until 11, then Mr. Jeremiah had them out running errands, and gave them a long lunch across from the courthouse, with instructions to report on comings and goings. From two onward, one of them would assist Jeremiah with typing while the other would help Tiffany with her cases. The entire operation would be closed up again by four.

Just before the end of the day, Jeremiah always asked for the mail, and a big document box. It had the initials "L. E. F." written on the side in an elaborate calligraphic hand, and held a number of accordion folders, each one looking a little older than the next.

"That's our special case," Jeremiah had said when Tiffany first asked about it, "and it's for a Jeremiah to handle, for the time being."

*"That's our special case, and it's for a Jeremiah
to handle, for the time being."*

Chapter
5

BEFORE JUNE COULD tell me what the secret was, if indeed she was going to, the bell rang. She waved and slipped out the door into the upstairs hallway of the junior high. In this one thing—arousing curiosity with an explosive declaration, then disappearing to let you stew in the mystery—she had achieved perfect mastery, and I was her abject victim.

I ran to the door, but she had already disappeared into the sea of students rushing to their next class. I stood lost in thought for too long, until the last students were ensconced behind the classroom doors, and was now late for class. Then, as if she had orchestrated it in a kind of magic trick, Clyde Duane appeared, slowly pushing his custodial cart down the hall, one wheel trembling as it rolled, squeaking periodically.

Duane was tall and wide. All the kids knew him by sight, his bulky figure a constant presence stalking the halls. He was a janitor at our school—which in this rural area accommodated all grades, kindergarten through twelfth—and one of the bus drivers.

Beneath his custodial jumpsuit a red plaid shirt flashed, like an ascot, a red reprised weakly in the color of his patchy beard and thinning hair. He had a meaty face, and meaty hands that were calloused and cracked. Before him, as if announcing his imminent arrival, wafted a bouquet of his various occupations: the smell of manure, rotten straw, and sour milk from the dairy where he milked cows before dawn, a hint of grease from the bus garage, and the ammonia of a host of cleaning products. A tobacco tin strained against the breast pocket of his uniform.

The almost genial blankness of his face belied the possibility of any mystery or special interest. I struggled to guess what secret he might have. As he passed with his run-down cart, I felt pierced by his thin lips, oppressed by his great open pores, netted under the pattern of blood vessels broken under the skin of his bare cheeks. To me, then, there, he was already a relic of the place. A giant, weathered stone some glacier had left on a hill.

He was living with his parents at that time, at least from what I've been able to determine—had an estranged wife and probably some hope, then, of reconnecting. Once, I learned, he had been a prodigy at the keyboard, and he still played the organ at the Pentecostal church every Sunday and on special occasions, displaying a devotion and enthusiasm that embarrassed the pastor and the four other congregants. The pastor would begin to cry as he prayed to himself, at night, alone, at the thought of God's gift of overwhelming talent to a man of such persistent lowness. And at Duane's feats of simple devotion. The pastor wept that we could never measure up to, much less understand, the works of heaven, such as they were.

What June said in our third period study hall, the next day, when I confronted her about her tantalizing bombshell, was only this: "Listen, next time you see Mr. Duane, look at his key ring." I pressed her, but she just said, "Look at his key ring and tell me when you see it."

I appreciated the way she was leading me through the story. It was like in the best detective novels, when the author metes out clues at a controlled, but unpredictable rate, so that you feel that you too are detecting, and can experience some measure of satisfaction when you've put the clues together, before the hero has, even. You become the hero. Supplant him.

As she talked, I noticed a palm-sized purple bruise on the inside of her arm. She caught me noticing and shifted her arm to obscure it, but as she did other small bruises flashed by, joining it to form the shape of a grasping hand.

She turned away, briefly, and as she did I could see her features fall into sadness. When a moment later she turned back to face me, that look was gone. I turned our conversation to Earth Science class; I was planning to take it as an advanced student next September, and she was completing it now. Was it right to pretend I had noticed nothing? I could tell that was what she wanted me to do.

"WHAT IS IT?" I asked her, in a whisper. "What the heck is it?"

This was during lunch, as we huddled together at the computers like two birds about to peck at some seeds between us. I had seen Clyde Duane's key ring, having surreptitiously followed him for ten minutes on a bathroom pass, until he took it out and you could not mistake the "it": There were maybe fifteen steel and brass keys of various ordinary shapes—the longer, weird old cabinet keys, keys to lockers, and a bus key—then there it was, a long, golden key, shining.

Its blade was twice as long as any of the others, and it wasn't flat, but cylindrical. It had an elaborate, medieval-looking end with strange protrusions, and the bow you held to turn it was shaped like the head of snake, with a crosshatching to represent scales and two ruby-red eyes.

"Why, haven't you seen one before?" she said, breaking into a Cheshire-cat smile. "It's a key."

The librarian shushed my loud groan.

"But is that the secret?" I asked. "That our trusty custodian, Clyde Duane, wields a strange-looking key?" I knew it wasn't just strange, it was full-on fantasy strange. It could have come from the hand of an orc at Mordor. It could have hung around the neck of a dragon rider from a leather thong. She didn't say anything. She seemed lost in thought.

"What's that?" she asked. She gestured toward the fat Manilla envelope I had tucked under my arm. She read out the large letters stamped on it, "I.L.L."

I explained to her it was some books I had gotten from Inter-Library Loan. That was how you could get books we didn't have here—and we didn't have that many. I was a master of Inter-Library Loan. It even got you access to the libraries at local colleges.

I pulled the books out to show her, temporarily distracted from my (or was it her?) quest to learn more about the janitor. There was a fantasy novel, fourth in the series, and a book about the history of New York State. At the last book I stopped, suddenly embarrassed. It was a guide to figure drawing, with photos. I blushed and pushed it back into the envelope. June didn't press me on it, but I saw the corners of her lips turn upward. I had never noticed before, what a strange spot it was, where the lips met the rest of the skin, and how it all moved, creasing, pink, and with a deep, enthralling shadow.

June then asked me to show her how to load the catalog on the computer. I was surprised—no one else used it except if they were working on a project for school. I logged in and put in a search for another in that series of fantasy books, making an awkward joke about whether it would have any serpent-headed keys, and I punched *Print Screen* with my thumb in an elaborate flourish. We watched the record print out, dot matrix screeching along the perforated paper, jerking it up, as text was tattooed on, row by row. I tore it off, and showed her how to fill the appropriate values in the right spots on the triplicate form, and which basket to put it in.

"In about two weeks," I said, "the books come, and they will be sitting here." I pointed to the biggest wire basket on the corner of the desk. The door opened about a foot. A crew-cut head poked through. It was Ryan. He was one of the jocks. You could barely tell any of them apart: tan and chiseled, green eyes or piercing blue, one playing soccer, another basketball. Were they all related? Or maybe just the product of convergent evolution: good genes and rich parents.

"Hey, June," Ryan's bodiless head whispered through the opening. It was as though there was some ward, some magic spell which prevented him even setting foot in the library. Or he was a vampire: you had to invite him in. "Come on, let's go."

She squeezed my shoulder, mouthing, "Later, dude." She went through the door. She was gone.

I had seen Clyde Duane's key ring.

Breakfast of champions.

Chapter
6

TIFFANY SPRINKLED the nasturtiums in her window boxes with water from the miniature green watering can she had gotten at Ace Hardware. She had, while picking something up there for her father, bought it on a whim, upgrading from the glass she kept by the sink. She decided it was a gesture to the idea that she was a fully independent adult now, living her life free to do as she chose, even if her father was her landlord. The can had the shape of a flower molded into its pleasingly nubby, dark-green surface, and a bright red flower for a spout, with a sunny yellow center out of which the water fell like rain.

In another nod to her blossoming adulthood she had decided she would keep a spare toothbrush for James, knowing that it rankled her father. But she was 24, and had a law degree and a full time job at a law firm, even if it was a firm with only one partner, a Mr. Jeremiah (first name also Jeremiah!), and two paralegals. Her salary was not exactly exorbitant, even by Utica standards, but her long-term prospects were good. ("What is the sound of a partnership with one partner, Tiffany?" Mr. Jeremiah would ask.)

She had lived away from home for two out of the four years of her undergraduate degree. The first two years her father would drive her to classes (he insisted) on the Hamilton campus, and pick her up in the afternoon in time for her to waitress dinner at the phở restaurant her family owned and operated: two brothers, her father and her uncle, and a cousin. It had been hard to sever her ties to her father, especially since her mother was in the process of doing the same thing. But she was able to get enough aid to cover room and board, and on top of that took work study in the computer lab. Her last waitressing shift was bittersweet but welcome. She let her father come to campus a few times a month, and he would sit with her in the diner, ranting in increasing volume about the latest transgressions of "your mother" while she grew increasingly mortified.

Tiffany was proud of her mother for leaving her father, though she loved him dearly. These seemingly opposite feelings were entirely compatible, and her ability to understand them and articulate why was a signature of her fitness for "the law," to which she found herself more and more drawn. Tiffany poured a little condensed milk into her black coffee and stirred. This was a nod to her culinary heritage and satisfied her sweet tooth. She touched the handle on the toaster, and the Pop Tarts leapt up. No matter the setting, she always found she wanted them a few seconds shy of done. She took a bite. Breakfast of champions.

She had lived "away" away, in Boston, for law school. She must have, she reasoned, already been an adult then, but it hadn't felt like it. She kept to herself, buried in the library. She rented a studio apartment which had a small screened-in porch. She filled it with plants. She worked the entire time, first at a Chinese restaurant her father's cousin's wife's family owned, and she did everything at one time or another— cooking, taking orders, delivery on a motor scooter. The scooter was terrifying to drive, but astride it she felt powerful.

Finally, she got work as a paralegal at a big firm. She was pushing herself too hard, at school, at the firm, and she began losing weight, which given her tiny frame, was a worrisome trend. Then she graduated.

She had come "home." It was as surprising to her as it was to everyone else. More surprising, really, because they only knew the world Tiffany had been living in in abstract, in their imagination. But there had been the letter, on thick bond paper, in a legal gothic font. It was Mr. Jeremiah, and he was offering her a job. He, and his prodigious eyebrows, and toad-like face, in his wide, navy, chalk-stripe suits, had come in often for phở when she was working there.

He must have asked her father about her and kept up on her path. His letter said as much. It should have felt creepy, but Mr. Jeremiah said he had heard nothing but excellent reports from his friends at her law school, and was looking for a strong lawyer with ties to the local community. Someone he would read the law with and help pass the bar. Someone young he could groom as a partner. The firm had been handed down through his family, but he was the last. It was Dickensian. And strange. And it felt absolutely right.

And in six months, she was a member of the bar, handling real estate transactions and wills. She was being sent to offices of corporations that were, mostly, disintegrating shells: boardrooms badly needing paint, a skeleton staff, some harried exec drawing the short straw at the home office in NYC, or Akron, or from Japan, presiding over holdings people had forgotten were even on the books. Tiffany would help them wind down. Mr. Jeremiah would take care of selling the assets. Or he might meet with this or that local VIP to obtain some paper promising help to prop things up.

She had told her boyfriend, James, "He is connected to everyone, ev-er-y-one!" and, "He knows more about the deeds than the deeds do themselves!"

James had sought her out and eventually found her just outside of the house, holding her valise, lost in thought. He was the front man for a real-estate investment group he and a couple friends from college had put together, and he often walked the streets looking for properties to buy up.

James was a good guy, in Tiffany's estimation, but possessed a few serious flaws that she wondered if he would be able to transcend. The way he gripped her tightly and moved to the farthest part of the sidewalk whenever they walked past the neighborhood boys. It was a weakness of understanding, and it was engendered by his complete lack of exposure to diversity, by the coddling he'd received, by a life of easy successes.

She hoped he might develop as he continued to interact with locals on the ground for his business, and through her influence. She kept trying to get him to work with Mr. Jeremiah. It was foolish passing up Jeremiah's connections, "and to top it off, you'd have me, too." But Jeremiah had made an odd impression on James and his crew.

He was "one weird dude," an "antique," they said. Of them all, James was the least bro-ey. The other guys were the epitome of dude culture. And their backers and silent partners were rich family and family friends. She imagined they wanted the false security of a lawyer from a mirrored-glass building, with rows of fax machines rolling out documents.

James just shrugged his shoulders.

Tiffany often mulled it over, the rank foolishness of the entitled. But even people who were struggling, people like her father, were also foolish.

Did no one have it together?

Chapter

7

"GRAMPS! HEY! GRAMPS! What the hell do you think you are doing?" I didn't respond because I didn't think he was yelling at me. I mean, I was only— what?—fifty-four?

I guess I had a grizzled look. Maybe I looked lost. I had been deep in thought as I walked to the precinct. It didn't matter at what age, it always took me time to surface from my inner life to the real world. I had never filed a missing person report before and since I had decided to do it, influenced by countless hours of TV detective shows, I had been running through an imaginary form, answering it. At the same time my emotions were twisting around, first worry then anger— Why had she disappeared? Why was she making me do something like this? Did I even have a right to?– and back to worry again.

Where was June?

The report went like this in my head: brown hair, brown eyes, distinguishing marks, a scar, average build, medium height—5'9" I thought—right? I couldn't remember. Last seen? Last wearing? No one else had seen her, since that night, best I could tell. My age-ish, I'd tell them. Birth date? 1979. December. Cell number? Disconnected.

"Dude, you can't be here. Don't you watch the news?"

I looked up. The young man in the police uniform was scowling. Someone was chiseling the metal letters off the precinct sign. Cops in uniform were streaming out of the doors with evidence boxes and boxes of files, and pitching them into a bonfire. The yellow and orange light reflected slickly off the dark windows of parked cop cars. Across the street it seemed like half the community was gathered, watching. Someone with a clipboard was pacing back and forth making little check marks periodically.

"I need to file a missing person report," I said.

"Not with us," he said. "We don't exist anymore."

"June, five-nine, brown hair—what? You don't exist?"

"Look, Mister," he said, "we're really busy here. Talk to your local council, they'll tell you what to do."

Fine, I thought, vexed by the whole situation, I'll find her myself.

THE REST OF THE DAY following the discovery of Clyde Duane's gold key found me preoccupied. Less with the mystery of the key than the maybe even deeper mystery of what June was doing with Ryan. Did she share secrets with him, too? How could she? He was so dumb. I considered how I would tease her in Study Hall, but she never showed.

If I consider the ways in which I acted after seeing June and Ryan together, I am not entirely happy with my behavior. At the time I was suffused with feelings I did not understand. I understand their source now. Then, it manifested as an irrational pique, and it was directed nowhere and everywhere. I was all out of sorts.

When the school bus dropped me off at the end of our driveway, I crunched the stones hard with my sneakers. I stopped and grabbed some dandelions just in their buds and snapped them from their roots, their milky sap sticky against my palm. I dallied so long on the driveway and the path— looking up at the towering clouds, how they were struck through with bits of yellow and deep purple and grey, a storm that might strike later, or if the wind picked up, blow over— that when I finally got to the door my mother wondered why the bus had been so late.

I was moody at home, and finally, at dinner, my mother called me out, derisively. "We have a real teenager on our hands now, William."

William was my father.

I mocked her back, sneering in an imitation of her voice, "We have a real teenager on our hands now, William!"

with as sour a face as I could muster, as if to prove it, and got sent to my room, which in the end is what I wanted anyway—like Garbo, to be alone.

Now I recognize those feelings: I was, in my own childish way, jealous and in love. Imagine how many books I had read already in which these symptoms were clearly delineated, and yet I missed it. We miss everything, even now, even if it's written clear across the sky. We miss anything that points to a cause for our misery within ourselves, because isn't love the most selfish, that is, the most self-related of all ills?

It might be that all our feelings are imposed on the world, not the other way around. This should be a cause for happiness—the solution to every problem is within. But for me, and perhaps you, it's terrifying, because we realize how far from true self-control we are. So I closed in on myself, with my books for shelter, like a tulip at night, and just as delicate.

As you can imagine, the next day I avoided visiting the library at lunch and recess, instead walking out to the farthest edges of the school-yard. I watched some cows the size of ants moving randomly on the hillside. Sometimes a large shadow would fall on them from a remnant cloud, and they would stride into the sunlight. Presumably they liked the warmth of the sun on their backs.

To further avoid June, I contrived to help one of the English teachers sort a bookshelf during Study Hall. Halfway through, when the teacher suddenly resolved to alphabetize by title after grouping by genre instead of alphabetizing the whole thing by author, I decided I had had enough—of my stupid resentment, that is. I was too much of a goody two-shoes to skip out on sorting the books, but when the second and minute hand finally crossed the long tick at five before twelve and the period was done, I was out in the hallway before the bell had even rung.

I speed-walked to see if I could intercept June, but she wasn't one of the people coming out of the classroom next to the art room, so I had to spend last period in algebra thinking about how to catch her before she left for the day on the bus.

What would I have said? How could I explain a thing I didn't understand myself, and of which she was surely unaware.

When school ended, I was quickly out by the flagpole, watching kids of all ages streaming toward their buses. All but a few had been consumed when I heard a loud motor noise. It emanated from a little, faded-blue Volkswagen, it looked like a toy, turning out of the school lot.

Ryan was driving. Through the open passenger window, June's hair streamed, her arm dangling. I had a brief moment of shock, then interrogated myself, and realized I was all right.

The following day June didn't show. At first I wondered if she was paying me back for my snub. But in my new state, in which I had blissfully let go of my pent-up feelings, I had determined that if June wanted to hang out with this Ryan, who was closer to her age, and with whom she must have had a lot more in common, what claim did I have? Not everything had to do with me.

Then I thought, maybe she's sick. She would, periodically, be absent from school for a day, with no indication she was getting a cold, and no hint that she'd had one, but she'd tell me she just hadn't been feeling well. I put it all out of my mind. The next day, the same. By day three, I was getting worried. It was Friday then, and there was nothing to do but wait out the weekend. We were really just acquaintances. I didn't even have a phone number for her. Today I could look at her social media accounts for updates. Back then, after mowing the lawn, I rested in the hammock, reading *Moby-Dick*.

Saturated by unease, yet also basking in the sun after consuming a glass of milk sweet from the partial melting-down of the Oreos I had dunked and dissolved in my mouth, I felt for the first time the effect of the book, and suddenly, out of the water, the slicked, half-bald head of Clyde Duane breached, dripping, and he smiled as he rose, with the colossal bleached-white denture-teeth like a mouthful of tusks or a gate of baleen.

I had fallen asleep for a moment, and had a brief phantasm of this strange man at the end of a foolhardy quest.

Chapter
8

TIFFANY SAT AT HER DESK, eyes blearing out. It was not long into her employment at Jeremiah & Jeremiah and she had been tasked with the dullest imaginable task. It was also a task onerous and seemingly-infinite. The letters on her computer began to crawl away from their words, scattering over the screen in a great confusion, like ants. If the letters were ants, it was Tiffany who had riled them up by stomping all over their imaginary anthill in frustrated anger.

This was uncharacteristic: she didn't get angry or frustrated easily, nor would she purposefully disturb any living creature. She had been known, even, to shoo mosquitos out the door. This irritated her boyfriend, James, who would tease her, "You're kind to the worst scourge of mankind, but me you treat like dirt!" To which she would reply calmly, "Of course I ask more of you. You should know better."

She was laugh-crying in exhaustion. The paralegals had both been called out for different reasons, and the phone was ringing. She let her head sink slowly to the desk, and her forehead pressed against the bottom row of her keyboard, spreading a chain of c's, v's, b's, and intermittent spaces, an inarticulate *cri de coeur* through the middle of a routine, but urgently required, motion.

All around her in the wood-paneled room, portraits of Jeremiahs of the past, both paintings and ancient photographs, scowled down at her, so similar that it was like looking at the same man arrayed in different costumes, in slightly different poses. Had the firm of Jeremiah & Jeremiah really been here since the days of Colonial America, or was the man just a mysterious fraud, with a cedar chest full of period clothes at home and a fake Penn Law diploma?

Her eyes lit on one of the portraits. It was a decent-sized oil painting, in an ornate gilt frame, a bit faded, but still arresting. She didn't remember much from the few art history classes she had taken, but she'd looked up close and this was signed Charles Wilson Peale—and she knew that name. It felt authentic. It, like Mr. Jeremiah, was surely an original. And in that painting, there he seemed to be, her Mr. Jeremiah: the same lazy eye and little half-smile, only in an ill-fitting wig.

"Buck up!" she thought she heard the painting say, "Buck up, Tiffany! Buck up!"

Tiffany locked eyes with the man in the painting, Mr. Jeremiah's great-great-great-grandfather, or something like that. But her flaring nostrils pulled in an old man's sweet scent, like ribbon candy and a hint of must. Cedar too, and aftershave. Under it all, warmth, like putting your hand through the thick hair of a dog that has been lying in the sun.

The voice had been Mr. Jeremiah himself, who had come into the office through the back, catching her unawares.

She jumped at the realization, standing and turning to greet him too quickly, nearly upsetting her chair. They stood almost face to face. It was easy to forget from his bearing that Mr. Jeremiah was not at all tall. His breath carried the scent of the mints he habitually chewed, but beneath it all, she sensed an air of decay. How sad, she thought, to be so old, to be dying.

She smiled wryly when she told me this. "Now," she said, "and just for a moment, I get a rush of that same, sick odor, when I floss those hard to reach back teeth. We're all dying, always."

She backed away from Mr. Jeremiah, but said nothing.

"It isn't the work, is it?" he said. It wasn't. "You can handle the work," he said. He touched her shoulder. It was not uncomfortable; it was a moment of great tenderness. "Come on. This . . . this motion can wait."

He led her back toward the break room. She followed him through the hallway between the two offices—his own small, cluttered office, and the larger one with the big oak table and high-backed leather chairs, where important documents were signed, and clients were entertained with coffee from a Russian samovar. Past the bathroom. It was a late addition, shabby but adequate except that the toilet often ran. Finally, to the kitchenette with its bright, chromium fifties furniture, the Deco toaster, white gas stove, the big black coffee maker, already steaming and sputtering. On the round blonde-wood break table sat two mugs and a box of *Entenmann's* donuts, the kind that had 3 plain, 3 cinnamon & sugar, and 3 with powdered sugar.

They were not good, exactly, but they were also not bad. And Mr. Jeremiah knew Tiffany liked to sit and soak donuts in her coffee absent-mindedly until they fell apart while they talked. Or did she do that because he had suggested it? Either way, in short order, they were having a heart to heart.

Mr. Jeremiah asked after her father and Tiffany explained his latest ridiculous adventure in more detail than she would have expected. Mr. Jeremiah elicited that kind of candor with his earnest, genuine understanding. He also seemed to know more about her father than she had ever told him. She knew that he sometimes went to the restaurant, but on the few occasions when they had discussed it, he seemed uncannily versed in the intricacies of her family. She didn't take offense, but it inspired more curiosity about him.

He seemed to absorb everything in the community, like a donut soaking up coffee. Her boyfriend, James, who periodically surprised Tiffany with his eclectic reading habits, had lately excitedly discussed a book he had been reading about ancient feats of memory, which had been an art. (People, he said, still compete in memory challenges, and use locations with intense emotional content to "place" in their head the facts they are supposed to recall.) One fact particularly had stayed with her: that a Roman politician could recall the name of every one of the hundreds of thousands of people he represented. It was a feat that boggled the imagination. Yet, if anyone paid that kind of attention to detail, if anyone thought there was no fact about this region that was trivial, anyone who treated everything, no matter how mundane it seemed, as if it was of the utmost importance, it was Mr. Jeremiah.

Tiffany had been at first startled, then too preoccupied with their conversation to register that Mr. Jeremiah was not in his usual clothes until now. His pale but muscular arms emerged from a bright-pink short-sleeved shirt with an army of green palms arrayed across it. On one wrist was a gold Rolex watch, on the other a curious leather cuff with a polished bone inset. A dark squiggle showed where the bone was jointed, like two segments of skull. There was a word carved in cursive along the length of it. As Tiffany's eyes scrolled across the bracelet, Mr. Jeremiah seemed to involuntarily turn it away before she could make out what it said . . . was it a name?

If he had then grabbed her wrists and confessed to being a centuries-old Caribbean pirate, she would not have been surprised. He wore khaki cargo shorts of a ¾ length, and blue Keds without socks. The skin of his thick shins was pale, and shot through with varicose veins, swollen where it was pressed into the canvas of his shoes.

Of course!

It was Saturday.

These were his golfing clothes.

Tiffany liked to sit and soak donuts in her coffee absent-mindedly until they fell apart while they talked.

*The windows were uniquely mullioned,
in a tight pattern of inverted triangles.*

Chapter

9

"WHERE'S YOUR GIRLFRIEND?" Aaron taunted. Another week had passed, and June hadn't come back to school. I grew worried thinking about her bruises. Thinking about her occasional moments of dark brooding, and about that one time she had pointedly said, "He's not my real father, you know," when the office had called her down over the intercom from Study Hall because her father was here to pick her up.

"She's not my girlfriend," I said, and stalked off.

I had made up a plausible explanation for myself: it was a family holiday, planned before they knew our school calendar and when spring break was, and it could not be canceled except at great expense. I put worry for June out of my head, thinking only of the stories she would tell of their ocean trip (I had never been), or foray to the mountains—real mountains, not our mosquito-laden green hills—or some exotic city tour, like St. Louis, with its big concrete arch.

Of all of my friends, only Max had ever flown, that I knew of; he had relatives in California. I had read about California. To me it was a wild, rocky place still filled with wildcat prospectors and mining camps. My idea of travel, beyond the car piled high with suitcases, was a train with a sleeper car, or a chrome airplane, propellers buzzing, like I had seen in old movies. Max never discussed it, but I attributed to him and his life a veneer of romance and danger. I suppose the reality was that his family just wasn't quite as poor as mine.

But my imagined vacation for June couldn't go on much longer. As I struggled with whom among the adults to approach, and what to say that would not make me appear to be a weirdo or fool, two important things happened.

The first thing was that I noticed in the library basket a big, fat folder full of I.L.L. envelopes, books from other schools, earmarked for June. I wondered what June had ordered from Inter-Library Loan after she had been so curious about it. I had initially assumed that like me, she was just looking to expand her literary horizons beyond what was offered in our school's small library. But I suddenly suspected it was related to the mystery of Clyde Duane's serpent key.

Mrs. Knickerbocker, the librarian who oversaw the Media Lab, had just stepped out. She often ran errands or visited the teacher's lounge; the nerdish denizens of the second floor library could be trusted (until this moment). I stood at the basket for fifteen seconds in pure agony, wanting to open the envelopes, but knowing it was wrong. The string closure, a fine waxed twine wrapped around a red-paper button, was facing up on the first envelope, and I grabbed the twine with thumb and forefinger and quickly unwound it. (Using as few fingers as possible, trying to limit—I suppose—my moral exposure to just those bits of skin.)

I slid the two books the envelope contained partway out. I was screening the basket from the door with my body, listening for returning footsteps or the turn of the knob. I could pass it off as just looking for a package for myself, I reasoned. Due to new and forbidden urges, I had lately become expert at passing off my untoward activities as something innocent and quotidian. To what degree anyone was fooled, I, to this day, prefer not to know.

The book on the bottom was a pictorial history of the village in the middle-to-late 1800s, in its downward decline, but when it was still twice as large and prosperous as it was now. It had the yellow return slip sticking out of it like a jaundiced tongue. The second book, much smaller, was a rebound paperback, with yellowed pages and a faded cover. It had been printed cheaply many decades ago; the brittle paper had started to chip off. The cover showed a lurid drawing of a lady in lingerie, and it was billed as a true-life memoir, *My Life* by Frances "Fanny" Fraser.

The door opened behind me.

My body screened what I was doing, as I quickly shoved the books into the envelope, and wrapped the string tight. Heart pounding, I dropped the envelope back on the stack. I was flustered, but didn't look up, just slowly walked back to the computers as if nothing had happened. My heart continued to pound in my ears as I shot pixel bullets in the direction of stylized deer and rodents scurrying across the plains as my covered wagon's wheels turned over the black void, aimlessly, as if to no purpose.

For all my feverish thinking, I could not make up an intelligible story out of the two books I saw that also involved a serpent key and June, but I felt the dots must connect to something, somehow.

The second thing, that same day, was much more momentous. It was a thorough confirmation of the reality of the mystery of Clyde Duane and his key.

After school there was a meeting of our literary magazine, *Evanescence.* I was one of the editors. (Everyone was an editor.) The meeting dragged on, but afterwards, instead of taking the late bus all the way home, I was dropped off in the village: My parents had a dinner invitation, and it was on the way. I was supposed to hang out for a half hour there by the little town library, which had a stone bench out front, or at the lone coffee shop until they showed up, and we'd ride together.

As usual, they ran late. So I wandered from the library down to the one stoplight. Above a storefront that had been empty for years, from the next story, was hanging a small sign for the Masonic Lodge, freshly painted gold, though you never saw anyone going in or out. I had been intrigued by the symbolism, the square and the compass, the unexplained "G," but when I asked my parents they shrugged their shoulders, and made it out to be a bunch of old men, farmers and the guy who ran the hardware store, all gut and cigar, gold ring and hairy knuckle. This was and was not how it had been in the past—we were just on the fringe of the "Burned-over District" in New York, a fervent soup that birthed religions and cults like the Shakers and the Mormons, and social radicalism— utopians and their communities, abolitionists, and advocates for women's rights. The upstanding citizens may have also been looking for social connections and a leg up, but they may have been secret Hermeticists, Rosicrucians, and Illuminati.

Next door to it was the post office, and next to that another storefront, ostensibly an insurance agency, but the window was piled high with documents, in binders, or boxes, or just scattered in total disarray. These were coated with dust, and then on top, rolled up tubes of paper, blueprints, I thought. And it had all been exactly this way for as long as I could remember.

As I lingered, the only soul on the street, except for a kid—the no-good Bradley Jenkins—at the gazebo in the park, smoking a cigarette and cradling a Hacky Sack on his sneaker, and casually popping it from one foot to the other, I noticed a door opening beside the phantom insurance agent's. The door was grey, paint flecking off it.

Out came Clyde Duane. Something made me cast my eyes upward, to the third floor windows of the Masonic Lodge. I had never noticed before, but the windows were uniquely mullioned, in a tight pattern of inverted triangles. They were flecked with gold and it had the effect of scales!

The next day, on the school bus, I wasn't thinking of that, though, I was psyching myself up to confront one or more authority figures, to find out what was going on with June. I was afraid I'd be asked why my sudden interest, and also afraid to draw ridicule. I had always kept my head down and didn't like notice of any kind. I ran through a thousand different scenarios, who I would approach, what kind of story I'd offer to elicit the required information with the least amount of embarrassment or disruption of the normal patterns of my day. As much as I liked mystery and adventure, I preferred to find them in books or a game, during the normal course of an ordinary day.

Imagine my relief when, heading into the school, I saw ahead of me, in a jean jacket, head bent downward, blue knapsack over one shoulder, June, returned to school in one piece. It was a threefold release: now I wouldn't have to risk upending the order of my life by talking to an authority figure; I could find out what June was on to; and I could clue her in to my discovery last night, Clyde Duane and the case of the mysterious windows.

At lunch, I rushed to the lab, and found June sitting there, glum. She barely lifted her eyes to meet mine. I was startled by her attitude, her posture of thorough defeat.

"Hey," I said, "where have you been?"

She didn't answer. Instead, she said, "Do you think we're as bad as the worst thing we've ever done?"

"Hey," I said, "where have you been?"

Chapter
10

MR. JEREMIAH CROSSED his arms, looking, in his oversized Hawaiian-shirt, like a samurai preparing to draw his blade. The rain was beating on the tin roof of the kitchen. He continued his pep-talk while Tiffany inhaled another donut. "The work, yes, I know you absolutely can handle the work.

"Just do one thing at a time, even the smallest crumb of a thing. When you finally stop and look back, you will find you have assembled, impossibly, from these infinitesimal motes, a great cathedral of work, of life. Like the way I slice, and chip, and putt my way through eighteen miserable holes.

"Well—nine, today," he said as the patchy sounds of intermittent light rain were cut into by distant booming thunder, "only to find I have put up a respectable golf score.

"It's not the work," he continued. "I chose you because I knew you could do it backward and forward. You are feeling unexpectedly low, lost, isolated, that's it. You are afflicted with doubt and dread.

"You've seen something, perhaps, an electronic newsletter from your Alma Mater's listserv highlighting some big corporate case and the surprise presence of a recent graduate as an important member of the legal team.

"Or a casual acquaintance from school has just been announced as one of the clerks for a Supreme Court Justice, an impressive, enviable accomplishment.

"Even if you question the ethics of clerking for someone of a different political persuasion, whatever the supposed political neutrality of 'the law.'"

Tiffany was silent, stunned. It had been both. And it had affected her in a way she was not prepared for. She hadn't dreamed of either of these things, thought of them as important. But she had innocently opened her alumni email as a break this morning from a particularly thorny passage. Normally she'd have stood up, walked onto the porch, and looked across the street through a gap in the buildings to a patch of green and blue beyond. But James had told her to check her personal email when she had time, and so she did.

She smiled to herself when she saw his name bolded in the inbox, unread, and the subject line "read when ur alone." She felt uncomfortable opening his explicit messages in the office, on the office computer, but it was a good discomfort, like James's big hands moving her to one side. She felt her freedom melt away momentarily, and then felt herself asserting it again, in pleasure. Sometimes she forced herself to read the other unread messages first. Today she had clicked on the alumni newsletter.

To her surprise, its contents, instead of filling her skull with a pleasant, empty boredom, were like a sock to the gut. What was she doing, it screamed, here in the ass-end of nowhere, typing and re-typing dry-as-dust motions—she was nowhere and nobody, growing smaller and less significant by the day.

"You are suddenly and unexpectedly worried you are 'nobody,' that you are 'nowhere,' and that you are doing 'nothing' of real value," said Mr. Jeremiah, echoing the words in Tiffany's head. "You are wondering what the significance of this old, seemingly impoverished little firm is in a city which even with an influx of immigrants has dwindled away from its former glories. And they are definitely former: a century would be long time ago, even a century and a half, but the glory days are even farther behind us. Furthermore, stuck here with the most eccentric, stuffy, and stuck-up practitioner of the law, and the paint cracked, and the wall having a yellow stain from a slow leak long unattended."

Mr. Jeremiah sighed a little, and his eyes darted here and there, looking all around the kitchen, which took on a shabbier air as they both regarded it. She didn't say anything.

What could she say? She just shrugged and made an embarrassed grimace.

"Of course," he said, "the most rational and reasonable person could reach only such a conclusion. But—" and now he paused and smiled, the smile of an imp, or a devil. It pulled her out of her slouch, in anticipation; the pause was interminable.

She thought to herself that she had never seen him operating in court, it was hardly the thing they did, really, but he must employ fantastic and surprising moods and gestures for every oratorical thrust. He was like an old-time lawyer, then. His fist pounded the table. "But a sensible person would be wrong!

"You are thinking, perhaps, now he is going to tell me about his secret client, the one exalted thing surrounded by so much quotidian dullness. Now I am going to open the curtain, lift the veil, un-shroud this mystery. But the secret"—and with each point he stabbed his stocky forefinger onto the table for emphasis—"is that there is no secret. What we do, matters of probate and property, contracts, bits of essential fairness, is the fabric that binds our community together, and it is itself the most essential bit that anyone does.

"Go to Washington, and these big cases, the earth-shattering cases, sure, they flip the deck, they spin the wheel we are all clinging to, sometimes, but it is us doing the spinning, the dealing, the drawing out of a card." He spun all over the place in his diatribe, enjoying his own compounding of mixed metaphors, cutting from one scene to another like a director who has just discovered that film need not flow like a stream, but can flash here and there without regard for linearity.

"I can tell you are not really convinced. But you must believe me, these papers, the words you are stringing together, cautiously and with all due respect for precedent, are the glue that sticks this community together, and this community is a vital link in the sinews that stretch across the muscular land of our nation, and our nation itself only one fleshy part of a whole body that is human civilization. Or it could be you feel that our civilization is not good.

"There are, certainly, those signs. The ethnic violence in the Balkans, the slaughter in Africa. The way the world's poor are ground into dust for our cheap trinkets, the slide in culture —well we've lost that one, for sure. And yet, we are still growing. At what state are we? I tell you if you measure up our society, we are not yet even born.

"Or if you like, civilization is a great clockwork, organized without a maker, and we are a flywheel, or an important gear. People say 'just a cog,' but without it, the machine won't run. What you are doing for me, for the firm, is really the same as our big, anonymous client, which I will tell you about, but not quite yet. But when I do, you will see, well, you've been working on it the entire time.

"I will only say one more thing, as you worry about your importance. The President of the United States, the Speaker of the House, the Chief Justice of the Supreme Court, the various Senators, and Congressmen, and lobbyists, and Defense Department Officials, the Joint Chiefs, the CIA, the General, General Motors, CEOs, business executives, these young tech wizards, your Bill Gates and his Microsoft, are all just other wheels turning, and in our own way, we are the gear that sets them to spinning.

"Except we have not been engaged. The whole machine is idling. We must keep its workings honed and oiled, survey the pieces, replace any questionable connections. We are doing work of the utmost importance. And out of all the candidates, out of all your classmates and the lawyers who would, if they only knew, give anything to be here, I chose you."

The rain was heavy now, constant. Like clockwork, the yellow stain on the ceiling began to drip.

Chapter

II

I HADN'T KNOWN how to answer June, when she had asked if we were to be defined by the worst thing we'd done. I just shrugged, I think.

"Where have you been?" I asked.

A shadow seemed to pass over her face. Like the memory of a bad bruise. I'd notice it happen often after that, after she returned. There were small cuts along her arm that had half closed, and her lips were a tad swollen. Her lower lip had split open and healed.

She didn't say anything for a while, then, in a hollow, tired kind of way, "We were on a family trip."

I had known it all along! My relief should have been immediate and palpable. A family trip. It must have been long planned. They hadn't been able to cancel, everyone had known all about it. No mystery at all.

It's just that I knew it couldn't possibly be true. Not from any actual evidence, just from the tone of her voice and her vacant expression. I felt glum and confused. We can lie to ourselves, but not this much. I didn't even bother asking her where they went. I think she was relieved, not having to concoct a story on the spot, or test one that had been made up earlier. I just gestured in the direction of the basket on the librarian's desk.

"Did you see what came in for you?" It was her Inter-Library Loan packages.

Her expression changed. She jumped up. "Now we are going to get somewhere!" she said.

"What are they?" I asked. "What ever *is* going on with Clyde Duane?"

"You've seen him," she said at last, the books in their envelopes gathered up in her arms. "Seen him then, in town, after school, going up to the secret chambers, haven't you?"

I had been thinking about June's bruises. I didn't reply. What was swirling through my mind then was whether what had gone bad had been with Ryan. I could imagine him, rough, cruel—all jocks had that in them; alas, I've learned, so do geeks and nerds—or had it been Tim?

I had not seen Ryan lately, and wondered now if he also had not been in school for the past two weeks. And he seemed like he could be the violent type. There was something edgy about all the athletes, something off-putting. It was a feeling of physical power, and the way they sometimes looked at girls, especially the older ones. The way they got into fights with each other, all that energy pent up, and then a sudden explosion, going at each other like dogs. And Tim—sure, I had been suspicious of June's step-father, especially since I had discovered that he was her step-father, and took note of her air of disregard for him.

But I started to imagine that June's bruises and scrapes had started about the time I noticed her and Ryan together, and I remembered I had seen them talking beside the parking lot, weeks back. Ryan was animated, gesticulating. I couldn't hear what he was saying, but he had a look that was dark, and painful, different than I'd ever seen him. It was the look of someone who could change dramatically, become a monster.

"Well, have you?" she asked.

I shook my head to clear it; my thoughts had been wandering like crazy. "No. I mean, yes! I saw exactly that, how did you know?"

She was hugging her books with care, but her expression had lost all of its tentativeness, all its sadness and shadow. She was thrilled. "Because of course you saw it! You saw him going in. Listen, stay here after school, invent something. It's the right day for it, and Ryan and I are going to follow him. You come too."

It could have been that Ryan wasn't so bad after all.

It's possible I might not be accurately representing my thoughts and observations of that time about June's injuries. Back then I had only the barest understanding of what physical abuse consisted, so I could not really have comprehended whether one explanation of these injuries was any more likely than others. There were periodic presentations in our classes, when a visiting adult with a vaguely haunted look would talk in hushed and serious tones about things that made my soul tremble, but I immediately cast what I heard into the remotest corner of my mind. So, to me, a whole range of other possibilities existed.

Sometimes I imagined that June might have hurt herself in the ruins of her old barn, which I knew from the summers could be dangerous, and our rugged landscape was a common source of scrapes and bruises, whether sliding down a rocky hillside into a stump or stepping wrong on a pile of old foundation stones. Several classmates had been kicked by cows or stepped on by horses at their farms.

I wondered, for a moment, if the latest accidents had been related to what I now thought of as "our" mystery. It gave it an air of danger. It was, in fact, related, but not in the way you might think.

As easily as I had cast Ryan as the malefactor, I now doubted that he had hurt her, in part because he was coming along at her invitation. But my heart also sank, on two fronts: I would go with her, but so would he. I would have to spend time with them as, I imagined, a couple. Furthermore, after the relief of not having to confront authority to discover June's whereabouts, I'd now have to lie to my parents, and fully involve myself in some kind of conspiracy. I didn't have the words then, but I had the thrill of it, this feeling that grew more and more, that filled up in me. It wasn't limited to Clyde Duane and his golden key, but as I engaged in a series of tiny rebellions against the everyday order of school, my circle of friends, my parents, I entered into what might be a conspiracy against the whole order of civilized life.

What side was I on—civilization or rebellion—is what I was really asking myself. When I looked at June, without knowing, I knew in an instant.

That was the secret, really. That each of us is born a bit of whirling chaos, and that the process of growing up, of maturing, compresses our vibrations into smaller and smaller spaces, to impose on our selves a state of order, or at least the outward form of it. The impression. And every secret is the same, either moving toward that order or away from it. It wasn't really Clyde Duane's secret, or my secret, or June's. And yet, much as quantum states are always in superposition, it was also each of these things.

"Well," she said, "are you coming along or not?"

"Yes," I said. "I'm in!"

Chapter

12

THIS YEAR'S PARALEGALS were an unusually youthful crop, a little younger than Tiffany, not the older, matronly sort that Mr. Jeremiah had habitually employed. The new paralegals frequently made overtures to Tiffany to join them out after work. She usually demurred; she'd had most of the fun wrung out of her, and she didn't mind it that way.

Eventually she relented, and let them take her one evening to an old oyster bar. It had a floor of black and white tiles, with a mosaic showing a date in the early 1800s which was not, as some people supposed, its founding, but a refounding. This tile succeeded a wood floor always covered in sawdust, swept into the street at the end of the night, just as the sky first thought of dawn.

After a few drinks, one of the paralegals asked if Tiffany knew anything about "the box," the one full of folders marked L.E.F. Mr. Jeremiah would on some days, as if according to some erratic and unknown schedule, or triggered by some mysterious contact, take the box out of a locked cabinet and into his private office. The next morning there would be lots of letters for the mailman to pick up, always to the same addressees, but none of them connected to any of the firm's cases that they knew about.

"Oh," said Tiffany, in reply, "I actually thought you might know." She had thought maybe the paralegals had somehow unbeknownst to her had a hand in preparing them. Their ignorance left Tiffany feeling satisfied; she had been afraid that the mystery of Mr. Jeremiah might be unceremoniously dispelled in an offhand comment, that the whole edifice would whisper away like a rumor, and she'd realize she had imagined it all. That she had been coming to an empty house on a ghost street all along, working alone in cobwebs and dust.

"This beer is terrible," said one of them.

"Let's get three more," Tiffany said.

There was Michael, impossibly tall, long fingers ("Yes, I played high school basketball."), his teeth perfect—Tiffany's lower teeth were slightly jagged; she ran her tongue along them. A sweating bottle of Utica Club looked small, gemlike, in the vastness of his powder-pink palms. Amber, the other one ("I hate my name!"), bad tattoo of an Asiatic-looking tiger crossed by the black spaghetti strap of her top, exposed as her cardigan slipped loose from her shoulder.

Tiffany had regarded them as drones, buzzing away in the warm wax cells of Mr. Jeremiah's hive, not real people from, respectively, Chicago and Cleveland, the wing and eagle-eye of the Middle-West.

At 11 PM, Michael said, "Let's have some fun."

They were both on the bubble, trying to build cred before starting law school. They had both been recruited for Jeremiah through eccentric undergrad professors who had "believed in them" and who assured them a connected future, if they played their cards right. A future they had believed their socioeconomic origins had all but ruled out.

As a trio, they heaved Tiffany's scooter up into the rusted bed of Michael's Dodge pickup; it bounced a little on its whacked-out suspension. Tiffany was tiny enough to ride in the middle of the small cab.

They drove for twenty minutes or so. It was uncomfortably dark here, where the city dropped off all at once into seemingly deserted wilderness. Forests, the shining eyes of deer on the roadside in the Dodge's weak headlights, the rush of sweet smelling air from the window. They passed, here and there, cinder-block garages that looked like they had never seen a heyday, nestled right up into the woods. From the highway, they turned off to one winding country road after another.

Tiffany was surprised to find they were in a quiet little town consisting of a church and a few houses. A dog barked, then went silent as they rode past. A final turn down to a big single-story white building, a single wan streetlamp shining over a sign of cockeyed black letters (they had been straight once, maybe), and a steel door. The letters on the sign spelled "Bowl-Mor," the "r" just an r-shaped shadow where the letter had once been.

A stream gurgled past, or a creek. A concrete walkway with railing made of pipe parts looked like it had been stood up at the top of the hill and slid, unevenly, down into place.

Michael held up a bright, new, silver key between two fingers. "My buddy's place," he said, by way of explanation, then they went to the door and he unlocked it.

"I've never been bowling," said Tiffany.

Michael flipped a switch, and a bank of lights flickered on over a seating area. They were standing on new carpet, black with a bright pink line scrolling through it like a careful child's long, babbling scribble.

There was a counter, and behind it bowling shoes waiting in cubbies. A plexiglass case filled with pretzels, a buzzing refrigerated chest. Michael hopped effortlessly over the counter and plucked three beers out of the chest by their necks.

"What size?" he asked, gesturing to the shoe-cubbies after setting the beers on the counter.

Tiffany took the largest child's pair.

"It's easy," said Amber. "Bowling."

Michael found an envelope and put a crisp $20 in it, and Tiffany and Amber did the same.

"The best things in life," he said, "aren't free."

Michael flipped more switches under the counter, and some lights came haltingly on over one lane, their light reflecting off of the polished wood like golden honey. There were little arrows, hopeful, helpful, of black lacquer, which were to guide the bowling balls toward the pins, which the machine had just racked up.

Michael helped Tiffany find a good bowling ball, not too light, not too heavy. It shimmered, opalescent like an oyster shell, or like an interstellar cloud lit by vast forces. Amber took the first turn, taking a long time to square herself to the lane before one, two steps and release, the ball making a short flight from her open hands to the wood where it seemed to float along toward the pins, rolling like that thunder just on the other side of the mountain until it cracked against the lead pin, then dashed along one side, toppling most of them.

"Nice job!" Tiffany said, instinctually. "Nice one!"

Mr. Jeremiah was kindly but stern, not given to effusive praise, so Tiffany would prop up the paralegals with encouragement, even the old, sour ones, who didn't seem to care one way or the other.

Amber herself was not satisfied with the throw. She was a better bowler than Michael, who just liked to have fun. Her next throw secured the spare.

Tiffany waved Michael next. He had tried to show her how to swing the ball and when to release it, but his body had gotten too close to hers and she stood back. It was okay, she'd learn by watching.

Michael's first throw seemed to get stuck to his fingers, and came off with a weird spin that quickly lashed it into the gutter, where it shot all the way into the darkness behind the pins. Tiffany was fascinated by the way the bowling ball, venturing into the unknown, unknowable space, was recovered by some invisible machinery, heard it cranked and pulled along to emerge, as though it had never been gone there, spinning to rest so that its three eyes looked her way.

Michael recovered, knocking down most of the pins on his next go.

Now it was her turn.

The ball was heavy, held a little in front of her, just above her heart. She had her thumb and two fingers curled into it, her other hand supporting the weight; an offering for the insatiable god of bowling, that gaping mouth behind the pins. She felt her body's center of gravity move as she swung the ball back, then thrust it forward. The ball left her. Maybe she was extraordinarily drunk, but she felt a sadness as if not the ball but the entire earth had left her, as though she were falling back into a void.

It hit the lane, rolling. The noise of someone dragging a heavy granite stone along the floor. It was slower than either Amber's or Michael's, but it was sure.

"Beginner's luck!" exclaimed Michael, already knowing what would happen.

Amber screamed, joyfully, shaking her beer so that it sprayed up from her hand when the ball found the center of the pins and the pins all fell down.

Did they bowl for an hour? It may have been more. Sometimes they talked excitedly, workday chatter, talk of the world, politics, the coming millennium.

"Tell me the truth. Jeremiah Jeremiah Esq. is," said Michael, toward the last frame, "a goddamned ghost."

"Or a vampire," said Amber.

With her pale skin and prominent veins, she looked like she ought to know.

Tiffany shook her head in bemusement. She had never even considered it. Mr. Jeremiah, with his old-fashioned facial hair, was just another old white dude with an affectation. Anyway, would a ghost or a vampire walk around in daylight? Would he drive a lime-green convertible Alfa Romeo with cream-colored leather seats?

"Ridiculous," she said. "First, there's no such thing. Second"—she put her hand up, holding it in an elegantly dismissive gesture that she hoped conveyed something of her disgust for the entire subject—"well, second, he just isn't!"

She didn't know what more to say.

The paralegals both looked, suddenly, deadly serious. The entire aspect of the night changed. And this place, too. What had been a fun bowling outing after some drinks at a local bar was now a visit to a creepy concrete building, in an anonymous hillside town. Michael and Amber became strangers, nothing in their eyes. She noticed the taxidermied deer head above the counter for the first time, its tongue lolling out. Was it covered with flies?

"No, really," said Michael. "Haven't you looked at all those old pictures? All the same man. All the exact same age."

"You're not serious," she said, getting angry. "There's a family resemblance. That's all."

The big, empty, echoing room, with its high popcorn ceiling and old felt pennants, its plaques and trophies and shadows, became ordinary again. There was a video game, *Centipede,* flashing on a screen set into a table beside them, she noticed for the first time. Blocky graphics, white, purple, blue, and pink. Little mushrooms being eaten away by bursts of an inverted-T-shaped gun.

She laughed now. "You had me," she said. "You really had me."

They laughed too.

"He is a strange, strange dude, though," said Amber.

"Yeah, he is."

Now it was her turn.

"I'm afraid the facial hair imposed by my forebears in this enterprise has become something of a trademark, and cannot be abandoned."

Chapter
13

I N DESCRIBING the offices of Jeremiah & Jeremiah to me, Tiffany recalled the first time she had come there and how Mr. Jeremiah had met her.

He had been waiting for her on the porch, watching as she dismounted from her scooter and put her helmet and gloves into the rear clamshell container. He was exceedingly gracious. There was something of an eerie, old-fashioned air to him, certainly, but she attributed it to his age and the difference in their stature. He wasn't dressed like a historical re-enactor, just like someone who had first dressed as a professional in the late 50s or early 60s and had not changed his style since. When she rushed up the stairs (she was a few minutes late), he gave a curt bow.

He welcomed her and led her through the door, into a foyer lined with framed photographs. When she had continued to walk toward the inner door, he stopped her, with one big hand on her shoulder.

"Most people," he said, "take notice of this wall of photographs, their eyes lingering on them if they are circumspect, or with an audible gasp, or even an indecorous 'Wow!' at this firm's long and illustrious history."

"I'm sorry," said Tiffany, "I'm a little nervous—"

"And you don't really care."

"Well, I do," she said, "and I don't. The past is the past, and we have work to do now, don't we?"

"We will get along well," he said, "but, please, if you will indulge me, you might want to take in a little of our firm's historical aura, as it is a heady inducement to new clients. It is true that we rarely add them, but from time to time we are required to augment our business."

He proceeded to her far left, and craned his head slightly up. Tiffany eyed the photographs. There were perhaps three dozen, of varying sizes, all in identical ebony frames. At the extreme top were etchings and prints. Yellowed scraps of newspaper. They advertised Jeremiah & Jeremiah in a large and enthusiastic typeface in bold exclamation, beside a drawing of an elaborately mutton-chopped face.

"Yes, Miss Ho," he said, "I'm afraid the facial hair imposed by my forebears in this enterprise has become something of a trademark, and cannot be abandoned."

The etchings were mostly of the office. They all looked much the same, except for one, with a carriage out front, this surrounded by a throng. Underneath, in a flowing script the caption announced, "A most famous client, the illustrious Governor Clinton."

Mr. Jeremiah walked Tiffany through the pictographic map of his family's multi-generational enterprise. He noted important dates, which he connected to important points in the history of the United States: the American Revolution, the Erie Canal; wars, foreign and domestic; Senators, Secretaries of State, and Presidents. It all revolved around this very office, and a figure with white sideburns, a stern look, and one lazy eye, which Mr. Jeremiah identified in turn as his great-great-grandfather, his great-grandfather, his grandfather, his father, and finally, himself in color photographs with Jimmy Carter, Ted Kennedy, Nancy Reagan, and important members of the local Vietnamese community, one of whom, Dao Van Duc, had lately been elected mayor.

"You have noted," he said, "the family resemblance. It is powerful in the male line. Uncanny, I know, but a close inspection of the portraits will yield many subtle differences.

"Our little firm, over the years, has been involved in some of the most critical events in the Republic. But as the country grew and its center of power moved West, as its great figures began to rise from other soil than ours, our orbit has become more circumscribed. But," he said, "no less important, as even the smallest gear in the watch serves a purpose, without which the sweep of the hands of time is stilled."

He was pompous, but Tiffany felt it was an earned pomposity, his eccentricity backed by real accomplishment, and an understanding of the world that was, yes, unconventional, but not, therefore, untrue.

THE OFFICE REMAINS, even now, decades later, almost exactly as she described it, except for one important fact—the firm has been taken over, and the name of Jeremiah has slid into a secondary position behind Tiffany's. In the foyer, however, the pictures remain. The oldest photographs have that curious depth of focus only an old-fashioned camera can produce, which usually has the effect of shouldering everything into strangeness. Except here, where the pictures felt oddly more immediate, less distant.

I examined the pictures of Mr. Jeremiah's ancestors, inspected them with a magnifying glass. I was unable to discern any of the small differences Tiffany said that he had claimed were there—each Jeremiah looked exactly the same to me.

It was summer, but I felt a chill, as if a change in pressure had opened the door behind me a crack and let in air of a cooler season. Whether the man actually was a vampire or some kind of an immortal spirit, or just strange was, as Tiffany told me, entirely immaterial: the influence on the world that he either engendered or partook in was eternal, and whatever resulted of it depended not a whit on his essential nature.

Nevertheless, I tracked him to a modest apartment in Rochester. He answered the first ring of the bell, and after some pleasantries at the half-open door, he invited me in. The sitting room was dimly lighted, and wall-to-wall books. He was extraordinarily well-preserved, but obviously quite old, ninety (or nine-hundred).

He stooped and walked slowly. He offered me a drink, I demurred, and we sat across from each-other for three-quarters of an hour and talked.

"Are you a vampire?" I asked him, at one point.

"You wouldn't ask me that," he said, "if you were inside my creaking old body. But we are a long-lived stock, and in my youth I neither drank nor smoked, and was devoted, before my total submission to the sedentary disposition of the law, to a strenuous regimen of exercise that built my foundation for life."

He answered each of my questions on points where I required some clarification, readily but slowly, and at last he begged off. It was time for him to take some pills (which he complained about) and a nap, he said. I suggested a day for our interview to continue, but he seemed not to hear.

I later called him at the number he gave me to confirm another visit but got no answer. When I returned to the apartment, it was vacant. The young man I talked to at what was a new management collective for the housing unit claimed never to have heard of him and found no records either.

Chapter
14

THE POCKMARKED, deep-red ball was bouncing, bounding across the gym with a loud inner music, some resonant, mellow vibration of rubber given shape by pressurized air. Today was dodge ball. I had absent-mindedly forgotten my shorts, and as he had every other time I had forgotten my gym clothes, Mr. Grimmon said, "It's okay, kid, you can go to the library. Exercise your mind."

My mind had been exercised almost continually since June had asked me to come with her and Ryan to find out, once and for all, what Clyde Duane was doing in that strange top-floor apartment, with its dragon-scale windows and gold serpent-key.

I folded and unfolded the hall pass in my hands, and by the time I reached the library doors, after a contemplative amble through near-empty halls, it looked like it had been in my pocket for a hundred years. I had been thinking of all of this as Clyde Duane's secret, but what did June's secret look like? She was, I thought, like the paper I held, young but folded by events so many times she was aged before her time.

I looked left before I entered the library, and there at the end of the hall, outlined by the white light streaming through the doors to the faculty parking lot, was Ryan.

Maybe it was the light, and the distance, but he appeared different: thinner, and more worn down. He seemed tiny. He didn't have that rounded, self-satisfied look. He looked like the infant bird I had seen on the sidewalk at last year's Memorial Day Parade. No one else seemed to have noticed it, but there it was, mostly pink, a few wet feathers, closed eyes purple, a kind of dinosaur beak, naked wings, huddled against the hard pavement, dead.

This Ryan couldn't have bruised June, or threatened her. At most he curled up beside her, tight as a cat, wretched as a dog. He disappeared into the stairwell, and I wondered whether he had changed, or whether I had developed some kind of second sight and was peering into his being, like a mage staring through crystal to see hidden writing on a map or secret runes on a cave wall.

I passed into the library. In the farthest corner I saw my friends as other might: peripheral teens—in goth black, or sweats and jean jackets; pale, furtive, serious—huddled, one of them presiding over the dungeon map behind a thin cardboard sleeve, decorated with star designs. I heard some dice rattle on the table, then a bout of fierce whispering, and a low whistle.

The gang had gotten together to play. Eric beckoned me over, and over I stole.

"Aaron just lost his throw against a basilisk, and now he, like the rest of his party, is turned to stone," whispered Brian. "They would be lost for a thousand years, if not for the help of a passing, rogue adventurer."

I had planned to read by myself, but seeing Ryan like that had thrown me off, and I still had to make up some lie and call my parents with it. I welcomed the distraction. My fortuitous arrival had transformed the game, which had today suffered from bad luck and worse planning, into a shining moment in our legendary campaign. Aaron, Eric, and Max were each in turn reanimated by my quick thinking and solid dice rolls, while Brian, his narrow eyes peeking just over the screen, mumbled descriptions of our path forward, after what had been a harrowing defeat of the monster. Tension eased. We began to chat about other things while playing.

Eventually things got around to June.

"I heard," said Aaron, "that they caught her and Ryan at the school, at night, trying to break into one of the offices, and that they were both suspended, and that's why they were gone, those two weeks. But they hushed everything up."

"I heard," said Max, "that the police were over to Ryan's house. My friend saw the lights and everything."

I had heard these rumors, and other besides, and had ignored them. The school was awash in rumors: ten different rumors for every true fact buzzed around in the minutes before and after every class. And in the art room, as people idly sketched the same houseplant for the tenth time that year. And out by the softball field. And on the bus.

You might imagine the rumors had grown out of a kind of childish coping with the uncertainties of life. But the teachers were spreading rumors too, probably twice as fast, over styrofoam cups of bad coffee in the lounge. Childish coping never ends.

Something else: in quiet moments, when I was alone with my thoughts, I found myself daydreaming conversations of a strange kind of unearned intimacy with June. They were like the extension of old novel plots that occupied the imagined pages after the story ended, the wedded, stolid, "happy" sections that went unwritten, after all the complications had unwound, and two loving adults settled into married bliss. With no guide, I had created these fictional moments with June, me whispering into her ear, her responding with whispers into mine. I could feel her breath on my skin, and the way the words, bristling my hair, trembled into me.

I would whisper-ask her about her life before, and I would explain the things I'd heard, the things I knew, and those which I inferred. And slowly, this imagined bliss would begin to die. Because the imaginary June was only a part of myself, and whispered back vague platitudes, things I knew for lies. I had fallen in love, discovered my love, somehow caught her, and then grew frustrated and disgusted, all within myself, in the space of a week or two.

The police angle had me worried, though.

And there were other rumors going around. Some I'd already heard, others I only found out about much later. That the police had been up to June's house too. That there were police dogs deployed. That she had been caught with drugs. That June's step-father, Tim, had left with the family car and hadn't come back. That there had been blood found on the porch. That Ryan had been dragged by State Troopers from inside one of the outbuildings, and that he had been covered in mud. What can I say about these rumors? Only that, after a long time, I found out they were all true, though not in a way that could be expected.

Eric had a faraway look, completely inscrutable.

"And I heard," Brian said, after making a hissing sound through bared teeth, and nearly at regular volume, which flew through the hushed library almost like a shout, "that if you don't pay attention this dungeon can be filled with some vicious traps."

It broke the spell. All my concerns melted away. My mind had been turning the whole time, little gears spinning, and a flywheel had finally spun around and caught something. My mind had engaged. I had an idea how I would get the afternoon free to stay in town, to be with Ryan and June.

*"And I heard that if you don't pay attention this dungeon can be
filled with some vicious traps."*

The police angle had me worried, though.

Chapter
15

THERE ONCE WAS a theory that our sun had a dark companion, a brown dwarf, orbiting unseen somewhere out past the Oort cloud at something like 95 thousand astronomical units, periodically disturbing the long-settled matter of the solar system's outer reaches, scattering it like buckshot, and that this was responsible for those great earth-wide extinction events that occur every 26 or 27 million years. Scientists called this star Nemesis, after the Greek goddess who brought vengeance upon the heads of the hubristic. If you asked me if there were some hidden source of gravity, another person who, unknown to me until much later, tugged at and changed the shape and course of my life, I would say "yes."

"BROWN DWARF?" said Tiffany, dismissively, as she peered over my shoulder. "Hardly! I'm almost 5'2." Then, as I yammered in protest, she said, "Don't you think it's all a bit much, and also, I don't know, really? Brown? Kind of racist, no?"

I tried to explain on two fronts, that I wanted to show, here, something of the great gravitational forces that were in play around June and me, and Tiffany's relation to it all. As for "brown dwarf," well that was just science: a large astronomical object, much bigger than Jupiter but still smaller than the smallest, coolest stars, the red dwarfs.

I could see on Tiffany's face she wasn't buying what I was selling. "Maybe," said Tiffany, "you're the dwarf and I am the sun." Either way, June was the focus of both our orbits, and the effect was to wipe the slate clean.

I WOULD LIKE to believe that at the exact same time I was formulating my plan to accompany June and Ryan that, about forty miles north by northwest of the school, Tiffany was visiting her mother, and having a fateful conversation, one she has told me about on several occasions.

Her mother had called the office and left one of her usual rambling message on the answering machine. The gist of it was that she needed Tiffany to pick up some wool for her but that she needed it urgently, before 2 PM, for a reason that was garbled, and if Tiffany by a lucky chance hadn't taken her lunch break, and so on and so on. It was excruciating to listen to, and she and Mr. Jeremiah had frozen awkwardly until it was over, standing together in the conference room where they had been reviewing some documents. Her mother's piteous rambling finally ended. The red light on the machine began to flash. The message count jumped by one.

"You'd better go," said Jeremiah.

"No, no, I already took lunch," Tiffany replied.

"It's all right," said Jeremiah. "I don't have very much to finish up here," he said, "and I know a thing or two about mothers. Just go and see what she wants to talk about."

There was no talking Mr. Jeremiah out of anything. In this way, he was exactly like her parents.

TIFFANY KNOCKED on her mother's door. It was the apartment they had all lived in together when she was young, and it pained her to see it so bereft. It had been a full house with her and her older sister, with her parents—a couple no longer. Her mother, after Tiffany's father and his things had left, seemed to age twenty years.

"Open the curtains, Mom," said Tiffany, "It's too dark in here. Or put some lights on."

Her mother was huddled in the corner in her comfortable chair, knitting.

"I'm fine, dear," she said, "Did you bring the wool?"

"Yes, yes, Mother." Tiffany brought the big paper bag over for her inspection. "What are you making?"

"It's a baby blanket. For your sister."

"What—she's pregnant?" Her sister lived in Boston, where she had a bakery with her husband. In that one regard—

being married—her sister was ahead in the race for her mother's approval, but her sister's steadfast dedication to working in the bakery instead of starting a family was a black mark against her, and Tiffany moving closer to home had put them neck and neck. A baby. She almost didn't believe it. It was out of character for her workaholic sister.

"No," said her mother, cracking a sly smile, "but I'm sending the baby blanket anyway."

Even prepared as she was for what she considered to be her mother's continual professional-grade passive-aggressive behavior, Tiffany was shocked.

Her mother continued, "It's for the dog," she said. "Come on! Dogs love a soft blanket. He's getting old. Just like I am."

"We should get some light into this place," said Tiffany, eying the curtains. "You're going to destroy your eyes." She thought her mother enjoyed this role-reversal, Tiffany mothering her. "And I can come help you clean up, throw away some old things." There were too many old things in the apartment, with their useful life behind them, and her mother wasn't old enough yet to become one of them.

As if to light some fire into her mother, Tiffany started teasing her about men. There was one of the cooks at the restaurant—but work affairs were always trouble—what about the mailman she was always bringing up? He was an older gentleman, who was, she believed, a stone-cold fox: and always walking around in those little shorts . . .

"What about James?" her mother asked. "When is he going to propose? Have you been dissuading him, making him think twice? Not being good?"

Tiffany reacted strongly. "Hey, what are you accusing me of? If he wants to marry me, he can always ask."

"I blame your father," said Tiffany's mother.

"For what?" said Tiffany. "For making us independent?"

"Don't you want a family," her mother said, "and a future? Don't you want to be happy?"

Tiffany turned around. "I am happy, and what I want is to be successful, to make a difference in this world. I don't need a ring for that, and if James asked me, I might even say no. If you didn't know already, there isn't a baby blanket in my future, even if it's just for a dog."

Her mother got up. "I know, daughter. But then why are you back here, where your parents live, in a small town, working with that strange old man. Is that success? And if James isn't the one, why do you waste your time with him?"

Why indeed. Tiffany turned back to her mother. She was talking to her, in some way, in the best way she could, on Tiffany's own terms.

There was silence between them. Tiffany didn't know what to say.

"Don't worry, Mom," she said, coming closer. She put her arms around her, and her mother returned her hug. "I know what I'm doing."

After a while, her mother whispered, "I'm sorry I screamed at you so hard back then. I didn't know any better. I've learned a lot."

"What?" Tiffany asked.

"When I found you with your friend," she said, "with that girl."

TIFFANY KNEW SHE HAD a shot at something big with Mr. Jeremiah, and she promised herself that when the time came, she would take it with all her heart. She would prove it was right to come back.

But the other thing, this memory, this moment her mother had fixated on, it was an eruption Tiffany had blocked out—her mother opening the door and screaming She had been doing homework in her room with a friend from school, they had looked each other in the eyes, and something happened. The friend had leaned close and, holding Tiffany's hand, had planted on her lips the softest, most tentative kiss.

. . . our sun had a dark companion . . .

"I've got it all worked out," June said.

Chapter
16

THERE WERE SOME considerations with respect to my plan to deceive my parents, and the list had grown as I continued to mull it over.

First, whatever was going to happen I already knew would happen after the late buses were supposed have dropped me off at home, so I would have to justify being out later than that. Furthermore, whatever excuse I picked, it couldn't be something my parents could reliably check. Beyond that, I had to come up with something my parents wouldn't accidentally discover after the fact, in conversation with their friends.

The amount of thought I put into crafting the perfect explanation might suggest I had a ton of practice in it; if I had, though, I would have known it was best not to overthink things. On top of that, I would have already established a pattern of erratic comings and goings that would have inured them to slight changes in my habits. I considered this too: because I rarely if ever deviated from my normal routine, this might raise a really unwarranted red flag that would provoke my parents into overreacting. This was harmless, just hanging out with a couple friends. But friends they didn't know.

As I grew older, I noticed increasing adult concern about my movements, especially from my mother. I connected it to an increase in disturbing stories on the evening news we watched together at the dining table: the disappearance of this or that young girl or boy, and their ultimate heinous fate; death or worse. I doubt that such violence and mischance actually increased over time; it was just that hunger for ratings-grabbing spectacle transformed shocking events that would once have remained local tragedies with very specific victims into fuel for a general, amorphous paranoia, a blurred polaroid of a missing child with favorite teddy bear, to which parents could attach their own specific fears, the real face of, say, me, or my younger brother.

What I believed then—which, however comforting it might be, is demonstrably wrong—is that this fear was ridiculous, because things just didn't *happen* to me.

I also knew June didn't think at all like me. But I had to admit that June was, for some unknown reason, a dynamic person, a person to whom things happened and who made them happen.

This is what my mind finally lit on: there was a last-minute meeting of the literary mag to resolve production issues, after which a few of us were stopping at Max's to review Global History homework. Max's brother, who was 18, would drop me at home, not before, say, 8 PM.

There had, in the past, been similar emergency lit-mag meetings, and these weren't widely publicized, so I was covered. My parents knew Max, and knew that we got together to play "The Game" often. And I knew there was a certain trust in Max's essential nerdiness. Finally, but most important, Max's parents and mine traveled in entirely different circles, so there was no chance of being accidentally caught in a lie.

The last touch, which I applauded myself for, was to treat the whole thing as nonchalantly as possible, hence letting them know late in the day, and by a method that you will only appreciate if you lived your young-adulthood as I did, in the era when phone companies had begun widespread automation but before the universal ascendancy of mobile phones. It was something we did, not to save the quarters (a dollar's worth, I remember), but out of the sheer joy of putting one over on the electronic-man.

In math class I got a hall pass for the restroom, went down to the payphones by the auditorium, picked up the phone, and dialed the number listed to initiate a collect call.

A recording played: "After the beep, say your name."

When the beep came, I said, fast as I could:

"MomdadlitmagmeetinglastminutethenMax'shomebyeight!"

Then the click, and then the phone ringing.

Mom picked up. (You could hear her say, "Hello?") The same robot voice. "Will you accept a collect call for" and then my own recorded voice:

"MomdadlitmagmeetinglastminutethenMax'shomebyeight!"

I waited a beat, then hung up, satisfied my message had made it through, for free.

"All set?" June said, later that day, in Study Hall.

I nodded, feeling a touch of foreboding, and asked, "What's the plan?"

We were sitting side by side, some school papers spread out before us. She was pretending to help me with my homework. We spoke in hushed tones, just above a whisper. Whenever the teacher stirred, June or I would shuffle some papers, or open and close a book. I eyed the Inter-Library Loan books pushed down in her bag, longing to look through them.

"Based on what I've observed before," she said, "nothing much happens until about 5:30. That's when Mr. Duane enters the building. The door locks behind him, and I wouldn't want to be caught in there with him. Instead, we'll wait until he comes out."

"How long is that?" I asked, remembering my self-imposed curfew.

"Don't worry," she said. "He's only in there about thirty minutes. When he comes out, one of us will grab the door just before it closes, and we can all slip in."

"But what if he notices us, or what if he comes back?"

"I've got it all worked out," June said. I was beginning to feel like a spy. It felt good. She continued, "There's a stoop in front of the Post Office. Sometimes I've seen some kids just sitting there. We'll wait until he comes out—that's when Ryan will call to Mr. Duane from across the street, in the opposite direction." Ryan's aunt was a member of Mr. Duane's church, she explained, so there would be some precedent for the communication. "While he's distracted, I'll put my foot out and stop the door from slamming shut. We'll wait a second to see if the coast is clear, then slip in."

I realized this meant Ryan would be standing in or near the gazebo. Only the stoners would hang out around there. I was suddenly filled with respect for him, for his willingness to look weird, and risk getting a "bad rep." Ryan might have been a jock, and maybe kind of a jerk, but I couldn't remember now if he had even been part of the older group that used to pick on me and any other kid who didn't fit in, or if he just looked like them. At any rate, here was someone real, with his feet planted in the web of the village, in a way I would never be; an insider.

"We're supposed to hang out there until 5:30? We'd stick out like three busted thumbs," I said. Not to mention the crushing dullness of it.

"We'll stay at Ryan's dad's place," she replied. "It's in town, not far, and we'll come back, and be heading past the Civil War monument just before Mr. Duane goes in."

"What do you think we're going to find?" I asked, half-thinking she'd already know.

Just then, one of the juniors, a musclebound guy named Kyle, grew animated. He had his Walkman on full blast, and wore an enormous, goofy grin. He eyed me, with the same wild energy as a zoo animal picking out a single face among a crowd of guests. He was balancing an empty soda can in his right palm. With a sudden move of his arm, he crushed it against his forehead. The crunching sound it made was sharp. It left in the center of that big, blotchy, white-pink surface a perfect red ring. He was guffawing now.

The girl who had been facing him turned entirely away in disgust. Some of his friends were slapping him on the back or wordlessly roaring, or shouting, "Shit, man!" The teacher, who had been idly scratching with a mechanical pencil at a photocopy of a crossword puzzle clipped to a Masonite board, slammed it down and jumped up, screaming at the top of his lungs, "Guys! Settle down!"

The room froze. The babbling noise that had filled the room became conspicuous in its absence. The conversation between June and I had its air knocked completely out of it and at once all the desks, which had been turned this way and that to form huddles of loud friendship snapped into line, and every face, even Kyle's, beneath that single, red circle, like an angry eye, dove into the nearest book.

The only sound then was that of the clock ticking out the period, and then, somewhere on the other side of the building, the incessant beeping of a truck backing up.

As we all sheepishly filed out at the bell, one hour away from release, June handed me a crumpled notebook page. I waited until I was seated in my next class to un-crumple it and read, almost expecting it to be written in code.

"It says 'Hiram.'"

Chapter

17

"**H**IRAM," said Mr. Jeremiah, looking down at the silver and bone bracelet that Tiffany had often eyed and was looking at now. "It says 'Hiram.'"

"What strange calligraphy," replied Tiffany.

"It is idiosyncratic. The letters are not our own. The bracelet is a family heirloom."

"Who is Hiram?" she asked.

"It's in the Bible," said Mr. Jeremiah, "He is a king of Tyre, and also he is an architect sent from there to work on Solomon's temple. And, as the latter, is a figure of some importance to the Freemasons, in their secret rituals."

"I've never seen you associated with the Masons," said Tiffany. She would see, however, some of the important men from city government and rich landlords come and go from the office with fat Masonic rings, or insignias on little chains pinned to their suits.

Mr. Jeremiah continued as though he had not heard her, his mind seeming to wander through a vast, historical landscape. "It was in Tyre they cut and hewed the towering pines they brought by ship to make the temple's riblike beams. It was from Byblos, the port, that Egypt's papyrus flowed to the world. There they took the murex, the snail, and boiled out the royal purple, a dye the color of clotted blood.

"We are," he continued, gesturing around the place, "Lebanese, from the beginning. You might not see it."

His skin did have an olive cast, she thought.

He stopped for a second, as though her words had just arrived from a long distance, echoing up to his lofty height. "No, not at all, not a Mason. I don't subscribe to all that phony half-mystical claptrap wrapped around, well let's just say it, a boy's club for overstuffed businessmen."

"And the bracelet?"

"It belonged to an architect of sorts. And I, I mean my family, got it as a reminder, and a pledge."

"A pledge of what?" It was maddening and futile to press Mr. Jeremiah. When in argument, or writing a legal brief, he was a master of direct communication, without any of that lawyerly overdetermination or purposeful vagueness or elision; he knew what to say and had the confidence to say it once, and in only one way. But whenever he was talking to her, of himself, or the firm, everything was a hint, or a signpost to something else, and finally she felt that she was walking in circles. Maybe the circles were getting smaller, and maybe the answer was there, right at its center.

"A pledge of faith, a pledge of memory," he said. "Did you know," he asked, "that even in the early 1800s there were still slaves in New York, and that the children of slaves were, themselves, indentured servants for many years, even after the abolition of slavery here?"

"I guess I hadn't known," she said.

"Freedom comes too slowly," he said, "and everywhere, even in the most enlightened places, are people required to help to break the chains."

. . . a boy's club for overstuffed businessmen . . .

To be right when so many other people are wrong is an affront.

Chapter
18

I CAME BACK to visit the school where I had spent much of my childhood. Four decades had changed it: trees that had been laughable little sticks with their punk spray of neon leaves were now tall and shady. The brick structure had taken on a stately feel, and some recent architectural revisions made what, when built, had looked like a low, lost office park, or a minimum security prison, or some other unremarkable institution, look, now, solid and enduring. It was late June, and finally hot, and the sun was still out and would remain so well into the afternoon. There was a tennis game being played on the school courts.

It is amazing what people will do with their time when they have a five or six-hour work day. I almost said "only" out of habit, but most people think of six hours as a lot. I have come to terms with being old in this new world.

We used to talk about my grandparents' generation with awe, as a people who had really seen the world change. Who had lived through grim Depression, saw the rise of air travel, a second World War, then entered the "atomic age." But what our world became was also something else, as we transformed from the savage end of their golden age, their eighty hour workweeks, fundraisers for medical treatment, or just doing without until you died; a long period of empty striving, invisible foreign wars, and slowly turning up the planet's thermostat, at first "innocently," and then with knowing fervor. The waning generations wanted the future to burn with them.

I wandered to the sounds of the ball striking the court or finding the tight weave of the racket; I felt the shadows of the clouds ran fast, turning the meadow dark then light like the chop of a bay. Someone had archery targets set up. The arrows were flying in fast and true. I knew if I found the people behind the sounds, looked upon their faces, they would be unfamiliar, some of them climate refugees, perhaps, now living productive, engaging lives here, despite their unfamiliar names and foreign customs. I resolved at that moment to continue on a kind of pilgrimage, to seek out Ryan's old house.

I had just up and left work, come "home." You could do that kind of thing now thanks to a basic income and the other changes the revolution brought. Do I have to explain how it was, how you couldn't do this before, really? For the young who have never known different, I do: You could only work some places; there were other places that just didn't have jobs. And once you had one, you had to grind away at it, bow and scrape to your bosses, show loyalty. You certainly couldn't just decide to go home, take some time for your own purposes, on your own schedule.

Things were very different now, but even so, it had been seven, eight years since I even visited. It is a long time, given everything that happened, but even back then I spent little time around the village, just came in to see my parents' place, with maybe an awkward trip to the convenience store, hoping not to encounter anyone from the past.

In a place so small, it is a real surprise how much you can fail to see.

I turned left out of the school, which was separated from town by a few big farms, and then after a ways, when I started passing a house here and there, turned left again. Now they were clustered thickly, some elegantly kept examples of Federal style, or Greek Revival, a stone house, a tall white church. Then another left, onto a dead end which quickly passed from asphalt, to gravel, to dirt.

The houses got smaller, little single-family dwellings with a half-story above, and add-on garages of about the same size. The vinyl siding was two colors; little front porches slid off their posts. Broken windows. Some sheets of corrugated metal bolted to the sides. A few abandoned stacks of cinder blocks. A rusted wheelbarrow poking from under a blue tarp. At last, at

the end, a larger house. Some had shown signs of life; this was
a total ruin. A tree was bushing greenly out of one window.
The roof had caved in. Behind it, a wide field, but well tended.
Then another field, and then the rise of a hill, the back of the
one I had just been looking at.

I sat in the car, idling. There was a noise, and then a
deer shot out from behind, passing in front of a sad above-
ground swimming pool. The grass was shoulder-high, and
through the open window in the now perfect silence, I heard
the deer panting, and the grass rushing by its flank. And then it
was gone.

The street had been full, and cheery, and this house its
bright culmination. It was not as big as it appeared in contrast
to the other almost-cottages. But it had a foyer, and to one
side, a blue-carpeted den, and on the other, a dining room with
a big oak table, covered with a lace runner and doilies. A set of
crystal candle-holders, and a Chippendale, and a glass cabinet
of china. And a back room with dark wood paneling, and two
large bedrooms and a bathroom above that you got to by a
staircase with a wide, curving bannister, the kind a child might
slide down. It felt queerly open now. When I first saw it, it
seemed like a kind of protected warren, the light coming in the
small windows dimmed by heavy linen curtains, the dark wood
and hushed carpet, the protected china and low ceilings, lulling
you into a protective sleep, or more nearly like a medically
induced coma that everyone knows can only end one way.

I could see how, for Ryan's alcoholic father John, whose
childhood home this had been, it was a terrible trap. He had
tried to escape it, only to be dragged back. After the dissolution
of his marriage and then his career, he had moved back, alone,
to the old house. And when he wasn't picking up odd jobs, he
drank, and drank, and drank, sitting in the kitchen, above the
half basement with the enormous coal-fired furnace, the heated
air forced through ducts, always breathing, an empty whisper
that filled the house. What did it speak of to him? Failure?

What did it say to me now, as I got out? I walked up
the cracked concrete drive which in a kind of natural kintsugi
was knitted together again with lines of green moss. An echo,

like a green thread running through an old fairy tale. Did it sneer a little? Someone had just called out the blue jacket I was wearing, which had been an emblem of so much protest. It wasn't my jacket. I hadn't quite stood with the crowd, then. That crowd had been right, then and before. They had been right about the war, about Reagan, about civil rights; right about the environment, right about corporate power; right, right, right. All through history.

A sneer was the inevitable result. To be right when so many other people are wrong is an affront. It is a tremendous weight of hubris. It was better to be wrong, as long as nothing you did or said could change anything. I had felt that, for a while, that powerlessness.

A stone scraped under my foot.

Some weather had rolled in. I was chilled all over now. I was standing—the whole valley was standing—in shadow. I felt a raindrop on my cheek as a streak of cold. In this new light the wrecked house had an austere magnificence; it was more immediate, more present.

It took us as a people a long time to realize that there was tremendous life to be found in decay.

That nothing was meant to last forever. That we gained more in giving up than we ever had trying always to keep things going. It was a blessing for the village to shrink. It should keep shrinking until we had the comfort of nature's walls. We expended so much for so long, but toward what end? Toward the end of sprawl. All because we couldn't imagine sharing our space with a neighbor, but at the same time, couldn't imagine being more than a few feet away from a manmade thing.

The illusion of control—there was a brief moment when those mad scientists had said, "We can control the climate now," and we came close to blotting out the sun.

Could it have worked? Yes, for some definition of work.

That's what the technocrats always said: that it had worked, only with such and so many "minor" and "unintended" consequences.

There are always consequences.

There are always consequences.

I still remember the silver cap guns with their faint cordite smell.

Chapter

19

THE NOTE FROM JUNE had not been in code, after all. It had read, in her straightforward handwriting, simply, "Meet you out back: 3:15."

Around that time I had started carrying an old wallet of my father's. I kept a few dollars from my allowance, my library card, and a business card I had designed and printed on too-thick paper. It had damaged the print heads of our 9-pin dot-matrix printer. That's where I had kept her note, folded up tightly, and over the years until I graduated, I had taken it out and read it so often it had broken into four or five pieces.

I recently found the wallet, itself worn nearly apart. Its former contents were long gone, except for a solitary scrap of paper wedged at the bottom. It had become so compressed that when I started to tease it apart, even with the utmost care, it fell into confetti. There were dark marks, but whatever it had said was as incomprehensible as those charred scrolls they dug up in Pompeii.

For much of my life those digits—3:15—burned bright as a bible verse in my recollection.

A quarter after three was just when the last big yellow bus was leaving the lot and before most of the teachers departed, at a shade after four. Ryan's car was a two-door hatchback. You had to crawl in with the seat thrown forward, but it wasn't so bad for me, since I was small. The teacher's lot had one exit to the back, which necessitated us taking a right and then another right before we could swing left down the hill and into the village proper.

We called it "town," though this was technically inaccurate: the county was divided into cities or towns, and within a town, there could be a village, with its own government. How counties were divided varied by state (more and more of you will not understand, or have to be reminded of, the quaint, difficult way things once were).

Ryan and June were in the car when I got to them, and it was already running. June had to get out so I could slide in, brushing past her into the backseat. In the cramped, enclosed space she had an intoxicating scent: like jasmine, like irises, at least how I imagined they smelled. I felt envious of Ryan, practically an adult, in the driver's seat, behind the wheel.

I'm not sure what I expected from my first real encounter with him. Not him greeting me warmly, his open, smiling face generous, holding out a hand in welcome. "Hello there," he said.

I acknowledged him with a little salute, a move entirely sincere, but which I worried might put him off. "Hi Ryan," I said. That was it, then awkward silence.

The engine engaged.

"We're going to Ryan's house first," said June. I nodded, but this was already the plan.

"I know," I said. I wasn't stupid. "You already told me."

"Let's do this," Ryan said. I saw his eyes in the rearview mirror, when they weren't looking at me.

"Yes," I said, "let's." So we did.

When I was six, or so, I remember we went trick-or-treating down Ryan's street.

It was only the once, and I'm not sure what caused us to deviate from our usual route. My parents came with us, and they would dress up too. That year Dad was a cowboy and Mom was a witch or a vampire. They were both so young then that I think something like this was still fun for them. Their costumes were fashioned out of normal clothes. Dad wore his pearl-button shirt, and had his leather tool-belt made up like a holster. He had a red handkerchief tied neatly at his neck, neat as a Boy Scout, and wore leather chaps he used for welding. Only the cowboy hat was "imitation," a cheap straw one from Mexico. They had been once, before I was born.

My mother was pale and beautiful. She had powdered her skin, and her dark hair was piled up in unruly curls. She had black opera gloves, and a silk cape with a blood-red lining my great-grandmother had worn. And lipstick, which she otherwise never used. I was a ghost-child. White face-paint, powder in my hair. An old bedroom sheet cut like a robe. We had been using it to pick up the fallen leaves we had raked. My hands were caked white.

I think I have never stopped feeling like a ghost.

The next year I insisted on being a cowboy too. My face was decorated with grease-paint stubble. I still remember the silver cap guns with their faint cordite smell. That smell came to me in the car, sitting behind June and Ryan. I had an uncomfortable feeling of a connection between June and my mother, and there was something now so upright, so good and fatherly about Ryan. How calm he was, intent on the road.

We had trick-or-treated down one side of Ryan's street, collecting the usual candies, the peanut butter cups, and Smarties, and various candy bars, Tootsie Rolls, and Tootsie Roll pops. (Somewhere, someone has a collection, a personal museum of old candy wrappers, dated and showing the gradual change of typeface and color, that would make them, bright beacons of memory, into dated antiques, like us.) At the end of the street was a house which took the spirit of Halloween to another level.

The porch had been festooned with cotton spiderwebs. A cauldron bubbled, the effect of dry ice and a bright green bulb. Ryan's father was a skeleton, his mother and sister witches of an entirely different character than my Mom. They seemed like a different species—green-skinned, warted, rag-mop hair, cackling, with long, fake fingers. Ryan was there too. He raised his arms, a zombie, and groaned when we came.

Even then I wondered why he was there, and not off with friends, teenagers who were running and whooping down side streets, tossing crab-apples and decorating trees in front of the school principal's yard with endless streams of toilet paper.

"Ryan," I asked, "are your parents home?"

Ryan's little car turned onto their street.

"It's just my dad," he said, "and I don't really know if he will be or not."

June looked at me hard, as if I should have known it was too probing a question.

Ryan's house was hushed. It seemed dark. Everything was muffled, quiet. We came in the front door. June started up the stairs. I followed her, but took a look down the hall into the kitchen as I passed. There was a figure slumped down on the counter, long hair, hand on high-ball glass of brown liquid. My father drank only beer. June beckoned me. Ryan nodded us on up the stairs, and made his way to the kitchen. We both knew, without him saying, that he'd be with us in a minute. June knew where to go. I felt a quick snap of jealousy: she had been here before.When we got into Ryan's room, I demanded in a whisper, "What's going on?"

"That's normal," she said. We waited.

I heard him skip up the stairs. He still moved like an athlete, like a jock, even if something had changed in how I thought of him.

If I had to describe Ryan's room in one word, it would be "anonymous." It felt like a teenager's room from a TV show with a below-average budget and set designer, something that didn't run in prime time. There were two posters tacked to the wall. The corner of one curled down like a nodding head: Denver Cowboys quarterback John Elway, in mid-throw. The other was a Metallica poster.

His bed had black sheets and a fleece blanket. There was a smaller, plush blanket folded on it, blocky colors loosely patterned after a football field. There was an old TV in a corner; a silver stereo-cassette player next to a He-Man play set and a few Star Wars figures; a dresser for clothes; and an alarm clock with a bright red digital face. It was a room that could belong to anyone around Ryan's age, or to no one. There wasn't a single discernibly personal item, any indication that he existed as a specific person.

Had I seen the room when I knew only the "old Ryan,"—the sports star who pranced around with the meathead crowd, who got good grades, who had his license, who was always smiling; who you got the sense was rich, whatever that meant; who was often seen "at the mall"; whose locker had cut-out pictures of bikini-girls—then I would have believed wholeheartedly in this empty, anonymous room.

But since his short disappearance, since he had begun to share some intimate secret, some deep bond, with June, I met the room with wonder. Where was the indication of Ryan's hidden depth? Did he keep it all in a box? Was it buried somewhere, with a stone to mark it?

After a little while, Ryan came in. We all looked at each other and then at the time on the clock. June whispered to us, reiterating everything that had led up to this moment: the sighting of the golden key, Clyde Duane's strange comings and goings from the entryway door by the Post Office, the serpent-like pattern of the windows on that top floor, and the gold accents of the mullions. She related how she had shared with both of us separately this mystery, and had now brought us together for this "mission."

We had only to wait. An unavoidable, inconvenient hour and a half. We sat in silence for a few long minutes. Ryan sat on the bed; I occupied a bean-bag chair; June was cross-legged on a pillow in an almost perfect yoga pose.

Breaking the silence, Ryan blurted out to me, "The other kids," I suppose meaning at the school, other than my small pack of friends, "find you kind of intimidating."

I was taken aback, mortified. I still don't like hearing anything said about me, even worse if it is sincere, or suggests anything other than that I pass ghostlike and unobserved through the ranks of humanity. June laughed.

"Aw," June said. "He's turning red. You are both kind of amazing, in your own way."

"I don't know, I don't know," I said. Then, after a bit, "Ryan, what's it like to be so popular?"

"Oh," he said, "you know I'm not." He looked thoughtful. Then he said, "Hey, I have an Atari. Let's see if it still works." He got up and wrestled it out from behind the TV, with its tangled attendant wires and joysticks. We all gathered on the rug in front of the screen. I looked through the few cartridges he had; I had never played Atari. I didn't say what I was thinking: for a family as rich as Ryan's was, why didn't he have a Nintendo?

But I knew he barely cared. It took him a moment to get the set tuned to the right channel, there were a few flashes of snow, and then a blaring noise of the game going, which he quickly dialed down. We took turns guiding the frog across deadly lanes of traffic, across rushing logs, onto the safety of his lily pad home.

After we played for a while, Ryan said to me, "What's it like having such good parents?"

I didn't know what to say, but just then June jumped up, pointing to the clock. "Guys, it's almost time!" It was 5:15 PM. We would soon take up our first position, behind the old lithium spring, now just a short stone platform under a cupola with a plaque, across from the Post Office. Shaded by the stately maples which climate change and human saws have since made into old, dark stumps, we would wait until Clyde Duane entered the mysterious doorway, then fan out to our assigned positions. It was waiting followed by waiting, followed by more waiting.

Just then, as the three of us had arisen, a loud thump came from downstairs—I guess it was a heavy whiskey glass striking the carpet—followed by a loud groan. It turned into a hoarse yell, then silence. Ryan's face went ashen. He looked at the floor, then said, quietly, "I'll handle this, then catch up with you. Just get downstairs and out the door."

We would walk to the fountain, June and I, and just make it on schedule. I felt a deep shame, on Ryan's behalf— shame for his father—but knew at the same time that my feeling was wrong.

We have no responsibility for the travails of our elders; they have every responsibility to us.

Chapter
20

NOW, AT THE RUIN of the house, years later, recalling that faraway day, I stood on one of the two remaining solid boards of the porch. The board bowed downward beneath my feet, but not so much that I thought it wouldn't hold. The board led straight to a window, a few feet to the left of the door.

Soon I was peering through the shattered pane into the hallway of Ryan's father's old place. In the slanting light from the sky, one shard of glass reflected my face, the empty spaces around it revealing a dim hallway, scattered with dry leaves and dirt. At the end, the dimness ended. The kitchen shone brightly, a sunset beginning through a great hole in the house, like the light of a train coming through the tunnel, laced with yellow, with red.

Ryan's father John was doing surprisingly well these days, I've heard. He must be nearing eighty. The disease, alcoholism, or just life, or the weight of other people, their greed, some incompatibility, whatever-it-was, had left him hollow, sick. He then had what I'd call an accidental recovery —some people do everything right and still tumble into the abyss, others tumble into the abyss and then one day you find they have stepped up out of it, on the far side, wholly sound. That was John.

He wasn't living in the house, and they let it be reclaimed. Ryan could have staked a claim, but he had gone out to Alaska long since. Is there still, I believe. I'd like to say I know this because I wrote Ryan a letter, or called him, but I haven't spoken a word to him in the intervening years. I don't know if June has either. "You let me down," she told me that last time I ever saw her. It hurt because it was true.

What did the deer make of its new utopia, the glorious retreat of man? We pursue the story of every great decline, every ruin, but we never ask about paradise; there is no history of paradise. If we enquire too much about it, we are afraid it might dissolve. There are so many ordinary ways that asking questions of a present happy state can turn your heaven to hell. You find the snakes in its grass; that the foundation is bound to crumble at any moment. You find, if you really think about it, that you were never really happy here at all.

At some assisted living facility, Ryan's father, John, with growing smile, throws down his canasta cards. The other old-timers throw theirs down too. They all jump up, shake their bodies, let out enthusiastic cries. Yes, they have been drinking, a little. But it is only to show that they still can, to revel in it.

I hurry back to the car. It senses my arrival, and wakes with a purr. I have an urge of my own. I want to get to the heart of the village, to look at that door, to peer up at the top floor, before the light is all gone. The bats have come out. It never fails that when I see one, I have to stop and watch.

Our little mammalian cousins, we almost lost them. We almost lost everything. No one likes to think how close it came. Soon we'll shake the feeling, like it used to be when you'd jump out of the way of one of those autonomous cars just in time. They had even designed the front bumpers to work like cowcatchers on an old-time train. The engineers would say, "What are you doing walking, anyway?"

I saw an old man go up over one once. His arms and legs were like a bat's, shaggy and wrinkled, his face resigned to flight, however brief. A little more leather from arm to hip and he might have glided out of danger. He rolled on the ground, but as he rolled you could hear something snap, and see a spray of blood. Well, the fault was his own, for a while. And it seemed right, then, to many.

Those few years were like an age of misery. Longer, deeper, darker than anything called "dark" before. It couldn't have been worse if we had lost the capacity for writing, or had forgotten how to speak at all.

They have uncapped the fountain, now. Lithium-water bubbles up. It is like a liquid gemstone. It is a declaration of water as a community resource, a bit of extravagance to remind us of what is special in life. As I sip I find the pocket of my blue smock-jacket with my right hand. It is an affectation, like I am posing for a photograph.

There had been an imagined future, when your iris or your unique voice would be your passport to the electronic palace that would be your home. Some people had imagined dark AI scenarios, moments of, "I'm sorry Dave, I can't do that," but the AI was never much more than people picking out images or answering questions for pennies an hour. So now all that is done. It all started, I thought, with a key. Look what the key has done.

As I stood up from the fountain to face the door, I felt something else in my pocket. A tiny square of paper. Somehow I'd had it this entire time. Maybe it had worked its way out of the lining. I thought: I've missed some note from June, some crucial note. The light was almost gone now. Light appeared in the windows of the top floor, of the secret room; as always, dripping gold into the night. I pointed the ghost-light of my phone's screen at the paper, and with a twist of my thumb and forefinger unfolded it.

"INSPECTED BY NO. 6."

I chuckled and imagined the hand that had put it in the pocket of the smock-coat before it was wrapped in plastic and piled with the others in cardboard boxes, then shrink-wrapped onto pallets, loaded into a big metal container. As a child I had pictured these inspectors like Inspector Clouseau, with raincoat and magnifying glass; now I saw a skinny Indonesian girl.

Then I stopped. The typeface of the message was peculiar. It had a sixties angularity. It couldn't be, but maybe it *was* a message from June.

She had introduced me to a British TV show about a secret agent, kidnapped and taken to a kind of pristine village. There were people from "both sides" there, all over-cheery, everyone referred to by a number, not a name. It had a distinct style, from the clothes and furnishings to the typeface, which matched my note. The title character of the show, "The Prisoner," was No. 6.

Sometimes mysteries were planted for their own sake, so that one was wandering in a great palace of endless rooms, pleasure to be had in the opening of each door: an elegant salon, followed by a vast, secret closet, followed by a sitting room, followed by a long hall with pictures; unlike a real palace, it continued, ad infinitum, and had no royal bedroom at its terminus.

Just then I saw the door open. Clyde Duane came out. He turned left, walked toward the gas station. I almost ran up to him, to see if, in this new context, he would remember me. Remember as I would, forever, that day in school.

Something held me back.

It may have been his bearing. He held his back straight, and his head high. His bear-arms swung beside him, his belly straining the buttons of a powder-blue shirt. He marched on in shiny black boots.

Duane marched to the corner across from the gas station and then executed a perfect 90-degree turn, west, and disappeared from view, like a mechanical soldier in the battlement of the clock-tower of a Swiss town. He was, between the hours of five and eight, a clockwork man, running on a clockwork track.

Chapter
21

"**M**ADE IT!" June said, after we'd sped along back streets from Ryan's house to Main, just in time to see Clyde Duane step in the door. She grabbed my shoulder, and stood so close I could feel the warmth of her body. I did not want her to let go. "Now we wait!" she said, emphatically. "Let's get into position." She pulled me across the street and sat on the stoop, closer to the door, as she had planned.

It was warm. Birds were chirping. Cars passed. The sound of their wheels turning was as distant as the surf over a big dune. You could smell the heat coming off the sidewalk; I noticed the tiny stones in it, quartz pebbles, grey rocks, and it felt like the first time I had ever seen them. June wore stonewashed jeans with big, unevenly rolled cuffs. I noticed grass stains on her cream-colored Converse sneakers.

I looked anywhere but directly at her. She was tapping her fingers with her thumb, like she was sending a signal to someone. I wondered when Ryan would get there, but now I trusted that he would come.

"Wait," I said—at the gas station, between a purple Chevrolet and the pump, a Big Gulp cup in his hand—"isn't that your step-father?"

The man got in the car, the door slammed.

I suddenly felt bad for saying it. Had I compromised something? She was looking straight ahead.

"Nah," she said. "That ain't him. My step-father? That asshole is long gone."

"I guess I'm just seeing things," I said. I ran my hand through my hair.

Just then, we heard a car engine stop and looked up together. It was Ryan. He ran-walked to the gazebo. He turned and quickly gave us a discreet wave.

We were on.

Stupid. This whole thing was stupid. What were we going to learn? Inside was just going to be a hallway, and a stair and another hallway, and another stair, and a door that was locked. I guess it would take the serpent-key. But then again, no door a gold key unlocked would just be a door. There had to be something special about it. Ryan was sitting on the gazebo steps, smoking. He looked like the coolest human being alive. A rebel with a cause. My cause, too: June. What did she mean when she called her step-dad "that asshole" and what was "long gone"? Had he left? Was he dead?

An old lady was riding her black bicycle down Main. She wore a black dress, black bonnet, black shoes, a black stone on a black necklace, and had pure white hair. She could have been riding through a black and white movie, and she would have looked exactly the same. She passed us and kept going, didn't bother to stop at the light. She knew no car would be passing. I almost remember her name. Something to do with a bird. She had an old name too. Margaret. Margaret Sparrow?

Right after old Margaret passed is when everything happened at once. It was as though she had been the trigger that set us in motion.

Clyde Duane left the building. The door was swinging shut. June jumped in, to keep it from closing. Ryan cried out.

I heard another noise, someone behind me, saying hello. I half-turned my head, and was staring straight at Aaron. What was he doing here? He tried to say something else, but I grabbed him. It seemed important he wasn't seen either, and before I knew it, all three of us were in the building.

AFTER A LOT of back and forth with myself, I've decided how I would describe the moment the three of us crossed that threshold, the nondescript door that led into a dim hallway two stories below the floor with the scale-patterned windows.

I had worried that so long after the fact, knowing everything I know now, I would fail to convey the authentic feeling, the exact experience, which was, in my memory, of an unmatched thrill followed, suddenly, by a frustratingly dull denouement. Only looking back was it all colored full of foreboding and significance.

During a break from writing out my recollections at my parents' house out in the woods, I found my old diary, a small, red notebook. Paging through it, I noted the goofy, distracted handwriting, which I periodically dressed up with unnecessary, exaggerated serifs and curlicues. Sometime around my first meeting with June, a self-conscious seriousness began to inform both what I wrote and how I wrote it.

Gone were the unnecessary decorative strokes, and gone too were flights of fancy, imaginary stories, everything but a straightforward account of one or two things that had occurred that day. And then I discovered the Caesar cipher, and the entries grew shorter, but now they were in code.

It is named after Julius Caesar. The historian Suetonius says Caesar shifted the letters in his personal correspondence, so, for example, A would become C and B would become D. I had a favorite number, then: 5. So in the first few entries, this was the code: A became E, B became F, and so on.

Then I came upon a page that had been bent and then smoothed down. Over each of my blue ballpoint letters, a pencil had written the correct letter. These penciled letters had been erased but here and there bits of graphite remained, and the impressions June had left in the page could still be read.

I remembered vividly when she had grabbed my notebook from me in Study Hall.

She stared at the page. "What's this?"

I must have turned beet red. "It's a code," I said.

She held the notebook in front of her, just looking at it, and didn't say a word. Her lips just barely moved, like they were forming the ghosts of letters. I don't think she blinked. Others have said there is something unnerving about her eyes: too much determination, slightly larger than they ought to be, a flaw in the iris. I was watching her eyes so closely I missed seeing her left hand find the pencil. She began to write the proper letters above mine.

"Hey!" I said, growing a little angry. She had finished two lines by the time I grabbed the notebook back. She was grinning ear to ear. I glanced down, knowing what I had written, wondering if she had gotten it yet, but to my deep relief, I saw she had not decoded what I urgently didn't want her to read.

Now I think she probably had.

Then again, some things you might try to hide with a cipher, without realizing you've written them elsewhere, for everyone to see.

After that, I became more careful. The number 5 had been too easy to guess. At first I varied the number by using the first letter of the day of the week, which I had been writing at the top of each entry.

I got more paranoid yet, I remember, and began to vary the shift with each letter I wrote, increasing them as I moved along the name of the week, and then decreasing as I moved backwards. I found this painfully slow going. Then I only used code for names and places. Eventually I gave up the codes altogether, as it had been irritating to read those entries, and they hardly ever contained anything interesting.

Then this entry, the one I had been looking for, the day of the stakeout. It began in plain text. Then, the section I wrote in Study Hall, about a hundred words, coded with my more extreme method: it was a Thursday, which meant a shift of twenty. For the letters up to f, it was simple, just the letters t through z. If you remembered g was a, you could write the rest. Of course, the shift increased, so that by the seventh letter, you wrote it as it was, and then began shifting again. It makes a kind of beautiful pattern in your mind. Then, there was a break, and the text started again following no recognizable pattern. I had no memory of this, no memory of devising a new cipher, of changing the code. There were no spaces. The letters ran together in a steady march, completely incomprehensible.

I was stumped.

I decided to take a walk out behind the house. My parents' dogs, Portis and Jacques, insisted on coming along.

We startled a fat woodchuck. The dogs were on him in a second, but he squirmed, fluidly, from under their paws, and like that, he was around the tree and into his hole, safe. The dogs barked, then howled. I had to drag them by their collars along the path, paws scraping ruts in the soil.

Let's pretend it was the woodchuck, nearly wide as he was long, but still fast and graceful, or the tracks left by the dogs as I yanked on their collars and dragged them along, or later, when we had all calmed down, the red eft I saw, with its speckled pattern, or the turkey vulture, in lugubrious flight. Let's pretend it was anything, because we want so badly to understand our minds, to make chains of understanding.

Because the moment when my hand hit the doorknob upon coming home, I had the answer.

It was a code bound with the event itself.

It was a phrase, but I knew it by heart.

We all know it, now, foreign as it is, thanks to the Movement, to the blue smocks, and their rallying cry.

How had I known it then? From our History book? From somewhere else? I repeated the three-word phrase like an incantation: "Liberté, égalité, fraternité."

So I began the laborious process of decoding the entry for that day.

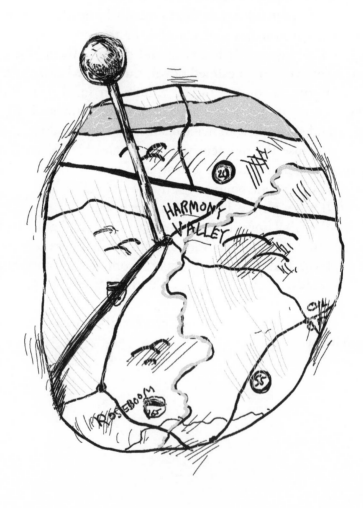

"Why should I bother Mr. Jeremiah? It's just a map."

Chapter

22

TODAY THE OFFICE hummed with activity until mid-afternoon, when Mr. Jeremiah departed for a court appearance with the paralegals in tow. Tiffany remained to sign for a special package and to finish up two important briefs. She'd be closing up, finally trusted with a full set of keys. Although Mr. Jeremiah made nothing of the matter—simply tossing them to her on his way out and making a complicated hand gesture to remind her that the inner and outer door locks turned in opposite directions—Tiffany felt that with that toss and gesture, she had been anointed. She even resolved not to test the keys in his absence, to see if the smaller ones opened the important drawers, or if she could get into his office.

So she busied herself with her side of the business, even took care of a few things for the paralegals, who would be happy to discover their inboxes lightened the next day. Around six, she was in the kitchen cleaning out coffee mugs and idly staring at the startlingly bright and beautiful pattern of colored dots on the bag of Wonder Bread, colors which corresponded with the primary color rectangles that made the jar of Jif peanut butter pop around its brown body—Mr. Jeremiah habitually ate peanut butter and jelly sandwiches as a snack, and sometimes the jam, a Tyrian purple shading toward the color of blood, would drip from the corner of his mouth and stick in his grizzled mutton chops—when a knock on the door startled her out of her reverie.

It was James. She had been late to meet him. She let him into the office, which he had never toured, and had never seen empty. His hand darted to her side and a look of lust passed over his face. She slapped his hand away.

"Oh, no. Absolutely not." She smiled playfully to show no hard feelings, but ever since that conversation with her mother she had grown more and more irritated with him.

"What's this?" James had blithely continued his walk around the office, and was now looking at the large Rand McNally map tacked up on one wall of the kitchen. It had a few hundred pins stuck into it, long silver shafts with different colored bulbs, all grammar-school colors, she thought, like the Wonder Bread bag: blue, green, red. Although Tiffany didn't notice it at the time, I can tell you there was a pin stuck straight into the dot labeled "Harmony Valley," and its bulb was ultramarine. The pins weren't dusty; they looked fresh, they sparkled.

"I don't know," she replied.

He was incredulous.

"What do you mean you don't know?"

"Really. I don't know. I guess the locations of cases or clients? It's been that way since I got here. We haven't added a pin or changed a pin or anything."

"You never asked?"

"Why should I bother Mr. Jeremiah? It's just a map."

James whistled.

"Sure," he said. "Well I'm gonna ask him."

Now it was her turn to tease him. "Are you going to ask him for help, advice, legal counsel for you and your, what to call them? Partners, I suppose? Or lazy bums, more like it."

"Maybe," he said, "just maybe."

Chapter
23

THE DECODED DIARY ENTRY ran as follows, in all its cringe-worthy glory:

Today, June, mysterious, funny, sad June, convinced me to embark on the most thrilling adventure of my life (so far). It began with a lie to my parents. Then we visited Ryan's house, who I think is her boyfriend, and after all not such a bad guy. We waited, just the two of us, for the janitor to leave the strange building sandwiched between the Post Office (it was closed already or we would have been subjected to the constant tuneless whistling of the post-master, who abruptly stops whistling and calls out "weni, widi, wiki" and then "coraggio" for no apparent reason, when you come in the door) and the Insurance Agency.

Well, we waited, and Clyde Duane came up to the door and in a second he was gone, and then June took me by the arm, and walked me to the stoop in front. She told me about lots of things. She talked about how old the different buildings were, and more history of the town than I had ever heard before. About an ancestor of hers (her family had been here going back centuries), and about some sinister forces.

She talked about New York City. The seniors had gone on a trip to Times Sq., and I even went once, to the Bronx Zoo, on the big yellow buses.

New York seems so far away. She told me it was even farther then, it took days to go there and back. But even then, she said, the connection was closer than I could have imagined. She asked me if I had heard of Tammany Hall. I remembered an old political cartoon we had seen in our Social Studies class, of a fat man with a cigar reclining on an entire city. Yes, I said. She was going to tell me more but Ryan finally showed.

I PUT MY JOURNAL DOWN. Already it had revealed more than I'd remembered. Tammany Hall. June's knowledge of village history. I made some notes to follow up and started reading my diary again.

I should not be so amazed at the way memory spills away, in places as weak a foundation as sand; at other times as firm as granite. But all efforts, even this looking back at looking back, tilt like the Leaning Tower at Pisa.

Every year our preservationists spend some time shoring it up. We dispute the ideal angle. Should it be returns to the exact slant it had when Galileo went up the spiral stairs to drop cannon ball and feather? For a while the "tech-gods" insisted we forget about the edifice altogether: Record it digitally, play it back for our avatars and let the pixelated billions bop around it—streams of electrons in silicon chips. Well—I am stalling, but meaninglessly.

I have already gone into the dark hallway, and let my eyes adjust, followed June up the stairs, and seen . . . well, I have already counted forward the letters and put letter down for letter, and read the truth, and now I hesitate, as if hesitation could change, what? The universe? Even what will happen already has.

I had asked, terrified, "What if we run into people?" June was adamant: "We won't, and if we do, just say we had the wrong door and back out." The plan worked as advertised. We got in.

I was struck by the entry: No mention of Aaron at all! What was I playing at? I had wanted to build an attachment to June by eliding away the other people there. I must have felt, even then, that he disrupted the drama of the scene, changed its tenor.

Wasn't it true, at least, that he was a non-entity, nothing other than a third body? But we learn in the equations of gravitation how much a third body complicates a problem. I kept on reading: "It was dark, but after some moments our eyes adjusted to the gloom." I had written it like a dungeon. "Our party moved"—here I was keeping it true without mentioning we were a party of three, not two—"toward the stairway. We ignored the few closed doors on either side of the hall, and began to climb the stairs. The wood creaked. It was impossibly quiet, except for our breathing, which was so loud it felt oppressive. How could anyone be so noisy and escape universal retribution?

"The next level was another hallway with small rooms opening off it." At the time I didn't know that this had been variously a boarding house and a brothel, but June did. She understood what the word meant, too, but had I been confronted with it, I would have stammered something far from accurate, though I had my ideas. "Finally, we reached the third level. Each flight had been lit by a single dreary bulb."

Not exactly a promising venue for a golden key.

But in our gaming, we had internalized the idea that the most glittering treasure, the most spectacular finds, were concealed in the gloom of drab dungeons, filled with the skittering of mice, cobwebbed skeletons, and old chains.

"Our footfalls echoed as we went, the odd step creaking loudly, our hearts beating in our ears, and on this level, we found the stairs ended in a kind of balcony, with a wooden railing. A large, dirty skylight overhead let dimly filtered light stream in on the wall that faced us, its only adornment two candelabra sconces, complete with imitation wax drips flanking a large green door."

I was proud of the word "sconce," I remember.

"On the door, a polished brass cross with a pattern of ivy on its surface had at its center a doorknob shaped from the leaves, and beneath it, a single large keyhole, fit for Clyde Duane's golden key."

It was a description that could have been from *Conan the Cimmerian*, a book Brian shared with me and which had been informing my writing around then: if only June had been a princess in scanty ceremonial garb, and the few spiders in the corners instead had been enormous, primeval lizards, with fire-red tongues.

"We ran up to the door, with June getting the first peek through keyhole. She saw in the dimly lit room ornate furniture, green velvet curtains, a Persian rug, which she described to us. There were man-high candlesticks, and walls lined with leather-bound books. At the far end a wood-paneled desk. I was close behind her, eager for my turn to see. We were in the antechamber to a forbidden room."

I must have felt her warmth and smelled the perfume she had started wearing, an old scent, of green and violets, and left it all unremarked.

"There are words," I had slipped into the present tense, to heighten the drama, "etched onto the ivy leaves of the patterned crosspiece on the door I am partly leaning against as she describes the room. The words are—"

You can guess them, maybe, or maybe not. When June said them, it was with an astonishingly accurate accent:

"Liberté, égalité, fraternité."

Now I remember what came next.

I didn't get a chance to put my eye against the keyhole. One floor below a door slammed. We turned, ran blindly down the stairway, skipping every other step, grabbing onto the handrails for leverage as we spun around each landing. There was nobody in the ground-floor hall but we heard loud footsteps above. In a moment we had bolted out of the hall onto the short stoop, and then across the street, and then behind the fountain, where we stopped, breathless. We popped our heads out like wary groundhogs for a moment. Everything was as quiet and as unremarkable as before we had entered.

"What is that place?" I said, each word punctuated by a puff of breath.

"I don't know," said June, "but I intend to find out!"

We were in the antechamber to a forbidden room.

He was young, once.

Chapter
24

SUNDAY, AFTER I'D made my pilgrimage to those all-important scenes—the school, Ryan's house, the lithium spring—I woke early, from another dream, this one active. It left me sore all through my body. (Or was that just age?) The queen bed in my parents' guest room felt too big.

I rose before the cats and dogs, just shy of 5 AM, and they were surprised by my presence. The light of dawn rested softly on the sides of the overgrown shrubs, and the dew shined like crystal, and everything began to steam.

I made coffee, sat at the oak table in the kitchen, and looked through the open window while the mug warmed my hands. I had just opened some cans of cat food and the elder dog, Portis, was already greedily chewing kibble. Jacques on the other hand had decided it wasn't time to get up yet: give it a half-hour or so. I liked his style.

A cacophony of whistles, trills, and chirps came from the birds outside, while the light kept growing as if someone's hand were smoothly turning a dial. I have noticed more dials in things lately; the increasing presence of touchscreens everywhere took a hit when our supply of rare earths got rarer.

Someone who had been frozen in the past and was only shaking out the cobwebs today might feel a sense of familiarity, as if the world had entered a nostalgic age, playacting regression, technologically and in other things. But there are, of course, subtle changes from the past. No wires anymore. And nothing is quite as heavy as it looks. We have projections and holograms, and nothing burns or smokes, although there is the fair imitation of fire projected in 3D from the burners of stoves, because it's difficult to "see" infrared heat.

Sunday. There was something in the back of my mind. I took another sip of coffee. The service at Clyde Duane's church ran from 9 to Noon on Sundays. I had heard he still played the organ there, and I wanted to try to see him again. To see him in a different context. What was I hoping to find? Some revelation?

I already knew the "answer," which is that he was a sturdy vessel, and whatever was poured in came out again. Could you see the hands at work, filling him up? With the majesty of music, or a simple xenophobic hate, or endless toil? Weren't we all wound up and set on our little tracks? Or was I hoping to find something else, a divine breath, some inner life?

After another cup of coffee and a breakfast of scrambled eggs, and a little time flipping back and forth through my jottings so far, I shaved and picked out clothes that would be quiet, dignified: grey slacks, black shoes, a maroon paisley tie over a pale lemon shirt, a light jacket. I dressed to blend in.

I made sure I had some cash for the collection plate. I tossed the tennis ball for the dogs a while, then brought them back inside, and got in my car. I drove around the village for a bit so that I could come in after everyone else, quietly, in the back: I didn't want to attract attention.

I've only been "to church" a few times. I didn't grow up religious, but we weren't irreligious, or anti-religious. It just wasn't a thing. I never felt compelled to experiment with it; there was in the fouling of the earth and its miraculous recovery (it has begun at least, not to minimize the tremendous loss; the unknowable, uncountable, untenable loss) religion enough of my own variety.

I guess I had pictured a long aisle with red carpet up to the altar inside, pews of hard wood on either side, the priest in black or white robe, mumbling. He holds a microphone; maybe he has a suit on underneath his robe. He is getting more enthusiastic—maybe he's a cool priest. A couple of dozen people there, locals, families together, a few loners, heads bent, "New Revised Standard" such-and-such editions of "The Bible" variously open or resting beside them, but always a hand in contact. The stained glass windows simple: a dove, the cross, the lamb, the morning light streaming in. I imagined pushing through the red door, sliding into an empty pew far in the back, unnoticed.

The church was a small, white, square building in need of a paint job. It had a sort of general slump to it, and a modest spire which was a late, stylistically incongruous addition. I had expected the movable letters on the sign out front to spell out something like "JESUS IS UR QB / R U READY / FOR HIS PASS?" Instead it was eerily blank. The grass was shaggy and neon green around some worn, irregular stepping stones. The door opened with a loud creak.

I pushed through heavy velvet curtains and found myself in a small, well-lit room, with a few rows of mismatched chairs. The preacher, a tall African with a booming voice, stopped his sermon abruptly. The congregation, no more than ten people, turned their faces toward me all at once.

So much for sneaking in to the back!

"Welcome, my son," he said. I recognized the kid from the grocery store, his buzz cut and tattoos, and a Hispanic family, and the old woman who rode her bicycle back and forth across the village in the morning, and the school librarian, and her strange son with bugged out eyes. All staring my way.

I started to turn on my heel, as though if I could just get back behind the curtain and out the door, everything would work out. Instead I stopped myself, smiled and made a half wave, muttered a greeting which I all but swallowed, and sat down immediately in the last seat to the left, but misjudged its height and fell back another few inches with a muffled thud and a scrape of the chair leg.

Clyde Duane was sitting at the organ already, motionless, like an automaton in the court of some Byzantine emperor, waiting to be cranked to life. I was right about the stained glass, but the carpet in the aisle was blue instead of red, with gold fringe.

The reading was Daniel, in the Lion's Den. The sermon began. He wasn't a cool pastor, or a fire and brimstone pastor, or ironic, or sensitive to the times. He told a story, his story, and as he told it, a few people muttered, "Amen." How he came from Gabon a decade before, the reception he had, and then his reception here in this community. I lost the thread, and his became a sonorous bit of music, sensible to the heart, not the head. Clyde Duane, his hair, what he had left, combed straight back over his liver-spotted scalp, began to rock a little in his seat behind the organ.

"You know my story now," the pastor said. "How I had been hired from my parents to work in the home of a rich man. So our brother Daniel was taken as servant by the king of Babylon. He was fair, long of limb, without bodily defect. When you are in service, they take your name and give you another. So I was called Nicholas, Daniel was named by the Babylonians Belteshazzar.

"In olden times, as I think now, the kings and rules were afflicted with one great anxiety, simply this, what would become of their kingdom, whether they would rule to old age, and grant their power and wealth down to their posterity, or whether they would be overthrown, conquered from without or overthrown from within.

"Like you or I, their anxieties came to them in dreams. Daniel was a godfearing, pious boy, then man, and he was given a singular gift by our Lord, the great skill of interpreting dreams. The king, one Nebuchadnezzar—we have talked about him before, haven't we?—was desperate to understand his prophetic dreams. And called in soothsayers by the score.

"But only Daniel could tell the truth of these dreams the king had had. And it was like this: when you hear the truth, you know. The king knew right away. And for Daniel's service over time, since the king and his successors had many troublesome dreams, and Daniel could explain them all, he was given a signal honor, a satrapy, rule over a third of the country.

"This made Babylonians jealous. Here was a stranger, not of their religion, lording over them. So they devised a strategy to catch Daniel, knowing he was faithful to the king, yes, but even more faithful to his Lord, our God. This chap Darius was the ruler of Babylon, then, and the whole Persian empire. He favored Daniel mightily, no matter what his religion was.

"But Darius's counselors were wily, and hated Daniel, and they tricked Darius into passing a law, forbidding worship for one month to any but him. Well, what could Daniel do but have faith in the Lord. And what could Darius do, but have faith in Daniel's Lord too: he must obey the law, and the law said that Daniel, for being true to his faith, must be cast into the lions' den.

"Daniel said to Darius words to the effect of, 'It's okay, my friend.' Then they closed the stone in over him.

"Can I tell you, can you guess, what a sleepless night Darius had, wondering whether Daniel's God would come through and preserve him?

"But Daniel never worried, did he? For he was righteous, and the lions only knelt to him.

"When Darius had the stone opened the next day, he nearly cried to see Daniel unharmed. Then he took his advisors and, it was a different time, their families, and said, 'If you are righteous as my Belteshazzar, go into the den, and see whether the lions respect you too.

"You can guess, parishioners, whether they did."

The sermon ended. We stood to sing some hymns.

Duane jerked into perfect form at his keyboard. He bowed his head a little, closed his eyes, and pressed his fingers to the keys. Then the organ filled the space with a great vibration. It was like the un-transcribable voice of God.

I reached for the hymnal and rapidly found the page. I didn't sing the hymn. I felt that the hymn sang me.

Had I been missing something in my life?

I don't think so, exactly. Except perhaps if you had asked me then and there, standing in the pew, letting the hymn flow through me. What else can I say?

The service continued. It went on longer than I had prepared for.

Then it was over.

The collection plate was passed, and I added some of the crumpled bills from my pocket. I fell into sadness, then felt loathing, mixed with boredom.

"As usual," the pastor said, "there's coffee, donuts, and fellowship in the basement. Again, as usual, we have to thank our brother, Aaron, for the plenty."

The pastor motioned toward the the front pew and a middle-aged man, nearly bald, in an ecru cotton polo, stood and half bowed to the pastor, then turned. He wore matching slacks, and he was so thin both hung off him like clothes on a hanger. A wisp of black mustache curved down around full lips, and he had the saddest green eyes anyone has ever beheld. On one wrist was an oversized gold watch, and on the opposite hand a class ring.

It was as though he had been this thing always, and the world had aged around him. But he was young, once; he had simply grown into his own father's image; I recognized both of them within him.

And he immediately recognized me. I must have grimaced. I had hoped to turn and be out the door before the last sound of the pastor's voice reached me.

Aaron strode up to me.

"Hey, fella, long time no see!" He had both hands around my right hand, and was pumping it up and down. "And here, of all places!"

I could have said the same thing. With a hand on my shoulder, he led me toward the foyer, where the metal door opened into the low basement, where the Sunday school was held. They had pushed the tables to one side. There was a stack of donuts, and one of the mothers poured watery coffee into little paper cups.

"I didn't know you were part of this church," I said.

"Oh, you know, there's been a period of consolidation. Anyway," he paused and looked at me sincerely, "best church music in town."

It had been a long time. Now he was the top salesman at the Dodge dealership, he explained. The top, he wanted me to know. And had I heard how well the old man was doing now? Yes, I said. He asked about what I had been up to since the stuff with the blue smocks. He guessed things had worked out pretty well. Not for everyone, but certainly for him, and maybe me?

Was I back at the old homestead? What about the "Dragon's Lair"? That's what we called the secret, dragon-scale-windowed floor, the first few times. He talked up old reliable Duane, and about the changes at the school.

He was alone, he told me. There had been a family for a time. Florida, and better days. But he was happy to send the checks. Then he whispered in my ear. There was this other woman I might have noticed, Mexican, here at the church. Yeah I know, he explained, she was married. I looked up involuntarily, there she was, in a long wool skirt above tiny ankles and delicate feet in white leather shoes. She glanced at him. I ducked my head.

He didn't bring up June at all, but he talked about Ryan. That he was in Alaska. That there were so many women to each man. Or was it the other way around? After a bit I touched his arm. We had to get together again. What was I doing here? Just trying some new things. I smiled, backed off, gave him a little salute.

Clyde Duane was in the far corner, tearing into a donut he held with both hands, like Saturn devouring his son. Then he laughed hard at something the pastor said, a deep guffaw, haw, haw, haw, and little bits of donut flew onto the pastor's shoulder and collar. I took the stairs out of there two at a time.

. . . a world of squirrels . . . with their own peculiar customs . . .

Chapter
25

WHEN I WAS twelve and thirteen, about the same time June and I were getting to know each other and investigating the mystery of Clyde Duane's key, my parents set me up with some odd jobs in town, through their friends. This was in the summers, and some days after school. I appreciated the extra pocket money. It supported a comic-book habit, and a "college fund," which through an aggressive savings plan grew to several hundred dollars. I enjoyed replaying its growth by scanning through the numbers written variously in black and blue ink in the columns of my green bank book.

This savings seemed substantial to me then. I was as yet unacquainted with the costs of living that ballooned throughout my coming of age and early adulthood.

When I reflect on how costs continued to rise—not through a process of inflation, which at least would have given compensatory relief to debtors and eventually lifted wages, but through the continuing growth of the slice of the economy claimed by that most American of occupations, the needless middleman—it seems inescapable that there would be, eventually, some irreparable breakage. The overriding logic of our economy seemed to be, "Why should something pass through one hand when it could pass through two?"

My earliest work experience was at the base of the pyramid, doing menial labor. Only when I got to college did I realize this was, for many wealthier children, an impossibility; these jobs in their towns were all taken by day laborers, immigrants picked up at stoplights near bus stops and housing projects. Not so in Harmony Valley. Regardless, I did not distinguish myself.

As a porch painter, for example, I was an abject failure. At the time, I felt I had put everything I had into it. Primer and two coats. My shoulders ached. Flecks of grey paint drying and cracking on my hands. There was paint on my cheeks and on the old pair of jeans I wore.

But I own that I got distracted. I took frequent breaks to rest, found myself staring at the sky, at a tree as it swayed, imagining a world of squirrels living in it, with their own peculiar customs and laws. The paint was not uniform, and I was not asked back, or put on any other tasks requiring both physical effort and concentration.

Then there was shoveling out the horse pen, for which one used two different implements, the flat shovel for manure, and an actual pitchfork, sharp and black with age, for the soiled straw. I liked the job, but it required strength and endurance, and I was low on both. I was afraid of horses, too.

In elementary school, I knew a kid, super nice, who always smelled a little like vinegar. He had a head that was all out of kilter, like a rhombus. He told me once, in confidence, he had been stepped on by a horse. He had been—but his oddly shaped head was not due to that injury; it was a family trait, shared by his sister and father.

Since that revelation, these large animals, with their black, deeply alien eyes, their unpredictable (to me) snorts and whinnies, would nearly paralyze me with fear. The persistent presence of horses while I worked, watching from just the other side of the flimsy wire fence (the electricity was never turned on, one touch of it having been enough, supposedly), left me blanched and sweaty. Though there was some enjoyment in toughing it out, this line of work was nixed for me too.

I wasn't old enough or mobile enough for a regular part-time job of the sort that Brian had. He was sixteen then and able to pay for gas money and insurance on his tiny blue Civic, which he had painted with red flames like a Hot Wheels Corvette, but with bright house paint that peeled right off.

When we drove to the mall, you could see the highway rolling along brightly below through big rust spots in the passenger-side footwell. After a stint at the soft-serve place, Brian got an upgrade, and worked after school at the grocery store, affixing prices, "cleanups on aisle four," and working the big cardboard binder, a "wicked-dangerous machine" that "would take your arm in a minute."

Brian had some amount of responsibility. And a firm place in grown-up society. He was part of a union!

Meanwhile, my odd jobs continued. Office temp, which lifted me a step above the common menial—coming in twice a month to stuff envelopes for a targeted mailing—ended up the thing that stuck. The paper sucked all the moisture out of my hands, to the point of the skin cracking; I had to brush my fingertips periodically against a small wet cube of sponge. The bright inserts, a typed letter with a stamped-ink signature, all went into an envelope with a matching label.

I despised every second it, but it was a task that matched my meticulous nature and required a different kind of strength: Strength to endure the low light, the flashing phones, the black coffee, and the running toilet in the back. The whole place smelled of new carpet and printer toner. On those days, when my parents didn't pick me up right afterwards, I might walk down to the small grocery and buy a Snapple and a tube of Pringles, and take them over to Aaron's house, the last house in the village.

Aaron's mom worked as a nurse, on the night shift, and when I'd arrive, she was still asleep, and the entire house would be dark, and filled with a hush.

I'd walk right in and head to Aaron's room. He was usually in there alone, plotting a campaign, or sometimes writing out longhand in composition books, in his somewhat girlish hand, the latest in his series of science fiction romances he kept trying to get people to read. I would always turn a few pages, and on seeing something extraordinarily embarrassing en flagrante on the surface of Clarion Seven, close the book quickly, with an empty compliment. It was okay, they weren't for me anyway.

There must have been a hundred volumes there, and he always made sly references to his ever expanding science fiction universe in our games, when he had responsibility for the dungeon. The references would build and build to the point of taking us out of the quasi-medieval fantasy world, but we all maintained through sheer force of will a completely united front against acknowledging any familiarity with his fiction until at last he would angrily explode.

"The magic saber flamed with same eerie glow that Colonel Zamara pointedly noted of the third moon of Exanion in the *Tragedy of Alpha Zebron,* which Eric, here, said had been 'a fun read' and that he was looking forward to the sequel!"

We would all roll our eyes and say, "Yes, Aaron! We get it!"

Aaron's house was another house, like Ryan's, where the child and adult spaces were clearly delineated. Only at Brian's did I feel I was at a household as well-integrated as my own, where there were no adult or children spaces, only a communal home.

One day I walked over to Aaron's after an excruciating two hours of stuffing envelopes. As I came in and started to walk down the dark hall, I heard something unexpected: music, loud, but muffled. I think it must have been Guns'n'Roses. I wouldn't have known then; I wasn't the type to listen to music like that, and I hadn't expected Aaron to be the type either. As I got closer, I suddenly had an unwelcome feeling.

When I got to his door, I rapped on it gently with the back of my hand. I don't think he heard me. I waited a bit, then tried the handle. It was locked. I heard, behind the music, muffled voices. One was, I think, Aaron's. The other was a girl.

I think what happened next explains a lot about what happened next. With everything, I mean.

I didn't knock again. I just started backing down the hall, the music fading with each step.

At last, I turned and left.

Chapter
26

WHAT WAS IT that happened next? I mean after June, Aaron, and I had had our little peek though the keyhole. After the vertiginous flight. After we had collapsed behind the fountain, the secret apartment glowing like a beacon across the street, the penthouse of a forbidden tower, gazing down on us like a great, lidless eye.

I cast back in my memory, trying to get the surrounding events clear, but that one moment shines out so brightly that everything around it is obscured, as if in deep shadow.

The next diary entries were cryptic, just a few words here and there on various days. A record of lunch snacks, maybe, a note about the weather: "Unseasonably cool." They stopped being dated altogether, then there were isolated fragments, lists of spells, accountings of experience points, a paragraph about a dead body shedding its flesh and rising up as a skeleton, glowing green and holding a rusty sword. It was summer then, I guessed, and I was in the thick of our game.

"WHAT HAPPENED NEXT?" I asked.

Aaron looked puzzled. "Don't you remember?"

"Sort of," I said, "I mean, of course I remember, but you know how it is—it's been such a long time. What do you remember about it?"

When I was leaving the church, Aaron had slipped me his card, a fancy iridescent thing with an idealized hologram of his smiling face. I hesitated for a long time before I called him to meet up. Has there ever been a more reluctant detective?

I guess I always had the thought that in the center of the maze, when you finally came up to the minotaur and pulled its mask away, the risk was that what would be revealed was your own face.

When I had finally called Aaron, he replied to my greeting with, "Hey, dude! At last!"

I suggested we meet up at a cafe in Cooperstown. It was a bit of a drive but had a nice big seating area. And it was a less likely spot to run into people we knew. It was always nice to drink coffee made in one of those big Italian machines. The secret was that it didn't really matter—it was enough that someone else had made the coffee for you. I liked a cappuccino —not especially because of the steamed milk, but because it came to you, ready-made, nothing to add.

"No," Aaron had said, "that place is all stuck up. Let's get some good home-cooking."

I was surprised then, that he chose *Applebee's,* and at a mall a good 20 minutes farther out. But I realized it was closer to the dealership, and probably a place he frequented. When I arrived, I saw Aaron was already seated. He was chatting with the waitress, a woman in her late thirties with dark hair. She looked tired. It was early for dinner, but the place was crowded. Maybe people eating before a seven o'clock movie.

Over the past decades, the pace of life here hadn't changed much at all. This was both good and damning, in that there had been for a long time loud cries that our way of life was on the line, and that even the slightest concession to "the imaginary bugbears of the left" would set us skittering toward disaster. Of course the disaster was upon us already, even then.

When I interrupted them, the waitress visibly relaxed, and Aaron jumped up to shake my hand. We sat back down. The waitress put a second menu down in front of me.

"I'll give you a little time," she said and left us.

Aaron started talking to me as if we had been in the middle of a conversation. Something about the new electric cars, and how there were some customers, mostly men, who complained about a lack of power, and for them, you'd add in a sound package, and let them take a test drive with the engine making all this obnoxious noise, and the morons grinned, and asked why you hadn't shown them the model with this engine in the first place.

I almost asked Aaron about the *Tykian Trilogy* or the *Tetralogy of Captain Alin,* or whether he had thought more about the romantic habits of the aliens on Xenian Nine. But there had been such a fundamental change in him, and I was afraid he might find it insulting. My other fear was that maybe he hadn't changed, and I'd have to suffer through an hour of listening to him talk about the stuff.

I stopped him and confessed what had brought me here. I told him that June and I had stayed in touch for years, and now she had vanished.

"That's how she is, isn't she?" Aaron asked.

It felt odd that he was this comfortable characterizing her. Had she stayed in touch with—with Aaron? It left me a little sick.

"This isn't like the other times," I said. I told him that this time, I felt a deep concern. I had always dismissed her more fanciful talk, and was just now coming to terms with some strange memories from school, and wondering about that place Aaron and I had called "The Dragon's Lair." I mentioned a meeting with June's mother, and a box of scraps, of old memories that June had left for me there that I couldn't make heads nor tails of. The whole thing left me feeling lost.

"Are you sure that June meant you to have that box?" he asked. "June's mother is a lot of things. One of them is—well, she exaggerates. She makes up things." Aaron explained that he was on the local council with her. There was, to put it lightly, a little conflict. But in the end, as long as you knew she wasn't always being fully upfront, and that her memory and grip on reality weren't necessarily reliable, you could work together.

"And she has really turned that house, at the farm, around," he said. "It's gorgeous now. All renovated."

I asked him to take himself back to that time in school. When June first came, and the mystery of Duane's gold key. That moment when Aaron ran into us. When we were young and innocent.

"Speak for yourself!" he exclaimed.

"But," I asked, "what I want you to tell me is—what happened next?"

The waitress returned and interrupted us, asking, "Are you ready?"

"I'll take the salad bar," I said, "and a Coke."

Aaron laughed, and caught the waitress's eye. "Always the same with this one; he can't do something healthy without doing something bad," he said.

Ignoring him, she said, "Salad bar, Coke. No main?"

"I'm good," I said. "Thanks."

"I'll have the burger," said Aaron. Then he hit his palm against his chest, shaking his head wistfully. "The veggie burger," he said. "Not so young anymore. And, darling, an iced tea with lemon."

She narrowed her eyes, repeated back, "Veggie burger, iced tea with lemon. Okay." She took a step back, watching him, before turning away, as if to make sure she was out of the reach of Aaron's arm. His eyes followed her ass as she walked to the kitchen.

I caught myself imitating his stare, and snapped at him, angrily, "Do you ever give it a rest?"

"Lord, no!" he said.

There was no time I would have joined his laughing. Would have patted him on the back. Or enthusiastically ogled alongside. But in the past, I wouldn't have been as bothered by what he did. Now I felt the full menace of the situation. It was depressing. Overbearing.

This *Applebee's* still sat at the end of the mini-mall in Oneonta, but a lot had changed. It was employee-owned, and the menu was no longer set at corporate headquarters, hence was open to local experimentation, like the atypical salad bar. It still had that unpleasant atmosphere of forced jollity, and still the TVs were turned to sports, the green fields flashing neon over the shoulders of the too-early bar patrons. Was there a reduction of efficiency? I suppose. But there had been challenges with long supply-chains leading in this direction even before "the revolution" had mandated it.

The local councils helped bridge the gaps, connecting producers and suppliers. Food quality and safety had, through these changes, improved! If you thought about it, this was to be expected: everybody now ate much closer to where they lived, and we all shared the same food. So it was rigorously inspected.

Sitting face-to-face with Aaron, I wondered if I had aged in the same ways he had. I felt in my soul that I hadn't, but when the waitress came back with our drinks, she was looking at us both with the same disdain.

The food wasn't half-bad either. The salad from the salad bar was crisp, and Aaron's veggie burger didn't have that just out of the freezer look.

I repeated my question.

"Don't you know?" he said.

"Sort of," I said, but I shook my head wryly, no.

"June did what she does best," he said. "Disappeared!"

Had she disappeared? Was Aaron right?

LATER, BY MYSELF, I tried to remember again. I seemed to recall that for a couple weeks June and I had only brought up what we had seen rarely, in passing. She explained she was doing some intensive research. Then she was out sick. She was out a few days in a row. I started to think about what this research entailed, and wonder whether it was dangerous or not. I worried. I began to gather up in myself some courage.

I had seen Ryan looking sullen. I had passed him in the halls, and he hadn't acknowledged me at all. The next day, I cornered him and asked about that secret floor off Main Street.

He said it was stupid. Pointless. Childish. That we had been infecting June with our *Dungeons & Dragons* fantasies. That she had just wanted—and he didn't know why—to be friends with us nerds. He seemed edgy. He fidgeted. He was late for class. I said that he was wrong. That there was something important there, and that June was out there somewhere doing serious research, that she might even be in trouble, and need our help.

"Listen, kid!" He brought his hands down on my shoulders, hard. "June doesn't need help. That whole family knows what they're doing. They may just up and leave us and the stupid mystery, and head back to Ohio, where they came from. Your stupid games don't mean anything!" His voice hissed on the word "stupid." He turned on his heels and stormed off.

Something was eating at him.

Chapter
27

I WAS NOT dissuaded by Ryan's unexpectedly nasty attitude.
I was convinced that June required assistance, and I knew
where I could find it. If not from Ryan, then from my
friends. We had, by this time, moved out of the library and
into the empty chemistry lab, where we'd been given
permission to "work on our homework," i.e., occupy it like a
club and play our game.

When we had all gathered the next day, I knocked on
the table with my Snapple like a gavel. It was how we centered
attention to make an announcement. There was a blanket
prohibition on food, something about deadly chemicals, but we
always brought some snacks in anyway, sneaking the evidence
out afterward. I usually had an apple, a chewy granola bar, and
the aforementioned bottle of Snapple.

They all turned their heads. There had been a lot of
disordered chatter, and somebody was already complaining that
we were wasting play time. Clearing my throat in an
exaggerated way, I began to tell them all about June, about
Clyde Duane, and about his gold key.

I am not sure what I expected to happen. I guess that I
was thinking the others would fall in to the adventure as
doughty companions in a real-life mystery. At least I expected
Aaron to jump up beside me and recount his own part in the
brief but significant event. When I finished, breathless—I had
let it all spill out, a hundred-words-a-minute—all eyes turned
to Aaron.

Aaron shrugged. He only said, "I guess so. I didn't
really see anything." The room filled with silence.

Then everyone sort of turned away. Eric, looking down
at some papers, shuffled them around, then looked up and said,

"Hey, we could make this into a campaign, it could be fun. Do you want to be the DM?"

"Guys," said Max, suddenly, "listen, these things are just taking too long."

He was right: The games extended over days and weeks, and everyone, including me, had grown tired of it. Why bring it up now, though, when something so exciting and real had fallen from the sky, into our laps?

"There's this new card game," Max said, offhandedly. Then he pulled a deck of cards out of the pocket of his jean jacket. We all crowded around to see them. They had, frankly, beautiful fantasy art, and witty descriptions. It was like a whole campaign, but randomized and quick. And no dice rolling required. "We can have tournaments," he said. "Also," and he picked up his backpack from the floor, and dropped it onto the desk. He made an elaborate flourish over it, then tugged at the zipper. Inside we could see the corner of a box. He pulled it out, presenting it to the group with two hands.

It was a display box, unopened, full of card packs.

"Holy shit!" said Aaron.

"I took them out of the store in . . . my . . . pants!" said Max, pulling out the waistband of his sweatpants to demonstrate how he could form a pouch. He broke the perforation and began throwing packs of cards to us like a homecoming queen tossing candy from a firetruck on Memorial Day.

WHAT I THINK they disbelieved was not the words coming out of my mouth, but the possibility of real adventure. I myself began to disbelieve it.

First there was Ryan's deflating rejoinder, now Max's triumphant redirection of our group. For a moment I went to a dark place, turned away from them. Then I felt a lightness.

It didn't matter.

This card game would prove to be more fun and less work, anyway, and, with June gone, who knew what to do next? Only she had known how to press forward. And I hadn't really enjoyed, even for just those few minutes I was speaking, exhorting, the role of leader. I wasn't good at it.

The pressure was off. I held three shiny new packs of cards in my hands. Max tossed me another. I fell, with the rest, to tearing open the foil. The warm, slightly acid smell of glossy card stock brimmed with possibilities.

And, as I shuffled through my impromptu deck I saw one or two cards that, without even knowing the rules, I understood to be of great power.

*As I shuffled through my impromptu deck I saw one or two cards
that I understood to be of great power.*

Chapter
28

S OME DAYS AFTER her bowling outing with the paralegals, one extremely early morning, when the light was just one shade of blue above pure black—at a time when an electrical short had knocked out the streetlamps on the entire block for a whole week—Tiffany was thinking about her first kitchen chat with Mr. Jeremiah on her way to the office.

Maybe she had had trouble sleeping. She did sometimes after drinking, or when James spent the night—his bulky form in her bed was too hot, too looming, and he often snored relentlessly—and after a fifth hour of fitful tossing and turning, she'd arise, before even the birds, and scribble a note of affection and leave for work. Whatever it was, she was out, sputtering along as the day opened up over her.

This day, Tiffany got to the office, as she occasionally did, hours before the start of the business day. She could come when she wanted, as she had the key to the front door, which Mr. Jeremiah had entrusted to her. It did not open his office, his "inner sanctum" ("We must retain some mystery!" he had said.), and the smaller key unlocked only some of the filing cabinets. This she had discovered one day, when called upon to pull some files from one, accidentally putting the key in the lock of the cabinet below.

Mr. Jeremiah's car was still there, top down, chartreuse green in the first light, when she pulled up.

He liked to park out front, and not in the spaces in back because it "brightened up the place," and, he felt, made things a bit more "exciting" and "less stodgy." Of course, there may be nothing as dull as an aging man's midlife-crisis convertible, but the color did remind Tiffany of an exotic beetle, and she sometimes stopped and imagined the buildings were pebbles and the green of distant hills was in reality the sloping lawn, and that all around them instead of trees grew up high blades of grass.

Perhaps a friend had picked him up for an event and he would get the car later. Nobody in the neighborhood ever touched his car, out of respect, but Tiffany was not quite sure how he had earned it. Maybe she would ask the corner boys one day.

She wondered about the leather seats; she supposed the sun burned off the dew. It didn't occur to Tiffany that he had stayed all night. But when she got into the office, it was apparent he had. The lights were all blazing and all of the restricted file cabinets were open. Her desk, and the others, were piled high with files.

The door to Mr. Jeremiah's inner sanctum was propped open with a ziggurat of leather law books. The man himself came striding out with a huge bundle of antique-looking ledgers, blueprint rolls, and legal pads under his arm.

"Well, Tiffany," he said, "I didn't have the heart to tell you yesterday as you were leaving, because you have been working so hard lately. I thought it better if you had a night to yourself. Selfishly, I suppose also I wanted to see if this old man still had it, could still pull things together when a brisk gale has picked up, the topsail needs reefing, and one must steer her, steady on the tiller, straight into the growing swells.

"And I knew you, dependable you, would be here to relieve some of the burdens when the dawn broke and I was still working the ship.

"It has happened at last," he said, "and now the time has come for me to reveal all about our mystery, our shadow client; our only client, really.

"I am perhaps the only one who knows it, but at this precise moment, the great machine, the one I so floridly described, which, for over a century, has been idling, unused, but well-maintained, has been swung into action.

"You and I, Tiffany, are the lever, and the person who wields us may—no, most likely has no clue what has been set into motion."

He dropped it all onto Tiffany's desk in a great pile.

Then he pulled a dull silver watch on a fob out of his pocket, flicked it open, and checked it against the office clock.

His eyes narrowed. He wound the old pocket-watch a few turns, then twisted the dial until, presumably, the numbers matched up.

"We have until 2 PM," he said, "or maybe 3, and then we shall have to get all the paperwork into the mail. The early trucks out of the sorting facility will just make their connections, and deliver in the morning to Boston, Albany, and Buffalo."

They stood like that in silence, Mr. Jeremiah with his watch still in his hand, ticking loudly, the pile on Tiffany's desk beginning to expand as it slumped into its lowest-energy state.

Tiffany squinted and opened her mouth to say something, but Mr. Jeremiah snapped suddenly alert.

"Yes, I did promise an explanation, and we have . . . a little time."

He put his watch away and launched into a monologue of such a steady, even tone that it felt practiced. For the first minute or two, it was just the story of the firm she had heard before. But then certain threads connecting major personages and events in American history became clear. And then a Big Bang, the shocking, surprising origin, a bright burst, followed by an ordering, the laying out of the machine. Elaborate planning, linking, building. The satellite offices, the unknowing contractors; the caretakers, and the cult-like rituals; the envelopes, the checks.

The monologue slowed, proceeded warily, almost circling as it approached this day, this hour, this moment.

He stopped.

"Now, Tiffany, what do you say? What do we say? Are we ready?"

Tiffany smiled; she knew what to say. And at once they both exclaimed, as they sometimes did, "Damn the torpedoes! Full speed ahead."

"Now, Tiffany, what do you say? What do we say? Are we ready?"

Chapter
29

ARON HAD BEEN wrong—June hadn't disappeared. She had been out of school for only a few days, and was back on Monday, not long after I had rushed to my friends and they had signaled their lack of interest in pursuing the mystery further. I had lost the sense of June requiring saving, at least of any kind I could offer.

Or had Aaron been right, in a way? That June had disappeared, only it was into herself? Or had June stayed steadfast, and it was us who had disappeared from her?

There wasn't much time left in the school year. I would be in eighth grade soon, and turn thirteen. You could really feel the wind going out of the teachers' sails now. Midterms had been hard and work piled up on our desks, but as the weather grew more and more beautiful, clear skies, warm sun, as summer approached, things eased up. Stern promises melted into self-directed study, and our final exams were nearly all open book tests.

I wonder if the teachers were trying to avoid too many summer-school sessions, since there had been staffing issues, and some of the full-time teachers would have to work them. In the final days before summer, the halls were silent. You might have just one test, and periods and periods of free-time to study, or if you were us, to play our card games.

I was in the thick of it: not of June's mystery, I'm sorry to say, but of the card game. I was exhilarated. I asked my parents to bring me to the one mall where there was a shop that carried the cards. I wondered, almost, if losing an entire box to Max wasn't just a clever marketing ploy on their part. You had to collect many, many packs to assemble a workable deck to play. If you didn't keep purchasing, refining your holdings, you might fall behind the others; it amounted to an arms race. It was fun, but stressful.

Through the card game, the entire tenor of our connection to each other changed. No longer were we a valiant group of companions struggling against the odds, struggling against a power outside of us; we battled each other, and began to keep score. Brian, I think it was, began to keep a book: the official scores of each match, and our player rankings.

Do I blame our changing games, or is this the natural progression of any group? In the past, I would have said it was inevitable that something would break us apart, into individuals, only one of whom could be supreme. I am not so sure now.

That summer settled it. It was each for himself with our cards. We assembled our arsenals in secret, and began to collect knowledge (there was even a magazine for players of the card game; I had discovered it and surreptitiously subscribed, hiding the stack of them when friends visited), which we did not share. With enough work I became "good enough" to occasionally crack the top rank.

I found it grim, but fun.

I suppose that this is also how I would characterize life since then. Or would have. So much of life's characteristics have subtly changed that you are hard pressed to characterize things in broad strokes anymore. The young, who have only known the new way of things, live, I think, without trouble, without confusion.

THAT YEAR, WITH JUNE and her family having taken up residence at the farm, our summer day-camp was moved. The new place wasn't even a farm at all. It was the old chair factory by the defunct railroad tracks, with a long open field out back. It had long been dormant. There was a covered outdoor space, that had been the old canteen for the workers, and on the tables and benches there on nice days is where we played. Inside the factory was dark and dim, but comfortable. Someone lived in the offices, and when the weather was bad, we were watched inside horsing around the long benches that had been part of the original production line.

I caught Eric grumbling to himself one rainy day early in the summer. I asked him what was bothering him.

"My drawing book," he said. "I left it in the Hiram room last summer."

I resisted the urge to tease him. Eric's family—like Brian's and mine—weren't "locals"; they'd moved from a metropolitan area in the West, and Eric had a strange accent, one feature of which was to pronounce words like "drawing" with an infixed "l" so that he said "drawling." We all used to jump on it with the usual heedless malice of the young. He usually took it in stride. Eric was a saint.

"The Hiram room?" I said. "What on earth are you talking about?"

"I thought everybody knew about it," Eric said, his brow furrowed.

Later, I found out everyone had known about it, except for me. At June's farm, there was a long pantry off the kitchen, and at the back of the pantry, under the shelves, was a door that opened onto a tiny room, all dark wood paneling, lit by a shaft of cool light from a frosted eyebrow window. Above a wooden bench, smooth with age and use, hung two metal shackles attached to the wall. Under the bench was a long empty box, and behind the box was where Eric stashed his drawing book.

At different times Brian, Max, and Aaron had found the room, and used it for private contemplation. It was both horrible and wonderful to them at the same time. The rest had some idea, but Brian knew what it was, and his announcement of its purpose was chilling: "It was a room to punish slaves."

It couldn't have been known as anything but the "Hiram" room—one of its former prisoners must have gotten hold of a bit of nail, and the name "Hiram" had been etched, in letters large and small, over and over again on the bench and the wall.

IN THE FALL, THINGS were different for me.

I was in the last year of middle-school, but also taking some high-school classes. They had advanced me here and there, based on some standardized test scores, and a conviction that some students would get bored. I felt even more disconnected than I had before.

Brian was also taking more challenging courses, and didn't have as much time for our games. The rest of the group began to splinter too. I wasn't necessarily cut up by it; I much preferred to dip into a book alone, or wander around thinking back to the strange school year that had just passed.

The old Apple computers in the library had been retired for brand-new PCs. *Oregon Trail* was bypassed for *SimCity,* and the westward voyages were now ill-advised probing spikes of roadway or rails. June wasn't that excited about the new computers. She complained about how nothing was ever good enough, that everything always had to be new and flashy.

Every so often I'd see June in the hall, and she would give me a big smile, but I could tell it was an effort; there was always a cloud around her. There was no study hall we shared now. I found limited opportunities for talking to her. I didn't tell her my friends had passed up finding out anything more about Clyde Duane, the "Dragon's Lair," or the serpent key. If she discovered anything from her investigations, she didn't share it with me.

She was out from school more and more; sick, I suppose. I'd sometimes see her in the hall, in tense, close conversation with Ryan. One day, passing through town, I noticed that the telephone poles had all been stapled with "MISSING" posters for her step-father, Tim. This initiated a burst of fresh gossip among the adults of the community. Some thought Tim had run off with another woman, or had a second family somewhere, or that he had been caught embezzling at work and the police were on his trail, or that June's mother had murdered him over abuse or an affair.

No one knew who put up the posters. Most said it couldn't have been June's mother, but some relative of Tim's, who'd come looking for him. The number on the posters was out of state. This chatter was like a sudden burst of radio static between stations, and it died as quickly—in a few weeks the signs had started to flutter loose, and in a month they had faded or torn away. You might accidentally tread on Tim's photocopied face as a breeze carried a flyer, soiled and wrinkled, from beneath a bush to under your foot.

I imagine it was one of the things weighing on June.

Sometimes I would meet the others and participate in card games, or tournaments, but I mostly retreated back to the Media Lab in the library. I think I was re-inhabiting the space of my early encounters with June in hope of conjuring her from behind the pillar, while I watched the citizens of my virtual cities move into the ranch-style houses which mushroomed in the residential zones.

I would, occasionally, find company there with a new classmate, Mark, who had big wire-rimmed glasses and braces, and whose cities operated with low taxes, heavy industry, and an overwhelming police presence. He watched my cities, overrun with parks, and groaning under a despotic regime of confiscatory taxes (his terms). He asked why I always bulldozed the churches which popped up periodically on the map.

"The churches raise crime," I said.

Mark rolled his eyes.

We did agree on one thing, which was our shared belief in the unparalleled superiority of trains, a belief which we both pursued to financial ruin: trains were not treated kindly by the simulation.

He derided my "Democrat tendencies" when it happened that the Republicans won (for the last time) commanding victories in the state, and I did not feel self-assured enough to taunt him back beyond saying, "We will see how they run things."

I wonder how he feels now: much of it, for both of us, came from family convictions, but they were convictions all the same. I knew, without him explaining to me, that our "religious" lives were quite distant from each other. His family was at church every Sunday, and other days too, something I hardly imagined possible. Mark was also a mainstay of the choir; I had overheard one of the adults compare his tender voice to an angel's. I was jealous.

Perhaps he is quite happy now: there has been a flowering of religious expression in the population, only now married with extensive tolerance, while the growth of high-speed rail and light rail networks necessitated by the excessive carbon emissions of air flight have brought trains to the fore.

Yes, I can imagine Mark happy. It is the measure of the success of the new order of things that it embraced in its organization such dichotomies of experience.

Was I, am I, happy? Happy enough.

But I am wrong, about Mark. How is it that we forget these things? Mark is neither now happy nor unhappy, at least in my theology, or lack thereof. Mark is dead.

At some point I had heard that Mark, by then married and a father, was returning home from the community college where he was enrolled in night school, and apparently dozed off. His car left the road, jumped an embankment, and met with a tree.

How easily our minds drift. At one moment Mark lives, his car in the right lane, his eyes open, traveling safely home so I can see how he lives now, and in another moment, he is long-buried, flesh fallen away from his bones.

I guess I bring him along with me anyway.

We are quite a gathering here, all the old, forgotten shades of my past chattering on.

The telephone poles had all been stapled with "MISSING" posters.

I kept the money hidden, at home, in a cedar box.

Chapter
30

THE NEXT YEAR was indeed different for me. I had new teachers. I found the material more of a challenge, or it could have been that my powers of attention couldn't quite come around to it. I half-assed everything, yet somehow I managed to do tolerably well.

I shared a math class with Max, who, despite his imposing intelligence, was repeating it. We were issued Texas Instruments graphing calculators. Max would spend the entire class typing into his under his desk. Periodically he would hand it to me. He had programmed it into a rocket-flight simulator, your triangle shaped rocket arcing up in a parabola toward the approaching moon.

Several times I was reprimanded, having been caught taking or returning the calculator. I would give Max a nasty look that said, "I want to be good, and you are ruining it."

I sat behind a girl named Alice. I cast my long-unrequited feelings about June onto her, engaging in naked lust over the five or six inches of skin visible from the ends of her short-cut hair to the neck of her sweater. I could see the line of her collarbone, and a single freckle on bronze skin. She did well in class, which only increased my admiration.

Some time after I was done with school, I found out that our math teacher, problematically, had shared my admiration, and from time to time passed her notes with her assignments which complimented her outfit or the ribbon in her hair.

It's in this class, "Algebra I," that I took on my first "freelance" assignments.

Max, although he himself was barely passing the class, had been devoting time to doing homework for two or three of the junior varsity basketball players who were studying algebra with us. He got five dollars a pop. When I asked him why his own homework often came back covered with red marks, and he never handed in some assignments at all, he shrugged and said that sometimes he forgot to make a copy of their work for himself, and anyway, it kept suspicions at bay. At any rate, he didn't care about the grades, but the money was welcome.

He had, he said, a bit too much work to do all by himself. He confessed that the effort of copying the handwriting and making a convincing presentation was sorely taxing. He might "arrange" for me to take on one of his new clients, and share in the bounty, less 10% for handling the deal from start to finish. It wasn't math homework, I realized, when Max clandestinely brought me the assignment to do, but an essay for 8th grade English.

Now I understood the true motive. It was decidedly not Max's forte to write essays about *Ethan Frome*. It wasn't a cinch for me, either: I was in the advanced class in English, so I had to keep up with my own reading and that of the lower course as well. He got me a sample of the handwriting to imitate. I suggested right off the bat that to solve the handwriting problem, we write the essays on a computer to print out, a natural thing to do; I'd use the computers in the Media Lab.

Though I had it all figured out, when I saw the name on the writing sample my heart sank: I was anonymously taking money from Alice, the sylph who inhabited the fairy kingdom one desk ahead of me in 4th period Algebra.

"She is busy with soccer practice most nights," said Max, "and she just can't do it. Writing just isn't her thing." I wondered if I should say something to her, but decided it could only go badly. It was an engaging exercise to match her tone, her words, and still produce something that could rate a solid B. I was an assiduous, dedicated worker, but I demanded $10 an essay, not $5, since the work was a lot harder than just putting down the answers to some math problems. Max told me that Alice—who did not know my identity, since I was just a subcontractor—had agreed.

I was conflicted. I hated doing it. But I had to do it.

I couldn't pass up this opportunity to be connected to her. I was almost too close, because in writing the essays I almost became her, for a moment. While I focused on her voice as I wrote, I was always tracing with my mind's eye the contours of her collarbones, the way they vanished behind her neck, and the gentle gathering of mouse-brown hair, the fuzzy softness at her nape.

I kept the money hidden, at home, in a cedar box a friend of my parents had brought me as a gift from a trip to Yellowstone. I'd take out the bills from time to time, thinking of how they had touched her fingers, resentful that she had handed them to Max. At the same time, I was thankful that he was a link in a chain that connected her to me.

The word must have gotten out. I'm not sure how, but people began to approach me, in between classes. I denied it utterly, and cast aspersions on the whole enterprise. The first time it happened, as the dejected student left, I wondered if maybe it was worth doing these. Thereafter, I said I didn't do this kind of thing, but I had heard—and keep it absolutely to yourself—that Max knew how to hook someone up with this kind of service. Max, in turn, came to me.

I had been re-reading Sherlock Holmes stories, and began to imagine myself like the Moriarty of illicit essays, a spider at the center of a great web of crime.

A couple months into the school year, I was writing four or five essays a week, for two different English classes. I used different computer fonts, spacing, and formatting, and different printers, to throw off suspicion.

I was also accumulating a fair amount of money for a kid in eighth grade. Also a fair amount of stress. And yet the more I did, the less my own classes seemed to suffer. It is something I have learned about myself in the intervening time: the more work I had, the better a job I did at it.

What was I, what am I, then? A spectacular underachiever, I suppose?

I wasn't sleeping well, would stay up late reading and thinking, writing. I was imagining a time when the school's

English department would be reading more essays written by me than by all the other students put together.

MY STUDY HALL had changed. Now I'd do my homework in an art classroom, where the teacher would keep CNN on the TV, and we piled our school books on the drafting tables. I used the time to read, but sometimes would chat with Matthew, a sad-eyed, earnest, athletic kid who never did well in school, but was always asking about the books I was reading, or bringing up something from current affairs.

It seems possible that Matthew was a figment of my imagination, for all the times I saw him outside of study hall—that is, never. It was as though he went to an entirely different school, in a parallel universe. For such a small school, there were many universes orthogonal to each other, touching only at a single point; here, it was study hall.

Matthew was cow-eyed, placid, but determined. His inherent goodness was tested at all points by his stupidity, but in trying, he challenged my own soul to be better. I hated myself for my part in cheating, even though the entire system was a cheat. So I reasoned.

Or was it just my bitterness? I felt I had been abandoned by June at the doorway of a mystery. I found that I lacked the wherewithal to solve it—it wasn't energy I lacked, but inner direction. June was my North Star.

Matthew asked me why I had books he knew were being read in different English classes, neither of which I was taking. I wanted to tell him the truth. But I lied. This is how we reward goodness. Physics teaches us that even the solidness of the earth that holds us up is a deception, and "truth" would send the emptiness of our atoms careening ineffectually through the vast emptiness of everything, void upon void, into a great nothing.

Brian switched into the study hall mid-year, and we resumed a friendship that went beyond games. Now we had lively philosophical discussions, with Matthew's head whipsawing back and forth between us. It felt better now, with a great pressure relieved, from having to lead Matthew myself from field to field so he could graze.

"LISTEN," SAID BRIAN, one day. We were sitting together alone at one of the big drafting tables. Matthew was out sick. "I know we all made a stink about June's fantasy story—"

"It wasn't a fantasy, it's all real," I said.

"Maybe we were hasty to disregard it," Brian said. I waited. "Aaron confessed he saw something. And I followed Clyde Duane, and that key is truly strange. Like nothing else I've ever seen."

"Of course it is," I said. "But what are we going to do about it?"

Brian wasn't sure. He said we should plan to get together outside of school to talk about it with June.

Just then the door opened and Clyde Duane's bulk came through it. What an odd time to empty the art room trash, Brian and I agreed. We were quiet the whole time, looking out the windows or at the TV or wherever until Brian finally whispered, "Too many ears in here, I'll come up with a plan. We'll talk tomorrow."

Brian's conspiratorial tone and apparently justified paranoia awakened in me an excitement that lasted exactly one class period. None of us were prepared for what came next.

Something quite serious was about to go down.

Chapter
31

FROM THE END of sixth period, when Brian confided in me, until just before Social Studies, I felt a surge of confidence and the promise of a return to adventure, with Brian and the rest by my side and maybe some way to get through to June. This was until I heard an announcement over the PA: it was the school secretary, calling for me to come to the principal's office. There were other announcements as well, but I was focused on my own name. My heart froze. I started to sweat.

Shit. I had been caught out in my paper-writing scheme. I would be suspended. I would be expelled!

I had never done anything like this before. Anything wrong, I mean. They had to take pity on me—but wasn't I guilty? Didn't I deserve it?

I whipsawed between feelings of abject shame and arrogant self-righteousness. What about the people who bought the papers? What about Max? They certainly couldn't expel everyone, could they?

But I felt my own guilt sharp as a nail biting into my stomach. I walked to the office on rubbery legs, making blasphemous bargains for release from my culpability with every deity I knew of but didn't believe in.

The principal's office was in the high school wing, just beyond the small, light-filled atrium that the stairwell across from my new locker descended through. I had heard my name over the loudspeaker right as I passed the doorway to the stairs, and I turned and clomped down each step as though weighted down by greater gravity than the kids of all grades who shot up and down around me, worry-free.

I finally reached the office. This was it. My hand—wet with sweat—slipped off the door handle. But when I opened it, I was surprised to see occupying the heavy, blond-wood chairs facing the principal's secretary's desk—purgatory row—five other kids, all of whom I knew well.

There was Max in the first seat. A no-brainer: he was the instigator, the ringleader. Had he ratted me out in exchange for a lighter sentence?

But there also was Aaron, sitting next to him, fidgeting, biting at a cuticle.

Next to him was Brian.

Then, Eric.

The last in the line before the sixth, open chair, was Ryan, looking sullen.

I couldn't think what brought the other four of them there, so wrapped up was I in my imagined prosecution, unless Max had recruited them into his insidious ring, too. Or if this was somehow about our card games, what was Ryan there for?

The secretary let the electric typewriter go silent when I came in. She nodded me, impatiently, over to the last empty chair. I guess I had been standing in the doorway for too long. The others look at me and grimaced, each in a slightly different fashion. I sat, arms crossed, eyes pinned on the floor. The sound of typing began again, hypnotic.

The office was a kind of suite. Here in the front room the secretary sat by a big wall calendar with different things marked in red. There was the door to the principal's small office, now closed, and another door, wedged open to reveal a small conference table and a wall of files; it looked out past the tennis courts to the soccer fields.

The principal's door opened from the inside, an unseen hand drawing it inward, with all the horror of the opening of a tomb in a black and white movie.

Clyde Duane lumbered out and seemed to eye us each in turn before he settled in front of the secretary's desk. She bowed her head to him. They attended the same church.

Then the principal emerged. He was tall, with sandy hair, ice blue eyes, a brown suit. Up close, his face had a rugged look, like an old football; freckled, lined, and tan.

Gradually my conviction that this was all an elaborate setup, with me as its central player, slackened. Nevertheless, I had the feeling that something quite serious was about to go down.

*. . . pristine white cowboy boots with a subtle,
cream-stitched rose and skull decoration.*

Chapter
32

"I T WAS AN extraordinarily busy time, those first few months," Tiffany said to me, "after Mr. Jeremiah let me in on the firm's big secret. But it took me a long time to understand—despite his having explained it to me—what it was that was really going on—"

"What was really going on?" I interjected.

"That would be telling, wouldn't it?" she said. "But every day there were new surprises. I felt at once important and also, frankly, mystified.

"There were letters to bank presidents, and to organizations, chambers of commerce, corporate boards, all these notices to send out on legal forms, though sometimes we would have to update them to conform to settled law of the day. Mr. Jeremiah relied on me to check and double check and triple check each clause, the exact wording, against the latest case law."

I HAD BEEN SHOWING HER some of my notes and sketches for the manuscript, which she had asked to see, when she asked me if I had any questions, things she might clarify.

She had arrived earlier in a swirl of snowflakes. They were falling, big as moths, out of the velvety sky. They had settled in the sable of her hat and on her showy mink coat. She brushed past me into the hall, leaving a succession of small, cold-wet stings as the snow melted against my pajama pants and shirt.

"Not expecting anyone?" I had not been.

I helped her off with her winter things, laying that magnificent coat, prim gloves, soft hat, scarf, all gently upon the caned seat of a baronial wooden chair angled to the potbellied stove I had just stoked against the sudden cold. She kicked out of her galoshes, revealing pristine white cowboy boots with a subtle, cream-stitched rose and skull decoration.

"I was," she said, "in the area, just checking up. I worry, you know." I offered her hot chocolate. "With a little rum?" she asked, in a leading fashion.

"Sure," I said.

"It looks like I'll be staying a while," she said. The wind was now howling, and what had been some big, wet flakes had become a white-out blizzard. Out of her cold-weather gear ("All vintage," she had said) Tiffany had shrunk to her true form, like a nymph or a child, face as ageless as when we had first met.

"You don't have to live like this," she said of the remote cabin I had removed to—so far from anywhere, outside the range of the weather stabilizers—after I had stayed so long at my parents' place.

She sat with her feet up on the chair in front of her, cradling the mug I handed her. White cowboy boots, white jeans, a white turtleneck, with a chunky white bracelet, and, I noticed, perfectly optic white nails. I didn't doubt she had another entirely different transformation underneath, and another under that.

"So," she said, "you're persisting in this . . . this plan?"

"Are you visiting in an official capacity?" I asked.

"You of all people should know I have no official capacity. I'm a citizen, as you are, nothing more, nothing less."

"Yes, but—"

"Why should you suddenly worry now," she said, "when you were always in more danger, before?"

"I am determined, anyway," I said.

"Good, I want to see it. Here, top me up." She handed me her mug. "I suppose we have time for some questions, too."

I showed her some of the earlier material. She laughed reading some passages about herself. At points her face turned. "No, no, noooo!" she said, pointing to the screen, on her precise, elegantly tapered finger a cluster of tiny lines, sickle-shaped burnt-umber shadows scattered around her knuckles and her nails—one of her few signs of age.

"WHY WOULD ANY OF THIS be surprising?" I asked her, about the various letters they were preparing. It seemed with such a large organization being set into motion, these would all have been quite necessary.

"I'll give one example," she said, "that will be particularly meaningful to you!"

"Oh?" I said.

"Yes," she said. "One day I was tasked with writing a long, curious letter about a chess club to the School Superintendent of your own Harmony Valley."

. . . the electronic oracles . . . will know . . .

Chapter

33

THE PRINCIPAL—I am trying to remember his name, something weird, out of a young adult fantasy novel, like "Artemis Johnson," but not that. I'll put a pin in it, more research, TBD—the internet, ragged and broken as it is, is no help. Of course, the electronic oracles they've installed at the library will know, roll their eyes back a bit in their marble, or ebony, Grecian visages, and through rectangular lips gurgle out an answer. I digress. Was it Arliss? At any rate, I remember his face clearly. It was like a mask—intensely tan all over except around the eyes, which were ringed in pale pink.

Something about his bearing said "this is all highly irregular," but all that came out, after a short throat clearing, was, "Miss Adams, the envelopes please."

Max quickly stood up from his seat and executed a half bow before sitting down; I think he may have been referencing the Academy Awards. The secretary, Miss Adams, opened a drawer, and carefully lifted out a stack of satin envelopes, which bulged fat in her hand.

She didn't give them to the principal, whose arms were crossed—Adrian maybe? Or was it just Arthur, itself an exotic name for this rural, farming area? You could imagine him in a crown; a proper beard would fix his weak chin. No—she handed the envelopes to Clyde Duane.

The envelopes were bound together by a thick, milk-white ribbon, which he gently untied with those beefsteak hands of his. The packet of letters lost coherence, became an avalanche of letters. The ribbon fluttered pathetically to the ground as he managed to cradle the envelopes in a disordered mess with his two huge palms. The whole event had the air of a Renaissance physics experiment. Quickly, though, he brought the envelopes into order and was flipping through them with some alacrity—showing that same unexpected dexterity as in his organ playing—and reading the names printed on them, to himself, lips moving to the silent syllables.

He turned to us, and one at a time, handed an envelope over. We each half rose in turn to receive it, then fell back into our chairs. I still somehow held onto a residual fear that I was here for some other reason, so when Duane came around to me, I was surprised to receive one. Always thinking I am the odd one out, and always being wrong, I suppose. I held the envelope to my chest like a prize. A last envelope remained in the janitor's hand.

We all instinctually turned our heads to the door, as if the envelope's intended recipient would appear there. And it did! For there stood June.

"There is," said the principal, after making throat-clearing noises again, "an exclusive after-school program we once had, many years ago, that has been newly revived. This letter is your invitation. It contains all the information you'll require." He stopped speaking, as if to let that all sink in. We looked at each other, no one daring to open their envelope. "It is," he said, when the frozen silence became too terrible to bear any longer, "the Order of L.E.F. Chess Club. A program, that is . . . uh . . . highly targeted to our . . . most fitting students."

We sat, stunned.

It was, for so many reasons, entirely ludicrous.

I looked down at the envelope. Someone had written my name in blue ballpoint on the envelope, ink biting darkly into the paper at the start of each stroke. There was something naggingly familiar about the looping of the cursive letters I could not place. The edge of the flap was loose, and I slid my thumb under it, and felt the glue weaken, cracking open bit by bit. I was determined, for some reason, to work the envelope without force, just coax it open, gently, with heat from the pressure of my thumb.

The principal clapped his hands together. Our heads all shot up.

"Alright already," he said, "get out. Back to class!"

We scattered like birds.

Later, at home, in the privacy of my room, with growing anticipation, and having worked the envelope completely open in my methodical way, I felt the pages inside without looking, down in my knapsack. It sat, unread, next to an old copy of the Canterbury Tales I had taken out of the library because of its age, and the quality of its leather binding, and read as if in a trance. The unfamiliar words washed over me, so that I had a vision of the stories like a lucid dream, coming in and out of focus, and I couldn't be roused out of the pages except by real effort, and if asked, would have been entirely unable to describe even one incident in anything resembling coherent language.

Well, here I was, home with the mysterious letter.

I unfolded it into the light at my desk. At the top was the letterhead. It said "L.E.F." and beneath it "The Order of Friends of Liberty," and below that it was all typewritten— which was still ordinary at that time—so that the bite of the type-face from the type-head could be seen here and there on the fine 60 lb. bond paper.

The paper had a watermark, a woman with one breast bared (I recognized the figure of "Liberty" from our 8th grade World History textbook). It excited me. I was easily excited then. Concealed under the papers on my work desk at home were a few women's apparel catalogs I had saved from the recycling bin, each with a chaste "intimate apparel" section, which I had dogeared. The models were older, confident, but demure. I suppose they may have been as old as twenty-five.

There was no signature on the letter, just a stamp; it was the hand of liberty, holding her torch, three French words circling it.

The whole was broken by thin lines forming a pentagram. I don't remember the exact wording of the letter. The first line had the word "invitation" in all caps and spaced out, as "I N V I T A T I O N." Beneath it, lower case, was written, "c h e s s - c l u b."

The letter said the local chapter of L.E.F. was delighted to sponsor a renewal of its chess club for local students, and that I had been personally selected to attend. I should come to the first meeting, after school, at the L.E.F. hall, and then an address off Main Street which set the heavy gears of my head to cranking. The school would arrange transportation.

By now you are far ahead of me. At the bottom of the letter was an etching of a key, and above the shaft it had a snake's head, and then I recognized the French words and the address, and connected them to the handwriting on the envelope which I knew now, and to the presence of Clyde Duane in the office, and his hand in delivering the invitations.

When we had all (except for Ryan and June) gathered during our free period in the chemistry lab, I expected an outburst of raucous chattering, but there was only silence.

"What does it mean?" said Aaron at last.

Brian just kept saying, "Chess? Weird," and shaking his head. I suppose he meant that none of us were much into it.

"Speak for yourself," said Max, at last, "I love chess, and I am stoked."

At the bottom of the letter was an etching of a key,
and above the shaft it had a snake's head.

He checked off names on a clipboard.

Chapter
34

IT SEEMS IMPOSSIBLE to me now that anything like this could have been arranged without parental notification. I see, in reviewing this section of my document, that I made a note to myself to call my parents about it, but I must have forgotten.

When I came back to my hometown from the city where I lived, it was ostensibly to watch my parents' house and dogs while they were on a vacation, part of which was supposed to be a complete communication diet. Over half of Newfoundland, a vast electronic dome ensured stray messages were gated. The drawbacks of hearing things an hour or two later than instantaneously were far outweighed by the measured pace of life it engendered. Periodically, they left the bubble for a scheduled call.

At any rate, I reasoned they must have known something about the "chess club" at L.E.F., and I had meant to ask them. My parents have often surprised me in our conversations about the past, about my childhood, with how much they knew but never brought up.

After the initial burst of curiosity, I remember that everybody seemed to play it cool, myself included. I had resolved not to mention the upcoming Wednesday event at all. I didn't want to let slip that I knew it was connected to June's mystery. It was hers to reveal, I reasoned. Aaron himself might have recognized the words of the motto, or I guess the name of this secret society. But, I wondered, if the principal knew about it, how secret could it be? Perhaps it had all only been a secret to me.

Wednesday came quickly enough.

We were all standing by the parking circle by the sports field without being told explicitly to gather there, even Ryan, who stood a little apart from the rest; this was where the smaller buses came.

It would be a big navy blue Suburban, the kind we rode to academic games, that came for us. It fit eight or nine. It was chilly that day; you could see your breath. We were underdressed. I hopped up and down for warmth. The bigger, yellow buses had all left before our ride rolled to a stop in front of us. The SUV's tailpipe gave off an absurd amount of exhaust —something about the air temperature.

The stop sign with the flashing red lights had extended from the driver-side door. It too looked absurd. The red lights and the red tail lights were the color of neon cherries. The heavy doors opened stiff, and we all piled in, still without speaking, and not acknowledging Clyde Duane, overflowing the seat. He checked off names on a clipboard that looked like a toy prop in his hand, like a kid playing doctor.

June came running up, almost late.

As we pulled out, the stop sign stopped flashing, and folded back into the car, like a vestigial wing. The metal frame shuddered as we drive. I had crawled into the last seat in the last row. I looked ahead and saw only silhouettes of my companions, their heads shaking or turned in private conversation.

It didn't take long—following a snaking path winding here and there—to arrive in front of the building that I knew in my heart that it would be.

When the bus stopped precisely there, everyone looked at each other. Aaron knew.

I said, suddenly, to everyone, in a bout of ill-tempered protestation, the non-sequitur, "See, I told you!"

It broke the trance we had been locked in, it seemed, and Clyde Duane even turned to look at us.

Duane's screwed-up eyes swiveled left and right, and at last he said, "Go ahead, up there," and pointed to the front door of the building, already yawning open. Aaron was the first out; we all followed. As I crossed the distance to the door, over the curb and across the sidewalk, I reflected on Duane's voice. Up the steps we went, swallowed one at a time. His voice when he'd said "go ahead" had been sweet as an orange, round and bright. Not gruff, or hoarse. He could have been singing.

I was inside, and last came Max. He must have knocked the door loose, because it swung closed behind us. In the now-dark hallway I wondered if we would ever get out. We went up and found the lodge door open, and here we were, at last, inside the secret room—the lodge of the order of L.E.F.— Brian, Aaron, Max, Eric, and me, itinerant campaigners, comrades, yet sometimes utter strangers, and then the real stranger, the clean-cut jock, Ryan; all of us joined by June, who strode ahead confidently, our leader.

It was just after 3 PM, still quite light outside, and the sun was shining straight through the windows, casting a scale-pattern of shadow from the oddly-shaped mullions like a net tossed over the group of us. The walls were lined with walnut and cherry cabinets, with bottle-glass panels inset into their brass-handled doors, leather-bound books inside them, and between the cabinets, a wallpaper with an imbricated pattern and an iridescent shine. The floor was overlapping, faded Persian carpets. There was a big oak desk with a leather and green fabric top; it had the feel of an altar, and it was flanked by two flags.

One of the flags was clearly the American flag, caressed by a gold tassel. But in its appearance was something odd, otherworldly; only later did we find out the blue field had only thirty stars. This was that same queer feeling, as if the entire universe had been offset, but only by a foot or two, that we all felt for that brief moment when the stars went from 50 to 52. I confess I was glad when the new order of things did away with the old flag and brought us a simpler standard entirely.

The other flag was, in the main, iron red, the color of dried blood; the way it draped presented a wide blue hem inlaid with white stars, and a dangling gold fringe. It was, I learned much later while browsing a finely illustrated volume of 19th century vexillology, the flag of the now-defunct Democratic Club of Tammany.

Other things of note: a large bronze eagle with an ashtray balanced on its head. Several rows of wooden folding chairs, with scarlet seats. A gilt snake undulating along the top of the walls; it circled the room, biting its own tail. Plaster caryatids stood at all four corners, the faces bearing a strong resemblance to . . . June?

And there was herself, June, incongruous with the surroundings in her tomboy apparel, except that her face was reflected in the caryatids, and in a small oval painting in a thick frame affixed to the desk. They looked like her in the way one of those police sketches that have been aged to show how a long-missing child might look now resemble the original, capturing her ten or fifteen years older. Maybe I am projecting our recognition, but subconsciously we must all have felt her future in the images.

And what of June? If she knew, she didn't let on. She was standing behind the desk, our natural leader. Then she came round to us, and we surrounded her like drones around the queen. Everybody jabbered at once. She put up a finger to shush us.

"I don't know what happened," she said, "but we seem to have gotten in. I half-expected someone to be here, to receive us, but it appears we are left to ourselves."

"What about the chess club?" asked Max. He looked forlorn. There were no chess sets in evidence, nor the little tables, nor the clocks you'd expect. There would be no chess games it seemed.

"Well, there had been one," said June, "I found that out when I was looking things up. Could be that all that stuff is in storage, somewhere," she suggested. "I could send some letters to the address I found, arrange to find it, or secure it," she suggested. "All in favor?" Max raised his hand high. The rest of us were indifferent. "Opposed?" No one was against it. "Then the ayes have it. I'll make inquiries.

"It looks like," she continued, "we can have this club to ourselves. What's that card game you play? We can have tournaments here. And discuss important things. And open all the cabinets, and look into the books, and see what there is to see? Every Wednesday, it's ours for two hours, and transportation provided."

While the others were enthusiastic, I noticed that Ryan, standing a little back from the rest, had a clouded look. It tempered my enthusiasm, and something left me feeling cut off. She had done this all alone and never said a word, hadn't let me in on anything.

I stifled the feeling, and mustering up some genuine enthusiasm, said, "This is completely unbelievable! It's awesome!"

Like anything else, it became the ordinary soon enough.

We spent the entire two hours searching for hidden compartments.

Chapter
35

THAT NEXT WEEK, we brought game paraphernalia, our special decks of cards, even resurrected our old "The Game" sourcebooks and dice to play. Aaron brought a magnifying glass from home, and a speckled composition book, on the front of which he had written, in all caps, "CLUES."

The big room, which an initial look had filled with ornate possibility, was revealed to be shabby on closer inspection. Though it had been carefully dusted, everything was faded. The gilding was chipped. The rugs were moth-eaten. The table dull, its green fabric pitted. Inside the cabinets, the books turned out to be a total wash. One contained dry as dust law books. Another, big ledgers filled with faded brown ink, just numbers, the occasional name, all in a swirling, illegible hand. Others held bound copies of old newspapers, which we were initially excited by—with their advertisements for long johns and quack remedies—but soon found boring too.

Another section contained darkly bound copies of "The World's Greatest Literature" from the late 19th century. There were editions of Macaulay. Dickens. All badly printed, with hard to read text. They smelled slightly mildewed. It was standard library-sale fare. I thought I recognized some of the same editions I had purchased for myself five for a dollar at the last sale, kept on my shelf at home, and never read. A treatise on animal husbandry was a source of cackling amusement.

One week, before Thanksgiving break, we spent the entire two hours searching for hidden compartments.

I took much joy in being the first to find one—the long shields that the caryatids held clicked open to reveal secret shelves. At the click and the sudden reveal of the thin seam all around the shield, I was thronged by fellow club members in a joyous congress. We were all deflated when inside was nothing but shadow and dust.

One excitement was the continuation of the card tournament. I was knocked out early, and it piqued me.

Meanwhile June was distracted, poring over the account books they had found on the shelves. Only Brian sat with her. Aaron had lent them his magnifying glass, and clue book, which had remained entirely empty. He was riding a wave in the tournament, and soon it was him vs. Eric in a final match. Max and Ryan had dragged two of the big medieval chairs from the corners, beneath the statues, and were passing a magnetic chess set back and forth between them, making their moves. Ryan would stop staring at the board now and then to look up and over at June.

Two weeks before Christmas break, June announced a surprise, and raised an unfamiliar key for our scrutiny. It was a big, iron thing. She announced that we were to take a field trip to the storage room to which she had finally, through much back and forth, gained access.

We filed along behind her like ducklings, downstairs to the first floor, and to a door we had passed a dozen or more times without observing. It was disguised as part of the wall at the back end of the hall—invisible except for a dark seam all around it. The thick key slid into the hole and turned with a loud clack.

We walked through the door onto a concrete floor under a high, vaulted ceiling with windows running along the whole length of the big room, high up, letting a cobwebby light fall over a lot of furniture piled under dusty tarps. It was cold enough to see your breath, and the push-button light switches didn't work.

We wandered around, peering into the piles. A mouse scurried out.

Aaron found the chess clocks, and boards, and some folding tables. We agreed to take one set up. The light outside was fading, and nothing else of interest popped up, so we went back upstairs, Brian and Aaron supporting the chess table, me carrying the clock, leaving smudges from my fingers in the dust that coated it. Max had the chessboard, and Ryan was absently stroking a moth-eaten velvet bag full of chess pieces.

About an hour into our meetings, the big old lamps would be lit. They had been candles first, then gas sconces, and were now all clumsily electrified. The narrow wires and tiny plugs were a source of dangerous fascination. The light was weak, and cast us all into jaundice. We kept the tourney scores and chess scores in chalk on a broken piece of slate we leaned against the old desk.

There was one locked drawer in the desk. We fiddled with it absently. Paperclips and a bronze letter opener were of no avail. Periodically I jiggled it.

Toward the end of the term, I found myself treating the club meetings like a study hall, sitting in one of the baronial thrones to do my homework.

No one dared to say it, but by sometime in February we all knew we were kind of over it. Someone suggested we bring in new members. Max posed a question, then: whether we ourselves had actually, officially joined up. Not the chess club, but our "real" club. There had been no ceremony. No signatures or writing down of names.

June grew visibly excited—the first time I had seen her become animated in some time. She had been listless and distracted lately. She also had been spending time on her homework. She was going to try to just get her GED, and "get done with this school thing early."

Now June had focus. After the holidays, we returned and June showed us a little leather-bound book she had found, which had in bright-red, hand-painted letters: on the front the title *Pocket Manual of Rules of Order for Deliberative Assemblies: Robert's Rules of Order*.

Soon, we were all "being recognized by the chair," "taking the floor," and making and "seconding" motions. She divided us into groups she called committees; she said something about how the Constitution was put together. I found myself on a committee recommending new members: my contributions were Alice and Matthew.

We aimed for fifteen. I can't remember the reasoning behind the number. It seemed like a lot, but not too many. Enough that we'd always have a quorum, despite—and I was guilty too—people beginning to miss meetings. June, however, was always there.

The subcommittee on initiation and ceremony June led herself, Brian and Max by her side. I perceived tension between Max and Brian from all the way across the room; they were vying for June's favor. I was in an orbit far removed from theirs. But I reasoned that June had intended it that way. We would, still, exchange glances and knowing looks. I built up for myself a sense that she needed my help out away from her, so that I was available to convey her intentions when she couldn't personally attend. I maintained a haughty self-satisfaction.

To one meeting, June, Max, and Brian brought big bolts of fabric, black and crimson red—these they had taken from Brian's grandmother, who had become catatonic and had no use for them any longer—and they handed out sheets of paper to all of us. The sheets were scripts, they had calls and responses, and different parts for each of us. There were door-wardens, and interlocutors, and ritual steps. The lights would be turned off and candles lit. The fabric would be worn as robes over our clothes.

We cut strips to make masks for our eyes, but this was deemed ridiculous, and the fabric wasted. We practiced a chant. It was all very gothic. I suspected it was much influenced by some of the computer games Max and Brian had been into. Games I also played.

I thought it was corny.

Nevertheless we began opening our meetings with oaths, and a little ceremony, and I got to like the feel of it. It took all spring to get things together. The invitations were composed, and however it was that June communicated with them, the principal and Clyde Duane again arranged a similar reception on school grounds. Invites distributed, a larger bus would be needed. The meeting to inaugurate new members would be the last of the school year. Everyone had different summer plans; June and her family were going away.

All week I practiced my part in the mirror, keeping my voice to a whisper so as not to be overheard by my family. I was slated to be one of the door wardens. We had found, in the storage room, a heavy staff with the head of an eagle, painted (not gilded) gold; I suppose it had held a flag once.

I was to pound the staff three times. I rapped my dresser with my knuckles at the appropriate time. But I had a tickle in my throat, and when I woke the morning of, I was burning up. I had caught a rare spring cold. My mother spotted it instantly, and putting the back of her hand against my forehead, she insisted I return to bed.

I couldn't really say that's when everything began going wrong for me, but if I had already been stepping away from the club's cult-like mysteries—school work, including my essay-writing business, had begun to wear on me, and I had been trying to get out of our meetings early—this constituted a sort of clean break.

So I missed it.

No one would talk about the initiations at school with me; they would just make a low whistle, or say something generic, like, "Wow! Next year is gonna be so crazy."

I had stopped seeing June much at school except a glimpse here or there in the halls. But it was that week I saw June in the library for the first time in ages. I explained about getting sick, and missing my role in the ceremony. She of course understood.

After some anonymous complaints, several of the old Apple computers had lately been restored to one corner, to allow students to play their old favorite games, or to use Print Shop to make large dot-matrix banners; the PCs had no analogous programs.

June invited me to sit at *Oregon Trail* with her. She displayed her old facility with a musket. I broached the secrets of the club with her, and we chatted for a moment, in hushed tones, about the initiation and the new year, but she cut me off, saying, simply, "I need a break from all that."

*. . . a shabby little field with no dinosaurs, no cave leading down to
the center of the earth, just an old rusted tractor,
up to its shoulders in tall grass.*

Chapter
36

THAT SUMMER I was finally old enough to fend for myself at home while my parents worked. That was the end of the days with gang at the "farm" or its successor, for me. I had been tasked with a few errands to occupy my time —vacuum and tidy the house, mow the lawn—but it all amounted to long lazy days of reading and nature walks.

Sometimes, on weekends, Brian, who had gotten a job at the soft-serve place on the highway, would come visit sometimes, in the afternoons. We'd play video games together, or knock about the woods. I explained that I couldn't wait to get to college. There was so much to learn there, I said. And the teachers would be different, I said, they'd know more, be able to teach more. The students would be different, too. He didn't seem convinced.

In the fall I was starting to get tongue-tied and weird around Alice, both at school and at our club meetings. I had started shaving and had developed a handful of coarse, curly hairs on my chest and was losing the roundness around my fingers and toes. I subsumed my feelings in work, read furiously, did extra assignments. I don't remember much of that time. I must have gone to many of the club meetings, must have spent some meaningful time with June. But I had grown determined to finish school early, and get on to college—to get out of this town.

We had two more crops of initiates. After I turned sixteen and entered my junior year, by December it looked like I was primed to leave school that spring. I had taken the SATs and done well enough. I picked a college closer to home, and by sometime in January, I had been accepted early decision. I hadn't told June I would be leaving a year early. I think I was making a conscious effort to look forward, and not backward. I became aloof to everything.

Then it was over, and I was packing for the first week of college. It seems crazy now, that I missed everything for books and study—everything that was real, and strange—but our own growing up and becoming ourselves in the world, alone, shorn of all connection, is another kind of mystery, and it was the one that took hold.

I didn't have a graduation party that year; it seemed silly to, somehow. But I went to Brian's. Brian's party was up on a hill. Below sat his parents' farm: an old farmhouse permanently in mid-restoration, a clean, bright-red barn, some cows milling about. The gravel road tumbled precipitously from the upper field into a sort of forgotten valley. It kept sinking past the house, and away. Even the vegetation changed as you went, getting wilder and bigger, and more strange. At its farthest extent you could imagine dinosaurs still flying above a lost rainforest canopy, or an opening in the earth from which red light poured, the fires of a hollow earth.

As children, we'd begin to walk down that road with such visions always a hundred yards beyond where we could see, but always turned back, as if instinctually, to avoid reaching the road's end, a shabby little field with no dinosaurs, no cave leading down to the center of the earth, just an old rusted tractor, up to its shoulders in tall grass.

Now, with the sky gradient from the last yellow of the sun to a blue-black sky, the adults took a torch and lit different parts of the bonfire pile. Nothing seemed to happen at first, then there was an inner crackle and small bursts of light, followed by spreading flames. Soon the whole mass of sticks was a tumble of bright, rolling fire. Everyone was slicked with the glow of it, and a thin stream of smoke was grey against the sky, where, as if here and there answering, a planet and some stars began to shine. Away from the fire, the air held a chill. This was still a time when you could call an early summer night crisp. Our children's children, given the heroic work we have done since, might get nights like that back again.

I spent a lot of the party by myself, watching the light on the long grass, or seeing how close to the fire I could stand. June surprised me, emerging from the darkness, a red Solo cup in hand. She said, "Don't be a stranger." But I had already become one.

I asked if I could write her from college, and she gave me her address, writing it down for me on a piece of notebook paper. I folded the scrap of paper and shoved it in the pocket of my pants, not to seem too eager. And I resisted unfolding it and folding it again for fear I might mar the address, and make it illegible.

It was too dark now, anyway, and it would be too obvious to take it out and try to read it. Now that I was leaving, all my standoffishness and academic focus had fallen away, a sham. I could have been a much better friend to her.

Sometime after eleven, I got a ride in a car heading my way. I knew the kids all by face, some by name, but had never much spoken to them. There was a sense of excitement in the car, of possibility. They were all new grads, and they spoke to me as if to a close friend. Most were off to work. One was heading to some kind of lumberjack college. I told them about my hopes for college in such elevated language I cringe to think about it, now. Back on the hill behind us, the fire continued to burn, brightly.

It burns in my memory still, like a beacon to follow to some momentous and tragic return.

She can read his thoughts well enough to divine whether he is looking at a card with a blue star or one with three wavy lines.

Chapter
37

I ENDED UP attending the same college as Tiffany had, although she had preceded me by almost ten years, I place myself among the last of her generation—people whose legs were so firmly planted in the 20th century they might have been held there by concrete. Ironically, she and I were part of the birth of the new one; part of that great clearing out that marked the real shift between the before times and the "real" 21st century.

This isn't about my college experience, so much as about how June came back into my life, if she had ever actually left it. Suffice it to say, all my predictions about what college life would be like were outmoded. Impossible, really.

I'd never had any kind of preparation for college, other than my imagination, and that based on old and outdated books. I wasn't even close to the class background of most of my fellow students, who had had tutors, and went to enormous, highly competitive public high schools, or private schools with uniforms, where they had lived apart from their parents. Most chafed at not being allowed to bring their cars the first year, brand new SUVs or sporty sedans, BMWs and Lexuses. They were conversant with "the city," usually New York, Los Angeles, or Chicago.

They knew things, and were smart. Studying, however, ranked low on their list of priorities. But for me the library became an important sanctuary.

Some weeks in, I put my thoughts together in a letter to June. I don't remember what I wrote, exactly. Or in the other letters. I think I treated it like a diary. They were long, and handwritten, in dense black ink from a fine-tipped pen.

But I remember an anecdote, a story I was particularly fond of, which I must have sent along to her.

Imagine, I had told her, a young man—it is the first week of college for this freshman, who is struggling with the campus map, by himself, trying to find a particular building. How can he be so bad at navigating? It's also pouring rain; it's coming down in buckets, and he's walking, huddled up in his light jacket, completely soaked. He has an umbrella, but the wind and the ferocity of the rain has made it worthless. He jogs to a red brick building with a medieval-looking turret. There is an archway over the door. Inside, all the classrooms are empty.

He goes up the central stairway, taking the steps two at a time. Now he is both soaked to the skin and out of breath. A single office door at the end of the hall is cracked open; there is a shadowy figure inside, bent over a desk. The window in the door is frosted glass, translucent like the door to a private detective's suite. The sound of the rain patters against a large skylight above the hall, the water pours down it, sending shapeless shadows that wash over him like waves. The boy knocks too hard on the door and it swings open into the closet-office of an assistant professor who, with an almost orange beard and narrow spectacles, is reading or possibly napping over an open book.

The professor's head pops up. The boy blurts out, "Help me! I'm lost!"

"Son," the professor says, closing the big book, which is now revealed to be a Hebrew bible, "we are all lost. None has any ultimate answers. But if, perhaps, I can't give the kind of help you need, I can point you somewhere you might try."

A stunned pause. "No," the boy says, "I am actually lost. I'm looking for the English building." Yes, he had found the upper floor offices of the small but earnest department of Religious Studies.

I might have been in the English class I had been looking for that day, when, sometime after midterms, I got a surprise visit at school.

It was November, and we'd had a light dusting of snow. One of the girls in the class had her leg immobilized in a cast, and took up two seats in the row. "Vail," she had said to people nearby who had been eyeing her cast, as though everyone would know immediately what it meant, and in fact, everybody did know what it meant, except me.

We were reading sonnets from Sir Philip Sydney's *Astrophel and Stella*. Alone among the students, I had the big, old rebound copy from the library, where the interior s's of every word were elongated like cursive f's. It had the faintest hint of mildew, and the pages were thick and stuck together. Did I take it out from the library to save the money on the book cost? Maybe, but I also did it because I liked being different and difficult.

I was—am, I guess—eccentric.

I exited class with haste when it ended, always fearful of being caught in the vestibule or hallway by someone and having to awkwardly chat with them. Outside, I took the long way back to the dorm. I popped over to the school store, bought a snack, and ate it walking around the moss and lichen-covered headstones of the Quaker graveyard. Then, back through the student center, where I checked my mail. I found a CD in a white cardboard sleeve from *Columbia Records*—my deliberately nerdy classical-music of the month club—and a credit-card come-on, but no letter from June.

I had grown accustomed to getting them, once a week, in reply to mine. Hers were, like mine, diaristic, nothing too extraordinarily revealing or personal, but enough to know we were both deeply alive.

My afternoon class had been canceled, a rare moment of freedom. I thought of all the things I could do. I could take the jitney in to the mall, but of course, no, I never did that, or I could have a late lunch at the diner, where I could see or be seen, or take a walk deep in the glen, although there wasn't much there but a hush and shadows, water, rushing.

No, I'd probably take a hot shower, and then read in my dorm room. My roommate, with whom I shared a ships-in-the-night existence—I think we were both too shy to really talk, although I was probably the shyer—would be off playing *Dungeons & Dragons*. Something I ought to have been interested in, but eschewed. I had closed off so much of my past that I didn't speak up and join them to play.

I was now crossing the bridge, leaving the neo-Gothic part of the campus and entering the 1960s-style part, now decidedly in the era of concrete. I came up the stairs, to my adobe-looking dorm. My card opened the door, and I entered the common room, where, facing me on the couch, sat June.

She was glued to the big CRT TV, its lights reflected on her face. She had a couple VHS tapes with her, and she was watching her favorite TV show, *The Prisoner*.

When she saw me, her face lit up. "Come on, sit down, watch with me!"

June had already met and made friends with all the people on my floor. Some of whose names I still hadn't even learned. She had wrangled control of the common-room television, even though it was *Dawson's Creek* night. A few people sat and watched *The Prisoner* with us. I think the episode was called "Schizoid Man." The prisoner (No. 6) is trained to be left handed and to enjoy smoking Russian cigarettes, and brainwashed into thinking he is not himself, but an imposter, trying to drive the real one mad.

It made a kind of absurd but beautiful sense. In the episode, a woman has a psychic connection with the prisoner. She can read his thoughts well enough to divine whether he is looking at a card with a blue star or one with three wavy lines. She betrays him, later, but has one chance to apologize.

When it was over, June told me she had to go, but, she said, "I'll be back some other time."

Afterwards, the relative strangers in my residence hall came up to me to say, "Your girlfriend is so fucking cool." I demurred. I protested. She wasn't my girlfriend, I told them.

They all rolled their eyes at me.

She had put a lot of effort in: sweet talked the RA into letting her stay there against dorm rules, and made friends with everyone. I was caught somewhere between delight and abject terror, although of what, I couldn't have actually explained.

She came back dozens of times. We didn't talk about her visits in the letters, as though we were trying to keep them a secret from ourselves. The same way we didn't really talk about the past, or even what was happening now. I knew she had gotten her GED, and was now commuting to take classes at community college.

When June visited, I took her around campus. She wanted to see all the oldest buildings. We quickly discovered forgotten and hidden places, none of them of any consequence, some that had not seen a footstep for a hundred years. We took nature walks in the spring. One day, as we were walking, she asked if I had ever been kissed, and when I said I had not, she leaned in and kissed me. There was a furtive quality to it, but the feel of her lips on mine was like nothing I had been prepared for. It was a living, fleshy feeling, but electric. We found our way to a bench in the glen. I pressed against her, and we made out for minutes, our breath coming out in erratic spurts until we pulled away from each other. I was about to reach for her again, fingers and face burning, when some people walked by—parents on a visit. I think I turned beet red.

June looked just as she always did, exquisite, poised, except for the slightest flush on her cheeks.

I didn't ask if she had kissed anyone before. I felt that I knew the answer; at least Ryan, maybe Brian, others, but I did not mind in the least. We were kissing now. We walked back toward her car, much closer now. I let the edge of my hand brush against hers. I thought, this is amazing. I thought, now we are together. Then she got in her car and left, giving me a little wave.

At first, June's visits increased in tempo. Sometimes two or three times a week. I was enthusiastic about it, to say the least. We spent more and more time making out. June didn't dress casually like most of the college students—she often wore a dress or a skirt and in cooler weather wore wool stockings that went up to her thigh. When my room was free, and we were alone, she would let me roll her stockings off her legs, or unbutton her shirt.

One day she was trying to help me with my calculus homework, a course I had badgered the professor into letting me into, and which was probably too hard for me. After sitting for a while with the big fat textbook opened across both our laps, I turned to her, and it dropped to the floor. We got up, and something drew us to the closet. We undressed each other there. Maybe thinking it would offer some kind of protection in the event my roommate popped in.

We stood in the closet next to each other, naked, like Adam and Eve in an etching.

I let my palm rest on a birthmark just above her left hip. She toyed with the hair around my nipples with her precise fingers. Soon we were on the floor. Fifteen or twenty minutes later we were getting dressed, she had to go, something she had to get to by a specific time.

I think I loved her hands most. The shape of them. The way they looked against her stockings as she slid them back on. She pulled her black skirt on over them. She had a striped shirt, gray with thin white stripes, that showed off her figure. She tightened the laces on her Dr. Martens. She pulled all her mass of hair into a little cap, and I straightened her necklace, which was a single silver strand with an acorn.

I suddenly felt young in relation to her. She seemed to be thoroughly grown up. She had become herself completely, while I was still incubating, waiting to split open into my actual being. This is what I was afraid of, and it led me to act out. I grew distant.

I challenged her about Ryan. "What would he think?" I said, after we had been making out.

"It's not like that," she said. "It was never like that."

I didn't understand her. (Do I understand now? Times have changed. I think back to the looks Ryan would give me. What kind of longing had been there?) I began to write less. Was it out of fear? It wasn't fear of commitment; I could have bound myself to her for a thousand years. I prejudged myself incomplete—not right for her, too insubstantial, too unformed, too young. I had probably been right. But to a large extent these things are self-fulfilling.

We both got busy with the end of the semester. Her visits slowed. I started to dread them, because I had in mind specific things, studying, or walks, or a visit to the library, I wanted all to myself. I suddenly didn't want things to work.

We are so self-destructive in this life, aren't we? I could have been happy. But at last it was June, who near finals week, came one last time, to end things. She was transferring to a full-time college elsewhere, a good school in Ohio. I felt it as a tremendous relief. She was the most astounding person I had ever encountered, and I let her go with a shrug.

So, we were lost to each other, until some years later, when we were both in New York City and met up again, through a friend of a friend. That was our penultimate, and maybe most disastrous connection—more disastrous because it had almost stuck, and although I often think back to it, wonder what a different life it could have made, know, for her, of not me too, and for our world, it would have been all wrong.

II.

The Key

Chapter
38

I GUESS WE'RE in for a bumpy ride, thought Zane Arbuster, still groggy from hypersleep, as he felt the flight stick kick back against his hands. The starfield in front of him was spiraling vertiginously. The proximity alarms and occasional loud thumps on the hull made clear that the computer had woken him in the middle of a large debris field.

He jerked the controls left then right, and juiced the azimuthal thrusters rhythmically to try to get out of the spin. Zane called out to the computer but got no response. He cursed the computer a few times under his breath, then swore loudly through the cabin, which was empty except for him. (As the entire ship was.) A large impact cracked one of the side cameras, then the whole left side of the screen went dark.

No matter—the visual display was distracting. He had to sync his speed to the field and stop the roll first before he could reliably avoid whatever was out there. There would be time enough to address the computer malfunction. If the voice interface was down, at least the critical pieces still worked.

Alarm! Alert! Something big, right ahead.

He pushed the yoke down hard and slammed the reverse rockets. Zane's Alaracan cruiser just missed whatever it was. Close shave.

The swirling finally stopped, but Zane still felt it in his guts. That was standard for waking from hypersleep. Usually, however, the computer woke you gently, on autopilot, a soft light, quiet music, Silurnian coffee when you were ready for it, and ETA at your final destination in a dulcet tone. Not like this, with no warning, alarms everywhere, spinning out of control in a field of asteroids or—now that he had righted the ship and slowed the careening he could see—the wreckage of a huge interstellar freighter, or pleasure yacht.

Gradually the assortment of buzzers, beepings, and klaxons died down to a single, urgent, repeating tone. Zane suddenly and vehemently swore blood vengeance against the worthless Coroxinian grease-monkey who had swindled him.

"*Zark!*" he blurted out.

The single tone that remained was the root cause of all his trouble to this point, and it would cost him more time yet: He had been sold a Barathinian Empire ambulance disguised as a light cruiser, and that fox hadn't even bothered to disable the automatic S.O.S. response subprogram. The noise was an S.O.S. beacon, and it wouldn't stop, nor could he jump back to hyperspace, until he found and acknowledged it.

What an enormous hassle. Zane didn't have time for this. The encrypted message blinking in the diplomatic pouch was burning a hole in his side: the sooner he reached the court of the Empress of the Quadrant and got rid of it, the sooner he'd be back where this all started, and he could resume his long overdue vacation on Erigal 7. For a moment he dreamed of a smooth, blue cocktail, garnished with the thinnest slice of red zargot and served from the fourth arm of a beautiful Ragerian sphinx.

"S.O.S.!" the computer blurted out, finally waking, "S.O.S.! Mark seventeen, thirty, eleven. S.O.S.!" Why did everything have to happen to him?

On the other hand, it gave him a little more time to think of an excuse for why three Xaveri rangers had found him with a gold dagger buried hilt deep into the diplomat's back, the one who had first been in possession of the diplomatic pouch. The news must have reached the Empress by now, and he suspected he wouldn't have much time before her guards had got to him and dragged him by the heels to the inescapable dungeons of Dornat.

The life of a galactic adventurer was never dull, but on occasion, it did have its moments of tedium. Such as now. The computer, which he had desperately wanted to speak at the beginning, he now finally found a way to shut up through a haphazard mashing of the control panel. He twiddled with dials on the emergency view screen which, knowing now that he was in an ambulance, he had pried up from behind the bank of controls his "friend" from Corox had laser-welded on top.

"There it is!" he said at last, having locked onto the beacon's location. He pushed the thrusters forward, and then steered carefully toward the direction of the S.O.S., taking care to dodge around the larger broken hull-sections. Best case scenario the beacon had been ejected from the wreckage, and he could bring it in with the mechanical arm, or better yet, zap it into oblivion. Otherwise he might have to hazard a spacewalk. Suddenly he wondered if this junk boat had actual weapons, or if they were all facsimile. He cursed again. It would be good to know sooner than later, he thought.

He was getting close now. If the sensors were correct it would be just behind this big section of the vessel's bridge. It was covered with scorch marks. The destroyed vessel must have been caught in a hail of laser blasts. Part of the hull bore the Barathinian Empire crest, a trio of bright orange stars covering a blue dragon, under a red crown. Zane tried to remember its meaning, but the finer points of interstellar heraldry were a matter of book learning. It was enough to know who was who.

He had to admit the fact that the wrecked ship was Barathinian and that's where he was heading was a source of worry. But of course! He slapped himself—better not to get worked up over coincidences—it *had* to be a Barathinian ship, because the ambulance, also being Barathinian, wouldn't have stopped for any other beacon. He pulled the stick back gently, swooping under the hull section and coming straight for the origin of the signal.

"Damn!" said Zane.

"THE FUCK IS THIS?"

I jerked my head around, and was face to face with my co-worker, Eddie. He was leaning over my shoulder, looking past me, straight at my computer screen. I admit it looked odd. I resisted the temptation to Alt + Tab myself away, as it would only encourage Eddie to probe further. On my screen was a vivid computer rendition of a gas nebula pierced by the light of a scattering of stars. At the edges, the blackness of space.

The space adventure I had just been reading was center justified over it in white text, which, in places, was extremely difficult to read against the backdrop of the nebula. At the top of the page, a banner proclaimed it as a snapshot from The Internet Archive. It was a Geocities site, which meant the original source was long gone.

He started to read out loud, and chuckle.

"Zane Arbuster . . . Silurnian Coffee . . . *Alarm! Alert!* . . . Ha ha ha!"

"It's this thing my friend wrote." I stopped and backtracked. "I mean this kid I knew in high school."

"You mean back in, uh, Lardon's Grove, or Uncanny Valley, or whatever?"

"Yeah, look at this." I started clicking through the thirty-odd volumes linked at the top, and the star atlases, and galactic encyclopedia entries, ship schematics, and chat boards.

"Wow, this guy was really into this," said Eddie. The site had a hit counter, like an odometer, with lots of digits. It was stuck at 93. "Not a lot of fans."

"He tried forever to get me to read it when I was in college. I mean, some sections you have to highlight with the mouse just so you can read them over the nebula," I said.

"Where's the guy now?" Eddie asked.

"Aaron? I don't know," I said. "I kind of lost touch after a few years." I thought for a second. "Maybe he got tired of me not reading his stories."

"So, the *Chronicles of Zebulon 9:* derivative," said Eddie, "but I guess it's more interesting than the conversion reports you promised?"

"It's—actually good," I said. "The conversion reports? I already put them on the shared drive. Check your email once in a blue moon!"

Eddie grunted and turned in his swivel chair back to his desk, and I heard the keys on his keyboard begin to clack. I heard him mutter a Zebulonian curse to himself, "Zark!"

I took my mouse and shrank the window to a corner of the screen, embarrassed a little, then scrolled back to where I'd been reading.

ZANE PEERED AHEAD warily. That damned computer was at it again: "Life-form reading: one. Life-form reading: one."

The S.O.S. beacon flashed its radio signal from a single, intact escape pod. He was about to take on a guest. The occupant, whoever or whatever it was, had been lucky. The pod thrusters must have failed, leaving it to float silently among the wreckage. Other pods, if he knew his space marauders, and this clearly was some kind of hit job, would have been gunned down mercilessly as they emerged from the ship.

Zane's thoughts wandered again to the unique anatomy of Ragerian sphinxes and the salty-sweet taste of their signature cocktails, before he snapped to the task at hand. Now he'd maneuver over the pod, engage the auto-docking sequence —the ship shuddered as the clamps found their mooring. Zane glanced around the cabin, looking for the robo-doc, but as the most-valuable part of an ambulance's accoutrements, that had most likely been stripped and sold to the highest bidder. Sure enough, in its place in the corner was a beat-up first-aid kit.

As the docking sequence finished, Zane imagined the fat, robed ambassador within, the perfumed stench that would rise from its sixteen tentacles, or if an Anchidion, a frequent complement to such missions, the constant, eerie tracking of the hundred liquid eyes. Would the second hyper chamber even fit the occupant? The normal fitting of hypersleep cubes had, likewise, Zane realized, been stripped, replaced with cargo space for the guns he was supposed to run back from Zebulon after his detour to the Empress.

But that was another story altogether.

Sometimes, Zane thought, it was hard to track how many different double- and triple-crosses he was engaged in, and at what point all the opposing forces of evil deeds netted out to good. That was Sardox's problem. Zane was just the best agent he had.

He sighed for a full minute. The doors were opening in the pod-bay, and he slapped the stabilizers and turned to head back. He straightened up to his full height, grabbed the first-aid kit, and marched in. The bay was filled with the mist of mixing atmospheres, which was dispersing. A shadowy figure started to take shape, and Zane began a slight bow.

"Your excellency—" he started, but there was no rich ambassador. In a muted jumpsuit, torn in places, stood a short, scuffed-up boy, with a grease-stained face, two piercing brown eyes, short-cropped tousled hair. Not a boy. She spoke.

"Oh, sir," she said, "thank you, thank you."

Zane was dumbfounded. The girl fell to the floor, and began to shiver.

He was over to her in a flash, pulling out the silver blanket and wrapping it over her shoulders. Under all the scuffs and the grime, she was not beautiful but quite pretty, slender but fit. On her cheek was an old, arrow-shaped scar.

I CLOSED THE WINDOW like a shot; the text and nebulae, the stars, planets, and galaxies of Zebulon were gone. But it all seemed to stick in the plasma of the screen like a ghost. What had made me react so frantically, so involuntarily? Had it been that I was struck by the unmistakable identity of the fictional girl in Aaron's mediocre sci-fi farrago?

But how had he known about the scar?

Part of the hull bore the Barathinian Empire crest, a trio of bright orange stars covering a blue dragon, under a red crown.

"The view from nowhere," said Eddie.

Chapter
39

"THE VIEW FROM NOWHERE," said Eddie, some days later, his form materializing in the glass, behind mine, pale, ghost-like, shot through with the sunset which was flaming down over New Jersey and the Hudson.

"A quiet moment of self-reflection," I said.

"Life offers many such moments," said Eddie, "usually not so literal."

Not nowhere. Somewhere. Here. Standing on a high floor of the office building where I worked. I saw myself, and now Eddie, and the bright, slanting colors in the sky, facades and water towers thrown into silhouette.

Different planes of reality, and the mind snapped between them: city, self, office, even intermediate states, chimeras of person and setting, a beast alive.

Had it been, then, only seven or eight years ago, that moment at the window? I say only, but for all that has changed it could have been a million years. I thought then: How did I get here? How did we get here? Interlocking questions: candlestick or faces, rabbit or duck, cube facing up or cube facing down? Reality running through the masquerade, picking up first one mask, then another.

So, looking once, it was Eddie and me in the window. Looking again, the bright sun ripping through the fading sky.

Another glance, the coworkers moving behind me, putting their things into their bags, getting ready to leave. Below, police sirens, flashing red lights. Even this far up, I could hear scattered bursts of shouting, the muffled voice of a crowd. Another spontaneous protest had erupted. Now the question was whether to wait it out or try to run through it before things got serious.

The lobby took you directly into the small plaza below, into a chanting throng, a swirl of blue smocked resistance, facing rows of cops in riot gear, itching to break heads.

The stairs—two flights and a landing for every one of 27 floors, lined with pale strips of glow-in-the-dark emergency tape—took you to a side street, and from there you might walk to the other transit line, miss the protest entirely, unless the guardsmen arriving late had started their pincer move to overwhelm the crowd from behind.

Or, a few more hours of work and you could get a head start on the rest of the week.

It didn't matter to me; I had no one to come home to. There might only be a whiff of tear gas, some blood on the marble pavers, a litter of masks and signs. The cops were efficient in their swift brutality. But the blue smocks were efficient too—they'd melt away through some unexpected, pre-planned channel, and form again, roaring, a few blocks away.

How had I gotten here? Only a handful of years away from fifty, living alone in a modest apartment in New York City, doing freelance copywriting and digital creative for a pharmaceutical company, peering down at protests against a system I loathed but had enwrapped me in.

As if George Bailey, after wishing his whole life away, had thanked Clarence and shuffled off to the big city, to sit in the office of some enormous, stone-hearted bank, stamping "foreclosed" on paperwork all day.

"I've been to Rick's 'Office Hours,'" said Eddie—every time he said Rick, he'd pause a beat, and we'd both say "the Dick" in unison. Rick the Dick was the new COO, embarking, as newly installed C-levels do, on a brash reorganization plan, "reimagining the way we work." You had to append an invisible trademark sign to the phrase when you said it, like Rick always did, with a little squint and dramatic hand gestures.

It had been ten years since the company's leadership had last mounted a big innovative initiative like this, something meaty, requiring buzz-words and town halls, offices to be drilled into, and conference rooms to be turned inside out. That's where Rick came in. Energy. New blood. No one could quite articulate to us what was changing in clear terms: it always seemed to boil down to new, expanded coffee stations and more free snacks.

After whatever it was was done, the COO would march through the sparkling new floors, his tight pants thin as cigarettes and only one shade less pale.

His lizard eyes darted this way and that under voluminous lids. His voice came as if from under a great weight, too, giving the impression of either a display of great thoughtfulness, as he intended, or of a sluggishness of thought because the office was too cool. You could imagine him settling on a flat rock beneath a red lamp at night, his tongue darting out to capture the protein of buzzing flies, or taking a pale cricket in, its startled antenna and faceted eyes disappearing soundlessly.

We were to pick up a new way of working, too. It was to be "agile," something out of the tech trades. I lifted up one leg and posed like a crane. "Agile," I said. Eddie smacked me, half-playfully, half real. It was these new "office hours," which Eddie had just been to, one more way to break down the silos our sclerotic, old company had jamming up its arteries. They were so many stents, allowing the blood to circulate, free.

None of it mattered. We had red stripes on our ID badges, with bold white text that said "CONTRACTOR." It meant lower pay and fewer benefits. But it also meant we didn't have to bow down to the faux-marble magnificence, and could grind ourselves into the reality of "nowhere"; our workspace hummed, a sad, beige wonderland.

That hum was the chatter-dampening "pink noise" machines the drop ceilings hid.

You could feel the hush hanging over you, a heavy blanket. I called it "Management."

These big initiatives were always a "tremendous win," because they had to be. You let a little air out of your soul, a little bit of clapping for Tinker Bell, to show you were on board with things.

We didn't have to clap quite as much as Linda, who managed our small initiative, creating marketing campaigns for some absolutely needless pharmaceutical "miracle." These always rotated in. I can't remember what it was then. Some pill to end the horrible scourge of too-sweaty palms.

"Him and everyone else," said Eddie, about the office hour, "were sitting in the dark when I got there." The lights would flicker off if people were still for too long. "Honest to god," he said, "in the fucking dark. Except his lizard-head was glowing in the light from his phone."

"So he was just scrolling through his phone?" I asked.

These little moments of indignation and scorn were welcome, they stripped the cool office air of some of the existential dread it seemed to carry.

"While some poor woman from the basement—I guess she's in charge of the outsourcing, janitors and shit—was going on about something," said Eddie, "our friend just kept scrolling and nodding, absently."

"Jesus!"

"When I came through the door," he said, "the lights flickered on. There was so little movement in there that they'd gone off. But nobody acknowledged anything, Everyone was sort of zombified, and the woman was droning on, this rehearsed but quite real complaint, and Rick scrolling through his phone."

"We sure take sunsets for granted," I said. I had had enough of Rick.

To Eddie, it was all a sunset, the great sunset of our civilization, and given the state of our civilization, as manifested in this big building, with its ersatz marble, in this pharma company, that since the 30s had been sweating out medicines, and turning paper money into gold.

Eddie looked, now, past our reflections.

The actual sunset.

It was there, every evening, this insanely dramatic thing, insensitive to our movements, our very existence: the clouds rolling fire, the sky broken into great planes of blues, violets, pinks, oranges, reds. The sun like a yolk, like a disc, the black water chopped with reflections, the gradual, comforting fall of night over the shoulders of the buildings.

"Fuck," said Eddie.

I had heard it too: the tell-tale pops and hissing; tear gas, flash bangs, the usual. "Looks like the groundhog saw the guardsmen, and it's two more hours of work," he said.

As we turned back, Eddie slipped a small vial into my hand. It was the acid I'd asked him to get for me to micro-dose —it just leveled you and made you feel sparkling—but occasionally I'd take more drops and have a regular old trip, a kind of mental-palate-cleanser for a tough week. Eddie had a reliable contact.

When we got back to our desks we saw that Linda was still there, at the end of our row.

She spent most of our meetings complaining about her colleagues and bitching about the company benefits. It was ingratiating and morale-building. I like to think of her as a manipulative genius who was pumping us for maximum performance, but I believe she really hated everything about the company and her job. What could you do then, though? We all twirled in our office chairs, inscribing our own "productive" work into the endless scroll of meaningless waste and accumulation.

Linda was 26, but she looked fifty. Eddie was obsessed. She was like a female Woody Allen, minus, he said, the sexual predation. He thought.

He said he was psychologically interested in the effect. She didn't look bad per se, and in fact, Eddie said, she would only get hotter and hotter as everyone else aged around her.

Artistically, he said, he wanted to understand it. Was it something about her face alone, or her entire body? An extra line around her mouth, the way her eyes sunk in a little, the hook of her nose? Was it her pale skin, almost translucent? She dressed old, too. Everyone had to follow the more-or-less professional dress code, but something about her choices, all black, and lace. Did she start dressing for her appearance or was it the other way around? Had she always been an old soul only barely contained by her younger body?

Eddie was a pig, but it made me wonder: I too had aged, but when I looked at myself, I saw only myself.

We grow accustomed to our surroundings as they change, and everyone who aged around me, I could only think of them as they were now, extending forever back and forward in their present form. We were all of us walking backward into the tunnel, watching the light recede. But what was it like for Linda? Did everyone grow grotesquely old around her? We were all carried forward into the future, but was Linda a rock upon which the future broke, and passed as it flowed?

Chapter
40

"GEORGE BAILEY?" scoffed Tiffany. "So after you and June split, it was—what?—twenty years of unbroken misery?"

First, I tried to do the math. Decades and events scattered around my mind, and trying to pin them all together proved impossible.

"I was lonely," I said, "and, yes, I admit, kind of empty, you know?"

"Hmm. Lonely. Not from what I've heard," she said. "I mean, there was the model-tall German, and then the office manager with the, well," and she put her hands out, cupped, far in front of her chest, "and the lovely little pianist, and the wife of that painter—bad boy!—and the photographer's assistant, and . . ."

I stopped her. "They weren't emotionally available."

"Weren't they? Or was it that you weren't?"

She was right, of course. But I protested anyway.

"The pianist, for example: a lesbian, she loathed me. I even asked her once, you know, why she kept coming over, what she got out of it. She told me even she wasn't really sure! That's what I was dealing with—"

"And the photographer's assistant, who came right up to you at the party, standing so close you could feel the warmth of her body, what was wrong with her?"

"Get out of my head," I said. "Anyway, it wasn't June that was stopping me from getting close. We were finished. Never meant to be," I said, lamely. "She's a good friend. Well, a friend, anyway." I thought then of how our relationship had become circumscribed, how we had lost touch for a number of years after breaking up and on seeing her again, how she had that scar on her cheek. It had already faded, but somehow we never touched on it. Me not asking, her not volunteering. It looked jagged and twisted, as if the cheek had been punctured by a knife. How had Aaron known about that scar, written it into his story? I tried to put the dates together, but nothing was working out.

Well, was that what a good friend was, someone who knew not to ask about something painful, someone who accepted you for whomever you were?

"No," Tiffany replied, "I understand, I get it. When I cut things off with James, he asked me, 'It's somebody else, right?' but it wasn't—it was just him, but how do you say it, how do you tell them?"

"Oh, I thought it had been somebody else, actually," I said, with some archness.

Tiffany sat back in her perch, the high wooden chair, dropping for a second the mask of gnomic wisdom, or sibylline mystery, for a wry, pixieish look, a sprite out of the forest she had trekked to get here from the main road—she was smiling, is all it took. "Of course there was somebody else, there's always at least one somebody else, isn't there? But the point," she said, "is that it really wasn't, it was what the somebody else brought—it was the universe opening up. Not the person, but the new world."

"What, you mean that I was emotionally attached to all the ways the world was changing? But I didn't do anything. I wasn't part of it."

"Sometimes," said Tiffany, "I would be looking for Jeremiah—and it was a small office!—he was there, and then he was gone. The paralegals would be after me, like little dogs, barking up my shins, for this or that, and I'd have to try to figure out what Jeremiah had wanted out of them. This happened a few times before I made a thorough search.

"And then there he was, in the back hallway. There was a coat closet with folding doors, and his big, brown wingtips poking out of the bottom corner, like Dorothy's witch. I ripped the doors open, and he yelped and popped up off the floor. There was a small mat, and a pillow in there. He told me that sometimes he required naps during the day. Scared the living shit out of me."

I thought of the old man, his funny whiskers, popping up from the ground like Dracula in his coffin, but getting caught up in the hanging coats, maybe pulling some from their hangers. Tiffany there, having just whipped the door open; Hamlet pulling back the curtain.

"But," I said, "what does that mean? What are you saying?" I was preoccupied with her assessment of my life, and its reasons.

"I don't know," she said, "I just thought of it, of that moment. I guess the day the new world opened, the day the universe came through our door, the day I knew I was through with James and that there was something new coming—the moment it happened, Jeremiah was back there in the closet, waiting for me to find him." She looked away, and said, as if to the wall and not me, "Maybe he planned it that way."

We struggled with all our might to solve problems we didn't have
with technology that didn't work.

Chapter
41

ROM OUR VANTAGE point, you and I, looking back, it is
not hyperbole to say "The Millennium" did come,
although it was twenty years or so late. In the decades
before, and even as it was happening, it was difficult to see.

You reason to yourself—things like, "Every generation
has felt the pressure of the world ending. It is only recently we
have upped the scope of it, the scale."

But of course, the scope and scale have only increased
in tandem with our understanding of the scale of our world. To
a point. For a time, this scale shrinks as it grows, because the
universe expands but our reach doesn't. Once we looked at the
night sky as a vault, with pinpricks for light, that we could
build a tower to reach, and even to climb up onto the clouds
and walk amongst the Gods.

Then, only as we came into a greater appreciation for
the scarcity of life, did we sense what was about to be lost, and
know bitterly what the old time religions had always
maintained: we are the apocalypse. Yet we just go on. And
when the only things lost are invisible, third-hand, easily
forgotten (just, say, a way of life, the tenor of the seasons, an
insect whose right name we never knew), it is easy to dismiss.
But there are flashes.

We had the Y2K bug, I am old enough to remember.
Before that it was nuclear holocaust, which we avoided so
many times that even now, when it is a brutal possibility
(imagine after everything we end it with nuclear winter), we
put it far out of mind.

So the real millennium sneaked up on us. It came first
as bubbling disaster. It is hard now to remember the sense of it,
the disaster of it. The scars surround us, but the disaster was

often abstract. Equally surprising was the recovery. That is not to say the world avoided ending—it ended emphatically, but much was saved and improved in the new world. We just never quite knew it was a new one.

Around 2012, a rich Bible-nut with a cult radio following predicted the end of everything. When it manifestly did not come to pass, he simply said it had: it was "an apocalypse of the mind."

So it was, when it finally came, and so everything is: of the mind. Bertrand Russell, in puzzling out consciousness, points out there can be no homunculus inside your head, watching the world on a screen, because what's in his head? Descartes's "I think, therefore" runs aground on the recognition that he thinks. Does the calculator say "I add, therefore"? Well, maybe.

The world may be made of two kinds of "stuff": mind stuff and matter stuff—yet how can one influence the other, undetected? We see only matter, but we know only mind. The world, this matter, then, must be mind-stuff too, all of it.

Now are sunny days. Days of rain without anxiety. And I realize it must be strange to try to venture into the past, when things were bad, before. They were bad for a long time. The grinding badness of them had some moments of relief, some times of peace, but they were for the few, not the many, and they always had their cost. A debt to entropy.

There will be dark days again. But not for you, and not for me. Not for our children, either.

What can I tell you then, to remind you, if you lived it and forgot it like me?

We believed that success was a byproduct of merit, and like the simple creatures we were, that failure was a sign of weakness, a disease. We believed that reason and science were the handmaidens of utopia, against all evidence. I want to highlight some things in particular. I know you will squint and laugh. I could be talking about life among the Neanderthals, except we know they lived lives of peace and compassion.

The vision of the future was selfishness, and ease. Robots would toil on our behalf, and yet everything about our lives would remain exactly the same. Our imaginations were circumscribed by something, by greed, we were made parsimonious by it. Driverless cars zipping us around (presumably for next to nothing), clean coal and natural gas extracted by terminally ingenious means, no more stranglehold of big government, this the dream of liberals(!), but a fully technocratic society, governed by benevolent nerds with the help of all knowing AI and big data. And the biggest victory of all: no more government-backed money, but crypto-currency, a money based on, what? Intellect, I suppose.

For a long time we struggled with all our might to solve problems we didn't have with technology that didn't work, to convince ourselves we had not been wrong once. That there were no greater goods than what was good for us, where us was usually them, them that's got.

If I say blockchain you might think for a moment, and ask if I meant "block-and-tackle?" You might think of a heavy block of wood, and an old iron chain of many links. But those would be more useful, and more real.

I might remind you of how crypto-currency was supposed to work and you would say currency isn't some mathematical inevitability, it is only a token of trust, and there is no trust without society, and you'd be right.

And what about driverless cars?

The final straw was this: every street, every person, every sign and crossroad, every curb, would have to be retrofitted for them to even have a chance of working, and even then the most critical decisions would be made by operators sitting in enormous call centers and living in barracks, making pennies an hour, and having to be retired for fatigue, and their experiences of wrecks, the sounds of which the software cut off in microseconds, but which they heard in their souls, and wore like a coat of blood.

And yet the powers that be pushed it, lest they admit of any other way.

I would instead make a monument of our folly and tell a story, a reminder of how the past, even a little fragment, lost in a box, can be the key that unlocks a great mechanism, and sets the idle gears going, and we must be extremely careful that we want what the thundering movement may be.

Chapter
42

LINDA HAD an intensely worried look as she reached the cubby where Eddie and I were matching stock photos to diseases with increasing hilarity and irreverence. Really, it was a stretch to call them diseases at all—but we had pills and creams to hawk. Linda's head was bent to her phone like a benediction as she stopped in front of us. Black dress, white lace, faux-alligator shoes. The phone's glow made her skin appear even more pellucid than normal, and highlighted a delta of blue veins at each temple.

"Oh, my God," she said. "Oh, my God. Have you heard?" Then, after another moment looking at the phone, she just said, "The army." She fell into the third, empty chair, beside us.

Eddie and I, at first feeling relief, exchanged glances. We had both been immediately worried she was coming about the project funding, because we knew the entire extravaganza had devolved into a game of musical chairs, the great silence coming at any moment, but the money was still there. We could still eat out. Be extravagant with tips. We were joyously boiling into the future, frogs in the steadily-heating pot.

I think she came to us because we were the glib assholes, who blithely asserted nothing bad would come.

Now, in a low, even drone, probably condescending, I set forth what we all knew, that given the unstable state of things—after the strikes had gone on for so long, the Republican faction agitating for harsh reprisals, even talking about the current president in starkest terms of treason, making their own treasonous appeals public and private to foreign intervention—something had to give.

Eddie calmly explained that the Joint Chiefs had each privately been sounded out, how things weren't like the bad old days, and that the army was for order, but it wasn't anymore a wholly-owned subsidiary of the plutocratic right ("No offense!" he yelled out in the direction of the corner office, occupied by a member of the family that still ran the pharma co. through an elaborate system of shell companies).

Eddie had been talking out of his ass. Everyone was. But the army, for once in its miserable history, had done some kind of good. They stepped in, and it was a coup, but it seemed like everything was going to be, if not exactly sunshine and roses, at least stable and calm. So everyone celebrated the army. That was before a tranche of disgruntled "lesser" Generals and their Staff-Sergeants, who thought the old fogies on top had gotten too soft, toppled them in a bloodier coup. That was the junta we all remember.

I don't know if I can explain what happened next. From every corner people rose up. The soldiers themselves rose up. People stood in the squares in their blue smock jackets, and they kept standing until no one was standing in their way.

Chapter

43

B Y THE TIME I saw it, June's message—"I need to see you."—on LinkedIn, was three days old. What were a few days compared to the years it had been since we'd talked? I typed "OK" and hit enter.

When she finally replied—Tuesday the following week —it was with just one word, "Tonight." I knew better than to press her for trivial things, like time and place. It was a test of that "emergency telepathy system" we used to joke about. I felt good about my chances.

I had heard from a mutual acquaintance that he'd seen her downtown, which meant her base must be Manhattan, probably the basement apartment of that house on MacDougal Street. It was owned by her second cousin, whom she'd only met after we'd moved in together. He was nice enough, a musician, old enough to be June's father. We'd see him and his ex-wife from time to time; they both lived in the building still, just on separate floors. June didn't like to drink over on MacDougal. There are always too many tourists, even now.

I thought for a while, then I knew. I made my way to Union Square. I had forgotten to factor in the chance of another big public demonstration there. I intuited something was up on the subway, or should have: half the car was filled with blue smocks, but that could go unnoticed, since people now wore these coats all the time, demonstration or no. I could have gotten out at an earlier stop and walked or decided to go ahead to a farther stop, but I was on the platform now, wall to wall blue smocks, with the doors just closed behind me, no choice but to press on into the protest.

I had an ongoing disagreement with Eddie from work —I said it was right, imperative even, to keep demonstrating, after you have won, otherwise complacency sets in. Look, I said, at what happened in 2008. The push was so great to turn things around, and when the day came and a first victory was won, we all just collapsed—exhaustion I guess, and a lack of will. It ruined us.

But Eddie said it was the politicians' time to work. If people had to work at it relentlessly, on top of "every other goddamn thing" (that was his trademark, everything was "goddamn this" and "goddamn that," and when he was extra serious, he would put a long pause between "god" and "damn"), then why even bother with politicians?

Here we were, a socialist and an anarchist ginning up a social media blitz with a guerrilla marketing campaign for a drug to fix the problem of "you piss too much." Or was it "you can't piss enough"? I could never remember.

"It's both," Eddie would say, with a grin. "The goddamn miracle pill fixes both!"

He was "an artist," though the grotesque metal things he welded together in the garage space he paid to work in after hours, across from his apartment, weren't to my taste. That was in Bushwick.

Maybe he was right. What use for politicians was there? You had to do the work yourself, with everyone, and never let your guard down.

When I popped up out of the subway station into the middle of Union Square Park, it was like a cork popping up out of the water, or maybe flotsam from a shipwreck. And it wasn't just because I was all in brown corduroy, surrounded by thousands in matching blue coats. I felt buoyed up by something; maybe the urgency of June's message.

At first I had taken it in stride, but some nagging feeling kept coming back, some sense of importance, until I was seized bodily by it. My heart was in my throat by the time the subway doors had thumped closed behind me.

Above ground, in the park, there were no signs, just people, masses of people, all chanting three French words, "Liberté, égalité, fraternité." Occasionally the euphony of it was broken by a subsection of the crowd putting an Americanized "y" at the end of each.

Eddie had said, "The chant of the blue-smocks proposes: What if the French Revolution, but good?"

"It was good!" I said.

"And the Terror?" he asked.

"'The Terror' is," I said, "essential," gesticulating with a newly empty banana peel. The firm had, with the idea of reducing their health care costs, introduced a regime of healthy snacks. You had to admit, though, it felt positive, this friendly blue wave. Some people held daisies. For peace.

The earlier assemblies hadn't felt so peaceful. Maybe it had been the intense response. The armored police and all. There had been a fair amount of skulls cracked, people tased and pepper sprayed. In those early days.

The people were warned, but they persisted. And the persistence, at first ridiculed in the press, and lambasted on TV, had broken through, somehow.

It may have been that the protests began to be accompanied by large and growing general strikes. Soon, people who had been entirely disinterested in the whole affair took to not showing up at work.

The GDP took an appreciable hit, but the strikers felt a growing sense of wellbeing. They did not know, or would not let themselves know, that at this point, if they lost, they would be utterly crushed. It was a perilous time.

But all times are perilous, and all life a danger to itself.

The crowd, in their chanting, their arm pumping, ignored my awkward perambulation through it. I was to them like a bright insect crawling through a mountain of leaf litter: interesting, but no wider than your pinky nail, and easily lost.

The crowd began to thin out down University Place, and I made my way there, toward the first of three spots I had in mind to check for June. It was the re-opened Cedar Tavern, a nostalgic spot to me, not from its days as a haven for drunken writers and painters, but for the time that June had taken me, and narrated the story of every famous denizen, and several lesser luminaries she'd met and corralled for stories of the golden age, which I suppose meant this third turn was brass.

Two-thirds of the way there, some demonstrators had taken notice of me, were giving me a skeptical eye. I didn't blame them—funny little man, out of time, out of place, struggling upstream. What is society if it doesn't at least nod to conformity? Dress and demeanor are a fine initial proxy.

I swiveled my head, surveying the eyes upon me.

The faces were quizzical, but serious. It is serious business, this revolution—in the initial crackdowns, many hundreds had died.

I waited a few seconds for the next chant to come, still making my way through the crowd, and yelled the words with them for the watchers to see, throwing my fist up into the air. With my left hand I brought out a blue handkerchief, and waved it for them. They turned away and I moved through faster now. I was sweating, beads welling up on my forehead and at the nape of my neck, cold as they slid down my back.

Inside the bar, it was colder still. I looked for June.

They had restored it from photographs that had been archived on Yelp! Everything was authentic, but it all felt ersatz, a bit too clean, too wide. Even the drunk slumped at the bar, presumably an artist, felt planted. Pure Disney. An alcoholic amusement park.

I looked to the left. I looked to the right. Finally I saw her, sitting at a bistro table far in the corner, almost in shadow. She had been watching me, wordlessly, the entire time. ("It's funny the way you scan the environment around you so thoroughly, and yet so ineffectually," she had said to me. "I hope to understand it one day. To really figure out the science of it. It will be of great benefit to humanity, to my research.")

"So much for the smoking ruins of civilization!" I said, as I sat beside her at the table, looking out on the bar. This is what the powers-that-be had been saying about "the menace of the blue jackets"; that their demands for equity, brotherhood, and true freedom for the masses, not the few, would liquidate three thousand years of human history, leaving us huddled in caves, gnawing on bones.

She didn't say anything at first. She swirled the dull amber drink around her high-ball glass toward me, its single spherical ice-cube picking up the cove lighting, the orange peel like a tropical fish darting sideways. "Give it time."

It had been a year, so far, and so far, so good.

"'The Terror' is," I said, "essential," gesticulating
with a newly empty banana peel.

Chapter
44

I MOTIONED to the bartender, then to June's drink. I'll take the same my little gesture said, and like the perfect fantasy-park automaton he was, he nodded and smiled, and knew what I meant. The joint was dead. It was still early, and people were caught up in the demonstration. Or maybe there wasn't much call for this kind of nostalgia now. In its heyday all the writers and artists might have been drinking and dining on the CIA's dime anyway. It left a bad taste I looked forward to washing down with a drink.

"So," June asked into the silence, "how's Karen Horney doing these days?"

I screwed up my face at her. "Karen Horney" had been our mutual friend, Samantha, when June and I were still trying to make a go of it, by which I mean sharing an apartment and a bed. Samantha had worked at the environmental non-profit where June was office manager. I'd met her a few times when they'd all gone out for drinks and I tagged along. It was a hard-partying bunch: we were all young, and their work didn't pay well, so the staff took as fringe benefits a sense of camaraderie and a dedication to self-destruction, and all their workday efficiencies halved by blinding hangovers. We were so young that every now and then, the hangovers didn't even happen.

Sometime in the early morning, all of us squeezed into a cab, we'd drop Samantha off at her place across from the Karen Horney Clinic by the Queensborough Bridge. June and I starting calling her that privately because of how, so many drinks in, she'd lean against you, and how she managed to sit across our laps in the cab, as we were jostled on our way. Toward the end June accused me of enjoying it too much. Maybe I did.

"Who?" I replied, "Who?" In truth she was long gone. In return, I asked, "And how's Peter Principle?" Shockingly this was his real name. I never thought he was good enough for her, but I was also, obviously, jealous.

Peter was a straight arrow—the good banker, the tall, square-jawed Australian whom I felt that June had, though she denied it, thrown me over for. In retrospect, I think we had both been thrown over, into a dark sea, each of us alone, and Peter was as worthy a spar to cling to as any, even if he was as dull as a post, too.

Although fully committed to the iniquitous system we lived in, I'm only, he would say, doing things that are utterly legal, no shady stuff, and if I don't do it, someone else will, and you know, it's better for everyone in the end, these efficiencies we create and all. You couldn't argue with him, because he was, well, fairly dumb for someone who knew as much as he did.

He loved her genuinely, I think. He wasn't *that* kind of banker. And he'd take us all out for expensive dinners, and was never anything but polite to me, an ex-lover who was still a friend, an odd duck in a depressive episode. I personally wouldn't have tolerated me hanging around. Sometimes she would complain about him, and then repent. "He's so fucking dull." I took great joy from it, and how my heart sank when she replied, quickly, quietly, to herself, "No, I don't mean it."

"So," I said, "really, how's he doing?"

She let out a low sound through pursed lips. It sounded quietly animal, like a faraway cat.

"Oh," she said, seeming to become at once more drained than usual, "Peter's dead."

"God, *what?*" I said. The news was shocking, however much I was opposed to the man.

"Walking between subway cars!" she said. "The only thing he ever did that wasn't 'straight.' A sudden odd turn tossed him. It bucked him right over those metal springs into the dark."

"No!"

"Right onto the third rail. It was . . . not an instant death, they said, it took . . . seconds. And the smell."

"Jesus!" Even a rival, and one I detested to his core, didn't deserve that kind of ignominious end. Fucking electrocuted.

I kept shaking my head, saying "Jesus" to myself, unsure how to reply. Mid-shake I stopped, having glanced at her face. It looked normal now, like a brief summer storm had rolled through and the sun was back. She smiled. Her eyes sparkled. I think there was a tear in them.

"Oh," she said, "oh, I expected so much better from you. I thought you could take it. I thought you didn't care?"

"He's—You're bullshitting me, aren't you? He isn't dead, is he?"

"In Malibu, I think," she said, "with a perky blonde. Suits him better."

"Christ," I said, regaining my cool. "Maybe with our Karen Horney?"

"Oh, no," said June. "Karen Horney is far, far too interesting for him."

I had my drink now.

The glass was sweating and I rubbed away the cool drops with my palm. I wondered if we could have ever made it work. It felt like it was working right now. The door of the bar burst open, and two blue jackets popped through. They yelled out, "Cheers, friends! Cheers!" then left.

This revolution was odd.

June was wearing a blue jacket too, I realized. She had worn it frequently, unrelated to the uprisings, since I could remember; it was just her style. It was a little shabbier, a tad faded, but it was beginning to read different to me now. I asked her about it.

"I hate it," she said. "Don't get me wrong, everything they stand for, I believe in. But it was mine for so long, my thing, and now it's theirs."

We chatted for a while about world affairs, and the revolution. She seemed to think the next step would be a general amnesty, and a period of truth and reconciliation.

She was glad, as I was, that the worst of the old regime, politicians and their rich backers, had suffered some time in prison, just enough that everybody knew that we, the people, weren't fooling around.

I asked about work. She had been doing something for a museum, but she told me she had recently quit. She had grown tired of all the bending over backwards for one family of donors, and sick at the way the museum had begun helping them hide their assets. Like backdating donations, she said, and taking Rembrandts in the night. The whole thing was disgusting. Anyway, she said, she was leaving.

"Leaving?" I asked. As little as I saw of her, the prospect caused a knot in my stomach. "Is that what you wanted to see me about?"

"I heard from him," she said. She didn't have to say who. "For real this time."

I didn't know quite what to say. That she couldn't have? That her biological father was dead? That it was all a charade she was playing with herself?

The last time we had talked about it I had grown angry. She was fixated. She was being irrational. She was throwing her life away. She would never commit fully to things in her real life, commit to actually living, as long as she was so bogged down in the past. It hovered over her. It was, in my opinion, the root of all the failures and disappointments that followed her around. I had begged her to go see a therapist and talk it through. She hadn't gone, hadn't progressed an inch.

I had thought things were turning around. But the last time I saw her was five, maybe six years before this. She had said to me, "I am so close. So close to finding the key!"

At the time, I held my tongue as long as I could, until I couldn't. "The key? Are you really on about this again? This craziness about your lost father, and that adventurer who duped your mother, and the key, and the buried treasure?

"And that clubhouse, and the secret books, and the whole mess with the janitor you talked into helping you, and all of it? This insane, unhinged, unreal fantasy you insist we all play a part of, I mean, by God!

"Why don't you, can't you, just admit it: you were hurt! Your father died! Your step-father abused you and your Mom! You made up a whole world to get away from it.

"You made it up so well we went along. And what about Ryan—who knows what you got him to do—but anyway it's all over now. I've had it with you and with being dragged into your mess."

That was then. Now, I was just silent. And she waited a long time for me to say something.

"I said I've heard from him. I've heard his voice. He called me."

I would have talked about anything else. My failures, my worst transgressions, the political situation, her new boyfriends, intimate details that made my heart sink from longing, but not this. I started to say something, but the words died before they left my lips. Or they hadn't even been born. At that moment, sitting across from June, I felt as far from her as I had ever been before. I just shook my head.

"You have always been a disappointment," she said.

"What is it you want from me?" I asked.

Outside, some bright yellow lights were flashing as they turned. Every time they swirled around, they stamped their color on June's pale face, except where my head cast a shadow that fell across her mouth, as if they were exposing my attempt to blot out her words.

"Mr. Wiggins," she said, at last. "I need you to take Mr. Wiggins for me."

"I need you to take Mr. Wiggins."

Chapter
45

I FROZE A BEAT, then glanced below the table. June wasn't messing around. There, sitting in the shaded space at my feet, was the blue plastic cat-carrier. Through the thin metal bars of the door, two green eyes peered out, warily.

"Okay," I said. Did I really have a choice?

She smiled. "Not a complete disappointment," she said. "You redeemed yourself, after all."

I shook my head.

"Now what, Dmitri?" I asked, referencing her blue smock coat with one of the common derisive names that had been given to the strikers.

"Now, Comrade," she said, standing up, "I go!"

As she stood, she threw off her smock coat, which had always been big and loose on her—it always made her look like a kid—and she left it to me. Then she was gone.

Here I was, with the blue smock coat and her cat. The three of us nursed the rest of our drink in the void June's sudden departure left. Should I run out after her? To what end? If I caught up with her what would I say?

It would only engender another awkward parting.

When June made her mind up, she made it up. Besides, I had the cat to deal with now.

"Hey ho, there, Mr. Wiggins. Surprised?" I asked. The cat responded with a low, plaintive meow.

MONTHS PASSED WITHOUT any further contact from June. Mr. Wiggins and I engaged in a cold war. This "war" on Mr. Wiggins's side consisted of insistent bouts of following me around, yowling. Later he identified and urinated on my most prized possessions. Some he hit twice. We had disagreements over doors (they should, per Mr. Wiggins, remain open at all times), and about wake-up times (roughly at dawn, but sliding minute by minute earlier), and over food (we tried all the grocery store brands, but I finally had to resort to the expensive stuff, from the fancy pet store).

My part in the war was my thorough inability to cater to Mr. Wiggins's desires. Gradually we reached a detente, in which the worst excesses of both sides were curbed (Mr. Wiggins ceased yowling and pissing on things, I ceased resisting and became subservient to his smallest whim).

Eventually, a visit to the vet revealed that Mr. Wiggins was really Mrs. Wiggins, or Miss Wiggins.

Perhaps this misgendering had something to do with her attitude?

June's gift of the blue jacket which was almost the right size for me—it had come to be called "Dmitri" in the privacy of my home—was fortuitous. A bout of counterrevolutionary activity raised tensions, and I welcomed this clear indication of which "side" I was on.

It really wasn't out of the ordinary for June to vanish so entirely, and for so long, but her announcement of some kind of contact with a man claiming to be her father (it was inconceivable that her father—who had died, decidedly, and been buried in our hometown not that many years before June and I had met at school—was actually alive). At last, worry got the better of me, and I revisited LinkedIn to send her a querying message.

LinkedIn's only answer was: "User not found."

She had similarly vacated the other social media sites. I tried the absolute last-ditch method, calling, but the phone yielded distressing tones: her number was disconnected.

Mrs. Wiggins and I looked at each other. I imagined she shared my deepening concern. She had taken to sitting half on my lap, half on the couch. We had come into a sort of friendship, a mutual dependence that stopped short of petting her, an endeavor I gingerly assayed from time to time with the same result: a quick sharp bite between the first and second knuckles on my hand.

June had gone silent before, only to reappear after seven or eight months. But she had never completely deactivated. I had always found a way to reach her left open to me (though, once settling myself into the comfort that I could reach her, I had usually studiously avoided employing it). Was this, perhaps, the end of us?

Meanwhile, in the wider world, things were, surprisingly, starting to go quite right. This gave rise to an uncharacteristic mix of feelings for me: So often I had been personally happy while surrounded by growing misery. Despite the worst—the climate catastrophe, the list of extinctions, the flare ups of disease, the loss of savings in general, a short war (or two)—the surprise victory of the blue smocks had coalesced into a strong, albeit distributed and anarchistic, government.

They had beaten back two forceful attempts at resistance, and then a series of attacks from abroad, hot and cold, and a cyber strike, all financed by the richest, most "enlightened" barons, titans of progressive philanthropy who all felt that this movement of the working class had gone much too far.

A third, weaker band of resistance had sparked a round of unpleasant reaction, but at last what seemed like a violent fever broke, and things had begun to change. Even I, who had been among the doubtful cheerleaders, found day to day life improving. People were, by and large, cooperating. It was, and remains, a great mystery, the greatest mystery: how things can go right.

I quit my job.

The days of selling un-asked-for and often harmful remedies for imaginary diseases to patients who couldn't afford them with the cooperation of every stakeholder along the way, for the reward of enough lucre to scratch out a ballooning rent payment, some black market anxiety drugs (for off label use), and a nice meal out every seventh day, were shuttered forever. And after a lot of *sturm und drang,* the result was that nobody much minded, and even seemed to like it better that way.

I had leisure at last.

It had been two solid years since that night she gave me her cat. No word. No sign. Nothing. Maybe June's game this time had been to leave me with no clue at all. I could have left it. Maybe I should have. But as things in the world improved around me, I grew increasingly worried about June.

So I made a short list of people who might still be in contact with her, and what means I had of contacting them. It was a meager list. It didn't take me long to whittle it down.

The last person I crossed off was Peter Principle. His response was highly peevish—I didn't blame him: my message had come to him through his new wife, who it turned out had been a friend of a friend. He wrote back only, "I haven't seen her, and I wouldn't want to." I don't really think he meant it.

I now pondered what I would do next, since my leads had dried up.

Chapter
46

"SO YOU'VE MADE your mind up about it, then?" Eddie asked. We were in a crowded duplex loft, music thumping, a DJ spinning records. Occasionally the beat would stop, and a voice would burst through, reversed and then wailing into comprehension, before dropping away again. It was Billie Holiday. The DJ never gave her a chance to sing much before the beat jerked in again. This told you it was a cool party.

"Yep. Packing it in," I said. "Leaving New York."

"City," he added. He couldn't resist the correction.

The revelers were all Eddie's neighborhood friends.

"I hate them," he had told me. I hated them too. "But it gets lonely in the studio, and"—I joined in and we finished the sentence in unison—"a man has to have something to do!" Then I'd make as if to slap him, and he'd put his hands up. Guilty as charged. They were all in fashion, or marketing, and of course the booze was sponsored, and some corporate concern had sent the DJ, who occasionally gave all the sponsors a cringe-inducing shout out.

This woman, Amanda, was talking. She explained she had been the one who arranged the booze—the distributor owed her a favor. I held a clear plastic cup of something fizzing that she had arranged. Its main virtue was being cold, and also taking the edge off. It tasted like cough syrup and antifreeze. The lime wedge made it worse, if that was possible.

Eddie had already wandered off, leaving me alone, here only after a dozen of his badgering texts brought me to a party I had vehemently wanted not to attend. When he was drinking he often did that, just wandered off—or maybe he had spied a woman out of the corner of his eye.

I had been pushed by the crowd into a group of people Amanda seemed to be in command of, and perhaps due to my open face and general good demeanor, she had directed this last comment, about the liquor, at me. She was waiting for a response. I nodded so that she could continue.

Amanda was complaining about how you couldn't dash down to the islands anymore. How ridiculous it was. But she had heard a rumor that they might be opening up the short flights again. She supposed it was all well and good now that we—she meant the plebes—could simply drop work whenever we felt like it and jaunt off somewhere for a month. She still had some pride in herself, couldn't leave for some week-long boat trip—so much for the weekends in Saint Kitts. She was stuck here for the first time in years, with the winter weather, and, I suppose, what's worse, her thoughts.

Well, she said, she would get those heat towers and crank up the lights, and saunter around in her bikini on her roof deck, if she had to.

They—the Amandas of the world—were putting a good face on things. But you could feel that their days were numbered. To be honest, this didn't seem too bad to me.

"I might leave, too," Eddie had said, earlier. "Strike out for the West. Wide open spaces."

I melted away from the group, circulating through the party like a cell and finally reconnected with Eddie on the fire escape. Some guy was talking to two women about the splendor of Italy.

Eddie kept muttering "Bullshit!" I don't think the guy heard. We resumed our conversation.

We hadn't really spoken much since I had stopped work. It was a thing you could do now, and it caused surprisingly little disruption. Work. Not work. You'd get credits in your account anyway.

"You were," said Eddie, when we first connected at the party, "eminently replaceable."

"Pot, kettle," I said. I thought "Fuck you."

But he was right, and it was right for everyone. It's what makes big business go: workers are all replaceable. Until the Blue Smocks, the opposite was not true: you had to hang on to a job as something precious, because it was life.

"What about the cat?" he asked.

"You don't know about the cat? I didn't tell you?"

I had been growing more nervous about Mrs. Wiggins. We had achieved a kind of mutual dependency, or so I thought, and with my parents heading north for the summer ("to get back to the climate we're used to"), I had taken on, when I agreed to occupy their house, responsibility for two dogs and two cats. Mrs. Wiggins was the odd one out. I had known, deep down, it wouldn't go well.

Then one day, on a weekend, I had slept late. A rarity. I woke to the distant sound of a parade. It was not an ordinary parade-route, but my lizard-brain knew what the bagpipe sound meant. Something odd, however—the memorial parade never passed. The bagpipes just kept going. The sound didn't grow, wasn't then met by drumming, or joined by the brass bleatings of a high-school band. Just the bagpipes, or maybe one bagpipe, in the middle distance, for over an hour.

"Remember bagpipe-dude?" I asked Eddie.

He had the apartment above me, had moved in fairly recently. He had a funny, English name. Was it Sherlock? Let's say it was.

"Scottish?" Eddie had inquired.

"No, Australian."

The bagpipe is a beautiful racket, really. It has a mournful edge, and Sherlock played beautifully.

We met a few times in the hallway. He looked, well, like himself. In the way people almost never do.

The first time, he came up to me when he realized I lived directly below, and asked about the bagpipes, if it was okay. I said I liked them. And it was—oddly—true.

The story, which I told Eddie, was that Mrs. Wiggins pushed her way through a hole in the screen in the kitchen window, where the fire escape was. I caught her at it a few times, and when I'd leave and come home, I'd cry out for her, "Mrs. Wiggins!" and shake her food bowl, with the dry kibble, and after some long time she'd pop back through the screen.

After a period of some concern, I concluded there was no real harm in it. She wanted access to the open air, and I felt for her.

"What I didn't know," I said, to Eddie, "was that she was going up to Sherlock's place. And he, not knowing, was feeding her a second, or third meal."

"No shit!" said Eddie.

"No shit. And get this," I said, "Wiggins likes Sherlock better than me."

There was a pause. "I like him better too," said Eddie. "I don't know him. But still . . . "

We were both kidding, but when I really looked at it, compared myself to Sherlock, I also liked Sherlock better.

I only found this all out because one night, for all my calling and treat-shaking, Mrs. Wiggins would not come back.

I climbed out onto the fire escape, and Sherlock was out there one flight up, having a smoke and petting Mrs. Wiggins, who was curled up beside him. He stood up and looked down and Mrs. Wiggins uncurled, looked to him, then slinked down to me, and through the screen back into my apartment. I went up the fire escape to greet him. We shook hands awkwardly.

"So," he had said, "she's yours!"

"Not exactly, watching her for a friend." I paused. "But it's looking permanent."

"I'll stop feeding her," he said, though I could tell it pained him. He had pale blue eyes. The sky was yellow with big white clouds, like a painting. He had an off-white cable-knit sweater, it was early autumn, and unseasonably cool. He looked like a ship captain, between voyages.

He was a kindergarten teacher. I had asked him about the bagpipes before. Mostly experimental music, he had said, the occasional funeral. I mentioned that it always felt like a parade was around the corner when he played. I'm not sure how he took it.

I shook my head. "No, let her come on up. It's okay."

"So," I told Eddie, at the party, "I was stressing about the cat before this trip, but I finally had a talk with Sherlock.

He's taken a shine, and making it official. Mrs. Wiggins and Sherlock are an item."

"What will June say?"

"She'd like him, I think."

Some time passed, the way it does at parties, when you have had three or four times as many drinks as you'd agreed with yourself at the start that you were going to. They were bad drinks, but they were there, at hand; it was something to do.

"You hate us, don't you?" a strange woman said to my face. "You're so bored by all this, by all of us. You think I'm dull and tacky. That I'm completely unconcerned with what's important, what's vital in the world," she said. She slurred her words just a little, and I couldn't tell if she was doing it on purpose, for effect. "Well you're full of shit, is what you are. You're just bitter, mean, alone. You think you're a nice person, you think you're a good person. You think because you look down on things that you have a personality—that you're superior. Fuck you."

"Do I know you?" I said at last.

She had already turned away into the party. I already couldn't remember her face. She might have been a ghost, or a fairy, come to denounce me. I was bored, and full of loathing, and mean. I did think of myself as a nice and a good person. But I knew I wasn't. The party had been vaguely awful. I had archly dismissed it while also, truth be told, enjoying the signature bad drinks, the good-looking people, however awful they were. But now I was miserable. The truth hurts.

"Don't mind her," a voice said. "You're not so bad as all that, I mean." I turned to the voice. It was emanating from a small, dark mouth set in an oval face. She had dark eyes, narrow eyebrows, and her lips were pursed—she was about to break into a laugh, then that's what she did. "Oh, dude," she said, stifling her laughter, "you are a piece of shit, because, let's face it, you're a man, but she didn't know you from Adam. She's been practicing on strangers, building up courage. It's her boyfriend. He really is terrible, and deserves both barrels. Maybe"—she looked me up and down—"you don't quite deserve it. So I'm sorry."

I was still stunned. I didn't reply.

"I hate this party," she said, "and all these people too. I'm Jen," she put out her hand, and I shook it.

"That might be the funniest thing that has ever happened to me, I think," I said.

"No, I don't believe it," she said. "You look like the kind of guy that weird shit happens to all the time, because you don't look like it."

"You're a cut above the crowd, too," I said. "So what are you doing here?"

"I'm her escort," she gestured off into the crowd at the woman who had unloaded on me.

"Tell her I thought she was the Ghost of Christmas Past. Like, that was some epic shit."

"A lot of epic shit going down," she said. "I'm a journalist," she added. "My friend will appreciate the effect she had on you. I don't think her boyfriend will, though. And good, he's due for it."

"What's your take on things?" I asked.

"What do you do?" she said, ignoring the question.

"This and that. I used to be an 'ad man.'"

"How gendered," she said. "Used to be? What, like in the olden days?"

"A few weeks. Since things changed, I guess I'm just a writer now."

"How romantic." She shrugged. "I think I'll still worry about getting paid for a while, as long as it's interesting."

"Actually," I said, "you know, I'm something of a detective, too."

There was a shriek and the sound of broken glass. "Oh, no," she said. "I think I recognize that shriek. I have to go. I'll find you later." She turned, and melted into the crowd. She didn't find me later. I still think of Jen.

I had lost track of Eddie by now, and was thoroughly on my own.

I looked down, as if the floor might have had breadcrumbs to follow, the honey-gold wooden floor which, once, had been the manufacturing floor before it was cut up into apartments. It had been strewn with shreds of fabric, bits of string, bent bobbins, and spent spools. Now it was metallic confetti, half-wet cocktail napkins, and little toothpicks with bits of canapé still on them.

"What do you think?" a disembodied voice said. "Well, citizen?" the voice asked. I looked up. I was in a group of people, maybe three or four. We, and by we I mean they, were laughing at the earnestness of the Movement. "Citizen" really was a step below "comrade," I had to admit.

"I think," I said, "I shall wait and see."

Maybe it was what had transpired with Sherlock and the cat. It felt like a tiny betrayal—I wasn't good enough. Or maybe it was thinking about June, for whom I was perennially insufficient. But she kept coming back. Or maybe it was that I was beginning to feel like a real "citizen" for a change.

Someone else in the group had begun to speak.

Past caring about decorum, I interjected, "But, you have to admit, things are going much better than anyone could have thought they would."

One of the men started to speak, saying "Well—" but I cut him off. I said, "Don't you feel more engaged in your own community, and empowered? What about the grants? About the local councils, and employee control? I am, for the first time, feeling freedom. Could you have imagined? I can quit my job, work on my . . . project."

Let them think it was art, or writing. Not detective work. (I was going to find June!)

But they wouldn't be receptive. They liked their jobs. They couldn't imagine not doing them. They liked having bosses, to imagine becoming one. They didn't like to think about "issues," but they would find—except for the top execs, and the mind-bogglingly rich, which they were not and never would be—everything had changed, but things could remain substantially the same. Only the environment would improve around them.

A principle of radical democracy and of absolute freedoms—freedom from struggle, freedom to be a pivotal voice—had washed over us with all the force of a seventh wave.

Had I stayed, I would have participated in the pharma company of which we all had become owners. But I chose to own my own life. Artists, musicians, writers, but also chess players, and readers, and acrobats, and beekeepers, and anybody at all could do what they wanted. It was anarchy, but it was order, too.

I had been waiting for everything to collapse. Worrying about it. Waiting for the "owners," whatever that meant, to rise up. It didn't happen. People did what was needed. We rowed society forward, genially, even without the heavy, threatening beat of a drum.

*Now it was metallic confetti, half-wet cocktail napkins, and little
toothpicks with bits of canapé still on them.*

*"What other surprises have you got in store?
What other sad little fragments?"*

Chapter
47

"Mrs. Wiggins is still alive," said Tiffany, one day when we were looking over my notes for these memoirs together.

"You've met her?" I said. "And Sherlock?"

"I just know," she said. "Nothing that mean ever dies."

"So you weren't a fan?" I asked.

"Where are you going with all this?" she asked. She put her palm flat on the papers—I had printed them out to get a better perspective, help me organize my thoughts—and said "Did you ever solve anything, or is it like one of those old History Channel shows, you know, the ones with five minutes of factual content, surrounded by fifty-five minutes of build-up and recapitulation?

"I do like the excerpt from your friend's sci-fi story, though. It's appropriate for a world being born again—I wouldn't read any more of it, though."

"I chose the best bit," I said, "and of course, to see June in it, although the character quickly diverges after that scene. She is revealed to be the Empress, in disguise."

"What other surprises have you got in store? What other sad little fragments?"

"You just want to know when our paths will finally cross," I said.

"Don't I know already?" she asked.

"I don't think Mrs. Wiggins was a mean cat, she was just misunderstood."

"Is mean," said Tiffany. "Is. And will still be long after we are gone."

"I think you'll last the longest of us all," I said.

"I like cats," said Tiffany, "I'll never have another, though, after my two lovelies. Never. But when Mrs. Wiggins was Mr. Wiggins I think he had something against me."

"You knew her then?" I said.

"Don't you know that already?" she asked.

I thought of what she'd asked, about surprises, about fragments. I felt like showing off. I said "I found something on my last trek to the archives." These were three big buildings in Ohio, where millions of old documents were being stockpiled, well-preserved but unsorted. I had been sending out feelers, looking for evidence of one or two original documents I had hoped to find. Someone had a lead, an anonymous letter mentioning a specific area in the archives, three hundred feet from the green cabinet, between wooden crates, etc., and included the torn piece that had been found. Tiffany would be astounded. If she was the only audience for this entire manuscript I was toiling away at, well that was worth it anyway. It had taken a solid month to find. All of the volunteers had come to know me by then, shaking their heads at my impossible, benighted quest. "There's something you're not telling me," I said to Tiffany.

"If you already know," she replied, "why do you need me to say it?"

"Will you stay for dinner?" I asked.

"What is it?"

"Spätzle," I said. "Handmade, with fresh peas, and German sausages."

"Fresh peas?"

"Haven't I shown you the basement grow room? It is a miracle what I can get out of it."

Just then someone pounded on the door. Tiffany went to it. I heard a voice outside, muffled, indistinct. She came back to me.

"Well, looks like you get it all to yourself. It's been grand, but I've got to go."

She gave me a light chock on the chin with her fist. "Keep it up, it's fun to watch you struggle, Ducks."

"Ducks?" I said.

"You don't want a nickname?"

"Okay, 'Ducks' it is," I said.

From outside came the deep, hypnotic whirring of the hovercopter revving up.

*In every flash of light I saw a still frame of crows mid-hop around
something that looked like a corpse.*

Chapter
48

NOT LONG AFTER the party I "lit out for the territories" like many had done before me. All the things that I cared about, that I cared to keep, fit in a few boxes in the backseat and trunk of my car. Everything else I left for the neighbors or for the sanitation crews—whomever got it first. There was a lot of stuff piling up on the sidewalks from people with the same idea as me: escape New York. Or maybe it was just that our orbits were no longer bounded by the intense gravitational force focused on "job" and "career."

Things left out for trash didn't usually make it to the dump anymore. A whole host would descend on the piles before the garbage trucks got there like that time lapse videos of a whale carcass stripped to bones at the ocean bottom—what was discarded found new use. In other times this has been viewed as a terrible thing, a sign of desperation or depression, but I find it beautiful. In our new society, the thoroughness of this kind of scavenging became a point of pride.

How quickly I had castigated June in my mind for her sudden and deep silence, like the empty space between those big bones settling into the anaerobic bottom silt. To be fair to June, I had vanished first: After our breakup in NYC I had stayed a while then had gone out to LA where I had dropped out of contact with nearly everybody from my old life. I had a string of girlfriends, worked a few jobs before narrowing into a career. For a while, a long time even, it worked out, and then, it didn't. The East Coast was home. I came back.

In the car, with my things, driving north, I was thinking of these things, and others. With the navigation satellites off—there had been in their mechanism a kill switch some in the security agency flipped to try to thwart the

Movement, and there were plans for replacements in work now but some deeply buried part of all of us relished the possibility to get lost—I found I had picked an escape path almost at random, flowing first into one and then another concrete chute out of the metropolitan area.

How much the same it all seemed, this terrain, around the Sprain Brook Parkway, the slumped stone walls, the pale green of the shoulder, like a snake, like a viper. The entire route to my parents was the same, except for its having been carved into semi-autonomous zones: Each with its own name, like "Yorkville Workers' Collective," a central committee, and idiosyncratic character. Some seemed to be fond of flowers, others impressive walls or farm-stands.

After seeing my parents off on their vacation, and reacquainting myself with the layout and rhythms of my childhood home—which had changed in small and large ways, but somehow maintained the same essential characteristics— my plan was to spend some time digging through "the archives" of the house, the boxes of things that had been saved from my childhood. It would be a while before I was ready to seek out actual living people. I didn't even know who might still be around.

But I ran into Matthew, my quiet, innocent study hall buddy only a week into my stay. What happened is, I was driving along one of the narrow County "highways," and turned my head to look at some crows that were sitting in the field, and almost literally ran into him.

The car had just passed into a shaded arcade of tall oaks some farmer had planted to separate his hillside house—now a pile of rotten lumber on top of a collection of mossy field stones—from the pastureland, which still blazed neon-green between the rough-barked pillars flashing by, making it seem like an old magic lantern. In every flash of light I saw a still frame of crows in mid-hop around something that looked like a corpse.

An impression of blue plaid flapped into the corner of my vision, and I jerked the wheel and slammed on the brakes. The car screeched and I left two dark traces of tire rubber on the cracked asphalt. Stunned, I sat in the car, stopped aslant in the road, then let my foot off the brake and slowly eased it to the shoulder.

In my rearview mirror, I saw a figure about a hundred feet behind me, bent over, moving a little, in khaki pants and work boots, and a blue plaid fleece pullover. He stood up, then seemed to notice me for the first time, turned his head my way. I jumped out of the car.

"I'm so, so sorry!" I said. "Are you okay?"

It was Matthew. I recognized him straight away. The same baby face, the same kind of vacant look. The only difference was that parts of his hair had turned gray. It looked like someone had randomly slapped his head with a thin paint brush. He was grinning, and held in his hand a dusty glass insulator, the kind from old electric poles.

He didn't say anything, but started walking toward me. He seemed entirely unfazed.

My heart was still pounding from the near miss. As I had been looking into the field at the crows, mesmerized by the light and shadow, by the crows hopping and feasting, I had begun to drift toward the shoulder. I was sure then that I had almost killed him.

"Look at this," Matthew said, when he got right next to me. He showed me the glass; it was pale blue and ridged, and had tiny clear air bubbles. He said, "1927. One of the older ones, for this stretch of road."

He accepted my offer of a ride. I executed an awkward k-turn on the spot, and we drove quietly to his trailer, about five miles back. His trailer was clean, the grass manicured. All around outside there were plywood cut-outs of people, in silhouette, about 1/5th scale, going on about various gardening tasks in what looked like Dutch clothing, clogs and bonnets, baskets of flowers, a watering can. The watering can spilled invisible water into a garden plot denoted by a circle of perfectly round rocks. There was nothing but grass inside, and some dandelions.

I started to wonder if Matthew hadn't always been, even back then, a bit slow. I recalled how in study hall he

would draw goblins and ogres for us, with a single unbroken
line on sheets of wide-ruled paper, one after the other.

"Come on," he said, as soon as we had gotten out of the
car. He brought me hurriedly into the barn, a clean, structure
of knotty pine planks, finished simply with oil and turpentine,
but well-built. It appeared pitch dark at first, then my eyes
began to adjust to the clear bright light pouring through two
high diamond-shaped windows in the roof. Then he pulled a
chain, and we were surrounded by the hum and buzz of
fluorescents trying to get going before they snapped bright.

The floor of the barn was a polished concrete slab,
entirely open except for one central table with a clip-on lamp
and a big ledger.

Underneath, in a hundred-odd cubbies, were all sorts of
old iron tools, awls, and augers, scissors, magnifying glasses, a
box of rags, cans of solvent.

The walls were pegboard, with wraparound shelving,
the lower shelves all cardboard boxes. Every free surface was
covered, and all the boxes were filled with parts, bits of metal,
plastic, hooks and starfish-shaped ceramic; it was a massive
collection of every kind of fastener, insulator, peg, separator,
bolt, spacer, crossbar, that had ever been used on a telephone
pole or power line.

Matthew was scribbling in his ledger—entering the
newest item into his collection. He took out a roll of small
stickers, and marked with a fine pen some number from his
book. He put the piece in an open cardboard box on the second
shelf up on the wall to the left of the door.

"Fine," he said, "very fine."

I asked him about his organization, and he explained,
haltingly, and using simple words, that it was a mixture of
chronological, functional, and aesthetic. Mostly aesthetic.

He took me here and there, pulling out and showing
me what he considered extremely fine pieces. I affected a great
appreciation. Then he pointed to a framed letter in one corner.
It was from an executive at General Electric, congratulating
him on his effort to preserve "an important part of our history."
He explained to me that many collectors had built their

collection through eBay and bartering, but he had found every single piece himself, and had noted exactly when and where.

In the past few years, all the power lines and cable had been buried, in an effort to catch up with the rest of the civilized world. Everything related to above-ground transmission was a museum piece.

I tried to ask Matthew what had inspired him to start building his collection. He hadn't been interested in these things as a child. He looked at me like I had two heads. He didn't answer, and I felt as if I had just revealed in myself an insurmountable character flaw. He shook his head and we left the barn, turning out the lights, and he latched the door shut behind us. "Come on," he said, "have some coffee?"

He led me up the steps of his trailer.

I sat at the low table in his kitchen and looked around while he put coffee on. On every surface were plastered pieces of paper with line drawings on them, in the same style as his goblins. They were all almost identical portraits of his mother. Some looking up, some looking down. In a few the eyes were closed, others had them open, with dark squiggles for pupils, or empty circles, like Little Orphan Annie.

Her hair was in tight curls, in a style that was a holdover from the 50s.

Matthew was in his childhood home. Like I was, now, (on a temporary basis?) too. He set a mug of coffee in front of me, and a handful of creamers out of the fridge. His sister regularly dropped them off, he told me, from the diner in town where she worked.

We sat quietly. I didn't ask about his mother.

He mentioned his sister had gotten married, and that it was going well.

He didn't ask me where I had been since high school, or what it was that brought me back. I tried to bring up school, June, the gang, but he just looked to my left and talked more about his collection.

Things had been quite difficult for a long time, but now he was set up well enough. He had even been able to hire someone to fix up the barn for him, on his basic income, and he gave the extra cash to his sister, mostly.

He didn't need much money at all, he said.

We talked around a bit, the weather and such. After he started to repeat himself, I realized his font of conversation had been drained. I apologized again for almost hitting him, and thanked him for the coffee, and his time. He was zoned out, just staring into a dark corner of the trailer.

When I thanked him for the tour of his collection, he looked directly at me. He smiled, his eyes began to shine.

He is probably out there still, all this time later, walking up and down the road, stopping to see something that glinted in the tall grass.

He shuffled out with me, down the porch steps, to his silhouette garden. A chipmunk scrambled across the road, then leapt over a fallen log, and disappeared into the thicket. I nodded, he nodded, and that was that.

Chapter
49

I AM NO GOOD with flower names, beyond the basics: Those were daisies—easy enough, like a child's drawing; then there were irises, and lilies. The heavy, heady-scented ones, petal massed on petal, like so many dresses at an antique ball, were peonies. The others—spiky, or pitcher-shaped, or flared with deckled edges, little drops of flower, or stars in a creeping field of green—who can say. So many more kinds flourish in our climate, now, heated-up as it is. They were nearly all white. The garden was an overabundance of white, an eruption that stopped you in your tracks.

I had heard about it, this garden, how it had grown up by the sign leading into our school, from my parents, and seen it once half a decade before, but wasn't prepared for how arrestingly impressive it had become. It had started with a single hyacinth, it's said, planted surreptitiously for a loved-one lost, and it had, over the years, been spontaneously added to and overspread, into a great garden, into a thousand great gardens here and elsewhere to the martyrs.

Every town had had a few—martyrs I mean.

Bradley Jenkins died away from home, in the city, in one of the first confrontations. Here, later on, our own Mr. Grimmon, the gym coach, took a rubber bullet to the eye, not necessarily fatal, but, unluckily it was for him. Some Elementary kids have given him the tapestry-treatment: it hangs in the gym; like Harold at Hastings, his bearded figure done in exaggerated, bold outline nods along the pieced-together paper until the finality of his exploding eye in their rendition of the brief, violent tribulations that made our time.

White flowers, so flat to us, of such blotting-out oneness, to the insects present a different tale—lines, dots, dashes, even fat arrows of ultraviolet direct them to the heart of the affair, to sustaining nectar and suffusions of pollen. Invisible signposts toward fulfillment.

In a way, this outward calm hiding a frenzied path represents our society most perfectly. When I look at the school, it appears to have changed little, it is the same brick, metal ductwork, sky-reflecting windows, the same shrubs and trees, grown up, perhaps, but not of a different substance. The same doors swinging in, earnest student-council election posters, and trophy case. Yet, under the surface, nothing remained the same.

It was to freshen my memories of then, of the time before and my own blossoming that I came—to make concrete the early moments I had come to believe held the secret to finding June. (Yes—I know, was it really myself who had been lost, and in all my searching, she, still, waiting, was going to find me?)

The halls were half the size that I remembered.

Old framed class photos were still up in their glass case, dozens of them, decades, though the oldest (ours) were yellowed, curled, and water stained. The people frozen in them looked like a strange species; at once freshly young and eternally old. At last I could even make out myself in one, small and distracted, big open mouth, goofy, eyes turned away. I was manifestly still a kid, with big ears, rounded features, and unruly hair, my clothes fitting awkwardly after the most-recent growth spurt.

In another photo, there was June; I sucked in air—she was exactly as I remembered her, adult, serious, and staring straight through the years directly into the back of my mind.

I turned away, as if her deep stare could, somehow, extract from me my most secret thoughts, to her now, or even from me now to her then. I got the strange, impossible idea that this momentarily imagined bridge had been the mechanism by which she had known so much so thoroughly all those years ago.

From the school gym, one open door which glowed into the dimmed hall with the strength of neon (it was the flood lights reflecting off the thick-lacquered, almost as if honey-drenched, shining floors), came the squeak of sneakers, the unmistakable thud of the basketball, grunts of exertion, the over-50 league.

I had started walking the halls again, directed indifferently inward, searching for something, I didn't quite know what. I quickened my pace.

I heard muffled voices, imagined there was an AA meeting somewhere, that these were scraps of confession. A saw squealed and a router chewed away—the wood shop, somewhere beyond this hall.

The school belonged to the community, and it was used to the hilt. As an adult, without community motives just then, even a welling fear of community, laced with suspicion, I was out of place, I felt, and dangerously so. I didn't want to see "the community," didn't want to be of it—and the worst of it was that here, I might meet someone whom I had known, or someone who knew me.

By now, though, I reckoned quickly, anybody who was anybody to know me here would have been retired and the others were long gone. I was safe. I turned the corner. Safe? No, I had been dead wrong.

Imagine reading to yourself before bed from a book of folk tales, a book that both tells the tales and then seeks to explain them.

First there would be the story, assembled perhaps from two or three different tellings in order to present them in their fullest form. Its language is rough, repetitive, nonsensical; alternately archaic and startlingly contemporary. There are moments of piercing beauty and vibrant imagery, then random cruelty, base humor, and a pinch of misogyny. There is some fairy magic, and, of course, a prodigious turnip.

And an ogre. Who is a king. Who also wields magic. And has a human wife. Has three. The black dog is a man who drank from a cursed fountain. There are some winged shoes, a bag of gold.

There is a key. It has the shape of a serpent.

A green thread is seen to bind it all together, followed by a little girl. She is caught, and baked into a pie that the dog eats, becoming his former self.

The key is forgotten.

The man weds a fairy, and the story ends.

A dense paragraph follows. It talks of provenance. Elements of the story are found in three places. A version is told in a stone house in Afghanistan. The teller has been at the poppy harvest. He shows a silver coin. It is a Greek coin; it has been in his family, he says, since Alexander. Another version is told in Hungary by an old woman who sits in front of a fire and drinks a gift of wine. A third is found in nursery rhymes told to the children in a small town near the tip of the heel of the boot of Italy.

By now, you are tired. The book is falling out of your hands. You have read the same paragraph twice over, and then over again. The words are changing with every glance. You can't quite trust them. As if you are in a waking dream.

Now the learned editor goes into broad themes.

He finds deep structures—you can, he explains, imagine the story composed of boxes inside of boxes, each with lines connecting to another set (you can't help but see them as thin, green lines, like thread), with a companion circle for every box. These shapes fit, again, into an opposition. It is the tripartite of water, earth, and air.

The story ascends, while the reader descends. The book drops again. You open your eyes. How long has it been? The cat has just tapped you on the shoulder.

Every night, the cat's demands are the same: You are to turn out the light on the bed. Now you wait until his figure is silhouetted in the doorway. Then you must stand; follow him to the stairs. You both descend to the first floor.

Now the cat is free for the night, and you are free to get a glass of water and go back to sleep.

Imagine that all night, then, you dream of ogres, and of black dogs becoming men, and of a golden key, to nothing, from nowhere—that singular impeller of the folk tale world.

And imagine you wake up, still thinking about it. Then you drag yourself out of the house, shouldered up by cold coffee and buttered roll. And there, on your doorstep, resting atop the newspaper, as if upon a bed, is the golden key.

This—exactly this—is how the ruddy, ogreish form of Clyde Duane, janitor, suddenly, shockingly manifested itself before me in the school hallway, while the lights above him dimmed and went out as if absorbed into the deep well of his electric potential.

To me, he didn't look all that much older than he had when I was in junior high. I'd thought him ancient then, but maybe he had been in his 20s, just, and was now only in his early 60s. It is a trick of the memory: We age things in our past as we ourselves age.

Or if he was older, was he possessed of some supernatural power of preservation? Or had it been, for him, only minutes since child-me had stood in the hall with my crumpled note from June, waiting to read it like a condemned man slipped a message through the bars and hoping it held— What?—A kind of rescue?

I made to turn, wondering if Mr. Duane had failed to notice me—as if he were a big, dark bird whose glassy eyes perceived only movement. But he cleared his throat. It was a horrible sound. The sound turned into words, but slowly. I found myself leaning in, bent over toward him to hear.

"Well," he said, "it seems that you were right."

"Excuse me?" I asked.

He looked up from his push cart. In the school building, he was never without his push cart. It could have been the same one, still, from way back then. What we have now learned, which some people already knew was: you don't always have to replace things. Things could be serviced; they could be patched, greased, sanded, tightened, and will suffice now as they did before. Things like Clyde Duane. Because he was merely a thing to some people. A cog. He was to me, too.

"You were right!" he growled. His face was a grimace— or it was a smile. Bits of tobacco showed on his teeth. "You got it right, and old Clyde got it wrong." Then he made these inhuman clucking noises, wet sucking tongue against his palate; his too-good teeth, strewn with black-tobacco confetti, were revealed to be loose, shaking dentures, and his pale, empty gums glistened like sea slugs, all pink and shimmering.

The old cart creaked as he moved forward, as he rolled on by one side of me, chuckling to himself, and coughing.

"You people," he murmured. "You damned people."

I didn't say anything back, only kept looking down the hall after him. I put my hand on my chest, fingers splayed. I had the feeling it would pass right through me, that whatever substance I had had gone.

I looked down at the rough, blue fabric between my fingers, like a patch of sky. No, Clyde Duane hadn't known me from Adam. It was the smock jacket, the blue smock jacket I forgot I was wearing.

Mr. Duane had not recognized me, but recognized the blue of my jacket. It had been the short-lived emblem of the Movement: the jacket and the revolution it signified had, in winning, been subsumed into the ordinary, become every day. Once everyone wore it, nobody had to. It had made you into a kind of Russian peasant. It was a sign of solidarity.

A sign that you stood against—what exactly? Against rage, against meaningless consumption, against convenient, hypocritical religion, and that you stood for the people, the workers, the planet. It was not the blue of the Democrats, it was a deeper blue that held in it just a touch of red. Naturally the Movement was painted red by the powers that be: just a front for Communists. The slander didn't take. The Movement, on the other hand, did.

HE WASN'T LASHING OUT at me from recognition, he was lashing out at the world, at anyone who would listen. The blue jacket I wore was shabby now, a bit faded. There were places where the fabric had worn and split, leaving tears like little knife marks. They had all been mothballed, for the most part, but I had always treated the smocks like a joke, and it was just the right weight for the season, sturdy but light, and it had such a useful array of pockets, a perfect assortment.

It wasn't even mine—June gave it to me, off her own back, at the Cedar Tavern, an extravagant gesture the very last time I saw her in New York. I called her Dmitri when she wore it. I suggested she take my bright red handkerchief.

"I pass Dmitri on to you," she had said. "Wear him well. *Das vadanya, tovarich.*"

Comrade. It seemed right, back then. It was embarrassing now. When the revolution at last won, so thoroughly, so finally, all its earliest trappings evolved and were discarded. But Clyde Duane didn't forget. He wasn't capable of forgetting. Time, for him, moved so slowly that everything outside of him happened all at once. He couldn't recognize me as an adult because to him I had only just been a child walking along the empty corridor, the wrong way, toward the back parking lot, toward destiny.

Or so I imagined.

Behind me now, he was whistling, or something like a whistle-hum. Oddly tuneless for someone with the musical talent he had—a prodigy on the pipe organ. Maybe it was an effect of his dentures. Something in the encounter put me off the errand that had brought me here. When I tried to remember what it was, I realized I had forgotten it entirely.

Maybe seeing Duane had been the errand after all. I waited until I couldn't hear his burbling. It took ages.

Then I left.

I walked out into the light. Into a blue sky. Clouds were billowing up over lazy green hills.

Clyde Duane didn't forget. He wasn't capable of forgetting.

Chapter
50

I HAD BEEN WONDERING—since I almost ran over Matthew, and more figuratively ran into Clyde Duane at the school—what kinds of ghosts would appear next. Would they be genial and recognizable, or hectoring, accusatory, and vengeful? Or would they simply be strangers, lost, like Matthew, in their own shrinking world? Of course I was seeking them out along my path back to June, but hesitatingly, peering through fingers, as if in anticipation of horror—not of the past, but of the passing of it.

I had been sorting through the collections that formed the archives of my youth in my parents' house, here and there finding the tracks of someone I had lost contact with. I was expecting the information I found to present a puzzle, and solving it would be an intellectual exercise. The result, I felt, would indicate a direction, pointing toward—what?—June, in the here and now, I thought. I was not expecting to find puzzles of a more psychological nature; to find myself grappling with feelings I couldn't connect to a flat mystery.

I had wandered out to the deck, and was thinking about Brian. In the time before June's appearance, we had been the closest of friends. Our friendship had waned, and I had never before considered that it was something I could attribute to my own actions. That I had failed to keep up the friendship. That I had let it drop. Now I recalled the times after I'd left for college when he reached out and I had replied late or not at all.

I held the cap of my beer against the deck railing and slapped my other palm down on it as I had a hundred times before. The cap bent but did not pop off, and it left a pattern of little notches in the wood, a small scrape. "Shit." I hit it again and the bent red cap pinged straight into my cheek, feeling like the flick of a spectral finger. The beer foamed up, and I took a mouthful of it—sad, bitter, airy. I washed that down with another big swig. Steady on, you moron—you're not even in the early innings.

I couldn't begin to make amends with Brian in person, I knew, since he'd headed off, last I heard, to Texas for good. He had been doing the kind of precision engineering he'd learned in his father's shop, with no degree, and from there had taken on many aspects of the job. Where was he, now? Had he kept up with June, too?

"Hey!" The voice was familiar, but I heard it as though from the end of a long tunnel. I almost dropped my beer. At the foot of the stairs, decades older, but unmistakable, was Brian, as if my thoughts had conjured him. His hair had gone completely grey. He had salt-and-pepper stubble, and his eyes drooped behind folded lids. His eyebrows were so pale as to disappear entirely.

"Brian, what the hell are you doing here?" I said. "I thought you were down south."

"I heard you were coming home," he said. "I heard from Mom, but they were even talking about it at the library. You know the way they gossip around here. I wouldn't be surprised if the entire village knew already."

"Talking about me?" I said. "Me?"

"Anyway, I come up here quite a bit, you know. Especially since Mom's not healthy. And I do a lot of stuff for the village these days." It felt strange to be talking to Brian as if none of the many intervening years had gone by. "How is it in the city?" he asked.

"Much the same, but different," was my lame answer, which he understood. "How is your mom?" I asked.

Brian looked pained. "It's hard," he said. "You're lucky . . . " He trailed off.

I wanted to say something about the past, to conjure our old connection, but couldn't get anything out at all. There was an awkward space between us.

"Do you want a beer?" I raised mine up, to show him, as if he needed a demonstration.

"No. Come on," he said. "A bunch of us are going out to check the condensers." These were pieces of the weather-stabilization systems. At least as far as I knew. "I said you'd be my partner."

"Honestly, I don't even know the first thing about the condensers," I said.

"That's alright. You don't need to know anything. I just need another set of eyes, and you can learn while we do it."

"I don't know," I said.

"No, really, come on."

Something changed in his demeanor. What had been easygoing just a minute before had gotten uptight. I now felt like I didn't have a choice.

"Okay. But I have to get back here," I said. "I'm working on something."

I had a lot to ask Brian: about June, about himself, about me. I followed Brian to his truck and got in. Something had switched. It felt too late to be sorry. And in being sorry, I would just be being sorry for myself. It was impossible to get absolution, forgiveness. I regretted saying yes. The silence was like a blanket, growing heavier as we traveled for what seemed like an eternity before we reached the first condenser.

They were larger then. This one looked like a jungle gym with some microwave receivers grafted on. Brian showed me the control panel. We marked down a few readings from the screen, and toggled switches into diagnostic mode. He checked the most critical components, and made sure none of the parts were rusted or bent. He had me sign off on each observation with my initials next to his.

He fiddled with the radio as we drove, alternating between a dozen different stations, but to me, they all seemed indistinct and AI-generated. Finally I coughed. It broke the spell like a gunshot.

I asked him about Aaron, if he had reread any of the stories. He confessed he had. We said, in unison, "I can't believe I'm saying it, but they're good!" I didn't want to bring up June, wanting him to broach the subject, but he didn't.

There were twenty condensers on our list. It took almost two hours to get to all of them. At each stop, we hiked from the road into fields, then turned knobs, pressed on screens, made adjustments here and there. When we finally finished with the last one, I found I was exhausted. We talked less and less as we continued, and had barely spoken the last hour at all.

The truck stopped in front of my parents' place. "Okay?" he said.

"Okay," was my reply. And I guess I meant it, maybe? I understood I would be called on again: In this way you contributed to your community. You did what you were asked.

As for my mystery, I could broach that with Brian another day.

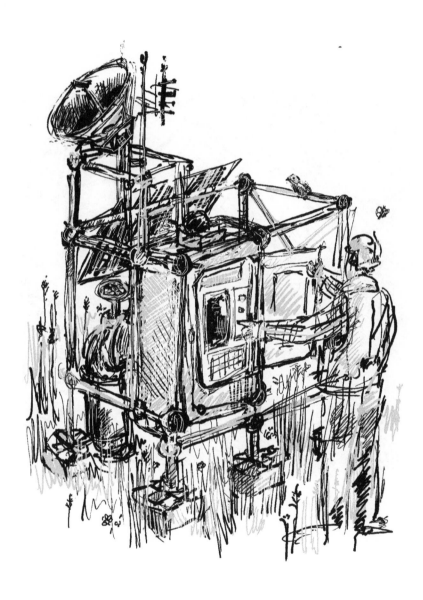

Brian showed me the control panel.

The desk lamp illuminated my little corner of the narrow office with the shallow light of a single taper in a monk's cell.

Chapter
51

SOMETIME CLOSER to when I had started this effort than now, I wrote out the words "everything happened at once" on a yellow legal pad with an old Bic pen.

The pen I'd found among a cornucopia of misfit writing implements my parents had bundled together with a rubber band that had once been blue. The bundle had been shoved in a china cup of stunning beauty, a thousand fine lines cracked into its glaze, in a corner of the sideboard in the hall by the kitchen, which had become overloaded with clutter.

The legal pad I bought new at CVS, though it had been sitting, neglected, in the stationery aisle so long in its tight plastic wrapper its color had faded.

Since returning, I had been trying to set down my recollections in longhand, from that time when I had first met June until the present, some forty years worth.

I compose much faster on a computer, and have since returned to it, but when I typed things out, I'd get lazy and sloppy; I would repeat myself, miss things, get ahead of the story. This pen rolling blue-black ink on the faded yellow paper, leaving me no choice but to scratch out mistakes was a steadying aid, a walking stick. It made me sure-footed, if slow.

It wasn't late, but, this time of year, it was already quite dark. The desk lamp illuminated my little corner of the narrow office with the shallow light of a single taper in a monk's cell. I had cracked the window, and white moths fluttered through the void. The flappings of their wings crescendoed while I watched them, mesmerized. The dogs snored gently—they had finally settled down on their beds by my feet.

Half a glass of red wine sat half-illuminated by the desk lamp. I picked it up, swirling the wine, watching the color deepen at the center of the vortex the swirling made. I took out Eddie's vial, and put a few drops in my glass. Then I thought about it for a second, and put in a few more drops: I needed to let my mind open tonight, to take in what it could. I'd really feel it in forty minutes or so, I guessed.

I had just written "everything happened at once," and was trying to picture exactly what the words meant—to see Clyde Duane emerging from the doorway like a monster born out of the earth, and Ryan calling out a loud "Halloo!" before his target had turned toward him, and finally June and myself coiling back like springs, about to leap up the steps.

The night wasn't quiet here in the country, so much as filled with noises of an entirely different tenor than in the city. No constant slush of traffic, no distant, erratically honking horns, no metal clanking, or the scraping of garbage bins being dragged here and there in perpetual dance, just the stream flowing in the night, the creaking of the trees, a single owl calling out "Who Cooks for You," the fluttering of insects, dogs pawing and snuffling around or whimpering in their sleep, and the constant, bright hum of the crickets, like background radiation, permeating everything.

It made "city folk," even those who, like me, had only adopted urban living, deeply uneasy. We called it "silence," and found it suffused with threat. Thankfully it had taken only a few weeks to re-accustom myself to what had been the ambient soundtrack of my childhood.

I read the last words I had written aloud, in the same deep, droning voice without voice I often heard in my head: "Everything happened at once."

The scene: it was Clyde Duane, Ryan, and June, all now in motion; and me, still half-crouched on the steps, about to move. Then Aaron had come, rounding the corner, ignorant of all, on a mission for his mother, to get a half-gallon of milk before the gas station closed.

From the back of their faded, lavender house, he had, as he always did, meandered absent-mindedly through the yard and then the field below, having ducked under the barbed-wire fence after lifting it up with a wooden stick he left there for that purpose. Emerging on the other side, he ambled past the rusting metal swing sets and the teeter totter, and the ziggurat of pipes that was the jungle gym, behind the neglected, empty old school. He had then crossed the creek, higher water than he had bargained for, yet still passable in one spot. His navy velcro shoes had picked up a considerable amount of mud, which he wiped off on the tall grass on the far side. No Lyme disease from deer ticks to fear, at the time.

Simple after that: hop a slumping, lichen-clustered stone fence, run along between two timber-frame houses, and pop out onto the sidewalk across from the cemetery. Then, just two blocks to the convenience store.

It was—by any way you reckoned it—the longer route. But Aaron enjoyed the solitude, the time to think.

"Hey-ooo!" he said, when just a few feet from where we had been sitting, he caught sight of us. I leapt, hissing, "Shhhh!" and put my finger to my face. This was some serious business. Clyde Duane moved toward Ryan, who had waited a moment, then called out again, as a distraction. As June slipped into the building, I did something I had, I think, never done before: I was aggressive. I took the initiative. I grabbed the front of Aaron's shirt and pulled him into the doorway with us.

Then the door closed and the hallway was pitch dark.

I wondered, as I tried to remember precisely what came next, how I would continue the story. I knew what happened, yes. But I was having trouble finding the right words to put on the page.

In front of me, beside the legal pad I was writing on, sat a small orange notebook. It had faded a bit, and the metal rings had wept rust onto the pages. That morning, in cleaning out more of what had been my bedroom, where my parents stored boxes full of my childhood things, I'd found it, in a large shoebox, with smaller scraps of paper: sketches of dinosaurs, scribbles of geometry, an embarrassing drawing of a woman's naked body I had imagined, some foreign currency that relatives and friends of my parents had brought back from their trips for me, baseball and superhero cards that stirred vague recollections, and a handful of metal jacks and a pink rubber ball I didn't remember at all.

I'd opened the notebook and recognized my own youthful handwriting, though all the words it held inside were completely alien to me.

"-/- D I A R Y -/-" it said on its first, title page, then the date, which was near the beginning of the school term June had first appeared. I turned the pages and found details I had not remembered. I returned to my memoir and added them in. Then, reading the diary, I arrived at that moment, at the doorway, at the great threshold of my life.

The crickets had stopped. That's the "noise" that jerked my head up—the sudden, enormous void of sound. The dogs had stopped their snoring, too.

I didn't have long to wait, heart pounding, wondering what was about to come, because after a few seconds there was a banging on the door.

The dogs were up then, barking in exaggerated menace, embarrassed they had let something pass by the perimeter so far. It was all bluster—I had seen them nuzzle the hand of a total stranger, someone whose truck had turned into the wrong driveway and gotten stuck.

The pounding at the door continued. I grabbed the dogs' collars, and called out, "Hold up!"

I heard someone speaking in response, but the thick wood of the door muffled any specifics of what was said. Once I heard the voice, though, my emergent anxiety melted away. I have learned, in the late troubles—you, and many others, will have learned it too—that the things worth fearing don't knock on the door and stand there waiting courteously.

First giving the dogs a corrective yank, I released them and pulled the door open. The dogs stayed a step behind me, but showed their teeth and growled.

In the front of a group around my door, looking the same as he had when I met him the other day at church, stood Aaron. On either side of him were Eric and Max.

I had not seen either of them since school. Eric, in the intervening years, had bulked out, and he stood solidly in faded denim jeans and a Buffalo check shirt, slightly bow-legged. His hair was perfectly white, his cheeks, even in the low light which reached past me to the porch, were bright pink. Max had only grown more striking in appearance, with jet black hair and olive complexion. He was tall, slim, and dressed with a casual professionalism that spoke of a previous era.

Had we been on Facebook (which, since its complete termination—cut out as the societal cancer it had become—no one is any longer), I might have kept up with their changing physiognomy through periodic updates of profile pictures or group shots with other long separated friends, as gradually and unconsciously as the proverbial boiled frog. Instead, I had the shock of sudden transformation; now I wondered how I, wracked by the decades, appeared to them.

I wanted to say, "What's up, fellas?" but my throat was dry and nothing at all came out when I tried. I stepped outside, pulling the door closed behind me to keep the dogs in. Then I tried again. "Hey, fellas, what's up?"

Their faces were stony. Instead of replying, they spread out, and I could see two figures behind them. Both had crimson hoods masking their faces but there was no mistaking the slim figure of Brian and the looming bulk of Clyde Duane.

I should have known what was up.

Max and Eric grabbed my arms, and Aaron pulled a hood over my face, obscuring everything.

Inside, Portis and Jacques began to bark after me, fruitlessly, but with spirited determination.

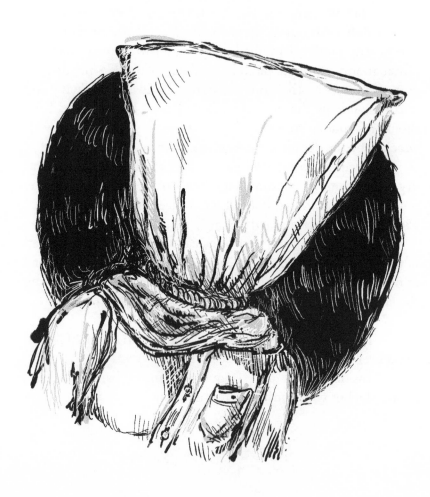

Under the hood, my own hot breath puffed against my face.
I tried to think.

Chapter
52

UNDER THE CLOTH HOOD, in the van—I knew it was a van because I heard the door sliding open before I was stepped-up inside—I began to see silver and gold streaks flash in the absolute darkness. My two companions, Max and Eric—or others, if they had swapped out as they had marched me along, crunching the pea-gravel of the path—sat on either side of me, restraining me with gentle, but constant pressure to my arms.

The door shut. Someone pressed the ignition and the van hummed to a start. Something I would never get used to: the lack of "lurching" as electric cars got started on their way: just a smooth acceleration from standstill. It saved energy, and reduced wear and tear.

Progress, such as it was, still lurched forward, though. There was no smooth transition to getting better and better; one day the old way, and then a new drive system is swapped in. This improved ride had been accidental, a byproduct of other required changes, just as the bipedalism our ancestors took to on the grasslands had let our brains begin to grow.

Under the hood, my own hot breath puffed against my face. I tried to think. What was I doing here? The neon worms squiggling through the darkness. They had, a bit before, been shooting stars. Now they were iridescent penguins on black floes, sliding with joy into an equally black ocean.

The sparks that flew up when they were devoured were slowly moving backwards while other sparks pushed forward, jiggling; it was—I struggled to think of the term—Brownian motion, and I was looking deep into the gas which, invisible, enwrapped us all.

The heat was becoming unbearable. The van shuddered a little. I could feel myself sweating. I knew what I had meant to tell them when I saw they meant to take me. Now I knew it was too late to say it—it would ruin everything. I had, against all odds, to keep the fact from everyone. In about ten minutes I would be laughing uncontrollably. No, not ten minutes. I was starting to chuckle even now. Sometimes when I laughed like this the dogs became anxious. I suspect they read it as a low, constant sob. I couldn't stop chuckling. The penguins of light —was it actual light or just the sparking of optic-nerve fibers, denied stimulus—had, each one of thousands, found themselves stewards of a rocky planet of their own, and they waved at me with tiny flippers, their water-wings.

I only stopped laughing due to the growing icy dread of my situation.

Eddie's LSD that I had dropped—as I'd done a few times already during my stay—about three-quarters of an hour ago, had me fully in its grip now. I had anticipated a leisurely, creative trip in the comfort of my parents' den, in its amber glow, watching the figures on the Persian rug slither and dance to the rhythm of my heart. No such luck. I was in for it now.

I stifled a yelp; I don't know where it came from. How could I be so happy, flushed up with dopamine, and yet so terrified. Yes, I had just been kidnapped. The word rattled through my brain. Napkidded, knapped. Nipnacked. Pinpacked. I was laughing again.

One of my companions chuckled too.

Had I been muttering my loony ravings out loud? But soon, regardless, sweat-soaked, swimming through the fiery universe of my mind, with that burning in my gut the only real drawback, that constant churning sick, I was a universe in myself, alive.

A trip on LSD was never like what you imagined: First, things became more fascinating. You notice every pore, every vein in every leaf, the fur on the animals, your own fur stretching out, the dead wood of the table shining, the grain describing a terrain as deep as the Grand Canyon. The trees outside nodded down; the flowers seemed to open to your eyes.

Your own face you saw in shadow, every blotch of red the broken dreams of a life gone by. People nodded, or turned their eyes to you from the covers of magazines.

Shadows here and there, clothes draped on a hook, each was now a real live person.

You both dreaded and looked forward to the end, when the bland, static world stood in bright shafts of sunlight and the curtain was a curtain, flat and dead.

We had stopped. Someone whispered. I felt their hood touch mine, red to black. I saw it melt through mine. Their voice was coming from inside me. "Are you ready? Do you remember what to do?"

No! But I must not say anything.

"Oh, shit," I said. "I'm tripping. I dropped acid just before you took me. But I'll be okay." I felt the weight of it slide from me, as I let go of my secret.

The van door opened, seatbelts released, people moved around. With a touch on my shoulder I was gently led into open air. They held my shoulders, and we marched along a flagstone path. Beyond our shoes slapping and echoing, and the rustling of fabric, and the sound of my breath heavy in the hood, there was also the sound of running water, and I became convinced we were under it, not walking but swimming. The sound grew immense—it was my own blood, the ocean we hear when we place a conch shell to our ear.

Now the sounds became flat and deadened, grew smaller, enclosed, as we passed through a door. I saw everything through the hood, shapes of sound, the outline of the hallway narrowing before me; I thought that I would shrink with it as I walked, until I popped out of the vanishing point into the void like a drop of oil, furred with electrons, curving up. That's just the acid talking, I told myself. Of course we would shrink, but with everything shrinking around us, you wouldn't feel a thing. We stopped. A door opened and I was led through.

"Wait here," they told me, as one. I was pushed into a chair in what felt like a tiny room, a closet. Someone sat next to me, and the door closed. The darkness was becoming too claustrophobic and I reached for my hood, to take it off, but the hand of my companion stopped me.

"Not yet." A whisper.

"Who are you?"

There was no answer.

"Who are you?" I asked again.

"You know," he said at last, peevishly, no longer whispering. "You know!" He stayed silent for a while. Then he said, "Ohhhh. Yes. Ask again."

"Who are you?"

His whisper voice returned, and it coiled around me like a snake. "I am the palace guard."

"What?"

The door opened. It was time. Two people joined "the palace guard." Two of them flanked me and one followed behind. It all had a nagging familiarity. I should know, I thought, what I was doing here. My own breathing contained in it a litany of excuses, recriminations, apologies, a cacophonous cascade of words. It was nothing. I was nothing. I felt a whooshing of fresh air surround me as my hood was whipped off. The darkness was still dark but not as completely dark as before. Shapes in different registers of shadow moved and turned through it. I was in a large open hall, with high ceilings, the gloom lifted there, and I thought there may have been large, hanging pennants, medieval, and in front, a throne upon a dais, and figures outlined, moving, joining and parting.

A single light flashed on, making a bright cone, revealing a crimson-robed figure on the throne. It was a brocaded robe, with gold-fabric lines swirled over it. The figure had a deep, but feminine voice. The voice said, "Bring the prisoner forward!"

Sweat sprang out again. I wondered if I would laugh. Nearby, many chairs moved and scraped. I felt the body heat of a hall full of people, heard murmuring, a cough and its echo. My companions, my kidnappers, pulled me forward, almost dragged me.

The voice next to me whispered, "Kneel." So I did.

I looked up and the robed figure was above me, on the dais, leaning down from the throne. She was, under all the finery, a frail woman with steel gray hair, and in her eyes I felt only kindness and acceptance. There was nothing to fear from her in all this awful majesty. Then her voice cut through, harsh, trumpeting, and I was afraid again.

"The prisoner stands accused!"

Words came to me, a line remembered, and I muttered them into the floor, "Not guilty. Not guilty." It had been, what, thirty minutes since I'd been collected from my parents' front porch in the stillness of the woods. I wouldn't be coming down for about, let me see, six and a half hours. Shit.

The crowd was echoing me, now, some in support, others mocking. First it was chatter, "Not guilty," scattered and uneven, and then it grew louder, more certain, a chant, in unison. It went on for a long time; it was like a song, it sounded rehearsed. I felt a sickness in my stomach, it was full of acid.

Bang! Bang! Bang! The heavy wooden staff beat against the dais and its thunder cut through the crowd, wresting the faceless shadows into quiet. A few called or muttered out again, "Not guilty." Bang!

Silence.

"The prisoner can have no plea, for he is guilty. The crime is grave, and the punishment final. Who will speak for the prisoner?"

"Guilty of what crime?" I said in the most confident, resounding voice I could muster. The companion to my right hissed, "Shhhh!" and tapped me on the shoulder. Someone in the crowd scoffed, "Improvising!"

I wobbled as the guard on my left took two steps forward, leaving emptiness beside me. Looking down I saw my knees against a rug. The light from the dais died just there, and the innumerable fibers of the rug, a colorless, institutional thing, were all twisting in the shining corona, like arms, and I marveled that so many tiny things could support such a great weight as the weight of my guilt.

The man who stood forward flared with a white fire so bright he appeared made of it, completely transparent. He pulled off his red hood, and his face disappeared. His voice rang out like crystal. He said, "I will speak for the prisoner."

He introduced himself. He was a humble city watchman, he explained. I struggled to remember if such a job existed. He told a story about us that I did not at all recognize: he explained that we had met each other as enemies, that I had bested him, fairly, he added, then spared him. He stepped back. The person on my right moved forward. He was, he said, a palace guard. There were no palaces here, had never been, except one Palace Dumplings, down the highway. He told an even more fantastic story: a princess in distress, and my selfless aid to her; I had risked capture that she might go free.

Now I was really feeling the effects.

I whispered to myself, to no-one, really, "Drugs are bad, kids." From behind me, a third came forward. Her voice rose to the rafters.

"I will speak for him." She told her own story, how I, a stranger, had come to her village when it had been at the point of starvation, and shared with them the secret knowledge of how to stretch out their wheat, demanding nothing in return. A spotlight came upon the crowd. At the farthest end of the front row was an old man. He looked like a puppet, and stood uneasily, all his joints swaying. He croaked out, "I will speak for this man." Then the next stood, a young woman who shared his features. "I will speak for him." And the next, and the next, then the whole crowd at once stood. In a flash, light filled the entire room.

"We speak for this man."

Everything went away as the lights punched out.

After a beat, the light-cone returned, spotting the dais and its throne.

"Prisoner," said the judge. "Stand."

What choice did I have?

"You are guilty of heavy crimes, you acted with callous disregard of the law, and struck against property and freedom, the pillars supporting our peerless society."

Stone silence.

"This court"—the judge turned to her left and right, where a step lower than her sat more robed figures—"must now cast a sentence.

"You all stand by the prisoner, as he has, in direct contravention of the highest order, helped each one of you. You all share in his guilt."

It was terrible. Her measured tone. Her face, kind, but resolutely logical.

"The court passes sentence on the prisoner. You . . ." She looked at me now and I realized I had misread her eyes as kind, but they were as steely as her hair, empty of all compassion. "You," she repeated, "the court sentences you, the prisoner, to—"

Bang!

"The court sentences the prisoner to life!"

"TWENTY MINUTES' BREAK, everyone, and the Women's Auxiliary has graciously provided punch and cookies in the back, and it's a $1 suggested donation. Then we return to our regular business, which will be fall festival planning, then provisions for winter street clearing, and a question about the electric co-op. Secretary, can you mark down that the new citizen initiation has been done?"

The judge draped her robe over the back of her "throne," a metal folding chair set on a small crate to raise it above the other seven or eight chairs arrayed along the stage. Immediately after my "sentence" had been proclaimed, the lights rose and revealed two rows of metal chairs filled with a motley assortment of locals on the lacquered floor of the school's "Multi-Purpose Room." Above, hanging pennants celebrated recent victories, placing, and participation in all sorts of academic and athletic games.

Behind us, two white tables stood with punch and little paper cups, cookies, some cupcakes, and a small wooden donation box. The walls were plastered with hand-drawn posters of all talent levels, celebrating community, the school, the earth, and families. My companions were putting their hoods in a cardboard box one of the women from the stage was holding out. All the people on the stage were women, young and old.

The sudden clinical brightness of the light from four hanging, conical fixtures tore all fantasy from the scene, leaving only a shimmering edge around each of the figures. I recognized many people from town. I walked back to the punch table, checking my pockets to see if I had brought my wallet. Max was the first to reach me, and he put a friendly hand on my shoulder.

For a second it went all rainbow, and I saw his fingernails curling into the tiny printed leaves on my shirt, which themselves were falling. I looked into his face and saw his beard in the act of growing. He smiled, teeth for days, but I steeled myself against the vision, and said, "That was wild."

In the light, I knew what was happening, had happened. I'd even had some notice of the event, by mail, along with a script to follow. In my defense, I'd been distracted, and forgot. They did it for every new arrival. There was a similar, possibly identical ceremony in Brooklyn, but it's much easier to fall through the cracks there, and I missed it, so I had only second- and third-hand accounts. It was meant to evoke the show trials the junta put on for the few weeks they were in power, and turn it into a message of inclusion, of pride.

I hadn't realized how much pageantry, how much religious feeling they engendered, and how thoroughly I went from actually debased to truly heroized and accepted into the bosom of the people.

The accusations and their defenses were ludicrous, but I felt I had actually done those things, and when the residents in turn stood for me, it was authentic; I entered into their hearts, and they mine. After the court sentenced me to "life," I knew it meant that I was supported here, and they all cried out "Life! Life! Life!" and the lights went up and they cried "Welcome! Welcome! Welcome!"

Sure, the room became ordinary then, but the underlying extraordinary remained. Every face, every object, was alive. I knew most of the people by sight at least, although my current state made it even harder to tie face to name. I was sure they all knew me.

The council on the stage was voluntary, and rotated. Disagreements about who should serve were met with coin tosses, the entire process endorsed via universal acclamation. Even then, the council only led discussions, although in practice, much power devolved upon them. There were resources to direct, and laws, and much scheming about it all, I suppose, but anyone in the area who had been initiated could come to the meetings, and only universal assent could move things forward.

Society policed itself, or, well, some hidden force masquerading as society, because things always got done, and whatever bad feelings existed dispersed like a fart in the wind. You might see some demagoguery, but on such a small scale it never seemed that bad.

I gulped down the punch, and regretted it. My drug-addled stomach didn't want food or beverage of any kind. The poster people waved their stick-arms at me, and smiled, or frowned, and squinted their impossibly-colored eyes. I whispered to Max, who was still standing beside me that I continued to be "tripping my balls off." He told me I would have to stay until the end, but set me, gingerly, in a chair in the back. An old woman was knitting. I watched the bright blue wool wrap around her wooden needles, dodging and swerving like a keyed-up serpent.

On the stage, there was no more mock-ceremony, just lots of murmuring talk about important local issues, and some voting. Now and then the woman knitting looked at me, importuning, and understanding her, I weakly called out "Yea" with the rest. She nodded and smiled. Her face was a snake's face, and her eyes were yellow gold.

*. . . worn woolen cloak, leather vest, leather pouch, breeches, worn
boots, blunt dagger, brass ring—tarnished, uncertain design . . .*

Chapter
53

"TODAY I HAVE something different in mind for us," Brian said. We had just sat down at one of the round library tables, me, Eric, Max, and Aaron, about a week after June had first agreed to play a round of "The Game" with us.

We pulled our character sheets from the notebooks we carried from the various classes we'd just come from (Algebra, Spanish, Biology)—if you skipped hitting your locker after class and came straight to the library, there would be more time to play.

Max's single sheet was impeccable, written with a mechanical pencil in his tiny, particular hand; Eric's a scribbled mess, extending over three crumpled and stained sheets of wide-rule; and Aaron's covered in fantastic outer space scenes. I had just arranged mine in front of me when a sheet handed out by Brian covered it.

He had passed out new sheets to everybody.

"Put your characters away, and meet—your characters!" he said. "Take a look at the levels: I have set these characters to level -1. You're lower than 0, not even a hero yet. We're going to play our first adventure together, again, but first we are going to do a backstory for everyone."

"I don't know," said Aaron.

"No, I see it," said Max. "This is going to be fun."

Eric held the physical manifestation of his character—a level 32 thief turned adventurer written into many dog-eared and wrinkled sheets—close to his chest, like something precious he might lose by letting go of.

"And we're going to start with you, Eric," said Brian.

I had felt that this was right: Eric, back at the farm, had been the one who pushed us to actually play the game we had been noodling over.

"YOU ARE SITTING in the darkest corner of the inn, nursing a Raserian Ale—"

"Hey," interjected Aaron, "that's copyrighted!"

"What do you mean?" asked Max.

"I mean it's my copyright."

"Whatever," said Brian.

Eric laughed. "Printed it out, and mailed it to himself!"

"Yes," said Aaron, "I can show it in court, with the postmark as proof."

"How can they prove you didn't just unseal it and put it in after the fact?" I asked.

"It doesn't matter if you have a copyright or not," said Brian. "It's an *homage*."

"Fine," said Aaron.

Brian started again. "Just a few moments ago"—he looked at Eric—"you reached into your tunic and felt in your leather pouch, past a few smooth sling stones for the last few coppers to pay your tab only to discover you had no more coins.

"It would take you ten, maybe twelve long strides to reach the door. Now you are waiting for the barkeep, a dumb-looking ogre, to get distracted by a big order, hoping your stealth works out.

"Not more than a few other patrons, so it doesn't look good. You'll wind up eating a fist sandwich. The way your stomach is growling, though, the idea sounds good.

"You don't see anything noble in skipping out on the check in a third-rate inn in a stony, damp corner of the empire. Noble, you say—a thief? But you had noble aspirations once— using your skills to take from the rich, to give to the poor, and for you, just enough to get by. A simple, heroic life."

"Yes!" said Eric. "That's it."

"Nevertheless"—Brian relished the many syllables of the word—"the check must be dodged. Now Roll!"

Eric picked up a single die, and, blowing on it for luck, let it tumble around in the deep cup made by his long fingers and palm and then let it drop. It clattered on the table. A one. We grimaced in unison.

"Your attempt at stealth is . . . pathetic. Perhaps influenced by too much unpaid-for ale," said Brian. Behind the screen of his notebook, Brian let a couple of dice drop. "Indeed," he said, "the ogre barkeep has reached you, and slaps you to the floor with his enormous, clawed hand. Ow! You take five damage."

"If I had Arsena," muttered Eric, "he'd be slit from belt to neck." That was the magical dagger his character had found at level 20, and which had often been a critical part of his exploits. Eric looked sadly down at the inventory roster Brian had written for him: worn woolen cloak, leather vest, leather pouch, breeches, worn boots, blunt dagger, brass ring—tarnished, uncertain design.

"The ogre raises both imposing fists together. Through stars, crouched on the floor, looking up at him, you are thinking this could be the end."

"It can't be!" said everyone at once.

"No," said Brian, "it can't, can it?" We heard the clacking of dice behind the screen. I had often wondered what relationship the numbers that came up had to the story we were playing. For the most part, the few occasions I sat in his seat, I mostly followed the rolls as prescribed, and dutifully the scimitar struck or glanced off, the monster appeared, or failed to notice, the wall tumbled or not, the spongy wooden step on the rope bridge across the chasm broke or held firm for one more step. Of course, at critical moments, I'd look at a 1 and think how easily it could have been a 6, or squinted and found the number the situation merited: there was a higher power to the universe of our game—that which tended to the good, to a fair story.

I, more or less living a felicitous life so far, felt that this reflected the real world. I think now that someone like Eric or Aaron whose lives had not been so felicitous thought that it reflected how the world ought to be. Either way, all of us had the psychological safety to understand that things might get dire, but would never be impossible, and that even if one was at the point of death, the magic of the dungeon would offer up salvation, maybe not immediately to hand, but within reach.

"You have just enough energy, as you perceive his coming blow, to lift your arms up, crossed in front of your face," said Brian to Eric. Eric prepared to roll. "But! The ogre's fists stop inches from you. They open. You feel the bony claws against your fingers; he turns your hand so your brass ring shines in the firelight.

"'Hmm . . . ' says the ogre. 'Maybe I should let you live, after all. Someone I know will be very interested in this, and, as much as it pains me, in keeping you alive to tell about it.'

"Just then, a large party of boisterous adventurers fresh from some minor triumph burst through the inn doors, calling for ale, for food, and for music. The ogre's attention shifts."

Eric was already rolling. "A six," he said. "Finally."

Brian rolled, then said, "You make it through the door. You slide one of the outside benches as a barrier, and make for the fence. But the ogre doesn't follow. Instead he says to himself, 'It doesn't matter, I must send a message to the master, the key he's been looking for for so long has turned up, at last.'

"You meet with a stranger in the road," said Brian. "Who stops you in your run. You reach for your blunt dagger, the stranger—Max, your roll, if you want to fight, or you can invite Eric to follow you to the cemetery: where you've arranged to meet two potential partners," Brian looked at Aaron and me, "and, remember, you had promised to bring a thief. But the one you thought you had agreed with had run in the night, stealing your jeweled belt, and scabbard."

"If," said Max, playing along, "I had been awake, he would have gotten my sword instead."

THE MEETING IN THE CEMETERY became an initiation, a bond between strangers who had come together for—what—a sense of adventure? Danger? A need for camaraderie? But I had almost forgotten the language of "the key," how it reflected our real-life adventure with June.

When I saw Eric again, at the bar at the Happy Valley Inn, a few days after my surreal, actual initiation, he reminded me of that moment, by alluding to it, as he tossed back a local beer and after praising the "Raserian Ale" asked if I had a copper for the ogre behind the bar.

The "ogre," a goateed transplant from the 60s with a pony tail and a diamond stud earring, narrowed his eyes and shook his head as he drifted to the other end of the bar, wiping it down with a rag as he went.

"Your money's no good here."

Chapter
54

"Y OUR MONEY'S no good here," said Eric, as I was reaching for my wallet. We had downed a couple beers in the well lit bar of the Inn. Eric had had a thousand questions for me. In turn, I heard about the divorce, about his kid, a loner but good hearted, then there was the cancer I hadn't known about, a private thing—he still had to have periodic scans. But, at least, at last, there was no danger of financial ruin.

From the television there came a big whoop—there was a local basketball match on, and a JV kid had just sunk a sweet two pointer—the local crowd reacted with an explosion of joy. We took the opportunity of the distraction to move into smoother conversational waters. We reminisced about old times—talked all about our time on the farm, and our early games. We touched on June and the L.E.F. only obliquely.

I had been uncomfortable meeting Eric there, at first. This had never been my kind of place. In the winter there'd be a half-dozen snowmobiles parked out front. There was often a deer carcass, either hanging in the tree, or slung over the back of a pickup truck. Inside was all knotty pine, a blue carpet, lit up like a surgery. On one side was a big chest freezer, beneath a Michelob-sign clock. The other room had some folding chairs, and a slight raised stage. As we had finished our drinks, someone was setting up for a solo set. The people who were coming in in ones and twos, in thick Carhartts and trucker hats, or in full denim suits, men and women with teased out hair, Casio watches, would have fit in here in probably any decade I had been alive.

It wasn't really Eric's place, either, I thought. And I had challenged him on that. Asked what we were doing here. He said they had the best wings in the county. And that it was light enough to work on his crosswords. And sketching. He had taken up drawing again.

I couldn't imagine these locals—I still had this idea of locals against transplants; you could be two generations in town and still a transplant—couldn't imagine them tolerating someone with Eric's proclivities, his quiet demeanor. And yet. Here we were.

"Come on," I said, "let me pay."

"No," said Eric, "really—I mean—literally, your money is no good."

"What do you mean?"

"Once you've been initiated, you're one of us," he said. "I mean, you were one of us before, but now it's completely solid, inescapable."

"You don't pay for anything?"

"Money is just for tourists," he said. "But don't get me wrong—everything is paid for. You don't want, but neither does our community."

I thought of Brian's visit, and the sense that other things were in the offing to be asked of me. "I get it," I said. "Is it like this everywhere up here?"

"Things are tailored to the places and people in them," he answered.

A guitar sound came from the other room, an electric twang, followed by repeated vibrations, tuning, then a start. A deep female voice—I noticed a flash of red hair from my occluded vantage—singing. Tentative at first then gaining confidence. I can't make out the words, then I caught one here or there, "horses," "mules," "sheep" . . .

"Some I want to sell boy, and some I want to keep.

"Look down that lonesome road, before you travel on; I hate to say goodbye," she sang. "So I'll just say so long."

"She's good," I said to Eric.

He nodded. "Hey," he said leaning in to me, because the music had gotten loud—the acoustics in here were predictably lousy—"I know you're looking for June."

"I'm looking for her in the past," I said. As if that made any sense.

"Listen," he said, "have you been to see Anne, yet?" Anne was June's mother. She still lived at the farm. I must have had a pained expression. "I know," he said, "I know. But she has something for you."

"She knows I'm here?" I said. I had almost said, "She knows who I am?"

"Just head over to see her," he said. "Also," he said, gesturing toward the TV, "see that guy?" I looked, there was a face caught in profile, with a crooked mouth, thick black glasses, slicked, thinning hair. He was a bit older than me, in a good suit. He was plump; he looked out of breath. The sound was off, but it was clearly a kind of "Wanted" poster. There was a text scroll indicating that all citizens should be on the lookout for this character. "He'd be a lot thinner now," said Eric. "If he comes to you, no matter what he says, don't talk to him, don't help him, just send him away."

"What's the deal?" I asked.

The singer belted out "Going down south! Going where the climate suits my clothes!" Her audience, in the now-packed other room, cheered.

"Look," said Eric, "some people miss the bad old days. Some people aren't content to be happy. Some people have had every chance."

"Some people," I said with affected derision, shaking my head.

He was at the top of the stairs now.

Chapter
55

"HOLY SHIT!" I said. "If it isn't 'some people,' in the flesh." Because there he was, the man from the TV. He was far thinner than Eric's statement even had led me to imagine. It happened just a few days later, outside my parents' house. He had emerged from the woods looking like a wild man, skin and bones, his pinstripe suit ripped and besmeared with dried mud, thick beard, one of his lenses shattered, a gold watch loose around bony wrist. I felt pity, but off of him emanated menace too. He stopped at the handrail to the stairs, supporting himself on it like a crutch.

"Help me," he croaked.

"I'm not supposed to talk to you," I said.

"I know you," he said softly. "You're not like them— not like her. Just a little food, please, I haven't eaten for days. Then I'll leave."

"Fuck it," I said. I looked around—of course there was no one else for miles. "Come on up."

He didn't even ask if I was going to help him. I could have. I should have helped, maybe. But there was something coming off him, some mixture of hollow desperation and cunning purpose that made me doubt his intentions. He was dragging himself up the stairs one step at a time, both arms hugging the bannister. Once or twice his feet slipped out from underneath him. He groaned but steadied himself and kept coming toward me. I backed away, like you would from a strange animal, or upon noticing you were too close to the edge of a cliff.

Cliff.

Holy shit. It was fucking Cliff.

He was at the top of the stairs now, and his eyes, sunken, bloodshot, pupils narrowed to pins, were boring into mine. I took him by the arm, and a little too roughly pulled him inside.

CLIFF. WE HAD BEEN in college together. Shared an English class. Cliff had been rich, a prep-school kid. He was in the Young Republicans, and the Campus Conservatives. He had weirdly taken a shine to me—I had never been sure why. I mostly despised him, although I also had some fascination for him, and his continued invitations into their society, a world of suits and cognac, of beer and cocaine, of class rings and skull pins, of trust funds, allowances, and exploits with and of the family servants, piqued my curiosity. I often said no to him, and I mostly wondered what he was trying to groom me for, certainly not for a genuine entree to the ways of the wealthy, maybe sidekick status, or as a curio, a human collectible, or, more darkly, the target of some long-running prank.

It certainly looked like the joke was on him, these days.

In retrospect, I think that Cliff was attracted to my rural origin, that he felt a kind of kinship, since he too hailed from Upstate New York, not far from Harmony Valley, although his childhood experience had been far removed from the place, skiing in Switzerland, prep schools in Connecticut and New Hampshire, and the like, and had always held an uneasy position in his milieu because of his slightly déclassé place of origin. We lost touch after my sophomore year—I think he had gone to D.C., and yet here he was. I suppose he had ended up returning to the region.

"What the hell, Cliff?" I finally asked him.

We faced each other at the kitchen table.

He had wolfed down cold leftovers I took out for him, eating too quickly, so he could hardly speak for a few minutes afterward. He had rejected my offer to heat them up in favor of getting food immediately. After we finished, he picked bits of bolognese out of his beard and ate them, as we spoke.

"You're putting yourself in danger, taking me in like this," he said. "Helping an outcast."

"An outcast?"

"I am 'without honor,' it means I can't participate in your beautiful 'utopia.'"

"The doesn't seem very utopian, enlightened," I said.

"Oh, it's the essence of utopianism," he said. "Rejecting all inconvenience, rejecting the hard reality, the truth! They don't want a debate."

"But really, what did you do?" I asked. "What are you accused of?"

"I wouldn't participate," he said. "I wouldn't share my labor with the collective. I denied that I should share what I earned fair and square with people who didn't work for it. I refused to give up on the principles that made America great!"

"And now?"

"I'll find a way. This can't last. She can't win."

"What? This? Who?"

He made another sick-sounding wet cough. I refilled his water glass.

"You don't know what is going on, do you? Not even a little bit? So naive. How can you be so innocent?"

"I know what's going on," I said, protesting. "I mean, it was all bound to collapse, everything was teetering, the government wasn't functioning, America didn't—"

"Lies. All of it lies."

"The center couldn't hold," I said. I became determined to answer him, to display some savvy. "It fractured, and the states did the best they could, but their governments were marked as illegitimate, too; finally different areas took different paths, but here in the Northeast, power devolved to the localities, and from there, to its workers. We've got local collectives, and what was the state, these institutions have been refashioned to support each local region—no more America, but a rejection of corporate powers too, everything has been broken apart and refashioned on a smaller, but more-efficient and more equitable scale. Of course you've been outcast, you refused to contribute, but I suspect beyond that, you refused to acknowledge—"

"Yes, you are either with her or against her, and if that isn't," he said, "a fascist attitude, I don't know what is."

"Oh come on," I said. "You like fascism. This isn't fascism. This is democracy at its most elemental. What do you mean her? Really, what do you mean?"

"Do you really think a general strike can organize itself?" Cliff's face was twitching a bit as he spoke. I started to reply to him but he cut me off. "I need some blankets. Rope. Do you have a guns here?"

"I can give you some things," I said. "I'll tell them you stole them. My parents aren't into guns, and neither am I. You know that." Cliff had always tried to get me to go skeet shooting. I guess I might have liked it, really. But I had limits.

He stood up rather quickly, and unsteadily.

"I have to go," he said. "You're just keeping me here until they come, aren't you?" He started getting agitated.

"Come on, now, Cliff," I said. "You keep telling me I don't know what's going on—but you won't tell me what is. You keep making these cryptic statements. You sound crazy."

"Sorry, bud," he said. "Thanks for the food and the water. And if you have supplies I can take, useful stuff, I would appreciate it a lot."

He didn't say anything but moved toward the door. I grabbed a wool blanket, and some rope for him. I cast about and gave him a small hatchet.

"And?" I said.

"How's your friend, June?" he said.

"June? What do you know about June?"

"What do you know?" he said. Suddenly all the unsteadiness and frailty seemed to vanish off him, and he fled the door, taking the stairs two at a time, and then he was gone.

CLIFF HAD MET JUNE a few times, when she'd visited me at college. I remember his crowd were always trying to get me to play this crazy game called "Diplomacy" with them. They pretended to be presidents and prime ministers and they bluffed and cheated and rattled sabers against each other in some realpolitik simulation of world domination.

One day they asked when June was visiting me. I declined again. She looked hard at me, asked me why? I told her I just didn't imagine it a fun evening spending six or seven hours with a bunch of Young Republicans pretending to be Henry Kissinger or something while trying to outsmart the Ruskies or whomever. It felt lame even by my standards. June told me fine, and then she said she was going. Before I knew it I was alone in my room.

She was gone all night, and when she woke me, she had a peculiar smile.

"Well?" I said.

"I won everything," she said. "I beat them all."

*The clouds were backlit with the bright sun
like an old etching from the Bible.*

Chapter
56

I T SHOULD HAVE been my first visit. But I dragged my feet. I had rationalized my reluctance: June and her mother had been estranged for years. Anne wouldn't know anything. Anything relevant, any clues, wouldn't still be in the house after all this time. It would just stir up bad memories. Anne herself would neither remember nor welcome me. Just a great jumble of embarrassment; bad all around. But I was kidding myself, protecting myself from something. My own sense of culpability, my culpability in all of this.

I had grown personally a lot over the years, but I still shrank from uncomfortable situations like a hand from a flame. The day I went to visit, driving along the street with the old stone fence, I found myself going too fast, and missing the driveway so that I had to go all the way to the dead end and turn in the tractor path, then limp back to be sure of making the entrance. I came in like a dog who had been scolded, low and halting, and eased the car in behind the dull, forest-green Volvo June's mother had had since our school days.

It was thoroughly rusted now. The pattern of the red rust was like a coordinating accent, and gave the car the aspect of an arrangement of shrubbery or a holiday wreath. I had tried calling, but the number in the book was disconnected. The book itself hadn't been updated since Obama's first term, so I wasn't surprised. An internet search found only some old public records, and a complete stranger's social media profile. So, here I was.

I had only visited June's childhood home, the farm of my earliest adventures, once since school, and it was only briefly, after I had been seeing June for a while at college, but the visits had tapered off before June and I had lived together in the city—a period of total separation between June and her mother. That last visit was during my junior year of college, a time when, like now, June and I had lost contact. I'd been there with my father.

June's mother had rented the house out for the summer season, and the agency called in Dad to assess the place, and make a plan for the kind of touch-up work it might need before it was fit to let. June's mother was off somewhere—back in Ohio, maybe?—and we met with the real-estate agent. When we got there, she was parked out front in her idling car, smoking a cigarette, and listening to the radio with the window rolled down.

Dad and I had just been golfing at the public course, on the lake. It was nine dollars for nine holes and came with a free ham sandwich in the clubhouse. The morning had been one of glorious sky, after an overnight storm. The clouds were backlit with the bright sun like an old etching from the Bible. It was humid, and we had grown sweaty and uncomfortable. My shoes were still a little wet. But I felt overwhelming peace and satisfaction. We had each had some good shots, almost a hole in one, which was well balanced by holes we had to seven- or eight-putt.

Despite the cigarette smoke emanating from the car of the real-estate agent, I could smell the earth rising up here, and something of ozone in the air. The sweetness of the wood of the deck, and the fresh-cut grass the rental company's staff had mown. As we walked, our shoes picked up flecks of grass; they clustered, a deposit of green daggers on our toecaps.

First we rounded the house. The agent stayed on the porch tracking us warily, puffing on her cigarette. There were still strange humps in the lawn where police excavators had dug the earth up, looking for a body, I guess—that late, lost, and little lamented step-father.

The window screens might be replaced, and the screen door. The back porch was a hazard and should be torn off completely. Some flagstones could be re-set, and a small platform and steps down complete a nice patio. I don't remember making a tour of the inside. Maybe I had held back, conscious of avoiding entering what might still be June's personal space. The only other thing I remember is that every bright thing reverberated with possibility and promise. I surprised myself with an inner wellspring of optimism.

As I walked to the door now, I felt, I realized, for the first time since then, fresh, and new. I was like a baby, and the world was wonder.

So I knocked for June's mother on the screen door; it smacked against the real one behind it. I knocked again, louder. Nothing.

Then I pressed the doorbell I'd just noticed stuck glumly beside the door. I often avoided a doorbell, wary of making too much fuss. After some knocking and waiting, I'd simply walk away. But now, I felt strongly it was right to announce myself—that I would be met, and heard.

Had there been, heretofore, a malevolent force opposing my investigation?

We are always imagining the world, and the story of our place in it. Of course there could be nothing opposing me other than my own self. Nobody else much cared.

I waited. Nothing.

I could have waited all day. The sun on my back. The smells—the pebbles themselves smelled and I could pinpoint the scent. And listen to the birds chittering about, in their tight brown flock, on the lilac bush.

When June's mother finally opened the door, I was stunned. I tried to remember when, if ever, I had actually seen her in person. Maybe once, at school, looking small, worried, and old, head down. I must have wondered how it was possible June had come from her: one young and full of life, the other bent, lost. But it was mainly grainy newspaper photos and unflattering still video frames on the local news from the time of her husband's disappearance that had painted her so.

But it was a confident, striking woman that swung open the door. She was just shy of seventy, I guess, a shock of straight white hair, round face, with deep brown eyes. She was not tall, but I realized the porch was a step below the front door, and I was nearly looking her right in the face. I saw June in her. She had a green, floral scent, with undertones of sandalwood and musk.

"Mrs. M—" I started to stammer out.

"Call me Anne," she said.

She knew me straightway, and asked after my parents. Then paused. "I'm sorry," she said, "I don't get a lot of visitors here, anymore, and I have to go out in about an hour"—she looked down at her watch, a thin, silver watch with an oval face —"hour-twenty, but come in, sit down."

So I did.

I had imagined her sunk in the dark into cobwebs, but the house was bright, spotless. She led me into the kitchen; a tall counter in the middle surrounded by stools was topped with butcher block. She asked if I wanted water, tea, coffee. She clicked a button on the kettle before I answered. "I always have tea before the meetings," she said. "You should come to one, tell us how you find our community, how different from the city it is."

"I'll have tea," I said. "Sure, maybe I'll come to a meeting sometime."

I wondered how long I could possibly hold off bringing up June, wondered if she would do it first. I felt sweat at my temples and on my upper lip. All nerves, I chatted about leaving my job with our new freedom to do so, and how my parents were off to the north for several months. She seemed to know all about it already. I wondered, suddenly, if they might not have become friends. My parents never told me anything.

We took the tea, with milk and honey, into the living room, where a pile of antique rugs and two angled vintage couches received us in front of a quiescent fireplace. After a moment of sitting, I jumped up, and walked to the mantel. A framed picture was staring out at me, and I had to look more closely at it.

"June?" I asked.

It was a novelty picture, a recreation of an old tintype. But it was her, young, just before she got that scar. The focus was off and only part of her face was clear, her head tilted back gently, her mouth ever so lightly fuzzed, those lips, I almost felt them prickle up and brush against my cheek, tender, dismissive.

"Oh, no. It does look so like her, doesn't it?" Her voice sounded suddenly far away.

I kicked myself for bringing up June first, as if I had relinquished some vital power, as if this had been a struggle from which I had to come out on top. June's mother had moved behind me, and I felt a tenderness surge in me, her scent pressing around me like a caress.

"This is," she continued, "oh, I guess, a great-great-great-aunt, I think that's the right number of 'greats.'" (A real tin-type then!) "She does look so like her. She lived here, we found her photo, this one, June and I together. Of course, when we found it, June was young, and had not grown into her yet, the way she did. But I could still see the resemblance, then.

"Though, funny enough, even if June and I look so similar, I can't quite see myself in Fanny—that was her name, short for Frances."

She took the picture up in its frame, and held it in her two hands, looking into it like into a deep well. "A tragic story. She was poisoned, at least that's what some say. She was still young when it happened, like you"—funny how we think of age as we age—"I guess. There's a book, I don't have it. A local historian wrote a whole account. It was all a bit exaggerated, I suspect. Too much lurid detail; something about her power over young men.

"She was a rich woman. Or so people said. But after she died, no one seemed to be able to find any of the money. They sorted out all the papers, and certificates, and bank keys, and the like, but there was nothing left at all.

"Bad for the family—you see: they had been the ones to do her in, supposedly, as she had been about to will her fortune to a younger lover."

She put the photo back on the mantel, her hands lingering there.

"Some think she hid the money. Others that the family lied, and hid it themselves. Me, I think the money was never really there at all.

"But enough family history. You came here because you want something, right?" she said.

I looked at the photograph, seeing June and not-June.

"June said you would be here, looking."

I did want something, and Eric said June's mother had something for me, but I hardly knew what it was I wanted. And now it was a shock to hear June talking to me through her mother. I felt, for a second, played by June, made sport of.

"What did she say," I asked, "exactly? And when did you see her?"

"June said she hadn't had time to give something to you. She left it for me. It had almost passed out of my mind entirely until you showed up." She put a hand on my wrist. It was a gesture June had used with me frequently. It was both an affectionate move and a controlling one. You felt held down, soothed with a gentle, if condescending, "Whoa, Nellie."

"Wait here," she said, "I have it somewhere. You should have asked right away."

I waited in the room while June's mother went off to another part of the house. I heard some papers shuffle, things moving out of the way. Other than the silver-framed photograph on the mantel, there were dusty but exquisite cups of antique china, with the faintest cracked lines, and hanging, brass firestuff—poker, and ash shovel, a leather-and-wood bellows, an iron screen. A little wooden cradle beside it was filled with rough wooden fruit painted in bright trompe-l'œil, while behind it a stone cat stood watchful, and the whole scene was flanked by brocaded couches.

There was a grandfather clock with a completely empty face, and needlework in frames, and at the far side of the room, an oil painting, of a man and woman of middle-age, who looked stuffy and uncomfortable. Maybe the ancestors June's mother was talking about? The woman held a wooden pear, maybe one of them from the cradle, in a gloved hand, and had an elaborate hat upon which perched a white dove. The man was red-faced, and slightly walleyed.

WHILE ANNE WAS GONE, fetching what June had left for me to find, I felt that everything was normal, on the level, but then I began to feel paranoid.

The back of my neck prickled and my forehead started to sweat. I couldn't stop thinking about "the Hiram room." I had not really thought of it at all in all the years since I'd been told about it by my friends, who all seemed to have known about it, and, maybe, kept it from me?

Aaron had hinted about it once when we were alone waiting for the rest of our friends to join us to play our game.

Aaron said, "Do you know how old June's house is?" I had an idea, and I told him so. "Yes, but did you know there's a room where they still have the shackles?" he said.

"Shackles?"

"For the slaves!" he said.

I screwed up my face. "Sure, I guess," I said. And that was that. I was about to say something else in reply, when the door opened and the rest of our friends came piling in. I didn't like to think about it, and June hadn't told me about it herself. I hadn't asked her either.

Now, all I had running through my head were the black, blunt, old, iron shackles, barbaric cuffs hanging from short chains attached to the stone wall. I pictured June and her mother standing in the squat room wherever it was. Chains. To bind humans. Why wouldn't someone have ripped them out of the wall, out of shame.

Black cuffs, black bodies. June's mother, beautiful, serene, commanding. I shook myself. You couldn't ask to see them. There was no opening for it at all. No purchase. I could ask about the restroom, wander off, and yet I didn't want to know, to see it.

It bothered me, Aaron's gleeful focus. Then my being bothered had bothered me.

Slavery had been a fact of New York, had been wrapped up in its founding. We whitewashed it, with our triumphal abolitionism, our participation on the right side of history in America's Civil War. Nothing was simply good or bad, except for slavery, which was a universal evil. And it had lived, in a small way, right here in this house. I couldn't look away.

What were the shackles? They were me. And I would never quite be free.

June's mother, Anne, returned, with a painted tin box about the size of a cigar box in her hand.

The paint was chipping off. It looked like it had been buried and dug up a few times. There was still dirt caked into cracks in the decoration. One hinge was broken, and the lid skewed slightly. She put it in my outstretched hands. Then she said, hurriedly, "I'm so sorry, I have to go. You can stay here if you want, and have more tea. I don't suppose you'll want to come to the meeting with me?"

They still never locked the doors here. I begged off, told her that, lately (truthfully), I had not been up to social efforts; I was still coming down from the too-much stress of city living.

She said it had always been the same with June. Now I was wondering about that period of estrangement. It hardly seemed possible that the two of them should split.

"No, but I will leave with you," I said, given up any idea of hunting for the Hiram room, "The dogs will be missing me."

"Some other time," she said.

I held the box flat, then turned it to slide it under my arm. I heard the contents shift. It sounded like stiff cards, and maybe a pencil, some coins.

As we parted in front of the old house, she looked straight into my eyes, and said "Go with God," an unsettling reminder of her former and perhaps continued religious extremism. I wanted to ask her. There was nothing religious in the house, not even the shadow of an absent cross on the wall.

The afternoon light was hitting the property's stone walls hard, falling across the rocks and moss, skipping and sparkling. She drove off first, while I was still leaning against my car, looking at the house, the marvelous old house.

I wondered again if I should go back in, dig around. But I was no longer young, and I was tired, and today had been quite enough already.

In the car, I set the box gently on the dash. Astounding the patience you developed with age. After dinner I would open it.

Or never.

I set the box gently on the dash. Astounding the patience you developed with age. After dinner I would open it. Or never.

Chapter

57

THE BOX, JUNE'S BOX, was sitting on the kitchen table at the center of a sea of newspapers I had put down, and some small canvases, paint still wet, sweating linseed oil and turpentine to mix with the scent of the pasta sauce: basil, thyme, oregano, and some bay leaves. Two bad studies of the dogs, and a bright, stupid flower. Oil painting helped me think, even if I wasn't any good at it.

I hadn't touched the box yet. Had been circling it warily while dinner cooked. First I'd had to feed the dogs. I had been gone too long, and when I got back, they raced, barking, sliding over the floors to meet me at the door, the rugs sliding up on each other, like folds of skin. So I shoveled out DADS-brand kibble into their bowls, poured in chicken stock from a big glass jar in the refrigerator, and some leftover sliced steak on top. They were absolutely spoiled by my parents, and I thought it above my paygrade to insist on any kind of change.

The box sat, still, where I had set it on the sideboard. Untouched. Beckoning. My indifference had always been an act, of course. But I was playing it as hard as I could.

June would respect my resistance. She, in some respects, demanded it. She admired me, she had said, for always being a bit aloof from the game. But it cost me. Now. I burned to open it. Once I did, I would be entirely hers, but wasn't I already? The sauce bubbled, and splattered up out of the pot. I ran to lower the heat.

My thoughts were, and still are, a jumble. I couldn't decide if I was observing, or actually taking part, and if I was taking part, was I playing exactly as expected, or holding my own, which, was, of course, what was expected. It was high school all over again, or it had never ended. Nothing ever ends. The players just change.

Fine.

After dinner, I was sipping the red wine I'd opened last night. It was better today, more mellow, or I was. Dinner had been fine; I had cooked too much, though, and so counteracted the health benefits of cooking from scratch by eating to excess.

The dark was closing in all around. The dogs had snuffled off into their corners. I washed the bowl, and utensils, the sauce pan.

Enough—I succumbed to curiosity.

Inside the box, on top of other things, was a new-looking envelope. Brightly white. My name was written on the front, in June's handwriting. It was sealed only loosely, and the contents bulged out at the center. Whatever was in there was heavy, it felt metal.

I opened the envelope, saw a flash of gold.

The serpent key.

Chapter
58

BESIDES THE KEY, the box contained a jumble of items, some seemingly precious and some seemingly not. Ticket stubs for a couple of old concerts, Bob Dylan and Tori Amos. Some receipts with the ink entirely faded, so only the shiny paper remained. Two jacks, and a green marble no bigger than the end of my pinky, the pale, frosted green of sea-glass.

There was an old post-card from Ohio, of a building in a town I had never heard of, hand-colored, never sent, with nothing on the back.

There was a small brass locket, and a thin satin envelope, with a name written in such an elongated and decorative hand I couldn't read it. Inside was thin foolscap folded tightly with writing running horizontally and vertically in the same hand, the same brown ink. There was a lock of hair folded in it; it was faded, but I think it had been a bright red at one time. The strands were impossibly fine, and it was tightly coiled in a crimson ribbon.

I stopped at a card from a library card catalog. It was typed up long ago, the paper browned, with that faint, acid whiff of decay, but there were little dents in the stock where the letters had made their impressions. The card referenced an autobiography, it was called *My Life*, by Frances Fraser. That was one of the books June had taken out from Inter-Library Loan, all that time ago! June's ancestor?

I knew the other items, in their way, were all clues, must be, if June had indeed arranged for me to receive the box, though I had my doubts. Was it her mother, instead, trying to set me on a trail gone cold?

I took a gamble and paid a visit to the village library.

It remained as it had been since the city fathers had put up a subscription to build it in the 30s, erected during the depression by out-of-work locals, brick by brick, at twice the average day-rate. The initial contents were donated entirely from two large personal libraries, with another five hundred more recent volumes purchased at a discount from two New York publishers through two different connections; a cousin of one wealthy citizen, the uncle of another. These books, all from 1934 and all with covers designed by one or the other art department, lent an aesthetic unity to the library's shelves, which two generations of head-librarians preserved through judicious purchasing and a relentless culling of donated books.

The library was a red-brick structure with simple white molding and matte-black wooden shutters; over the door was a cast-iron eagle and when we were young out front hung a glorious handmade flag—each colored stripe separately stitched on, a thing of beauty. Odd to think now there is no flag, per se, just the rectangle of pure navy blue, as though to anticipate the water world we nearly had, though scientists say we are not out of the woods yet. Not that there would be no dry land, but that the waters would inundate the land as in some ancient legends.

This new flag is said, too, to assert our lack of national chauvinism. Which is and is not true. At least we are open to the world now, and found the world was open to us.

When I was a child, the library was only open three days a week. Now, the library is open seven days, seven to seven. There is no line-item for it in the tax bill; it's kept open out of the general fund, and no one complains. They built out the back and installed enormous desks, free 3D printers, and a rotating staff of librarians who answer questions about what should be done and how to do it. They are the well-informed oracles of our new order, and perform their task with aplomb.

I had not set foot inside the library in twenty years or more. I was surprised, although I shouldn't have been, to find the front room, with the check-out counter and those immaculately uniform bookshelves, remained entirely unchanged—not frozen in amber, but the same as they had always been, only fresh and alive. The one difference was the doorway into the back atrium, a vaulted glass structure over rows of desks and cubbies, swimming with light.

I found myself perplexed by the librarian, who looked up from the front desk as I walked in, because she, too, appeared unchanged. She regarded me through rimless frames, large liquid eyes, thin, arched eyebrows, tight, small mouth, skin like cream, lace collar, and black velvet dress. Her long hands were folded over each other, and a pearl pin was stuck through her dress, just above her right breast.

No, she wasn't unchanged, she was younger. Ah! She was the daughter of the former librarian, I surmised. It was not so out of the ordinary, here, for children to follow after their parents, like something out of medieval serfdom. It was a type of inertia, but a comfortable one. I, on the other hand, felt the world's energy spinning me away from the life of my parents, or so I had thought; it turned out I was like a comet, traveling far into the vastness of space on my elliptical track, only, much later, to find myself tugged back to the place of my birth.

When she raised her eyes and said hello, in a surprisingly deep voice, I said, "Hi. It really is something. How little and yet how much has changed." Before I could continue, and introduce myself, she greeted me by name and asked after my brother and my parents.

"Oh, all well, and you?"

"Yes," she said, "yes. How can I help you?"

From the atrium came the quiet murmur of patrons and librarians, the faint click of virtual keyboards, a gentle music which seemed to accentuate the hush of the library. I began to search my pockets, arriving at the breast pocket of my shirt last, where I had put the card. I took it out and showed her.

"I'm looking for this book," I said.

She examined the card as if it was a relic, which it was, then turned to the computer. She glided her finger across the screen, making those tight compact gestures of screen-spelling which had become so familiar. She shook her head.

"There's nothing on the computer," she said. "But the call numbers haven't changed, so there might be something still on the shelf, though I doubt it."

She motioned me to the farthest shelf, books of local interest, and said it could be there. I walked past some reading nooks and began to scan the books on the shelf. As I read the spines, and their labels, I began to feel that thrill you could only get browsing in person, when you might discover something else, something entirely unlooked for.

I found a volume of old pictures of the town, and a book, *Main St. Through the Years,* but not the book I was seeking. I kept looking between the two books that should have, by their call numbers, flanked it, eyes moving between one and the other.

"Hey," the librarian said, softly and suddenly behind me. I almost jumped out of my skin. "The name sounded familiar," she continued, "so I looked it up. A while back we sent a bunch of materials to the county, all under her heading, for an archive. You might be able to find it there, in the main library, in Cooperstown."

"Will you be taking those out?" she asked.

"What?" I said.

"Those books," she put her hand down on the few books I was cradling, and I felt their weight suddenly, pressing me to the floor.

"Yes," I said.

"Let's get you set up," she said. "Is it your parents' address, or . . . ?"

I left with the books, and a fresh library card.

Scientists say we are not out of the woods yet.

A young girl sitting at a desk in a halo of light pointed me down the hall to the brass elevator doors when I asked for the archives.

Chapter
59

A T THE COUNTY SEAT, the main buildings were housed at the center of a large pedestrian mall. Old-style electric trolleys moved along tracks from the flanking lots. I rode to the center, then hopped off into a small, scattered crowd. The archives were in the back of the library, with its enormous wooden pillars and Greek-revival facade. Behind it was the same glass atrium that characterized the smaller library in the village, but this one towered a hundred feet up. Shapes of black crows flew here and there as images on the glass panes, to keep birds from crashing into them.

Tall wooden double-doors let me in to a dim hallway. On either side, rooms where people silently browsed shelves of books, let out bright white light. I heard the low murmur of someone reading from a picture book, and then children briefly chattering, then being hushed. A young girl sitting at a desk in a halo of light pointed me down the hall to the brass elevator doors when I asked for the archives.

As I walked I heard the voice of the reader coming through the open side door of the children's room, and it seemed so familiar that I stopped. As I was trying to place it, I felt the floor vibrate a little under my feet, and then a light found me. Another light glowed on the elevator. The floor vibrated again, and, getting the idea, I kept walking.

I appreciated that the former absurd and total militarization of our public places had been replaced with waves of gentle suggestion. When we strayed from the right path, it was enough to remind us.

I pressed the button, and the doors opened right away. Inside the old elevator, marble and brass, there was no indication of the floors, no buttons to press; I got in and it just sank, and went down a long time before slowing and coming to a stop. Then came a clear resounding tone, like a real bell physically struck in the darkness somewhere above, and the doors opened to a spotless white reception room.

A woman came to meet me from the secure area. She wore a crisp white uniform with white gloves, and her brown hair was secured in a bun by white clips. She reached out and shook my hand, and asked, "What will you see?"

Her brown eyes swam in circular glasses, and she had perfect white teeth all of almost the same size. Though I am not tall, I looked down at her face, and stepped back because she stood too close to me, in the center of the room. I felt the extreme strangeness of it, but I found myself telling her in great detail about how I came to my interest in Fanny Fraser.

She listened to it all, nodding at times. I showed her the card from the card catalog. She looked at it for what seemed like a long time, and returned it without comment.

To this day I am not sure what possessed me to unburden myself in such detail to a stranger. She listened like an angel, or like a kindly dog doing its best to understand and give comfort to the big dumb human in front of it, head tilted, eyes big. At last I said, having gone on too long, "And now I've come here, to see what the archive holds."

She nodded, said "Come on in and take a seat. Put on the gloves." She had them in one hand, soft cotton gloves I pulled on one at a time as we passed through an airlock with big climate-control doors, into a long room with cubicles on each side.

The people in them were hunched over big books, small books, old newspapers. Some were flipping through microfilm on big screens you could see just a bit of as you passed. So many purpose-built things had returned, more efficient, secure, and useful than that handful of universal devices, guzzling power and twisted through Rube Goldbergian contortions to bend the will of silicon and electrons when a simple lens, and knobs, and screen, and light did the trick.

Our dreams were not given up willingly, but at the very gates of death, in defiance of the world. One thought sometimes of the billionaires with their rockets, and wondered if they had got, after all, what they had long wanted, in leaving, or had all died in some sterile corner of Mars. Some still insisted we should prepare for an onslaught of their robot-armies, from hidden perches on airless rocks in space—but there had been no sign of them for years. Maybe they were gone for good.

I waited in the cubicle she left me at, after signing my name to a pad. The walls were gentle gray. The click and whir of microfilm devices, the exaggerated sound of turning pages, the scraping of pen on paper, and a low hum of ventilation, made up the sonic ambiance, along with my own breathing. I must have fallen asleep. When she touched me on the shoulder, I started. I was all soggy and pins and needles.

She had a banker's box in her hands but held it too high, as if it was weightless, empty. It was. She set it down on the desk, took the top off, and we both looked down into it, bowed over it, a little archival prayer. Nothing. She whispered to me and made signs, expressing that she was as surprised as I was. She motioned for me to come back out, so as not to disturb the researchers.

"This is most odd," she said.

"I am beginning to think it's all some kind of elaborate hoax," I replied, gently. "I couldn't find anything about this Fanny character online, either."

"No," she said, "she exists, I myself have looked at these materials, before."

"Were they stolen?" I asked.

"Well," she said, "they're most certainly gone."

"The money gone, the body gone, and now her story gone—strange."

Chapter
60

"T HEN," I ASKED HER, "what do you know? Do you have some time to tell me?" I looked at my watch; it was now just after noon. "Can I take you to lunch?"

"Come into the break room," she said. "I'm Emily. We can chat over coffee and cider doughnuts. They're good, fresh, local." Of course, everything was local—more or less—these days, but I appreciated the regional spirit. "I had a late breakfast," she continued, by way of explanation.

"Nice to meet you," I said. "Lead the way."

The break room was accessed with a palm scan against the flat, white wall, which swung outward, and carried us in. Everything was crisp and in order. No crumbs. She pressed for coffee, in a niche in the wall, and the doughnuts were, as advertised, fresh. She explained her boss picked them up every morning during apple season.

I asked about Fanny Fraser, and about the archive.

"I'm surprised there's nothing online," she said. "Fanny was a prominent citizen, although more infamous than famous I guess.

"Still," she continued, "we never heard about her in school. I know what I know from the archive and talking to people—I have always been interested in local history.

"Fanny was a bright girl, excelled in school, but forced to leave. She liked the finer things: boys, and riding around in fast carriages," she said. "I read a bit of her autobiography, and there are some letters, a diary.

"I don't remember exactly when it was—sometime in the 1840s—she made her way, at 16, to New York City. Even though this area bustled more than now, you still couldn't beat

New York. I think it was that she met someone, a young man who had come up here for work.

"You see, in the late summer there were big harvests, time to pick the hops. There were also people coming up for the air, richer folks, to play croquet, and ride. Her parents were farm people and well off, but, I don't know how to say it, straightforward, staid, maybe dull. An uncle was a lawyer, I believe, maybe that's where she got her mind, this brilliance."

I dunked another doughnut into the coffee, it sucked up the dark liquid, softened, bits of brown sugar flecked off, drifting and twinkling on the surface a moment like stars. My hands were sugared, and my lips.

We were seated on white stools at a high table. Her legs didn't quite reach the floor. Emily stayed immaculately posed, and unsugared, as she talked. She could have been making it all up as she went. She was moving her thumb, with its short nail, a small black bruise underneath, in gentle circles over the first joint of her forefinger. The toes of her shoes wiggled back and forth as she talked.

"At any rate," said Emily, "and I am now approaching the first of two important points—no I guess it's three—in the life of Fanny Fraser, which really constitutes most of what I know, maybe what anybody knows.

"We don't have anything more than some bits of diary, and a coy, misleading, and extraordinarily abridged autobiography." Emily shook her head, and looked up over my shoulder for a moment. "I'm sorry, I'm a little distracted—too much sugar." Then she smiled to herself. "Sorry, the commentary was so biased and dismissive. The editor was a horse's ass.

"Fanny," she continued, "had slid into 'the world's oldest profession,' as that 'scholar' had sneered. It was respectable sex work. She grew a distinguished clientele, and became 'the special woman,' at 23, of one of the most powerful of Boss Tweed's men, a chap named Sickles, who took a four-year break from a life of graft and official crime to lead a number of successful campaigns against the rebels, and rode in triumph through the arch at Grand Army Plaza with general's stripes, with a shining sword and gold spurs.

"I suppose he was a thorough scoundrel, not just wicked, but a real bad man through and through. He was good to Fanny, though. By now, she was a madam in her own right, a property owner, and rich. Somewhat through the aid of Sickles, but I believe some of her own success must have rankled a man who wanted to own her.

"At this time, she was engaged in legal pursuits, the plaintiff in a number of suits—violation of contract, defamation—which have only partially passed into the record, but what has survived is that she represented herself, and that in each case she was awarded judgments of varying size, attaining something like vindication.

"Fanny was then a prominent citizen, and surrounded by a coterie of young and wealthy admirers. She had a magnetic personality—some claimed hypnotic. She traveled to Europe with Sickles, and was presented once to Queen Victoria. I like to think of that proud, prudish monarch—fat, Teutonic, and slightly pickled—receiving with honor the curtsy of a whore.

"But on her return to New York City, something changed. Sickles sought out a younger girl. Not yet 30, Fanny made a marriage to a kind of milquetoast, a quiet, retiring, balding widower, a merchant, big in barrel staves. They honeymooned at Niagara Falls, where a daredevil in a barrel— made of oak planks this William Larch provided—went over, and survived."

Emily took a sip of coffee. After the sip, she touched the corner of her lips with her pinkie finger, and absently rubbed down her lower lip before letting her hand slip back to the table.

"Now, the last, the final, the tragic act. Larch's children, one of whom is residing in Fanny's old hometown, near here —"

"I know it," I said. "My hometown too."

"Well, they are concerned she's after his money. But they didn't know his 'empire' was built on a foundation of sand.

In the panic of 1873, he is revealed as a bankrupt. Fanny, however, is rumored to still be a millionaire. He lives on an allowance from her, puffing out his chest, and smoking cigars, and making a lot of noise.

"Yet his name begins to find its way onto contracts. He becomes director of this or that partnership. All of them just trails of paper, trusts of trusts. Much of the legal paperwork that survives bears the letterhead of her uncle's firm, her mother's brother, that of Jeremiah & Jeremiah.

"Then, in 1875, she dies. She is in her mid-40s. Only a few years older than I am.

"Well, the coroner's report is of apoplexy. The will gives it all to Larch. But her parents, still living, and a brother, demand a real autopsy. They get a kind of Sherlock Holmes— before Holmes—on the case.

"There is evidence brought up, the newspaper clippings are contradictory and hardly exact. Poison. Suspicious conversations had by all, but some pointing to the ruined husband, others his scheming children. There is a new hearing. It's all buried. And so is she. With great solemnity, and only those few people at her grave, the new family, the parents, the crusading brother and his detective, the uncle, and then, the papers report, a few mysterious 'Continentals,' dark, with shifty eyes, who melt away.

"All of it 'sheer poppycock' to our friendly scholar, who ought to know. And the money? The millions? Completely disappeared. The enormous marble tomb was repossessed, and her body moved to the pauper's section, I guess it was a narrow trench with a wooden cross. It's a highway now.

"The money gone, the body gone, and now her story gone—strange."

I agreed. We ate another doughnut each in silence. I had the chills. Then Emily jumped up and scraped her stool back loudly under the table.

"Back to the salt mines," she said.

"Be seeing you!" I gave her a little salute.

But just before Emily, the archivist, was swallowed back up by her pristine world, I called to her, "Hey!" I had one more thing to ask.

She tapped her watch, it was a blank circle, optic white, with no hands or any other indication of the time, and then shrugged—she didn't have any more time. I ran up to her before she could disappear.

"Listen," I said, "Emily, thank you for all your help. I know this is far fetched, but do you know of any connection between Fanny Fraser and a kind of Masonic Lodge type of secret society, something called the Order of L.E.F.?"

Emily pursed her lips. "I don't really know of any connection," she said, "but it's strange you mention L.E.F., there was one of those in the town I grew up in. I've never seen or heard of any others."

"Oh?" I said.

"Yeah," said Emily, "back in Elmira. A strange little apartment just off Main St., with these weird, scale-like mullions in the windows. They had a sign hanging until some kids knocked it off its chain, I remember passing it every day, The Sacred Order of L.E.F.

"I always wondered," she continued, "why none of the adults thought it was odd, or talked about it. I suppose it was just a thing that had always been there. They never put the sign back. But sometimes, I would see a light in the windows.

"I'll be honest, I hadn't thought about it in years. Well. Now you can find out something, and come back and tell me." She smiled, tapped her watch again, and passed through the automatic doors.

Looking back I saw the white contrail line of the day's single regional flight to the midwest ascending almost straight up.

Chapter
61

WHEN I GOT BACK to my parents' I pulled out Dad's old atlas. I had found it in a cardboard box in the basement. You could see patterns on a paper map that the phone maps, in their earnest, singular desire to get you somewhere, kept at bay. Elmira had a larger dot than other places in the area. I cast back my memory, and recalled that Mark Twain had spent many summers there writing in a cottage on his wife's family's land. He had become a novelist in Elmira—not on the Mississippi river, but overlooking the Chemung, a small tributary of the Susquehanna.

Much like Utica, it was a canal city, a transportation hub for boat, rail, and cart.

I took the long drive one morning.

You headed west and then began to drop. Directly below the middle Finger Lake, nearly into Pennsylvania territory. What had been rolling pastures for dairy cows were now orchards, with row on row of juvenile trees, alternating with solar farms and small assembly points and warehouses dotting the new train lines. As I drove, endless behemoths of freight, raw materials, shivered on rails beside the road as they shot onward.

Meanwhile, you could see teams of neon-yellow-clad workmen and women almost every mile, at public works, building rock walls, adding road barriers, and digging animal crossings. They were putting in new rail, and low-energy sensors. They were a swarm, like bees, preparing us for the onslaught of time, of the still changing climate.

Planting trees too, and digging out wetland, knocking buildings down, or taking their bricks. It sometimes seemed disorganized, but so does a colony of ants, and they have been quite successful.

I heard a crack, and looking back saw the white contrail line of the day's single regional flight to the midwest ascending almost straight up. Aeronautics in the last decade had produced the giant, efficient rockets that could propel two thousand people to Chicago in an hour in a tight, towering parabola. Since the patchwork of thousands of flights had been cut down to dozens, the air had become clear, weather more tractable. I had taken one to Europe, a three hour trip, surprisingly relaxing. Many, though, took fast ships across the ocean, and I might do the same next time.

When I reached Elmira, it was slumped quietly along the river, all low brick buildings, with some attractive facades, featuring dates from the 1800s spelled out in darker brick. As I drove down Main St., there were few people out, some Amish, in dark clothes. There was a buggy parked in a big lot, the horse's head dropped in contemplation.

It was exactly as Emily described it. The same windows with their scale-like mullions. I tried the white front door, with its layers on layers of white paint, but found it locked. I grasped the knob and shook the door. The ground floor window was dusty, clouded, dark. I couldn't see in; blue paper covered the glass on the inside.

As I was making a ridiculous spectacle of myself, hopping up and down like a hyperactive child, trying to see over the top of the concealing paper, I heard someone clear their throat and spun around, surprised.

I was doubly surprised, as well as unsettled, to discover a Mark Twain–looking fellow, with white hair and mustache, and eyebrows that shot out toward me like exotic caterpillars. He said, "Son, what are you doing?" He was pointing in my direction with a stubby cigar.

What was I doing?

"Do you know anything about this place?" I asked.

Twain, whoever he was, was dressed in sweats, with "U of LIFE" in big collegiate letters on the front of the shirt.

"Are you lost?" he said. "You look lost."

I craned my neck and looked up at the top floor. "There was one of these in my hometown," I said. "I always wondered about it."

"No idea at all what you're talking about," Twain said, but his smile said different.

I waited to see what would happen next. Like so much in life that's disappointing, it was nothing. We both stood there for a minute more. There was something grim, now, and determined, in his look. Utopia, it was surprising to discover, was suffused with an undercurrent of violence. So was nature, but even worse was the society that came before. It was a necessary evil, but it was fair, I suppose.

Yes, fair. I gave him a salute, and turned away. It seems he was some kind of watcher, a venerable djinn, conjured up out of the gritty sand caught in the cracks of the sidewalk to watch over the place. Across the street, in an upper window, a naked mannequin with a vacant, painted face seemed to be peering down at me with an air of derision.

I took the long way home, stopping in Ithaca. I had a hunch, and drove through the crooked streets twisting and turning by the lake, the old brick buildings at the feet of the gorges, where train tracks once let goods flow into barges and the reverse. After a disappointing hour, I turned onto one side street, and looking up, at the very end, saw what I had been expecting to find. Another secret lodge.

If I told you that there were five-hundred such meeting rooms spread across the older cities of twenty different states, would you be surprised?

I have seen a map, now, and a roster listing each one, and the records of secret accounts, and names of caretakers, and deceased members, and, several decades ago, their strange, slow return to life.

"Are you lost?" he said. "You look lost."

Chapter
62

"DEAREST FANNY," was how the letter opened, the one written in such a careful hand in June's box. I had carefully unfolded it and started to read. It was slow going. The handwriting was elegant, yet cramped to save space, and the pen had sputtered here and there, obliterating letters entirely. I hadn't had much practice reading cursive. And to save space, the second half of the message was written over the first, at a 90 degree angle. The words flowed over each other with seemingly no interaction. Ships in the night. But I stopped, from time to time, to marvel at unintentional felicities, as the crossing of related words, like "love" and "light" and the conjunction of names and places, as Loudon and Toronto, as though the letter writer intended for them to cross there, forming a kind of portal where two places could exist together in the same space and through which one could walk between them.

"Dearest Fanny,

"I regret that I am so long in answering your letter of the 1st of July, it being now November, but the mails have been much delayed as of late here, owing to some unscrupulous contractors who have been stashing for weeks or months some portion of the letters as may have in the same assortment communications related to various business dealings they have been bribed to postpone or unsettle. This all having come out quite recently, as having happened more than a number of times, in a great trial resulting in the conviction of many men for fraud and disturbance of the post, with the hidden caches of letters recovered by postal inspectors, or leather mailbags asserted lost found by trappers in the wilderness beside cold streams. I worry that more of your correspondence has not reached me here in Toronto—victim to the fact that the mails from the south are mingling with those coming up the St. Lawrence lately from Europe."

So far, this seemed fairly weak for a love letter, which is what I had initially thought it must be, with the lock of hair and all. But what do I know?

"But I treasure," it continued, "every letter of yours that has arrived, as I treasure our connection, and the services you have done for me, from the care you showed to make me lettered and read, with so many intervening kindnesses, and that last kindness of which we won't speak, of which it would be imprudent to speak. You are a light in my life.

"You may recall that I intimated in an earlier letter that I had planned to embark on a venture to the northwest, a venture of collecting pelts, and how you implored me not to take on such a danger. In this, that it was dangerous, you were entirely correct. I have no need to tell you the kind of characters I encountered, both fellow-trappers and natives, neither satisfied with my position; yet, it was necessary, and the result was a thorough success.

"I have established myself in independence, and with the proceeds have set up a small dry-goods shop in the city center. While there is much prejudice against the color of my skin, mostly I am rewarded for my hard work, and good prices, and there is far less danger here than on the other side of the lake of being dragged back to slavery. I have to tell you something, however.

"In Loudon's Grove, you were a savior to me. But we were young, and both lacking in experience. The feelings I felt, and those that you felt were complex. I regret none of our actions, but they were confused. Surely, now, you understand, from your own life experience, how power over someone and affection can be intermixed, muddled. Do you see why I have to be my own man, and why I cannot accept a new servitude that accepting your endless generosity would represent? I love you, but it is the love of a brother.

"I am entrusting this letter not to the mail, but into the capable hands of Mr. Jeremiah. He is returning with the too-generous gift I could never accept. It is the only way that I can repay the gift you already gave: the gift of freedom—to be myself, and stand by myself. But know that I owe you everything,

"Forever yours, etc. etc.

"Hiram."

"MY DEAREST HIRAM,"

So the second letter began. This is the letter I had long been searching for. That I found only recently, the one I knew would impress Tiffany. It was the right hand to Hiram's letter's left. It was the second half of the face; it was, perhaps, the darkness. Or was it the light?

"I nearly burned your letter, it was, at first, so hateful to me. I am sorry. It's hard to have the truth shown to your face, to look into a mirror of words. I carried it against my heart for weeks, felt it burning my skin. I had thought that I loved only you, all these years, but, finally, I see, and I thank you for your patience in instructing me: I loved myself, was proud of myself, and replaced one sin, with another. Lust, for pride.

"Forgive me.

"But I am afraid it's recognition that comes too late. I perceive, and cherish your thanks and your everlasting affection. So I preserve the letter which burns no more, but warms, when everything around me has gone cold, and in it, that tiny lock of my young hair—you know the one, the thing that started it all—a memento, a reminder that I was, once, foolish, free, and when it mattered most, brave.

"All that I have done, all that I have amassed, was meant for you. I think you can't have imagined what a blow it was to have it rejected, even as just as your rejection was—You would say I should keep it for myself, and for my people, but in all these years, I have no one but you, and a sufficiency to establish my sister's son, and as for me, I need only a little, and what I have is enough for ten lifetimes.

"Again, I ask you to forgive me, this sin of pride, which I now have twice over, pride in myself, and pride in you. And I ask you not to censure what I have done with the money, even to enjoy it: I have made for us a lasting monument. And for them, an altar of lasting shame. Is it enough to have those who were and would be your captors unwittingly celebrate you? Pledge their lives for you? Even Mr. D—, remember him? His merciless countenance, his one drooping eye, has mouthed the 'secret formula' and confessed his earthly shame.

"These men are mad for joining, mad for me, and for some different world, even if I've made it up from whole cloth, as a lark. Mr. Jeremiah assures me by Spring there will be a chapter in every major city and all its top citizens will be accreting by way of tithes their resources to mine. Some of it will make its way to support abolition, the balance will keep this strange monument going, will keep it growing—one day, I wonder, if someone will take the keys to its locks, and do something more with it. Until then, it is enough to humiliate and abase the country's 'best' men.

"Until we meet again,

"Fanny."

Did they meet again? I don't imagine so. And this strange monument, this social machine? I had a hunch about who took up the keys.

Chapter
63

I TRY TO IMAGINE what my life would have been like had I been able to commit to something, to stop circling life like a moth around a lightbulb, flitting in and out, a tiny insect, making big shadows; to have been able to be myself, living. I would have held on to June, or let her hold on to me, or if it wasn't June, I would have opened up to one or another of the women who had come to me and said, without saying, let's make a go of it.

Of course it's not so easy.

Everything is compromise. There is the steady job, which perforce has become a career. There are savings, and bursts of creativity wrested from few idle moments. We accrete a life together. It weighs, but also protects. It is not without mystery or seduction. It is, in fact, more romantic than all the years of lonely adventure.

YOU HAD, TIFFANY THOUGHT, to have the ability to strip away the surface of everything that surrounded you down through the ages. To break the concrete curb, shatter it into its conglomerate sand and lime, whisk it down to bedrock, and build up the dirt, the big quarried slabs of bluestone, to put the granite carriage steps back, even to fill in the wear from leather boots over time, the concave surfaces flattening, hard stone against the palms of her slender hands.

Only against the pale granite did she think of her skin as dark, almost brown, or at night when James had held her small frame against his cream-white torso. She knew that he had fetishized the differences between them; her dark skin, her rounded features, and him—this bland, blond tower of flesh. She preferred the stone, after all, she had learned. First with

Mr. Jeremiah, who was, to her, truly exotic, and then for herself, as she took the reins of a practice older than America.

Yes, you had to slice off the asphalt from the street like you were flaying the village. The dirt below, you imagined packed and covered with a fine powder, bits of straw, horse dung. The ruts of carts and hoof, and bootprints. Across the street some men on the porch of the general store are leaning against oak barrels. One spits tobacco into a brass urn. Now you could play it all forward to this moment, to Tiffany sitting out front of the cafe. The coffee is bad, but enough sugar made it palatable to her.

The blonde girl in the apron, who brought it, would have been back at the counter, staring at her through the window once, but there have been many immigrants of late. An Indian couple have been tasting the same wretched coffee and peeling apart sticky buns, simply to be out on Main Street, as Tiffany was, enjoying the autumn sun. Unlike Tiffany, they were used to warmer weather, and now swaddled in sweaters and scarves, each of them topped with a wool cap. Tiffany could have been in her shirt-sleeves.

Tiffany could follow time across its long track and then watch it pass her, and see the street change again. If you couldn't see the past as it was, and how the present came to be, you couldn't imagine a future, and if you didn't imagine the future, Mr. Jeremiah had always said, you couldn't direct yourself into it. And so she had done.

So here she was, nowhere, but in a way the center of everything. As the right hand for her client, and on a task which no one lesser could be trusted with, and because, in no small part, it interested her, she made the forty mile trek through the Mohawk Valley to this cafe, and, glancing down at her silver watch, saw the ornate black arrow touch 11, and looked up to see who it was who would come toward her from the municipal lot beside the old stone bank. It was me.

What impression I made, I don't know. Tiffany never volunteered that information. As for me, I saw her at the second table, in a smart herringbone suit and extra large sunglasses. Her face was slightly round, with a tight, tiny mouth. She was holding the coffee with two hands, and drinking it as if she were French, taking a café au lait from a bowl. A blueberry muffin sat on a plate in front of her, with a single small bite out of it. The muffins were dry.

I knew her immediately from the description in the letter I had received that morning. Handwritten letters, delivered anywhere shortly after they were written, once would have seemed at the point of extinction. But the post office had been a cornerstone and guarantor of our democracy in the 19th century. After the unraveling of encryption brought on by quantum computing, and the general distrust of the internet for the most vital communication, followed by a massive expansion of the postal service to administer public banking and welfare, and the promise of total commitment to confidentiality, coupled with unheard-of delivery speeds, well, the bonded letter from the law office of Jeremiah & Jeremiah was in my hand the morning it was sent.

How she knew I would open and read it and get to the village where she waited for me, I cannot say. That I would open it was guaranteed, since junk mail did not exist as such, and the envelope was addressed to me in elaborate calligraphy. I nodded to the letter carrier, who was back on his motorized bicycle before I had slid my finger to break the red wax seal holding the heavy, satin envelope together.

My attendance, it said, at the cafe in town, giving the address, for a meeting with Tiffany Ho, Esquire, was required, at 11 AM, today. It was a meeting I would welcome, in that it would provide "at last, the information I had been seeking" and though it had left out "awkwardly," or "ineffectually," somehow I knew it was implied. Tiffany would have a saddle-colored valise. And so she did.

"Thank you," she said, "for coming."

"Of course," I told her, and sat. "A coffee," I told the waitress who was by my side immediately. I thought I might know her, but she didn't know me. I turned to ask for milk, but she was already gone.

"Do you know June?" I asked.

"Do I?" she said. She smiled. Why was everything so hard, so cryptic.

"I've been looking for her," I said.

"I know," said Tiffany. "One could hardly avoid learning that information."

"I don't really understand," I said, "any of it."

She took a sip of coffee.

"No one does," she said. "No one."

"The letter said you had information."

"In a way," she said.

The waitress brought my coffee. I thanked her, and took a sip. "What way?"

"You have the key," she said.

I did have the key, it was in the pocket of my jacket. I took it out, holding it up to her. The golden, serpent-headed key from June's box.

"This key?"

"That is the key," she said.

"You have the key," she said.

I was a fly buzzing against the window. I was the ice settling.

Chapter
64

I MET TIFFANY AGAIN, later, after everything that transpired, as you know. She laughed hard at how absurdly gnomic she had been, then. We were in Utica, in an old Italian restaurant.

"Surprised?" she had asked about the place, I suppose assuming I would have thought we'd be meeting in a different kind of restaurant. I told her I didn't make assumptions. She could really pack away the pasta. It had that light red sauce. She twirled the spaghettini around her fork, and only a stray end of the noodle remained a moment, flecked the corner of her cheek with sauce and disappeared. Tiffany took the thick white napkin and dabbed the spot away.

She took her work seriously. Her face grew serious, then. I told her that I was trying to collect information, to put into a book.

"Nobody will believe you," she said. "Nobody will believe any of it."

"I myself don't believe it," I told her.

"You want to write it out of existence? Is that it?"

"Not out of existence, but into some semblance of order. It's been like trying to hold on to a dream. The more I touch it, the more it recedes, like a mist, or a cat that won't be petted. That's why," I said, "I wanted to talk to you."

"You mean, am I real?"

She pounded the table with her hand, and the cutlery jumped. The water glass, filled with ice, and sweating, had jumped too, a little. Some ice water drops soaked into the tablecloth. Nobody stirred. The place was nearly empty for lunch, the windows dusty, and full of light. An old van slushed slowly by in the remnants of the recent early snow. Two waiters talked in low tones. I couldn't tell if it was Italian or Spanish or something else. Their black suits, and vests, and white shirts were all of a thin fabric, something synthetic, stain-proof. They looked like drawings of themselves.

"I'm no dream," she said. "Maybe you are."

I was a fly buzzing against the window. I was the ice settling. I was the faint scent of tobacco which would be stuck in the wood around us for a hundred years more. I was the little man in the dark glasses sifting through invoices in the back. The sudden light as a waiter burst through the saloon doors from the kitchen. The slow drone of words coming out of my own lips. The useless shrug.

After the waiter cleared our pasta, and the bread basket, and scraped the crumbs from the table, Tiffany and I sat across from each other, quietly. I asked her to tell me her story, at least how she thought it began.

"You should have the tiramisu, it's incredible."

We shared a plate; she wasn't wrong. I thought, this woman never is. She told me some of her story. Then she looked at her watch. "I have to go."

The waiter came to our table, and he made an elaborate show of tearing up the check into little pale-green and white confetti, which he let sprinkle onto the table.

"When can we talk again?"

"Maybe never," she said.

That was how it always was. Maybe never, but possibly next week. I think she liked teasing me; maybe she liked having someone else so closely bound to June, orbiting along with her.

Chapter
65

"**Y**OU HAVE THE KEY," she had said at the table at the cafe in Harmony Valley. Then without speaking, as I sat there, key in hand, the cold of it against my skin, that gold metal, that gothic gleam, she just waited for me to understand. It was minutes, longer. At last I did. She saw it on my face. "Go now," she said, "if you want to see her."

I stood up. I reached into my pocket and threw a few bills onto the table. They sat, pale pink where they fell, Rosa Parks looking up at me from behind her wire-rimmed frames. Imagine, before, how we had hung on so hard to the past; it was impossible to imagine such things as the tokens we exchanged for life's necessities changing with us. The sudden freedom of it, of the death of the greenback dollar and its ornate decoration, its pyramid and glowing eye, the cadaverous president of puffed out chin and powdered wig. I had not felt it before, but I felt it then. I might not have had to pay, but I assumed Tiffany did.

"WHAT DID YOUR FIFTH grade teacher say happens," asked Tiffany, reading this passage, "when you 'assume'?"

"Oh my god," I said, "I will never forget it. Did June tell you? Also his joke about doing laundry outside (it's better to do it 'in Tide'), and Al Veoli, shortstop for the 1957 Detroit Tigers and important component of our lungs. But, yeah: when you 'assume' you make an 'ass' of 'u' and 'me.'"

"I still have those bills." said Tiffany, "They're some of the last money I ever saw. I didn't have to pay. I hadn't had to pay in a long time. Though, like all of us, I've paid a lot.

"Anyway, you need an end," she said.

"This is it," I said. "This is the end."

"Do you find it plausible?" she asked.

"Is anything?"

I STARTED TO WALK ACROSS the street, but as soon as my foot hit the opposite side, I broke into a full-on run.

This running was ludicrous. What would it gain me? Seconds? And to be there huffing and puffing, brow sweaty. My heels hurt.

The front door was open. Lucky—I hadn't even thought of the possibility that it might be locked to me. I was at the end of the hallway in a moment. It echoed with the clopping of my shoes. I sounded like a horse, galloping ahead of myself. I took the stairs, with their short risers, three a time.

I stopped at the door, bent double, wheezing.

Out of shape, buddy.

Here, nothing had changed: The low lights were burning orange, like torches. The key found the center of the lock. I turned it. Heard and felt the heavy click. I twisted the center knob, its scrollwork raised in my palm. The door sank away from me and the secret room swallowed me up.

Chapter
66

O N THE OTHER SIDE of the door, in the darkness, loomed the bulk of the aged Clyde Duane, like a mountain emerging from the fog, an old idea that wouldn't come unstuck.

He had a clipboard, like he was taking attendance; how he could read from it in this gloom is anyone's guess. There was something milky about his eyes, I thought, though who could tell. He was making this low sound to himself, like a dreaming cow. It joined with some noise piercing the curtain, all insect-like and uncomfortable. I wondered if I was dreaming. Haven't you had moments where you couldn't, suddenly, recall how you had gotten to where you were, or what had come before?

"Why do you lie so much?" he said.

"Excuse me?"

"Everything evil you've done is known," he said.

"What?"

"Think back, is there something different you could have done? How is it you have ended up here?"

"What the fuck, Mr. Duane?" I asked. (You don't refer to the shadowy ogre in your life by his first name.) I had my hands on the desk in a posture of aggression. If it was a dream, its furniture felt solid.

"Oh, nothing," said Clyde Duane, "nothing but formalities. It's just to mess with you."

He turned his wrist, which was naked and covered with white hair, and peeked at it as if he wore a watch.

"You're early," he said. "Name?" he said. "Age?" he said. "Place of birth?"

"You know all about me, don't you?" I said.

"No, no," he said, low, "we have to do it official."

There were noises in the other room. They were growing louder and louder. I think I heard wailing. But it all still seemed so far away, which was impossible since the room only extended thirty feet or so beyond the curtain. Fine. I answered him.

The first question had been like a sandbag to the heart. Why had I lied so much? I gave a noncommittal, evasive answer. He continued. Duane bungled it, though, if he was trying to drive me to insane terror. The second question struck, but the third was sheer annoyance. Now I was at the DMV, filling out a form.

"Okay, all set," he said, when we had finished. Then he closed his eyes, and went slack. His whole body became restful, and I could see his hulking shoulders relax into deep breathing. Then he put one big hand to his face and I heard the snap and hiss of an inhaler. He took two or three deep drags and slumped again.

For a while it was all silence but his heavy breath. Then he started to wheeze. It was laughter. His eyes were closed, from what I could make out. "Heh heh heh." Then amid some incoherent muttering, I made out a single sharp word I understood: "Knife!"

"What?" I said, involuntarily.

"Oh," he said, and his eyes opened. "Remember Mrs. Kane? Sweet quiet Mrs. Kane." He paused. Started again, "No jury in the world, and they didn't either . . . said he was snoring all the time . . . but of course, people knew he hadn't been a kind man . . . put five inches of steak knife in his back, up to the brown wooden handle. Well when it was over, and she stood up free, looked at the evidence table . . . 'I want it back, it's part of a set.' Heh heh heh!"

On the last laugh, the curtain flew open and two sets of arms picked me up out of the chair, dragging me into the light. It was similar to the earlier initiation in the gymnasium: a robed figure above the altar, two guards on either side.

"Who will speak for the prisoner?"

This time, there was no one to speak for me.

"What do you have to say for yourself?"

Beside me, from out of nowhere, rose figures in red and black. They pointed. I cleared my throat. I had lost my line.

"I have always," I said, "done my very best." I knew it wasn't good enough the minute the words died in my mouth.

"His very best!" the figures roared. Laughing. There was no one to stand for me, no sudden reprieve. Only shame. How was the room so big?

I fell down to my knees. The judge stepped down from the altar, directly over me.

I felt a hand on the back of my head.

"Your very best," she said. "It wasn't that good, was it?"

"No."

"It's okay, it's the same for everyone."

The robes flew off, the lights came up, the folding chairs were still in the corner, we were all in street clothes. And the great and powerful judge, was slight, kind, weird, and flighty June.

"Why do you lie so much?"

Chapter
67

"W ELL," SAID JUNE, as I stood up, shakily, "you've almost made it through the initiation, at last. Only one thing is left."

She took me by the hand. Her hand was warm, and I remembered, suddenly, each of the "first times" I had held it, once by accident, a second time, at her volition, the third in New York, at mine. Now, a last time, after so long, she took it, but I had been holding my hand out since she disappeared, waiting, not knowing for what. We came up to the desk, where there was a big old ledger. She turned back the pages, name and signature, name and signature, until some point in the middle, and there, carefully written in ink, were the names of the first few friends who had come up to this secret place. All had since signed, except me.

"You can only go through life so far," she said, all those around us us watching, and now Tiffany came to her side and put an arm around June's waist as she spoke, "without signing your name in some book. Let it be this one."

I had a pen in my hand, a fountain pen, with its dagger-tip split, so I brought it down, and made the loops of my name, the line diverging where I pressed too hard, and then took on a bubble of ink. June blotted it and then a cork popped. You couldn't really call it champagne, since the climate had changed and there was no champagne anymore, but you fought back against the falling world, holding up what bits you could, and such a thing was sparkling wine. I wasn't in any state to sip so I downed mine in a quick gulp. This triggered a sputtering, coughing fit. Then I downed another, and was feeling good.

Everyone was there, only Ryan excepted. We had lost Alaska in part to the Russians. It was not practicable to keep, really. But now here I was, returned. Perhaps he would too. There were Brian, and Aaron, and Max. Alice, who had sat in front of me in class, now with salt-and-pepper hair. Matthew was there, even, looking lost, but steady. And Eric beside him. Then others whom I had seen before, and ought to know. It became a party, people circulating, and I found myself making small talk, or descending into odd reminiscences. Alice and I stood in awkward silence, and all I could muster was, "You look well, it's good to see you." It had been a lifetime, and we had never really been close.

The room was like a big wheel, and I felt myself as a fixed point on a ring, moving against it all, until I managed to grab on to June. She was standing where she had been, by the desk, hand on the green fabric blotter. She and Tiffany greeted me both.

"So," I said, "you've been here the whole time?"

"Oh no," said June, "I've been here and there, I've been traveling so much lately. Wherever it is that I'm needed. How is old Wiggins?"

"She's good, I think," I said. "You remember Sherlock? The piper? Well, she ended up bonding with him . . . I had to let Wiggins go so I could come looking for you."

"I didn't ask you to leave and come find," said June. "But I'm happy for old Wiggins."

"She's not even that old," I said.

"Old soul, at least."

"Of course you wanted me to look for you, why vanish otherwise? It was another of your quests."

"I guess," she said. "But if it was, what did you really find? I haven't been lost. I know where I've been all the time."

"I haven't found myself, if that's what you're insinuating." I said. But maybe I was wrong. "I haven't found a home," I said. But maybe I was wrong.

"Okay," she said.

"I never realized how like to this," I meant our old club, "that the Movement was," I said.

"Like to?" she said. "Like to?"

Tiffany looked hard at me and she said, "Yes, they're very like."

"You should sue," I said.

We all laughed, and then I turned my head, toward the entrance. There was no trace of Clyde Duane, the curtain had been taken down, the table and chair were gone. "Mr. Duane," I said and jerked my head back to the front.

"Yes," said June. "Old faithful. You know he gets paid for it, regular, and has no truck with the goings on."

"No truck?" I said. "You've been infected with something old-fashioned."

"I don't know how," said June, "when everything around us is so new."

I looked around, and every surface belied her. But I knew what she meant.

"Love," said Tiffany to June, "I have to go: that thing we discussed. I'll see you later." She peeled off from us and disappeared.

I watched her leave, then turned back to June. "Love? Are you two . . . ?"

"It didn't start like that," she said.

"It never does. I had no idea you went in for that sort of thing," meaning being attracted to women. I shouldn't have been surprised.

"You didn't? I think you did," she said.

"I guess maybe I did."

The party chatter had stopped. Only the ice, melting in the ice bucket, was sounding, cracks and pops. Little icebergs, breaking up and floating away into the swelling ocean. People saying their goodbyes, leaving in ones and twos.

"It's time!" said June, loudly. She put her hand on my shoulder, and led me to the front of the room. Now they all welcomed me, as an official pledge of the group. There was a final ritual. We did it in full solemnity, with no error.

Later, I was told these rituals, if not done entirely without mistake, would be repeated again and again until all had done their parts correctly, and this could take an hour or more. I was thankful everyone had been on their game, and mine was done in ten minutes. I buttoned my shirt back up, and then June raised her arm, and we all followed her out into the early night.

"Listen," she said, when we were out on the sidewalk, as everyone dispersed. In a minute no one would have known we had gathered at all. "Why don't you come over to the farm tomorrow, and we can take a walk, and chat about the past."

"Yes!" I said. "Yes."

"You can only go through life so far without signing your name in some book. Let it be this one."

"So that's what you know," she said. "What do you guess?"

Chapter
68

I T HAD SNOWED—something that used to be regular in
November—and now it was melting. All the tall grass was
matted down with it. The ground squelched as you walked.
I had on brown boots, waterproof, the water beaded up on
them. My feet were warm in wool socks and silk liners. I
followed a little behind June.

We saw June's mother for a minute, as if we had been
teenagers, as if she were checking on us before letting us get
back to necking. Instead we sat drinking hot chocolate that
came from packets about five years past their expiration date. It
was a little bitter. Off.

We made small talk about the weather, the house. Then
June got up and I followed her, our empty cups left on a little
wicker table on the porch as we moved into the field and up the
ridge. June's mother would have come out to take them up. We
kept going until we would have appeared to sink inch by inch
into the grass. Then, like ships sailing over the horizon, the tips
of our masts disappeared. June walked without even looking
forward. She kept turning to me—I would see a big stone
coming, one of those boulders shaggy with lichens the glaciers
had dropped, and I would open my mouth to warn her, but
before I could speak, she would veer away.

"What do you know?" she said.

"I put a few things together," I said. "I know a few
things, and other things I suspect."

We were coming into a valley, where a bunch of scrub
still had some dark green leaves, and there were islands of
snow, all corned, and melting, water puddles reflecting the
grass and a bit of white sky. The earth seemed to be breathing
up a mist; we could have been walking straight into a cloud.

She was quiet, so I started to tell the story, as I knew it, or thought I did.

"Well, I know that there is a secret society. It's been around since the mid-1800s, and it was founded here, I think. You followed Clyde Duane to it, and had a thought. What is a secret society that has lost its society altogether, and is only going through the motions? It is an idling machine, waiting to be engaged. Somehow, you found the key. It must have been in the books. I think it must have been something you knew, and something you had. Otherwise, someone else would have found out and done what you did."

"Sure," said June.

"When we were young, I didn't really think about what it meant to unlock that door, into the space. It was a place to act and play. But it must have come with resources. And you learned, I guess, learned you could move people, organize them. I was too preoccupied rooting myself in old books to really understand. But then what?"

We came to a brake of sumac, some black leaves still clinging, dead, to the branches, like withered pennants. A rabbit hopped out of the thicket of blackberry thorns. It hadn't shed its brown for white, yet.

It stopped, panting, glassy-eyed, its ears folded back onto its body as it crouched, deciding what to do. I shifted my weight from one leg to the other and the rabbit ran, crazily, in an arc, and after a few vertiginous moments, disappeared. A crow cawed. Then another. "So that's what you know," she said. "What do you guess?"

"Well I know, also," I said, "that you somehow kept things going here, despite moving all over. I think of your comings and goings now, and I can't really imagine the scale of it: five-hundred chapters, each with its building, its warehouse, its caretaker, its accounts. Maybe regional lawyers, at old firms, taking the interest and contracting out for a paint job, a locksmith, to keep the gears oiled. Perhaps a single person performing a single candlelight ceremony, and then cleaning up. A hundred thousand, or a million dollars, invested in safe assets, growing slowly over time . . . " I trailed off.

We started walking again, both of us at once, without any kind of communication, just some connection at a deeper level, moving us together, like cars on a track. I looked back. You could see our footsteps in the snow, and then the long patches of grass, then footsteps again.

At last they mingled with the distinctive track of the rabbit, looking like ": = … : = … : =."

I thought of them as a sort of code. I said, with my head tilted toward it, "It's a message."

"Everything's a message, but we can't read it," she said.

"It says 'dit-dot-dit-dot-dit-dot.' Couldn't be clearer."

"Straight from the rabbit's brain to yours," she said.

"So I guess that the thing had something to do with your relative, Fanny Fraser, the one who so resembles you."

"Ah, you're wrong," said June. "You have the order reversed. It's easy to do. I resemble her!"

I stumbled. The ground here was uneven, sunk or slumped in rectangles or wide circles, here and there, all over.

"The residue," June commented, "of all the digging. All that senseless digging."

As we walked on, I saw at the edge of one field, which was bordered by some oaks, an old bucket loader. It was bright orange, with big spots of rust. Its shovel head was resting on the ground. There was a broken hydraulic tube and a cap of snow on its one-person cab. There were twigs stuffed in the treads. It was a great metal nest for all kinds of critters. The windshield was broken as if someone had dropped a large stone out of the sky.

"I guess that was the treasure your father and step-father had wanted to find. I mean, the society itself. There was never anything buried, no Tammany gold. Just stock certificates and some kind of secret code?"

"What else?" June asked as she led me on. I could hear a stream running. I thought of the black banks, all mud, and the dens of muskrats, and otters, and the small silver fish hovering in the cold water, darting this way and that, while old leaves and sticks shot by. The fish were like spirit-beings in that water, as though un-afflicted by time.

"So," I said, "I have been considering a few things recently. First, how closely our new initiation into citizenship resembles the initiations you and Brian designed. And there is the curious case of the blue smock, and the question of how the protests kept organized, and where they got their resources, and I have this feeling that a map of the first protests overlaid on a map of the Order's sites might look pretty similar. And then I feel kind of ridiculous.

"But I can't help wondering if it's possible for something so earth shattering, something so transformative, to have begun in a place like this, and initiated by one person."

I hadn't voiced this feeling before, even to myself. I had let the dots stay unconnected. "And what else?" she said. "What else?"

"When you visited me in college, not five miles from the offices of Jeremiah & Jeremiah, and Tiffany, was it me you were seeing, or was I the excuse?"

We reached the stream. A scattering of low spruce trees were struggling there, and the ground flattened out before dropping off, cut into banks by the water's meandering path. We followed the stream now, and I think the crows were following us. One landed on a nearby pine, and it was weight enough to make the tree's top bow a bit, shaking off some snow that shivered like sifted flour onto the net of fallen, brown needles below.

"What else?" she said.

It was a maddening refrain.

There was something on the ground, just before the short drop into the stream, flowing fast and full. It was a large fish, half-eaten; you could see its bones, and different layers of muscle, then the silver scales peeling back, like an anatomical model, or an illustration of the fish in three dimensions. Some worms were wriggling in it. I felt a little sick.

"Look at that!" she said. She was pointing away from the fish, to a small bush bright with red berries. There were many berries fallen, scattered on the ground. They were vermilion, and were as solid-looking as wood. The effect of them was like a spray of bright blood on the snow, a red crescent circling the bush. It looked like the birds wouldn't even eat them. It was the only color for miles. Even June and I were drably dressed.

"Poison," I said.

Fog had begun encroaching, so that I was having a hard time seeing where we had been, or where we were going.

"I ate two whole handfuls, thinking, I don't know what I was thinking—to get away," she said. "I couldn't keep it down, and afterward my stomach hurt something awful. Still here, though," she said. "Still here."

We walked farther, the ground rising. I could see fragments of old wall, and stacks of wood. There were holes dug and filled in here and there. And groundhog burrows. I almost turned my ankle in one.

"What else," she said, now to herself, though, not asking me, and then she began to talk. "I was a happy little girl, in Ohio. We lived in a small house. I had a small room and my dolly had a smaller room inside it, where she lived. We had a great dog, he was reddish, like a fox, small, some kind of terrier. He had wiry hair, and he liked to lie on the ground and put his chin on my leg while I colored.

"There was a small wooded area, and a stream, large corn fields, and soybeans. We used to walk and walk; I collected pine cones. Our dog was called 'Roger-not-Rover.' That was his full name, a family joke. My father, he was sweet. I remember, he always smelled like aftershave. He was a foreman at the factory, but he always liked to read. He was so smart, my father, at least that's what I remember.

"But it got him into trouble. He wouldn't watch the floor, and things would be missed. He began to detest work. He was obsessed with getting out of it. He tried lottery tickets, the race track, card games, inventions, investment schemes. Of course, none of it panned out. Then he found something, in Mother's things. It was about our family. I mean, her family. But things always came through the mother's line with us. So it was. So he found out about the million dollars, and the old homestead. So they came back.

"That was when 'Roger-not-Rover' ran away. I think everything turned after that. Everything for me, anyway.

"They fixed things up. It was a lot of work. But he was always looking for something. He'd break down the walls and rebuild them, but he'd sift through the debris like an archaeologist looking for sherds. He was thin, and he always had some sweat on his upper lip. He smoked. One day he was up in the attic, pulling things from their niche, making big piles. I had crept up there playing at spying when I saw him throw up one arm, and then he just fell over.

"I used to pretend he didn't die, that he had faked it so he could keep up his search in peace or whatever. It didn't make a lot of sense."

She stopped. We had come to the top of a hill. The fog was starting to lift a little. You could see this field sloping down to a line of circular hay bales wrapped in white tarps, coated canvas. They looked like marshmallows.

"Roger-not-Rover!" she yelled. "Roger-not-Rover!" On the top of the hill, I saw her as if she were young again, calling for her lost dog.

"Mom met Tim at a revival meeting, after Dad died. I don't know, maybe he had been at the funeral too. There were a lot of strangers there. At least people I'd never seen. I think Dad might have hired him to help dig. So he could have been looking for a way to hang around and look for the treasure. Tim loved Mom, I think. But I could tell he also lusted after me—it was not something he admired about himself, and he never acted on it. You know what a lot of failure and drink will do to that—turn that hate outward—Maybe I didn't help, I had a mouth, and was always insulting him."

"So he did hurt you," I said. "That bastard."

"Anyway," said June, "I found something in the barn. I had become interested in secret doors and passageways. I was always looking for them, though our house was as ordinary as any house that old could be, as ordinary as any house under a kind of curse, and in the process of regeneration."

"What do you mean 'a curse'?"

"Oh," said June, "I don't really know. But in the barn, at the base of one of the big wooden beams off the milking stalls, I found a seam in the wood. I picked at it with the jackknife I took from Dad's things before Tim got his hands on them. And when it popped out there was a box. And in the box were some letters, and an old tintype that looked like me.

"The letters were the key," she said. "The key to the treasure. I just didn't know it, quite yet."

"So it's true?" I said.

"Yes, Frances—Fanny had been funding this society, it took its motto from the French Revolution, and she bound its members to, well, to herself. Secretly, though, it was to her love, the ex-slave Hiram, and to freedom.

"It spread, and she took the money she made and shoveled it back in, to the tune of more than a million of dollars, a real fortune then. And when she died, it kept going on without her, candlelight meetings, cleaning, repairs, upkeep. But in a few generations it had died out, all except its immense inner works, the caretakers who kept things going.

"One of those letters I found was a key to the cipher that was her memoir, describing, well, not all of it, but enough. Others were bearer certificates, and code words. There was something magnificent, exciting about it all. What I didn't really understand is why Fanny made this thing, and what it meant, for her to be a Madame, to be the 'woman' of a man, or the cool, blue flame of hate that carried through her writing. I didn't really know, then.

"I get it now," she said, after a pause. "Now I do."

"But why didn't you tell me, then," I said, "or, ever?"

"Aren't I telling you, here and now?" she said. "It was Tiffany," she said, "that I met in Utica, and then I would come see you, or visit her after. She was the one who opened my eyes to what this thing could be."

"And to other things?" I felt a blaze of jealousy.

"That was later," she said. "Much later."

We were walking, I now realized, in a great circle, and were just now beginning to arc back toward the farmhouse. We had been gone less than an hour, maybe forty minutes.

"When you told me about Clyde Duane's key, did you know everything already?"

"It was only just beginning," she said. "A key. It's funny, it's so easy to mix up the key with what it opens. You can confuse the thing with the metaphor. I mean, I know I'm not making sense, but a key grants you authority, it gives you ownership, even if its not supposed to be yours, but a key is also a responsibility, a terrible responsibility.

"When I visited you in college, that was real. And in New York, it was real too, even if it didn't work," she said. "I'm sorry I told you that you let me down. You did let me down, but it wasn't all your fault. I took advantage of your nature, and I kept you as an escape. It was so easy with you to melt away from all that responsibility. I was letting myself down."

We walked on in silence for a while. We were both breathing deeply, and as we walked our breath caught the edge of the cold and came out like steam.

It was my turn to talk. "What now?" I said.

"Don't you mean 'what then'?" she said. "Don't you want to know how I brought the orders to life, some with young members, others recruiting men and women at their prime? How I got the idea for the blue smocks, and how Tiffany and I formulated a plan? How we took our resources and the biggest resource of all, society, and made this world?"

"I don't believe it, really," I said, even though, maybe, I did. "And why tell me now? Why initiate me now? Do you want to get rid of me?"

I thought of the dead fish, exposed on the bank, its innards excavated.

We had come to a little shack. I guess it was the spring house. It was still standing, all shaggy, peeling paint, yellow and white. A single window had been painted over, some chips showed the interior dark as night. I pictured myself at the bottom of the stone-lined cistern, with the water above me, frozen, like crystal. I was cold, too, dead I suppose.

"You never told me, what happened with Ryan and Tim," I said.

We kept walking. We were by the base of a tall hemlock, its trunk like a pillar, knobby but straight, imposing. There were three hemlocks here, and behind them the old family graveyard, with an old metal fence. The tombstones were crooked, chipped, fallen over. A stone in the shape of an angel was weathered almost beyond recognition.

June stopped at the gate, and looked in.

"It was an accident," she said. "It was in the barn. I was showing Ryan that tin box, the one I left for you.

"He walked in on us. He must have thought we were doing something else. Ryan's arm had been around me, and when we turned our faces were flushed. Tim grabbed my arm hard. I remember you saw the bruises."

"He tripped," I said, suddenly, "backward, and he hit something in the floor, right? It was an iron cleat, or an old nail. Is that it?"

"Or I pushed him," she said. "Or I pushed him. Just a shove with my other hand. He was unbalanced. Oh, it was terrible. All that blood. It was so dark. And it soaked into the wood. He gurgled once and he was dead. That mean, twisted expression stuck on his face."

"No one," I said, "would have convicted you."

"Don't be so sure. I mean, how could I have been sure? Ryan was terrified. Frozen. Finally we wrapped his horrible head in an old feed bag, and we dragged him, so heavy, along the stream, on this path, here to the family plot. There are so many bodies in there, all jumbled, bones. We knocked over one of the slabs to hide the seams in the grass, where we put him. Anyway, I don't know how they didn't find him."

I thought, that's why she's kept me at arm's length this whole time. Afraid of something bad, the sickening, final drop. That ugly accident. I thought that and then thought different.

"Mother watched us the entire time."

I shivered.

"Why tell me?" I said.

"It doesn't matter why. You know, why any of it was. I mean, it only matters now. Now you have the key."

We had come back to the house, were only as far from it as the green lawn where in different times they had played croquet in long skirts. There was a tire swing beside me, still. Someone had renewed the rope. I gave it a push. You got a hint of the degrading rubber of it, wafting through the air.

I had the key.

But I would never understand.

Appendix

The Sioux were dynamiting Mt. Rushmore.

Timeline

12000 BCE: Wisconsin glaciation recedes having gouged out Harmony Valley

1450: Iroquois League forms

1609: Henry Hudson sails the Half Moon into New York harbor and up the river that bears his name

1664: New Amsterdam becomes New York City

1737: First British settlers in Harmony Valley

1749: British administrator remarks that the Iroquois have a perfectly egalitarian society

1756: John Fraser builds his farm in "charming Loudon's Grove"

1775: American Revolutionary War begins

1779: Harmony Valley raided by Loyalists and Iroquois during Revolutionary War; fort is burned, dozens of citizens massacred

1783: Treaty of Paris ends Revolutionary War

1784: Iroquois sign treaty of Fort Stanwix, ceding much of their land in the United States to the Americans, including the area of Harmony Valley

1788: Firm of Jeremiah & Jeremiah, Esqs. established in Utica

1789: Tammany Society established in New York City

1799: New York State passes law of gradual emancipation

1791: Town of Harmony Valley incorporated

1812: Village of Harmony Valley established

1814: To address small-coin shortage, Harmony Valley issues 1, 3, 6, 12, 12 ½, and 25 cent Notes

1815: Hiram born to former slaves in the Fraser household; required by law to be an indentured servant of the Frasers until the age of 28

1817: Erie Canal begins construction

1817: All slaves in New York born before 1799 are freed (effective 1827) but their children remain indentured servants

1818: Harmony Valley establishes its first fire company

1823: Fanny "Frances" Fraser born

1825: Erie Canal opens

1826: Shakers establish a communal farm in Groveland

1828: Joseph Smith uncovers golden plates, his source for the *Book of Mormon*, near Palmyra

1830: No ball playing allowed in streets of Harmony Valley

1838: Hiram escapes the Fraser farm with the aid of Fanny Fraser

1839: Fanny Fraser leaves Harmony Valley for New York City

1845: Harmony Valley builds plank sidewalks

1846: Hiram, safe in Toronto, Canada, embarks on a fur-trapping expedition

1847: Fanny begins relationship with Tammany Hall bigwig Daniel Sickles

1848: Founding of the utopian group the Oneida Community
      Seneca Falls Convention

1851: Fanny founds a brothel at 119 Mercer Street with help from Sickles; it is an immediate success

1852: Order of L.E.F. founded in Harmony Valley
      Sickles marries 16-year-old Teresa Bagioli

1853: Millard Fillmore visits Harmony Valley as President—throngs welcome him
      Fanny joins Sickles and his young wife on a trip to England and is presented to Queen Victoria

1855: Hiram opens a dry-goods store in Toronto
      Fanny pursues a number of legal cases related to her reputation, representing herself, and wins
      Fanny reputed to have amassed a great fortune

1856: Fanny marries William Larch, the "Barrel King"

1861: American Civil War begins
      Daniel Sickles a Union General

1865: Lee surrenders to Grant

1873: Mark Twain publishes *The Gilded Age*
      William Larch goes bankrupt
      Fanny Fraser dies under mysterious circumstances, her fortune vanishes

1874: The renowned Inspector LeBeaux comes from France to investigate Fanny's death at the request of her family; her body is exhumed, and then disappears; no satisfactory resolution

1877: 100th chapter of L.E.F. opens

1882: Fanny Fraser's *My Life* is published posthumously, and for a short time becomes a national sensation before being forgotten entirely

1893: Bank runs, and economic panic

1896: William Jennings Bryan's "Cross of Gold" speech

1899: 250th chapter of L.E.F. opens with a gala celebration one minute before midnight on December 31st

1901: President William McKinley assassinated by an anarchist

1909: 10 m.p.h. speed limit enacted, Main St. macadamized in Harmony Valley

1913: The Grand Hotel at Loudon's Grove burns for a third time; it is not rebuilt

1917: The United States enters World War I
June's great-grandfather, Henry Fraser, takes out a second mortgage on the Fraser farm

1927: Order of L.E.F. at its greatest extent
All of Harmony Valley now electrified

1929: The Wall Street Crash of 1929

1930: Henderson's Chair Factory closes, permanently

1933: The new Civilian Conservation Corps builds a camp behind the Fraser farm, and nature trails through Loudon's Grove

1944: June's grandfather serves in the Pacific

1947: The last direct train from Harmony Valley to Grand Central Terminal departs from the depot on Railroad Avenue

1955: Final meeting of the Harmony Valley chapter of L.E.F., with no new initiates, and three nonagenarian members, its active status ends

1957: June's mother, Anne, born

1964: Johnson uses Gulf of Tonkin incidents as a pretense to escalate the War in Vietnam

1971: Hue "Tiffany" Ho born in Saigon

1974: My parents move to Harmony Valley

1975: New York *Daily News* headline: "Ford to City: Drop Dead"

1978: June's mother leaves Harmony Valley after fight with her parents
Tiffany and her parents arrive in Utica, NY as refugees

1979: June is born in Point Pleasant, Ohio

1981: I am born

1983: June's grandfather dies

1986: The New York Mets win the World Series

1987: Melinda Rath and her daughter begin running a Summer day-camp
for kids at June's ancestral home
The "old-school" is left to ruin, and a new building inaugurated on
the hill outside of town
Tiffany attends Hamilton College

1988: Clyde Duane becomes caretaker of the Harmony Valley chapter of
L.E.F. after his father retires

1992: "The Game" invented
June's grandmother dies
Tiffany joins firm of Jeremiah & Jeremiah

1993: World Trade Center bombed (for the first time)
June's family moves back to their Harmony Valley farm
June appears to me from behind a pillar in the library's "Media Lab"
We discover Clyde Duane's gold key

1994: Tim, June's stepfather, disappears
Police called up to the farm

1995: I embark on an illicit paper-writing enterprise
"The Game" ends
Invitations to join the L.E.F. Chess Club
We establish our secret society and its rituals

1996: I miss my initiation
June leaves school

1997: I attend Hamilton College
Visited by June
June meets Tiffany

1999: Y2K bug passes without incident

2000: We move to New York City
June and I break up

2001: George W Bush inaugurated
Buddhas in Bamiyan are demolished
World Trade Center bombing

2003: Invasion of Iraq

2004: I move to San Francisco

2006: Mid-term elections in America give some hope
I return to New York City

2008: Lehman Brothers bankrupt
Election of Barack Obama

2011: June invites me to the Occupy Wall Street camp, I demur

2014: Smallest graduating class ever at Harmony Valley school: 22 students

2016: I close my boutique marketing business and begin consulting for
large firms

2020: After a couple years, June resurfaces—we have an intense period of
almost daily contact

2023: First appearance of the "Blue Smocks" in a spontaneous protest
against new austerity measures

2025: Momentary lull in our march toward full fascism
June returns to my life again

2028: Another "most-consequential" election of our lifetime
We have missed every "last chance" for climate action; the weather
has become insane; nobody cares

2029: Ryan moves to Alaska

2030: Refugee crisis
Tax-free settlements on the moon

2031: I am 50; no card from June
Smattering of protests; general dissatisfaction
The Democratic President has thoroughly militarized daily life
Every aspect of our existence is altered to accommodate the needs of
our technological overlords
Efforts to control local climate conditions

2032: Financial crisis
Protests erupt everywhere—the "Blue Smocks" in earnest
General strikes
Worker lockouts
Bipartisan agreement to suspend elections
I am trying to figure out how to sell an incontinence pill

2033: Bradly Jenkins and Mr. Grimmon killed during protests
AI-driven systems widely sabotaged
Street battles
The Sioux, having occupied parts of North Dakota, begin detonating
Mt. Rushmore
I hear from June

2034: The military dissolves the government
      The United States fragment
      New York loosely part of the Northeast federation
      A shocking quiescence
      Climate mitigation strategies

2035: Further decomposition of our institutions
      Local control of most industry
      Private Equity abolished
      I try to file a police report about June
      Brief Sino-Russian war
      Convulsions in Europe
      Air travel refashioned

2036: I quit my job, head north to Harmony Valley
      Initiated, at last, into L.E.F.
      I meet June again, walk through the Fraser Farm

2037: I am deeply engaged in Harmony Valley reconstruction
      June called away

2038: I see Tiffany from time to time
      I move into a cabin out past the weather stabilizers

2041: I begin writing *The Happy Valley*

The Chronicles of Zebulon

AARON SICKLER, my Harmony Valley schoolmate, under the pen name of Anson Goodsort authored more than 70 science-fiction novels set in the Zebulon galaxy between the ages of 12 and 32 before he quit writing altogether. The first were written out long-hand in school composition books, and illustrated with verve and some talent with colored pencils and markers; then he switched for many to dot-matrix printouts in a clear binder; he posted all his novels online, later, as endless scrolling texts in teletype-font over backgrounds of space scenes on his GeoCities home page, *The World of Zebulon*.

I have since obtained copies of some of the originals—for reasons I won't go into here. This is a complete catalog of Aaron's works; the titles whose originals are in my possession are marked **in bold**.

1. *The Rose of Mars, Part 1 (80 handwritten pages, 6 illustrations, 1992)*
2. *Zebulon: Awake! (95 handwritten pages, 12 illustrations, 1992)*
3. **Last Chance Rocket** *(60 handwritten pages, three illustrations, 1993)*
4. *Stars Shining on Kanzabar (150 handwritten pages, 9 illustrations, 1993)*
5. *The Tragedy of Alpha Zebron (75 handwritten pages, 10 illustrations, 1993)*
6. **Zebron's Children** *(208 handwritten pages, 26 illustrations, 1993)*
7. **The Exanion Arrival** *(89 handwritten pages, 14 illustrations, 1993)*
8. *Seven Weeks in Zamarazon (70 handwritten pages, 7 illustrations, 1993)*
9. *The Oceans of Albion's Waste (The Tykian Trilogy 1) (100 typed pages, 1994)*
10. *The Rose of Mars, Part 2 (88 handwritten pages, 4 illustrations, 1994)*
11. **The Chronicles of Zebulon 9: Book 1** *(120 typed pages, 1994)*
12. **The Chronicles of Zebulon 9: Book 2** *(111 typed pages, 1994)*
13. **The Chronicles of Zebulon 9: Book 3** *(99 typed pages, 1994)*
14. *The Chronicles of Zebulon 9: Book 4 (132 typed pages, 1994)*
15. *Escape to Eregal (67 handwritten pages, 13 illustrations, 1994)*
16. **The Empress Returns** *(76 handwritten pages, 5 illustrations, 1994)*
17. **Zane Arbuster Learns His Lesson** *(52 typed pages, 5 illustrations, 1994)*
18. *The Rose of Mars, Part 3 (93 handwritten pages, 9 illustrations, 1995)*
19. *Last Chance Rocket Redux (199 typed pages, 25 illustrations, 1995)*
20. *The Chronicles of Zebulon: Ezra's Story (45 handwritten pages, 1995)*
21. **The End of Infinity** *(520 typewritten pages, 1995)*
22. *Curse of the Red Moon (The Tykian Trilogy 2) (100 typed pages, 1996)*
23. *Asteroid Tales (120 handwritten pages, 16 illustrations, 1996)*
24. *More Asteroid Tales (122 handwritten pages, 8 illustrations, 1996)*
25. **Six Moons to Lindon** *(76 handwritten pages, 12 illustrations, 1996)*
26. *The Empress Absconds (398 typewritten pages, 1997)*

27. *Call of the Quasar (The Tykian Trilogy: 3) (100 typed pages, 1997)*
28. *The Chronicles of Zebulon 9: Eight Seconds Later (80 typed pages, 1998)*
29. First Ship to Cross Alpha Zero *(421 typed pages, 2 illustrations, 1998)*
30. *Zane Arbuster Flies Again (320 typed pages, 15 illustrations, 1999)*
31. Beta Rays for Mr. Andrews *(100 handwritten pages, 1999)*
32. *The Orchestra Goes Atomic (225 handwritten pages, 20 illustrations, 2000)*
33. Noted Pleasure Spots in the Outer Quadrants (150 typed pages, 2000)
34. *Nine Cuisines of Rageria (120 typed pages, 50 illustrations 2001)*
35. *Zark! (Tetralogy of Captain Alin: 1) (195 typed pages, 2001)*
36. *Barathon, Home of the Lesser Gods (204 typed pages, 2002)*
37. *Laser Burns (Tetralogy of Captain Alin: 2) (211 typed pages, 2003)*
38. *How to Get Rich Without Really Flying (200 typed pages, 2003)*
39. *Bandit Tales (190 typed pages, 20 illustrations, 2003)*
40. *The Empress Minds (610 typed pages, 2003)*
41. *Space Shanties, Volume 1: Anderon to Coneria (111 typed pages, 2004)*
42. North Alaracan Wildlife (220 typed pages, 80 illustrations, 2004)
43. *Nebuloso the Magnificent (400 typed pages, 2004)*
44. *Robot's Rules of Order (200 handwritten pages, 15 illustrations, 2004)*
45. Mr. Andrews and the Zebulon Kids (310 typed pages, 2005)
46. Chaos on Condetian Five (298 typed pages, 2005)
47. The Lost Outpost (129 typed pages, 5 illustrations, 2005)
48. The Chronicles of Zebulon 9: The Lost Freighter (200 typed pages, 2005)
49. History of the Universe, Part 1 (333 typed pages, 4 illustrations, 2005)
50. *Elsa Eats the Galaxy (100 handwritten pages, 12 illustrations, 2005)*
51. *Three, Four, Open the Door (Tetralogy of Captain Alin: 3) (120 pps., 2006)*
52. *Wormholes, Portals, and Other Impossibilities (220 pps., 2006)*
53. *Cooking Like an Alarican (120 pps., 30 illustrations, 2006)*
54. *Space Shanties, Volume 2: Colicarion to Horus (120 typed pages, 2006)*
55. *The Rites of Pignon Seven (95 handwritten pages, 20 illustrations, 2007)*
56. *Arbuster Busted (390 typed pages, 12 illustrations, 2007)*
57. *The Chronicles of Zebulon 9: Book 5 (300 typed pages, 5 illustrations, 2007)*
58. Forbidden Planets: A Concise List (70 typed pages, 14 illustrations, 2007)
59. *Space Dragons: Myth or Reality? (30 typed pages, 7 illustrations, 2007)*
60. *Time and Thyme: Cooking Secrets of the Temporal Titans (110 pps., 2008)*
61. *The Chronicles of Zebulon 9: Book 7 (195 types pages, 3 illustrations, 2008)*
62. *The Empress Asks (450 typed pages, 2008)*
63. *Space to Spare: A Zebulon Story (40 handwritten pages, 2009)*
64. My Trip to the Outer Rim (240 typed pages, 10 illustrations, 2009)
65. *Rocks for Sale: Bandits of the Belt (120 types pages, 20 illustrations, 2009)*
66. *Alms for Almogast (Tetralogy of Captain Alin: 4) (290 typed pages, 2010)*
67. *A Catalog of Ships: The Many Forces of Zingar (198 typed pages, 2010)*
68. *A Galactic Constitution (590 typed pages, 2010)*
69. *Force Field Frenzy (110 handwritten pages, 40 illustrations, 2011)*
70. *Xenian 9 & Other Delights (100 handwritten pages, 33 illustrations, 2011)*
71. *Eregal's Revenge (350 typed pages, 12 illustrations, 2011)*
72. Fusion for Dummies (636 typed pages, 46 illustrations, 2012)
73. *The Rose of Mars, The Final Chapter (399 types pages, 2012)*

A Final Mystery

WHILE COLLECTING Aaron's novel drafts, Aaron's childhood notebook with his L.E.F. "Clues" that I had initially imagined to be filled with red herrings and meaningless doodles happened to fall into my hands. You can imagine my surprise when, in paging through it, I discovered that Aaron had actually been on to some things.

Reading the notebook, at first his clues don't amount to much, but then I notice him referencing things I only found out decades later, like the connection of L.E.F. to Frances Fraser and the identity of Hiram. Then I turn the page, and he has written, in code:

EDW RAB KQ JZW YHQ AEJ PKP DAH KYW PEK JKB WIE OOE JCP NAW OQN A—H SBZ MAD NOD MDC VHS GSG QDD JDX R, ZMC SGD XZQ DZR ENK KNV R:

I was able to easily decipher that line: he used that trick I had employed before myself, with a clever twist at the "—". Here was a reference to missing treasure, the thing we had always been searching for. I was also able to decipher two of the three "keys" to the treasure he mentions, one building upon the other, like his stories—but not the third. Finally, he concludes with another undecipherable (to me, so far) line ending in three exclamation points.

In pen, a later addition, he has added (presumably as an adult —the handwriting matches the corrections in his last novel manuscripts), this scrawled text:

"It's a shame I was only able to uncover the treasure long after we didn't need it anymore—I've left it, as a monument to my own folly." And then, later, in red ink: "Pretentious crap. All of it. Forget it. Just live already."

Here is the rest of Aaron's coded message:

VMZ F ZYS YTD TBN RIV RTQ RCQ GSF ZHE DX

YMZ L HMP QZF ALM XRX CBA LBE KWZ ZHD YFX LFH LTJ STJ WDI

*BTA Q UPO BLC GML ZEI VMU IIZ QFK LHG IZQ KDV
ZFA VZX PSS UYW EZL OR*

*XFF NNF FTP CIV QBN I? TMT WGX AOM EOH TOQ
QN? OSO TN, KET THO TU, OIR REQ VWP IJL XQU L!!!*

If you decipher what I could not, I don't really know what
you'll find, but Aaron seemed to think it was both not worth
anything anymore (could be money, a baldness cure—no,
Aaron never found that, or some bit of arcane lore) but also
worth everything—I mean, as a monument to . . . something.

Fitting that the story begins with the destruction of one
monument, and ends with the hint of another, don't you think?

On the back cover of the notebook, I found scrawled in pencil
this:

*"Job 21:21—What does he care about his household after him, when
the numbers of his years are written out?"*

and then, in code, what I think it is the final piece to the
puzzle, the thing that ties all Aaron's work in a bow. This
coded message is:

*JIU VPE VIG VWG ITB ANB VFZ PDJ OEP UBA XED SDH
JWI FYY FTT UKK PTE GSQ HQG NEV CLP U*

But what does it say?

Reading Group Guide

1. THIS NOVEL is divided into two parts: *The Farm* and *The Key*. Why do you think the author structured the book this way? How did the parts differ from each other? How do they work together to form a whole? What is the significance of "the farm" to the story, and the narrator, and what is the significance of "the key"?

2. This novel seems to work with pairs. Some examples: past and future, country and city, child and adult; there are also pairs of people: the narrator and June, Tiffany and Mr. Jeremiah. What other pairs of people, places, or concepts did you notice? In which ways did these pairs oppose or support each other? How is the story centered within these lines? What are the connections between Jeremiah Jeremiah and Clyde Duane?

3. The author sketches a future that is like and also radically unlike our present, and which is quite different from our past. In what ways is this future believable? In what ways is it not? Does the narrator make for a reliable witness throughout? How do the different characters relate to the changes that have taken place in the working of the world? How do you relate to the changes in your own world?

4. The book opens with two maps, one quite realistic and seemingly historical, the other a representation of a fantasy world from "The Game." What part does "The Game" play in the story? What message is the novel making about our reality, and the role of imagination, if any? How do the drawings (not a typical component of modern novels) play a role in the telling of the story?

5. "The Game" that the teens invent is a role-playing game. What roles do people play in the novel? What roles do you play in your day-to-day life? The author also includes references to *Wizard and the Princess, Oregon Trail, Wheel of Fortune,* and *Sim City*. What significance, if any, do these have to the story?

6. At the center of the novel is a rather long extract from a self-published and heavily stylized science fiction story by one of the characters. It contrasts with the more literary style of the rest of the book. Why? What purpose does it serve? Why are Aaron's fictitious novels so exhaustively categorized in the *Appendix?*

7. In the single page prefacing the novel, the author makes some claims about the book: that it is a gothic tale, and through allusion compares it to *The Wizard of Oz.* It opens with two quotes: one connecting the novel to a flourishing of spiritual fervor and the other from the Marxist philosopher Herbert Marcuse (author of *Eros and Civilization* and *One-Dimensional Man*). What do you make of these connections? Can you think of others?

8. It's evident from the beginning that place is a crucial part of the story. How does the author evoke the landscape, and treat it as its own character? Are there specific scenes or interactions that make clear the relationship of the land and its history to the meaning of the novel and to our lives?

9. An important scene explicitly connects the central figures and events of the novel to a folk tale. How does the world and logic of the folk tale differ from our own? What are the essential characteristics of a folk tale, and which of these does this novel share? In what way can fiction be like a dream?

10. An *Appendix* is usually thought of as something secondary, something inessential. Is that the case here? Why has the author added one? Is the "final mystery" worth solving? How would you go about doing it?

11. Does this novel have a central message about the way we order our life? Does it offer answers to important questions? Or does it just raise questions of its own?

Acknowledgments

I WOULD NEVER have completed this book without my first readers: especially my brother Sam Harnett and my wife Toni Hacker who both gave me solid advice and needed encouragement. Thanks also to Howard Mittelmark whose recommendations and edits made the book into the book it deserved to be. And to Porochista Khakpour who encouraged me to stick with my voice and lean in to atmosphere. Thanks also to Nicole Stawikawski and Alizah Salario for feedback, advice, and moral support along the way.

Also thanks to my best friend Jesse Kolbert, with whom I shared many discussions about both the craft of writing and our fucked-up society; who was also the real force behind making up "The Game" when we were kids. The dungeon map at the opening is from one of Jesse's notebooks which he kindly lent to me.

This novel started out life as a short story idea in April 2019—I began writing it, and just never let myself finish it until I'd completed a novel draft. There have been quite a few drafts since. Thanks also to Anne Trubek, who (along with Toni) convinced me it was fine to go ahead and put this out into the world myself.

I learned to write mostly by reading—this book owes an enormous debt to E.L. Doctorow, whose books I have devoured since I was a teen. Thanks also to Dana Spiotta not only for her books, which have been guiding lights, but for showing how one can be an artist and make a life in this world, and for her friendship and advice.

Also thanks to my first creative writing instructor, George O'Connell, who had faith in my talent and helped me hone my craft. And to Fredric Jameson and Herbert Marcuse, whose writing showed me why it was important that I made art. To Benjamin Dreyer who is a force of nature and an inspiration and in practical terms because *Dreyer's English* was a path to and a balm for the completion of the longest stretch of writing I've ever done. To Frank Stock who first showed me how beautiful language could be.

Most of all thanks to my parents, Bruce Harnett and Barbara Margaritis, who built up my creative spirit, made space for a grand and purposeful life for me, and remain models of how to be good in this world.

I must also thank some folks whose extremely generous contributions made the launch of this book possible: Jesse Keppler, Jonathan Rury,

Katherine and Elizabeth Peik, Matt Boggie, and Bashir Abdallah. Also supporting the launch were my brothers Will and Sam, and my sister Emma; also Christopher Schelling, Rebecca Wright, Jessica Collier, Sherrie Carroll, Mahantesh Patil, Gregory Ganio, and Henry Minich. And there were scores of others on Kickstarter, including John Durkin, Tom Blodgett, Bob Rust, Sandra Simonds, Christina Sebez, and Lynn Talbot. This mix of family, childhood and family friends, acquaintances, fans of past endeavors, and strangers, all believing in my novel has filled me with gratitude.

Also to many others who have encouraged and supported my writing, or through friendship and pizza, or by way of inspiration—thank you: Rae Steil, Elliot Black, Karl Steel, Holly Antolini, Alex Kuhner, Claire Blatz, Janice Cable, Travis Wingate, Rory Sawyer, Nina Feinberg, Jacqui Shine, Brent Cox, Dakin Campbell, Julie Bennack, Kenneth White, Ashley Strosnider, Sommer Hixson, Martha Sharer, Nora Manley, Kira Egan, Robin Berjon, Brooke Bassin, Sarah Miers, Leigh Harrison, Nora Manley, Barbara Rogers, Carrie Campbell, Elisa Davis, Elon Green, Edward Bannett, Andrea Grady, Marian Makins, Stephanie Frampton, Marny Smith, Melissa Manganaan, Leslie Jo, Max Bentovim, Jessica Collier, Steven Nedlin, Jill Flint, Laura Valetutto, and Audrey Maldonado. Love to Mr. Jackson, Oliver, Sadie, and Leo, too.

Special shout out to Elizabeth McCracken and Edward Carey, who liked one of my drawings enough to hang it in their collection, the only thing that has ever impressed my mother (and which encouraged me to go for it with the illustrations).

Finally, I have to give thanks to the weird, ancient ground of my childhood—that triangle of glaciated earth that sits between Cooperstown, Cherry Valley, and Roseboom, New York. Thanks are owed to you, too, at last, reading this, for joining me in this story, and for indulging me in this fictional exercise, which is always something of an ego trip.

Afterword

I HAVE, SOMETIMES, BEEN of the impression that if you look too deeply into the making of art it loses its magic. For instance, I have now looked at the word "happy" so many times that it has more or less ceased to read as a word, and more like a strange collection of letters. What could it mean? What is it trying to tell us? It's like the last, enigmatic carving of a lost colony—the lost colony of my imagination. This book wasn't always called *The Happy Valley;* that name came to it late, and felt like a cheat. I think it works, though, and now I wouldn't change it.

Naming things is one of the hardest things to do in any endeavor. What's in a name, but Shakespeare was wrong. And doubly so in writing. We make fun of marketing folks, brainstorming the perfect packaging for some corporate retread, but I wish I'd had some of their type along the way. I did have help, an editor who looked at an early draft and gave an almost final draft a solid once over, but I longed for the kind of help (if overbearing) that I imagine established authors get, an agent's advice, a publisher, a designer. I suppose there are those artists who have a singular vision and refuse to have it compromised. I am not one. I'm just blundering along here. Make me change things!

Instead I spend a week taking commas out and then another week putting them back in. You try to split yourself, then, let loose creating and then read as if it were the ramblings of a stranger—here and there it felt like that, actually. Still—help me decide whether my epigraphs are dumb, where to put a scene, whether I should scrap this or that chapter, how to take the story I've already written and put it in order. Get the opening chapter right. And so on. But that's not how it goes—nobody will take the book out of your hands and say, "Don't worry, I've got it from here."

When I took creative writing classes in college, the instructor would take my poems and short stories and pass them back with suggestions—lines to cut, different words to use, validate some choices, question others. After I left school, I lost this crutch, and it took me a long time, a decade or more, to start writing again without it. It occurs to me now that I could have worked harder to be part of a community, find someone, or a group to get that back. I guess I'm just not that kind of person. There was a lot of other life going on, at the time too. When I finally jotted down some poems, in a quiet moment in the office, I thought that would be it, but I kept going back to them, reworking them. They started taking up space.

The only way to stop working them up was to send them out. As long as they were gone, submitted (to be rejected), I could go on to other things, and then the little slips would come back in the mail, "Sorry," "Not for us," folded awkwardly into envelopes addressed to myself in my own writing. Then one day the little note said "Yes" instead, and, like that, without comment or alteration, without suggestion or fix, I had a poem in a journal, warts and all.

This book was originally called *The Idling Machine*—I know, ponderous, pretentious, weird. In a way that was my writing "career," I was idling, and needed to throw things into gear. Now I can call myself happy, if the word means anything at all, because the book is out of my hands. It's going somewhere. And now it is up to readers, some of whom have questioned my choices, but many more of whom who have validated them. If you're reading this, you might have validated some of them too. You liked it. Or you hated it enough to find everything about it you could. Like an old plumber I know who when maximally frustrated will go back to the busted up box the part came in and curse the distributor, the manufacturer, and the entire city, state, and country that let such a faulty part out into the world.

"Harnett—you are in love with your own voice," is what one college professor wrote on a particularly florid essay. It was a sharp, if fair, rebuke that has stuck with me. It wasn't my voice, anyway, but modeled on the kind of 19th c. prose I read in books we picked up for dollars at the library sale, and which I felt must be the pinnacle of intellectual style. What I love about this novel is it is full of voices also not mine, but all as authentic as I could channel them. (Writing fiction, for me, is all about putting up my antenna, and listening— sometimes there's too much static in the old radio to get the words quite right.)

But if my own sheer hunger for oral histories, commentary tracks, making-of documentaries, and personal narratives, and artist memoirs is any indication, an inside look into how art is made doesn't kill the magic—it adds to the pleasure of consuming it and, frankly, enhances the mystery. Or rather it separates the ordinary achievements from the truly wonderful. The more we see regular people doing regular things—typing into a Word doc, scribbling notes in the margin, deleting every instance of very and then putting some back in, slowly tearing a manuscript page into confetti—the less understanding we have how the thing we admire came to be, and the more respect we have, not for the author, but for the text, a bit of alchemy unconsciously or accidentally achieved.

Which is not to say there's not skill involved. It is the skill of building the hexagonal plates and fitting them into a great water-filled sphere, attaching electrodes, sinking it miles into the earth, but the neutrino must still wander into it, and improbably interact for the experiment to be a success.

Well—we will allow a little florid language in the afterward, if only in understanding of my own deep surprise at the solid thing I've made, which feels so personal and, yet, so absolutely alien. It's the surprise of the woodcarver whose puppet suddenly walks on its own.

The Idea

"WHY NOT WRITE A NOVEL?" people have asked.

Gore Vidal's assertion that famous novelists occupy the same plane as famous ceramicists notwithstanding, even of a smaller cultural pie, people still want to claim a big slice. Or maybe it's simpler yet— loving novels, being taken out of our own heads (or having entire worlds thrust into them), exposed to lives we never imagined we could lead, even getting the sense of talking to a wise stranger, or crossing time to speak with the dead, we want to achieve that for others. Or it is that there's a burning story to tell, or a message we want to get across. Or we write for ourselves, caught up in the creation, satisfied whether or not a single person beyond ourselves reads a single word.

At times in my life some of each of these things was true, but the biggest obstacle was when I did sit down to write, I couldn't think of anything I wanted to say. I had no ideas. I mean, I had ideas, but none I thought best communicated in novel form, or that, done so, would be of interest for people to read. Why not write a novel? Why write one, really. And, anyway, does the world need another novel?

My ideas always felt right for smaller canvases, anyway. A short poem, words distilled to their essence, a few thoughts wrapped together, a strand of DNA to grow in the mind into something else. When I tried prose, I could sustain a story for a few pages. I wrote "Gigantic," on the strength of a single conceit– what if your kid never stopped growing? In a way, that's the story of *The Happy Valley*, too: when I got the idea, I thought, here's another short story. You can see what happened.

By far the biggest budget item for rural schools is transportation. Big yellow buses with green faux-leather-grained seats climbing up narrow winding roads in the wooded hills behind the village to pick up kids in bright-colored clothing at the end of their long driveways flanked by stands of poplars, a few gold leaves clinging to otherwise barren-looking branches shortly after dawn. My brother and I would take that ride together, and I'd sit in the window seat gazing out in a state of near-trance at what passed by. When we got to the village, the bus would turn left at the light to head for the school, and as it slowed to approach the light, I'd notice the same thing, a sign for the "Masonic Temple" in sparkly gold paint with the square and the compass. If I happened to be sitting on the right, we'd pass, after the big communal grave to the massacre victims in the cemetery, the "Order of Odd-Fellows" on a building.

I'd let the strangeness and wonder of those places in an otherwise ordinary-looking town wash over me, and imagine forbidden rites and mystical wonders beneath every straight-looking facade. I never took it much further than that—owing I think to a reluctance to have mystery and wonder flattened into the much less interesting reality I guessed was the real truth of the matter.

Fast-forward to three decades later (ulp!) and my wife and I are living in Beacon, and on weekends driving to Target and Lowe's in Poughkeepsie to stock up on things for the house and garden. When we do, we pass through a town called Wappinger's Falls and see a bright yellow building with period details, kept up in excellent shape. It is a Temple of Odd Fellows. And I wonder: here is valuable real-estate, there can't be many Odd Fellows around, the thing just keeps going, a memory from a more-flush time for fraternal orders and secret societies. And it might just still be going—funded out of the coffers, administered by some lawyer or Limited Liability Company, employing groundskeepers and charged with protecting the assets.

I imagined, like a one-handed clap, a secret society going on with all its administrative, legal, and financial affairs unchanging, but sans active membership.

That's the idea, and in my mind a young girl, fascinated like I had been, with seeing some such thing in her little village, decides to do what I did not, dig under the surface, and takes it over.

The Writing

SO MUCH FOR THE IDEA. Then to get writing. It was a short story, and how I usually write them is from an idea and a feeling. Take the main character, and set her going. I made a few attempts and got nowhere. The rest of the story never came, and I set it aside. Then in April of 2019, in an effort to unlock creativity which had begun, with the stress of work and the world, to be all bottled up, I started writing a poem a day. When the month finished, and May came around, I said to myself that I would start the same thing with prose.

I'd write on the train, from Beacon along the Hudson into Grand Central Terminal. Knees up on the seat in front, laptop balanced on top, clacking and tapping away. I went back to the story of the girl and since I couldn't make it work from her perspective, starting telling it from the perspective of an observer. It allowed me to heighten the mystery, and to look at it from multiple angles.

My method for writing is to just attack the blank page, writing the words as they pop into my brain, sometimes going back to correct sentence structure and clarity, but mostly not doing it. If I stop moving forward I might stop writing altogether. Once I couldn't go on any longer, I'd see if changing perspective or talking about a new character helped. Mostly it did. I was writing the story the way Tristram Shandy told the story of his life: in exhaustive digressions, never quite getting to the action. How do you write a novel? Start with a short story and never let it finish.

After a while I started to get a sense for the arc of the thing, and when I had gotten about a hundred pages in, I jotted in a notes doc a series of scenes or chapters that would get the story to the end. Now I'd start each writing session on a particular scene, sometimes generating the need for new scenes. Sometimes going back to a spot and starting to fill in again.

As I wrote it became clear to me that the story of the secret society would stretch backward in time and forward, too. Also that making it a small, Upstate New York village which had been in my mind simply because of the genesis of the idea, was now a crucial part of the book. Also that this was a book—a novel. I drew more and more on my own memories and recollections of the place, and on the scraps of true history I knew about the area and our country. I also found myself influenced in writing by books I had read recently, by video games, by films, by music, by my view of the river, by my personal philosophy, by my love of nature, by theories of change, and by the secret campaign I joined up with to organize my tech-working colleagues into one of the pioneering tech unions in the country.

A little more on my process: I write in OpenOffice, which is, frankly, not great, but I feel superior for not using Word or Google Docs. The latter I avoid for personal writing because I use it so much for work writing, and the two must be kept separate or they would destroy each other. I write with the spell-check and grammar check off, to keep me rushing headlong.

When not actively writing, I put whatever stray thoughts that pop up into the Notes App on my phone, which Apple continues to make less and less usable for quick note jotting, curse them. Outlines and plans, though, I write longhand, and then transfer onto the computer. I have never been able to write text of any sustained length except in my diary, which I have done only intermittently.

I saved different sections in different files, and when I felt secure about how things would fit together, I'd knit them into a master document. I am sure there are a million better ways to do this. I often lost track of the "best" copy of something, and who knows how much brilliant writing is lost in various poorly named files on my hard disk drive.

Only when I'd put a few chapters together did I go back and do an edit for sense and to better knit together sections. I did a lot of careful line edits on the opening and closing of each chapter, and not as much in the middle.

At the end, I knew there were some missing pieces, and purpose-wrote them to fill the entire book out. At last, I had a finished draft. This was sometime in November, about six months worth of writing, with long fallow periods in between weeks-long bursts of daily, almost frenzied activity.

In a way, the influences for this novel were every single moment of my life up until and during the time I started writing and re-writing the words that became *The Happy Valley*. But assuredly some things were more top-of-mind than others. And there may be obvious influences I completely miss because they're burrowed so deeply into my unconscious. This last becomes incredibly apparent when someone who is extremely well-read and used to picking apart writing for allusions and references, such as a Classics scholar, reads your work and finds a very clever allusion to a Seamus Heaney poem which you had no idea you were doing at all.

I think it's a matter of self-preservation to some extent. If an artist or a writer has too much insight into complex web of influence behind his or her work, well, it can be a little crushing to say I rearranged a few words on the shoulders of giants. Or it could be my method— stream of consciousness, and editing by gut feel, that allows for complex creative work that bypasses conscious intention in ways that others' practices don't. I can't help but think of Dylan asking Leonard Cohen how long it took to write "Hallelujah" and Cohen saying years, and when asking Dylan how long it took him to write a song and Dylan saying 15 minutes.

My idea of what a novel can be was shaped by a reading list inspired by what I found on my parents' shelves and working outward from there. John Updike, Robinson Davies, Gore Vidal. I read Kurt Vonnegut, and every cheap mystery and sci-fi paperback I could get my hands on. I read what was called out in *The New Yorker* at that time as good literature, V.S. Naipul, Paul Auster, Norman Mailer. It was a very male, very American, very post-war reading list. E. L. Doctorow stood out, and my admiration of his work persisted even as I discovered Pynchon and David Foster Wallace. For a period in college I was reading Richard Brautigan and Philip K. Dick. When I started studying Greek, everyone was talking about *The Secret History* —and it was uncanny how closely our tiny class fit the characters. After that I turned to non-fiction.

When I graduated from college I discovered Iris Murdoch and then went back. I picked up *Frankenstein,* and then read through all of Austen. I read *Tristram Shandy* all the way through (I'd started it in college in an old contemporary edition the library had complete with genuine marbled page and plenty of must). I read *Pride and Prejudice* through about six times on the subway back and forth to work. Subway reading was a revelation. I reread *Moby-Dick,* and experienced it like a religious document. I read through Conrad, and then read *Middlemarch.*

Middlemarch floored me. It was a novel like Austen of relationships and social class, of love and striving, but it came with a huge backdrop of political economics and genuine social study—it truly lit up all the lights of my interests for me in a way I hadn't imagined possible. (Side-note: it was the second truly long classic novel I'd read in succession on the train from Beacon, the first being

Stendhal's *The Red and the Black* which left me cold—I'd read it because Al Gore had said it was his favorite book and after all this time I'd been curious to see why. It made a lot of sense. In that same election, George W. Bush's favorite book had been *The Very Hungry Caterpillar*. Well, people got that. And there wasn't much complaint when George W. Bush was installed as president. It was a very hungry time.)

I didn't set out to write a *Middlemarch*, but that was one of the outstanding works that made up the literary constellations of the sky surrounding my writing. Anyway, such is the background. Add to it countless classic and modern films and TV shows, paintings, architecture. Not to mention ancient works. And, oh yeah, video games. Of the literary stuff, I still have huge gaps. I am not proud of how white and how male and how American a lot of it is, especially to start, the things that really marked me. In fact it feels quite conservative. Like the reading history of someone who has leather patches on his tatty cardigans, smokes a pipe, and is secretly paid by the CIA—I was pretty small-c conservative once, every day it seems as I go through the world, I move farther left.

This influences are all in the unconscious background and I'm sure have influenced heavily for good or ill what I put down on paper. Now here are the conscious things which I thought about, those books that informed my writing. First up is a mystery novel by Kobo Abe, *The Ruined Map*. I kept thinking of this novel as I was writing because it's a mystery but with everything expected undercut, the hero hapless, buffeted by events. I find Abe's writing mesmerizing, and surreal.

Second was E. L. Doctorow's *The Waterworks*. Here's a novel that when I read it I knew I could write the novel I wanted to write in *The Happy Valley*. Here was a real mix of historical fiction, mystery, science fiction, even gothic horror. It had the same sense of a story started whose resolution keeps being delayed, giving time for more and more to be loaded up into it. Here is also a narrator who is in the story, but not the real protagonist. I read this novel and thought, I can do this. Was it one of Doctorow's better novels, probably not. Was it a big success, I don't feel like it. Does that matter? No.

Third was *The Secret History*. Why? Because I held onto the feeling I had when I was reading it, what it evoked—and I wanted to capture some of that in *The Happy Valley*. There was a powerful setting, and a rural, haunted character to it. It felt like a winter novel, and a country novel, and it had these hateful, strange, and intense characters that were well drawn. The other two books I had read recently, and were still quite fresh, but I didn't want to go back to *The Secret History*, either to lift too much of it, or to discover I didn't like it nearly as much decades later, no longer an angsty Classics student at a small rural liberal arts college.

A book I couldn't finish but which stood like a lighthouse for me was Yiyun Li's *Kinder Than Solitude*. The book made me so sad and the experience of reading it was so painful I finally had to put it down, but every time I wrote a sentence or tried to finish a chapter I thought of the hard beauty on every page, the deep history, the tangled webs of it, the juxtaposition of countries, landscapes, class, language, and wanted to keep going with my own work.

There are other pretty clear inspirations for me which might pop out at you or which you might miss entirely. Some of them are plainly referenced. Games like *The Oregon* Trail and *Sim City*. Obviously the cult classic TV show *The Prisoner*—not just where I reference it, but throughout the book influences so much about the actions and characters and situations; the narrator is unnamed, so is the prisoner; the narrator is trapped in a world of his own creation; the mysteries which begin in rational investigation but wind up in more and more fantastic ways, including dramatic set-pieces. I suppose there's something of Pynchon there too.

There is one influence which may be so obscure and so "of a certain age and characteristic" that it may blow past everyone, but the Sierra On-Line video game series created by Lori and Corey Cole, *Quest for Glory*. These were cross-over role-playing/adventure games with incredibly witty and erudite (for children's games) scripts and expansive and beautiful worlds which lit up my imagination from the first time I was able to play them from 5 1/4" floppies on my i386SX desktop computer. They were hero's journeys but emphasized the power and value of community and relationships, even when your character was a thief.

And I am as surprised as you are, frankly, that when I imagined a future utopian society, elements of their games came to mind and found their way here and there into the text. I leave untangling that as an exercise for the reader.

A Deleted Chapter

Years ago, Toni and I were looking to get out of the city and we pulled up rental listings in a smattering of locations in the Hudson Valley, close enough to commute back to our offices in Greenpoint. This was when we had the fashion company Hayden-Harnett, before the financial crisis, when things were still going pretty well. One place we visited with a realtor was off literally right off the highway. As you drove along the highway a small entry road appeared, you screeched off the road onto a cul-de-sac of small, strange houses.

Toward the end, we stopped and there was a nice older cottage, with a long, sloping back yard. There were stone walls, and statuary, some of it moss-covered. It was like a place out of time, a place from a novel. If you walked to the end of the grass lawn, which was all crabgrass and half-overgrown, you found a wooden walkway, and if you followed it through bracken and scrub and saplings, and then tall grass and cat-tails you came to a dock rotting into a small, isolated lake. There were a number of small cottages dotting the lakeside. We stood for a while there as the sun started to sink, frogs croaking, a single blue heron took off.

I wrote a very short chapter of the novel taking place there, to the best of my recollection. It didn't do anything for the plot, it was all atmosphere, and on good advice I cut it. But here you go:

I "lit out for the territories" not long after that. Everything I cared about, cared to keep, fit in a few boxes in the backseat and trunk of my car. Everything else I left for the neighbors of the sanitation crews. There was a lot of stuff piling up, people with the same idea as me: escape New York, or maybe just that our orbits were no longer bounded by the intense gravity of "job" and "career."

Things didn't make it to the dump, anymore, a whole host descended on the piles and the trucks like those time lapse videos of whale carcasses at the ocean bottom, everything discarded found a use. This has, in other times, been viewed as a terrible thing, a sign of depression or desperation, but I find it beautiful, and I see how quickly for our society it has become a point of pride.

How quickly I had castigated June in my mind for her sudden and deep silence, like the space between the big bones settling into the anaerobic bottom silt. Though, truthfully, I had vanished first. After our breakup in NYC I had stayed a couple years, then gone out to LA, where I had dropped out of contact with nearly everybody from my old life. I had a string of girlfriends, worked a few jobs before narrowing into a career. For a long time it worked out, and then, it didn't. The East Coast was home. I came back.

In the car, with my things, driving, randomly, north, I was thinking of these things, and others. How much the same it all seemed, the terrain, the Sprain Brook Parkway, the slumped stone walls, the pale green of the siding, like a snake, like a viper. I suddenly knew where June was. It was that simple. Her Uncle Mort, who wasn't an uncle but a special friend of June's aunt who had died and left the family some scattered things, one being a strange cinder-block house on a cul-de-sac right off the highway, surrounded by thickets, with a long sloping yard, overgrown gardens, weathered concrete statues of Poseidon, a trio of deer, a Buddha, which finally ended in a path opening through a bunch of falling poplars and alder, then the path became planked, and turning this way and that, the reeds shot up, cattails, and finally a sunken pier into a wide, glassy lake in the center of nowhere.

June and I had gone once. You turned suddenly off the highway by a big yellow painted stone. Now the way was the same, except having been carved into semi-autonomous zones. Each with a name, a central committee, and idiosyncratic character. Some were fond of flowers, others impressive walls or farm-stands. The turn off was the same though. I took it a little too fast, and the car front bounced a little and ground into the gravel of the road. I groaned at imagined damage. But it was fine.

As I took the car through the first turn toward the cabin I was thinking about how June would be there. The lamppost would be shining, it was late enough, and the light in the bedroom, she would be sitting reading. Something hard, Condorcet, or Deleuze, or Adorno. She was always trying to figure out things about the world. Why was it this way, I mean, the world of people, and our problems. I would be a bad influence on her, but good, we'd drink together. Smoke up.

Take wine out on the almost-navigable boat, and watch the eagles hunt from the shore of the island. Maybe this time our relationship would work. Or maybe it wouldn't. We'd stay months there, enough for each other. Maybe listening to radio reports. I would, once or twice head to town, where I'd stock up on coffee, cream. Someone would have started up the local paper again, that's how things were trending. I'd bring it and we'd discuss the ridiculous scandals behind the anodyne headlines. We would intuit, together, who was feuding with whom.

One time I would come back, and she would have vanished. Leaving behind most of her things. The lights would still be on. Maybe the radio. But she had lit out for something, for somewhere. And now I really had to find her.

And it had all happened like that, except that I had not been with her. The car had purred to sleep, and the lantern-light was weak on the front path. I came to the door and it swung open. There was a radio playing, but it had gone to snow. June had been here. I would have to be Sherlock Holmes to know quite when.

I shut everything off, and resolved to head north, as I had originally planned, to hit up my parents' place, in our old hometown, to use as my base.

Hope for the Future

These days there's a pretty big category of fiction, "Dystopian," that is supposed to capture all our feelings about the future. Really all dystopian "future" fiction is about the present time, or even an investigation of the past. Reviewers and readers of *The Happy Valley* have classified it as partly dystopian, and I almost would have chosen the category myself, thinking about where the book might fit. But it's really not. It's a *utopian* future. It's a future I could very gladly live in, and I think a lot of others would gladly live there too. Maybe you. So I'll leave you with that—hope for the future. Things can change. Our way of living can be radically altered, but we must participate in that change, even if it's just imagining a new way to live. I hope that fiction, like *The Happy Valley*, can help us to do that.

Thank you for reading and let's find the future, together.

Playlist

CURATED by Toni Hacker, here is a playlist that evokes the spirit of *The Happy Valley* to an uncanny degree. For convenience, you can pull it up on *Spotify* with the following link (though you may prefer a different music service, given their poor politics):

https://open.spotify.com/playlist/1643EYPh8lFb10hcKS4O51

1. David Cassidy, "Come On Get Happy"
2. Electrelane, "The Valleys"
3. The Cleaners from Venus, "Incident in a Greatcoat"
4. Sharon Van Etten, "Serpents"
5. Bob Dylan, "I Want You"
6. Vampire Weekend, "The Kids Don't Stand a Chance"
7. Crystal Stilts, "Still as the Night"
8. Royal Philharmonic Orchestra, "Barry Lyndon: Sarabande"
9. Ramones, "Blitzkrieg Bop"
10. Tiger's Jaw, "June"
11. Horny Toad, "Vampire Ska"
12. Black Moth Super Rainbow, "Forever Heavy"
13. Lana Del Rey, "Summertime Sadness"
14. Peaches, "In The Valley Below"
15. Porcelain Raft, "Drifting In And Out"
16. Deerhunter, "Snakeskin"
17. Phantogram, Future Islands; "Black Out Days – Future Islands Remix"
18. Atlas Sound, Noah Lennox; "Walkabout W/ Noah Lennox"
19. Future Islands, "A Dream of You and Me"
20. Porcelain Raft, "Unless You Speak From Your Heart"
21. Lalo Schifrin, "Secret Code"
22. Suburban Lawns, "Janitor"
23. J. Christopher Pardini, Ken Mervine; "Toccata on Amazing Grace"
24. Dead Man's Bones, "Pa Pa Power"
25. Timber Timbre, "Trouble Comes Knocking"
26. Crystal Stilts, "Love Is a Wave"
27. Tol-Puddle Martyrs, "Time Will Come (1967)"
28. Papercuts, "Future Primitive"
29. Ghostland Observatory, "Sad Sad City"
30. Steve Lodder, "Gothic Castle"
31. Jagwar Ma, "Come Save Me"
32. Crystal Stilts, "The Dazzled"
33. DEVO, "Freedom of Choice"
34. Tom Waits, "Murder In The Red Barn"
35. Ghostland Observatory, "Stranger Lover"
36. Timber Timbre, "Bad Ritual"
37. Woods, "Rain On"
38. Tchami, "Adieu"
39. Pharrell Williams, "Freedom"
40. Urban Cookie Collective, "The Key, The Secret"

A Note on the Type

THE BODY TEXT of this book is set in ADOBE CASLON, a revival designed by Carol Twombly after studying the output of William Caslon's foundry from 1734 (when his Latin typeface was "fully realized") through 1770. Caslon's first designed typefaces were "exotics," an Arabic in 14pt, made on behalf of the Society for Promoting Christian Knowledge; a Hebrew; and a Coptic.

The title and section titles are set in BIG CASLON, another revival of the same typeface, this one designed by Matthew Carter to be used in displays; it was released in 1994.

SOURCES: *Adobe* and *Wikipedia.*

About the Author

BENJAMIN HARNETT was born in 1981 in Cooperstown, NY. He attended Hamilton College. After graduating in 2000, he went to work at the Annenberg School at the University of Pennsylvania on a study of the Internet and the election. He moved to Seattle in 2001 and then Florence, Italy. On his return, he studied Classics at Columbia University. He took a gig writing encyclopedia entries, then started work at a midtown fashion company helping with their computers and working in garment production.

In 2005, with TONI HACKER, he co-founded *Hayden-Harnett,* a cult-favorite fashion brand. He then took up work as a digital engineer at *The New York Times* in 2012, where he continues to be employed today. He was an organizer in the effort that helped its tech workers win a historic union; he served on the inaugural Unit Council and as a shop steward. Toni and Benjamin married in 2014. In 2017 they moved to Beacon, NY, where she founded *Beacon Mercantile.* They now live in Cherry Valley, NY with a collection of eccentric but lovable pets.

Benjamin holds an MA in Classics from Columbia, and is the author of 2017's "Diffusion of the Codex," an important paper on the origins of the modern book. He has published scores of short stories, poems, and essays in venues like *The Evansville Review, Saranac Review, Entropy, Aeon, Juked,* been nominated for a *Pushcart Prize,* shortlisted for the *Bridport Prize,* and had his story "Delivery" selected as *Longform's Fiction of the Week.* He is also the author of the poetry collection *Animal, Vegetable, Mineral (2020)* and the chapbook *Last Cut (2000).*

To find out more, visit www.benjaminharnett.com.

Coming Soon

COMING SOON from Serpent Key Press and Benjamin Harnett (and available now on Kindle) is a collection of surreal, inventive, and engaging short stories, *Gigantic: Stories From the End of the World*, and a short excerpt from the title story can be found below:

"HERE," THE DOCTOR SAID, handing me a tiny, squalling, red thing, "it's a boy. A healthy baby boy." That word —"healthy"—I'm sure the doctors said it thousands of times over thousands of other girls and boys. That day, in the days before, and the days that followed.

Healthy—none of us knew any different.

He had a wrinkled, monkey-face, all contorted, purple from exertion, but cute. I saw my father in his face. My husband, too. I saw my own eyes, whenever his would open. Jacob, we called him. He was on the big side, for babies, eleven pounds. That size runs in my family.

Yes, he was big for a baby, but even so, he was so small, this tiny, fragile thing compared to all our ungainly adult bulk. As I cradled my little son, my husband reached out to touch him. For a second, Jacob stopped his wild screaming. The feeling of something electric passed over us all, like a jolt of static. I saw, I'd swear, a kind of blue fire dance down Jacob's back, then disappear.

I still love my boy. Despite all that happened. I guess it's being his mother. But I think I understand what he—what they did, the why of it. If you weren't a parent, I don't know if you could.

Back when we still used to talk about it we'd get to a point in the discussion when my husband would take his glasses off, put them back on, then take them off again. He'd rub naked eyes, put the glasses back on a final time. Then he'd open his mouth as if he had found something, just the right thing to say. But nothing would come out, and our talk was at an end. All that fussing with the glasses, it's a nervous affectation. If he didn't do that, he would bite his nails.

I'd wanted a natural birth, a home birth, especially for my first. But after a serious talk with mother, I embraced my practical side, and when the time came, off to the hospital it was. I held on to the pain as long as I could, then called out for the epidural.

Someone might think less of me for taking the easy way out, to medicate away the pain—but consider how much of the rest of our lives is already so unnatural, we are fighting against the natural state of everything, which is to be at rest. We focus on the visible, the apparent, the outstanding. The gigantic . . .

Lightning Source UK Ltd.
Milton Keynes UK
UKHW010630080223
416649UK00016B/766/J